David Peace was born and raised in Ossett, West Yorkshire. He now lives in the East End of Tokyo with his wife and children. His first novel, *Nineteen Seventy Four*, was published in 1999, *Nineteen Seventy Seven* in 2000, and *Nineteen Eighty* in 2001. *Nineteen Eighty Three* is the final novel in his Red Riding Quartet.

Praise for *Nineteen Seventy Four*

'Peace's stunning debut has done for the county what Raymond Chandler and James Ellroy did for LA . . . a brilliant first novel, written with tremendous pace and passion' *Yorkshire Post*

'Peace's pump-action prose propels the book's narrative with a scorching turn-of-speed to an apocalyptic denouement . . . One hell of a read' *Crime Time*

'This breathless, extravagant, ultra-violent debut thriller reads like it was written by a man with one hand down his pants and the other on a shotgun. Vinnie Jones should buy the film rights fast' *Independent on Sunday*

'The sheer ghastly flair brings to mind noir supremo Elmore Leonard, with good reason. Superb' *Big Issue In the North*

'*Nineteen Seventy Four* takes the direct approach: straight to the heart of Ellroy-land, turning his native Yorkshire of the early seventies into a pustulant, cancerous core of complete corruption' *Uncut*

Nineteen Eighty Three

David Peace

Library of Congress Catalog Card Number: 2002110944

A complete catalogue record for this book can be obtained from the British Library on request

First published in 2002 by Serpent's Tail, 4 Blackstock Mews, London N4 2BT.

website: www.serpentstail.com

Phototypeset by Intype London Ltd
Printed in Great Britain by Mackays of Chatham plc

10 9 8 7 6 5 4 3 2 1

For William Miller, John Williams, and Pete Ayrton –
thank you.

'Oh, this is the way to the fairy wood,
Where the wolf ate Little Red Riding Hood;
But this is the riddle that you must tell –
How is it, if it so befell,
That he ate her up in that horrid way,
In these pretty pages she lives today?'

– Traditional

The last beg

Yorkshire –

The Summer of Love:

Jimmy's dog is barking and the boys are crying, Michael screaming; Martin slaps him across his face and says:

'Do you want to be next?'

The boys close their eyes.

He is going to teach me a lesson.

They tie my hands behind my back and kick me to my knees, forcing my face into the sod; Leonard's dad pulls down my pants and asks:

'Do you love me Barry?'

I close my eyes.

He is going to make me learn.

Part 1
Miss the girl

'History does not repeat itself, only man.'
— Voltaire

Chapter 1

'No more dead dogs and slashed swans for us,' whispered Dick Alderman, like this was good news –

It wasn't. It was Day 2:

9.30 a.m. –

Friday 13 May 1983:

Millgarth Police Station, Leeds –

Yorkshire:

Waiting in the wings –

I pushed open the side door, the Conference Room silent as I led this damned parade out:

Detective Superintendent Alderman and the father, a policewoman and the mother, Evans from Community Affairs and me –

The Owl:

Maurice Jobson; Detective Chief Superintendent Maurice Jobson.

We sat down behind the Formica tables, behind the microphones and the cups of water.

I took off my glasses. I rubbed my eyes –

No bed, no sleep, only this:

The Press Conference –

This same, familiar place again:

Hell.

I put my glasses back on, thick lenses and black frames. I sat and stared out at my audience –

This same, familiar audience:

These hundred hungry hounds, sweating under their TV lights and deadlines, under the cigarette smoke and last night's ale, their muscles taut and arses clean, tongues out and mouths watering, wanting bones –

Fresh bones.

I switched on the microphone. I reeled back from the inevitable wail.

I coughed once to clear my throat then said: 'Ladies and gentlemen, at approximately 4 p.m. yesterday evening, Hazel Atkins disappeared on her way home from Morley Grange Junior and Infants. Hazel was last seen walking up Rooms Lane towards her home in Bradstock Gardens.'

I took a sip from the warm, still water.

'When Hazel did not return from school, Mr and Mrs Atkins contacted Morley Police and a search was launched early yesterday evening. As some of you are aware, the police were joined in this search by more than one hundred local people. Unfortunately last night's freak weather hampered the search, although it did resume at six o'clock this morning. Given the inclement and unseasonable weather and the fact that Hazel has never gone missing before, we are obviously concerned for her safety and whereabouts.'

Another sip from the warm, still water.

'Hazel is ten years old. She has medium-length dark brown hair and brown eyes. Last night she was wearing light blue corduroy trousers, a dark blue sweater embroidered with the letter *H*, and a red quilted sleeveless jacket. She was carrying a black drawstring gym bag, also embroidered with the letter *H*.'

I held up an enlarged colour print of a smiling brown-haired girl. I said: 'Copies of this recent school photograph are being distributed as I speak.'

Again a sip from the warm, still water.

I glanced down the table at Dick Alderman. He touched the father's arm. The father looked up then turned to me.

I nodded.

The father blinked.

I said: 'Mr Atkins would now like to read a short statement in the hope that any member of the public who may have seen Hazel after four o'clock yesterday evening, or who may have any information whatsoever regarding Hazel's whereabouts or her disappearance, will come forward and share this information with Mr and Mrs Atkins and ourselves.'

I slid the microphone down the table to Mr Atkins as the hounds edged in closer, panting and slavering, smelling bones –

His daughter's bones –

The scent strong here, near.

Mr Atkins looked at his wife, his four eyes red from tears and lack of sleep, a night's guilty stubble in clothes damp and crushed, and from out of this mess he stared at the hounds that waited and watched, waited and watched –

His bones.

Mr Atkins said, said with strength: 'I would like to appeal to anybody who knows where our Hazel is or who saw her after four o'clock yesterday to please telephone the police. Please, if you know anything, anything at all, please telephone the police. Please – '

Stop –

'Let her come home.'

Stop.

Silence.

Mrs Atkins in tears, shoulders shaking, WPC Martin holding her –

Her husband, Hazel's father, his fingers in his mouth –

He said: 'We miss her. I – '

Stop.

Silence –

Long, long silence.

I nodded at Dick. He passed the microphone back along the table.

I said: 'That is all the information we have at the moment but, if you would excuse Mr and Mrs Atkins, I will then try and answer any questions you might have.'

I stood up as WPC Martin and Dick took the mother and the father out through the side door, the dogs watching them go, still hungry –

Hungry for bones –

Mine.

Alone with Evans at the front, I said: 'Gentlemen?'

The stark forest of hands, from their whispers a two-word scream:

'Clare Kemplay . . .'

More bones –

'Coincidence,' I was saying, seeing –

Old bones.

'Coincidence,' I said again, knowing –

There is salvation in no-one else.

Upstairs, a cup of cold tea in one hand: 'Where are the parents?'

Dick Alderman: 'Jim's taken them back to Morley.'

'We should get back over there.'

Dick: 'Take my car?'

I nodded.

Dick put out his cigarette. He reached for his coat.

'Dick?'

He turned back round: 'Yeah?'

'Where is all the Kemplay stuff?'

'What?'

'The Clare Kemplay files.'

'It's a coincidence,' he sighed. 'You said it yourself. What else could it be?'

'Where's the fucking stuff, Dick?'

He shrugged: 'Wood Street, probably.'

'Thank you.'

*

The Dewsbury Road through Beeston and along the Elland Road until it became Victoria Road and Morley –

Dick driving, me with my eyes closed –

Just the sleet, the windscreen wipers, and the radio:

'Parliament dissolves amidst excitement and relief ahead of 9 June poll; search continues for missing Morley 10-year-old; body of a boy aged three found on Northampton tip; 18-year-old found hanged in police cell; Nilsen to be charged with more murders . . .'

'How many you think he did?' asked Dick –

'Not a clue,' I said, eyes still shut. 'Not a bloody one.'

It was snowing in the middle of May and Hazel Atkins had been missing nineteen hours –

Lost.

Morley Police Station –

Four o'clock –

The Incident Room:

Maps and a blackboard, markers and chalk, grids and times –

One photograph.

Lists of officers and their territories, lists of houses and their occupants –

Gaskins out in the fields, Ellis on the knocker –

Evans in and out with the press –

Dick Alderman and Jim Prentice sat waiting.

The chalk in my hand, the smudges on my suit –

The egg sandwiches covered in silver foil, uneaten.

I took off my glasses. I wiped them on my handkerchief.

There was nothing more to say:

Outside it was still snowing and Hazel Atkins was still missing –

Twenty-four hours.

Her parents back on a sofa in the cold front room of their dark home –

The curtains not drawn –

All of us lost.

There was a knock at the door –

I looked up.

Dick Alderman: 'Nightcap, boss?'

I shook my head. I closed the file, glasses off and on the desk.

'Clare Kemplay?' Dick said, looking at her file.

'Yep.'

'*Evening Post* mentioned it,' he mumbled.

'Kathryn Williams?'

He nodded.

'What did she say?'

'Nine years ago, same school,' he shrugged. 'Bit about Myshkin.'

'What about him?'

'The usual bollocks.'

I picked up my glasses. I put them back on, the thick lenses and the black frames. I sat and stared up into his eyes, thinking –

I am the Owl:

I am the Owl and I see from behind these lenses thick and frames black, see through everything –

Unblinking –

The usual bollocks –

Everything.

Chapter 2

New Hope for Britain:
    Saturday 14 May 1983 –
    D-26.
    Fog and sleet from Wakefield to here:
    Park Lane Special Hospital, Merseyside –
    A *rotten*, un-fresh place.
    You switch off the radio and the election debate and wind down your window.
    'I'm here to see Michael Myshkin,' you say to the guard at the gate.
    'And you are?'
    'John Piggott.'
    The guard looks down at the clipboard in his hands, tilting it towards him to keep the rain off: 'John Winston Piggott?'
    You nod.
    'His solicitor?'
    You nod again, even less sure.
    He hands you a plastic visitor's tag: 'Follow the road round to the main building and the car park. Report to reception inside. They'll take you from there.'
    'Thank you.'
    You drive up the black wet road to a low grey building, modern and barred. You park and get out into the dismal cold light, the sleet and the rain. You push a buzzer and wait outside the metal door to the main building. There is a loud click then the sound of an alarm. You pull open the door and step inside a steel cage. You show the plastic visitor's tag to the guard on the other side of the bars and tell him your name. He bangs twice on one of the bars with a black and shining truncheon. Another set of locks moves back. Another alarm sounds and you are through to the reception area. Another guard gives you a slip of paper with a number. He nods at a bench. You walk over and sit down between a couple of old people and a woman with a crying child.
    You sit and you wait in the grey and damp room, grey and damp with the smell of people who have travelled hundreds of miles along grey and damp motorways to be told by overweight men in grey and damp uniforms with black and shining truncheons to wait on grey and damp government seats for nothing but more bad news, grey and damp, as the bolts and the locks slide back and forth and the alarms sound and the numbers are called and the old people stand up and sit

back down and the child cries and cries until a voice from a desk by the door shrieks: 'Twenty-seven'.

The child has stopped crying and its mother is looking at you.

'Twenty-seven!'

You stand up.

'Number twenty-seven!'

At the desk you say: 'John Piggott to see Michael Myshkin.'

A woman in a grey uniform runs her wet, bitten finger down a biro list, sniffs and says: 'Purpose of visit?'

'His mother asked me to come and see him.'

She sniffs again and looks up at you: 'Family?'

'No,' you say. 'I'm a solicitor.'

'Legal then?' she spits at you with sudden English hate, crisp and vicious.

You nod, vaguely afraid.

She hands you back your visitor's pass: 'First time?'

You nod again, her breath old and close.

'The patient will be brought to the visitors' room and a member of staff will be present throughout the visit. Visits are limited to forty-five minutes. You will both be seated at a table and are to remain seated throughout the course of the visit. You are to refrain from any physical contact and are not to pass anything directly to the patient. Anything you wish to give the patient must be done so through this office and can only be one of the items on this approved list,' she says and hands you a photocopied piece of A4.

'Thank you,' you smile.

'Return to your seat and wait for a member of staff to escort you to the visiting area.'

'Thank you,' you say again and do as you are told.

Thirty minutes and a paper swan later, a lanky guard with spots of blood upon his collar says: 'John Winston Piggott?'

You stand up.

'This way.'

You follow him to another door and another lock, another alarm and a ringing bell, through the door and up an overheated and overlit grey corridor.

At another set of double doors, he pauses and says: 'Know the drill?'

You nod.

'Keep seated, no physical contact, no passing of goods, ciggies, whatever,' he says anyway.

You nod again.

'I'll tell you when your time's up,' he says. 'If you've had enough, just say so.'

'Thank you.'

The guard then punches a code into a panel on the wall.

An alarm sounds and he pulls open the door: 'Ladies first.'

You step into a small room with a grey carpet and grey walls, two plastic tables each with two plastic chairs.

There are no windows, just one other door opposite –

No tea and biscuits here.

'Sit down,' says the guard.

You sit down in the grey plastic chair with your back to the grey door through which you've just come. You lean forward, arms on the marked plastic surface of the grey plastic table, eyes on the door opposite.

The guard takes a chair from the other table and sits down behind you.

You turn to ask him: 'What's he like then, Myshkin?'

The man looks over at the door then back at you and winks: 'Pervert, same as rest of them.'

'He violent, is he?'

'Only with his right hand,' he mimes.

You laugh and turn back round and there he is, right on cue –

As if by magick –

In a pair of grey overalls and grey shirt, enormous with a head twice as large:

Michael John Myshkin, murderer of children.

You've stopped laughing.

Michael Myshkin in the doorway, spittle on his chin.

'Hello,' you say.

'Hello,' Myshkin smiles, blinking.

His guard pushes him forwards into the grey plastic chair opposite you, then closes the door and takes the last chair to sit behind Myshkin.

Michael Myshkin looks up at you.

You stop staring.

Myshkin looks back down at the grey plastic table.

'My name is John Piggott,' you say. 'I used to live in Fitzwilliam, near you. I'm a solicitor now and your mother asked me to come and talk to you about an appeal.'

You pause.

Michael Myshkin is patting down his dirty yellow hair with his fat right hand, the hair thin and black with oil.

'An appeal is a very lengthy and costly procedure, involving a lot of time and different people,' you continue. 'So before any firm embarks upon such a course on behalf of a client, we have to be very sure that there are sufficient grounds for an appeal and that there is a great likelihood of success. And even this costs a lot of money.'

You pause again.

Myshkin looks up at you.

You ask him: 'Do you understand what I'm saying?'

He wipes his right hand on his overalls and smiles at you, his pale blue eyes blinking in the warm grey room.

'You do understand what I'm saying?'

Michael Myshkin nods once, still smiling, still blinking.

You turn to the guard sat behind you: 'Is it OK if I take some notes?'

He shrugs and you take a spiral notebook and biro from out of your carrier bag.

You flick open the pad and ask Myshkin: 'How old are you, Michael?'

He glances round at the guard sat behind him then back at you and whispers: 'Twenty-two.'

'Really?'

He blinks, smiles, and nods again.

'Your mother told me you were thirty.'

'Outside,' he whispers, the index finger of his left hand to his wet lips.

'How about inside?' you ask him. 'How long have you been in here?'

Michael Myshkin looks at you, not smiling, not blinking, and very slowly says: 'Seven years, four months, and twenty-six days.'

You sit back in your plastic chair, tapping your plastic pen on the plastic table.

You look across at him.

Myshkin is patting down his hair again.

'Michael,' you say.

He looks up at you.

'You know why you're in here?' you ask. 'In this place?'

He nods.

'Tell me,' you say. 'Tell me why you're in here?'

'Because of Clare,' he says.

'Clare who?'

'Clare Kemplay.'

'What about her?'

'They say I killed her.'

'And is that right?' you say, quietly. 'Did you kill her?'

Michael John Myshkin shakes his head: 'No.'

'No what?' you say, writing down his words verbatim.

'I didn't kill her.'

'But you said you did.'

'They said I did.'

'Who did?'

'The police, the papers, the judge, the jury,' he says. 'Everyone.'

'And you,' you tell him. 'You said so too.'

'But I didn't,' says Michael Myshkin.

'You didn't say it or you didn't do it?'

'I didn't do it.'

'So why did you say you did if you didn't?'

Myshkin is patting down his hair again.

'Michael,' you say. 'This is very, very important.'

He looks up.

You say again: 'Why did you say you killed her?'

'They said I had to.'

'Who?'

'Everyone.'

'Who's everyone?'

'My father, my mother, the neighbours, work, the lawyers, the police,' he says. 'Everyone.'

'Which police?' you say. 'Can you remember their names?'

Michael Myshkin stops patting down his hair and shakes his head.

'Can you remember what they looked like?'

Head still down, he nods once –

But you stop writing, looking into the uniformed eyes of the man behind Michael Myshkin, another set of uniformed eyes behind you –

You say: 'Why did they tell you to do that? To say you killed her?'

Michael John Myshkin looks up at you. He is not smiling. He is not blinking. He is not patting down his hair –

He says: 'Because I know who did.'

'You know who killed her?'

He looks at the table, patting down his hair again.

You start writing: 'Who?'

He is patting down his hair, blinking at the plastic table.

'Michael, if it wasn't you, who was it?'

He is patting down his hair. He is blinking. Smiling.

'Who?'

Smiling and blinking and patting down his hair and –

'Who?'

Michael Myshkin looks up at you.

He says: 'The Wolf.'

You put down your pen: 'The Wolf?'

Myshkin, in his grey overalls and his grey shirt with his enormous body and oversized head, is nodding –

Nodding and laughing –

Really, really laughing –

The guards too.

Laughing and nodding and blinking and patting down his hair, the spittle on his chin –

Michael John Myshkin, murderer of children, is laughing –

Spittle on his chin, tears on his cheeks.

Outside in your car, you switch on the engine and the radio news and light a cigarette:

'Thatcher names defence as nation's priority; ten Greenham women arrested as council bailiffs move in; boy aged fifteen to appear before Northampton magistrates charged with murdering three-year-old boy; Hazel day three, the search continues; Nilsen charged with four more murders: Kenneth Ockendon in December 1979, Martyn Duffey in May 1980, William Sutherland in September 1980, Malcolm Barlow in . . .'

You switch the radio off and light another cigarette and listen to the rain fall on the roof of the car, eyes closed:

Fitzwilliam, three days ago. You waited in the same piss for your Pete to show. He didn't so you went inside and cremated your mother. Stood alone at the front and bit the inside of your cheek until the blood wouldn't stop and the tears finally came.

Mrs Myshkin was there, Mrs Ashworth and a couple of the others –

But not your Pete.

Ma Myshkin had caught you back at the house, cheap yellow margarine from a stale ham sandwich on your cheap black suit. She sponged it off with a thin flowered handkerchief and said: 'You'll see him then?'

You open your eyes.

You feel sick and your fingers are burning.

You put out the cigarette and press the buttons in and out on the radio until you find some music:

The Police.

'Mrs Myshkin?'

You are in a working telephone box on Merseyside, listening to Mrs Myshkin and the relentless sound of a hard rain on the roof –

'Yes, he's fine,' you say.

The rain pouring down, car lights in the middle of a wet Saturday afternoon in May –

'I will need to see you again.'

The kind of wet Saturday afternoon you used to spend round your Uncle Ronnie and Aunty Winnie's over Thornhill way, eating lemon curd tarts and custard pies in their kitchen with his old British motorcycle in pieces on the cracked linoleum, afraid –

'Can I pop round sometime early in the week?'

Sitting in the sidecar in the garage with Pete, listening to the rain fall on the corrugated roof, the shells in the wall outside so sharp and full of pain, listening to the relentless sound of the hard rain on the roof and not wanting to go home, not wanting to go to school on Monday, dreading it –

'Tuesday, if that's OK with you?'

That vague fear even then –

'Goodbye, Mrs Myshkin.'

That fear again now, less and less vague –

She hangs up and you stand there, in a working telephone box on Merseyside, listening to the dial tone –

The dial tone and the relentless sound of the hard rain on the roof, not wanting to go home, not wanting to go to work, dreading it –

That fear now:

Saturday 14 May 1983 –

D-26.

That fear here –

Dogs barking –

Getting near.

Wolves.

Chapter 3

Rock 'n' Roll –

Record on jukebox is stuck. BJ not dancing.

Eddie Dunford is pointing shotgun at BJ's chest.

Eddie asks: 'Why me?'

BJ say: 'You came so highly recommended.'

He drops shotgun and turns and walks down Strafford stairs and Eddie's gone –

Eddie's gone but BJ still here –

Here:

Strafford, Wakefield –

Now:

Tuesday 24 December 1974.

Think, think, think –

Heart racing and gasping for breath, eyes wide and looking about:

Grace behind bar screaming and shaking, Old Cunt over by window in fucking shock not moving or anything, hands still up in air –

Craven stood there in centre of room, shit running out of his ear, his mate Dougie crawling towards bog in his own blood –

Paul on his back, eyes opening and closing, dying –

Boss man Derek Box already there –

Dead.

'Fuck,' BJ say, thinking –

Think, think fucking fast:

Over to Derek and open his jacket and take out his wallet, have his watch and rings for good measure –

Paul still whistling air, BJ take his money and his watch –

'Cunt,' he hisses.

'Shoosh,' BJ spit back –

Then sirens, BJ can hear sirens –

Fuck –

BJ leave him pennies and BJ say to Grace: 'We got to get out of here, love.'

But she's still all shock and screams, blood on her blouse and blood in hair –

'Come on!' BJ yell. 'They're going to be here any fucking second.'

She doesn't move.

'You don't want to be here.'

Behind bar to give her a shake but it's no fucking use so BJ grab night's takings from till, shouting in her face: 'They'll kill us all!'

Nothing –

BJ slap her –

Tyres and brakes and car doors outside –

Fuck, fuck –

BJ jump bar –

Fuck, fuck, fuck –

BJ can't go out front, BJ have to take back –

'Grace!' BJ shout for last fucking time. 'Come on!'

But she doesn't fucking move –

Fuck, fuck, fuck, fuck –

Fuck her.

BJ head down passage and push open back door, hit night and stone steps running when BJ hear:

BANG!

Sound of another shotgun –

Fuck, fuck, fuck, fuck, fuck –

Down stone steps, bottom of stone steps when BJ hear another:

BANG!

Another gun –

Fuck, fuck, fuck, fuck, fuck, fuck –

Across empty car park, crouching and running through puddles of rain water and oil, out back way then flat in a doorway as police car circles past, ducking over road and down side of bus station, thinking what the –

Fuck, fuck, fuck, fuck, fuck, fuck, fuck –

Fuck BJ going to do now?

Through shadows of deserted bus station, into coach station when thank –

Fuck, fuck, fuck, fuck, fuck, fuck, fuck, fuck –

BJ see it –

See it standing there, all lit up in silver and lit up in gold:

A coach.

Panting, BJ ask driver: 'You running?'

'About six bloody hours behind.'

'Where you going?'

'Preston via Bradford and Manchester.'

'When you leaving?'

'Now.'

'How much?'

'Ticket office is closed,' he winks.

BJ smile: 'So how much you want?'
'Tenner?'
'Done,' BJ say and hand him a stolen bloody note.
'A Merry Christmas to you too,' he says.
BJ get on and head for back seat.
Two other folk; one sleeping and other pissed off.
BJ take back seat and get BJ's head down.
Coach pulls out of station but heads back into Bullring –
Towards Strafford.
BJ want to look but BJ dare not.
Coach slows –
Fuck, fuck, fuck, fuck, fuck, fuck, fuck, fuck, fuck –
Driver opens door –
Fuck, fuck, fuck, fuck, fuck, fuck, fuck, fuck, fuck, fuck –
'What's going on?'
Fuck, fuck, fuck, fuck, fuck, fuck, fuck, fuck, fuck, fuck, fuck –
'Been a shooting,' comes copper's voice.
'Shooting?'
'Strafford Arms.'
'You're joking?'
'Looks like a robbery.'
'Robbery?' repeats driver with his stolen tenner burning a hole in his unwashed pocket and his jelly heart –
Fuck, fuck, fuck, fuck, fuck, fuck, fuck, fuck, fuck, fuck, fuck, fuck –
'You'll have to go down Springs,' says copper.
'Will do,' says driver.
'Some bloody Christmas,' says copper.
'Aye,' says driver. 'Hope you catch the bastard.'
'We will,' says copper. 'We always do.'

Driver closes door and coach turns left and heads down Springs and out of Wakefield, snaking its way through Dewsbury and Batley into Bradford –

Sat on back seat, BJ suddenly shaking and crying and BJ can't stop shaking and crying because of all things BJ seen and all things BJ done, things they've made BJ see and things they've made BJ do, all those fucking things they've made BJ do and BJ thinking of Grace and BJ shaking and crying because BJ know what they'll have done to her and what they're going to do to BJ, all people they've killed and all people they're going to have to fucking kill, and BJ know BJ should have done it right, should have done bloody lot of them because now BJ be truly –
Fuck, fuck, fuck, fuck, fuck, fuck, fuck, fuck, fuck, fuck, fuck, fuck, fuck –
Fucked forever.

When he pulls into Bradford Bus Station, driver comes up to back.

BJ close BJ's eyes –

'Get off,' he whispers.

BJ open BJ's eyes: 'I want to go to Manchester.'

'Don't give a fuck where you want to go,' he spits. 'It's all over bloody radio and all over your fucking face.'

'I . . .'

'I don't want to know,' he says and chucks Derek Box's tenner at BJ.

BJ pick it up. BJ walk past him down aisle.

BJ get off. BJ stand on freezing platform.

BJ watch coach pull out and away.

It's three in morning:

Christmas Eve, 1974 –

Three in morning, Christmas Eve 1974 when BJ remember Clare –

Scotch Clare.

Fuck, fuck, fuck, fuck, fuck, fuck, fuck, fuck, fuck, fuck, fuck, fuck –

Holy fuck, no.

Chapter 4

Wakefield Metropolitan Police Headquarters –

Day 5:

Monday 16 May 1983 –

Five thousand buildings searched, thirty thousand folk interviewed –

Widening search radius to twenty-five square miles, frogmen dragging rivers, sewers;

Family flattened, relatives leant on –

Dawn raids on the perverted and recently paroled.

'Go straight in,' said the Chief Constable's secretary. 'He's expecting you.'

'Thank you,' I said, adjusting my glasses.

I knocked once. I opened the door.

Chief Constable Angus was sat behind a big desk with his back to the window and another grey sky. He was writing. He glanced up. He nodded at the seat across from him.

I sat down.

'Any news?' he asked, knowing the answer.

I shook my head.

He stopped writing. He put down his pen. 'What about the Press?'

'Reconstruction would keep them quiet.'

'Bit premature that, don't you think?'

'Anniversary Check.'

'You want to do it Thursday?'

'Long as we can let them know today or tomorrow.'

'The Press?'

'And the family.'

He nodded: 'Fine.'

'Could go National?'

'Thought you reckoned it was local?'

'Still do.'

He shrugged.

I opened the file on my knee. I handed him a black and white photograph: 'Remember her?'

'Very funny, Maurice,' he said, not laughing.

'Seems like a lot of folk do.'

'What?'

'Remember her.'

'Heard you were sniffing around.'

'You blame me?'

'It's a coincidence.'

'There's no such thing.'

'He's behind lock and key,' said Angus. 'Where he belongs and where you helped put him.'

'What if *he* had help?'

'He'd have said.'

'He says he didn't do it.'

'He never did before.'

'We never let him.'

'Maurice, listen to me,' he pleaded. 'Michael Myshkin might have been soft in the head, but his heart was hard, rock hard. He did those things, killed them girls. Sure as I'm sitting here and you're sitting there.'

I said nothing.

'You know it in your heart,' he said. 'You know it in your heart.'

In my heart –

I shook my head: 'So it's just a bleeding coincidence then?'

'Like I say.'

'Well, like I say, there's no such fucking thing.'

Ronald Angus sighed. He slapped his hands down hard on the top of his big desk. He stood up. He walked over to the window. He looked up at another grey sky over Wakefield.

It was starting to rain again.

His back to me, he said: 'That's not to say he might not have a fan or someone, way these animals are.'

'I want to go and see him,' I said.

He was nodding at the grey sky.

I asked: 'That a *yes*, is it?'

He turned back from the grey sky. 'Just keep it out of the bloody papers, that's all.'

I stood up, adjusting my glasses.

It was raining heavily against the window.

I picked up the black and white photograph from his desk –

Clare Kemplay smiling up at me, out of my hands –

In my heart.

I took the motorway back into Leeds, odd and sudden patches of sunlight falling from the dirty grey sea up above, childhood memories of sunshine and cut grass drowned by voices; terrifying, hysterical, and screeching voices of approaching doom, disaster and death –

'A young girl doesn't simply vanish into thin air.'

The odd and sudden patches of sunlight gone, I came off the motorway at the Hunslet and Beeston exit, past the terrifying lorries, the hysterical diggers and the screeching cranes. I took the Hunslet Road then Black Bull Street into the centre and Millgarth, my hands shaking, knees weak and stomach hollow with approaching doom, disaster and death –

'Someone somewhere must have seen something.'

It was Day 5 –

1983.

'Now?' said Dick. 'This very minute?'

'And not a word, not even to Jim.'

'Can I get my coat?' he asked, standing.

'Meet you downstairs in five minutes.'

'Right,' he said, opening the door.

'And Dick,' I said.

He stopped.

'Not a word, yeah?'

He nodded like, *this is me Maurice, this is me.*

'I mean it,' I said.

'I know you do,' he said and I hoped he did –

Hoped he fucking did.

He drove.

I drifted, dreaming –

Underground kingdoms, forgotten kingdoms of badgers and angels, worms and insect cities; mute swans upon black lakes while dragons soared overhead in painted skies of silver stars and then swept down through lamp-lit caverns wherein an owl guarded three sleeping little princesses in tiny feathered wings, guarded them from –

Waking afraid of the news:

'Police today continued their search for missing Morley schoolgirl Hazel Atkins, as Chief Superintendent Maurice Jobson, the detective leading the search, admitted that so far the response from the public had been disappointing . . .'

Afraid of the news:

'A young girl doesn't simply vanish into thin air. Someone somewhere must have seen something.'

I took off my glasses. I rubbed my eyes, that taste in my mouth –

Meat –

Afraid.

*

We waited on plastic chairs, listening to the doors and the locks, the shuffling footsteps and the occasional scream from another wing. We waited on plastic chairs, staring at the different shades of grey paint, the grey fittings and the grey furniture.

We waited on plastic chairs for Michael Myshkin.

Five minutes later the door opened and there he was –

In a pair of grey overalls, fat from institutional living and sweaty from institutional heating –

Michael John Myshkin.

He sat down across from us, eyes down in front of a full house.

'Michael,' I said. 'Do you remember us?'

Nothing.

'My name is Mr Jobson and this is Mr Alderman. We're policemen from West Yorkshire,' I continued. 'Near where your mum lives.'

He looked up now, a quick eyeball at Dick then back down at the chubby hands in his tubby lap.

'How are you, Michael?' asked Alderman and I wished he hadn't because now Myshkin was fair wringing those chubby hands of his.

'Michael,' I said. 'We're here to ask you some questions that's all. Be gone before you know it, you tell us what we want.'

He looked up again, my way this time –

I smiled. He didn't smile back.

'Been a while,' I said. 'In here a while now, yeah?'

He nodded.

'Must miss home?'

He nodded.

'Know I would; my family, my mates?'

He nodded.

'Fitzwilliam, yeah?'

He nodded.

'Just you, your mam and dad, wasn't it?'

He nodded.

'Dad was a miner?'

He nodded.

'Passed away, yeah?'

Another nod.

'Sorry to hear that,' I said. 'Been sick a while, had he?'

Two quick nods.

'Where's your mam now?'

'Fitzwilliam,' he whispered.

'Same house?'

He nodded.

'Bet she's keeping your old room for you,' I smiled. 'Keeping it just the way it was.'

He nodded again, twice.

'Comes here often, does she, your mum?'

'Yes,' he said, a whisper again.

'How about mates, they come and all, do they?'

He shook his head.

'Hear from them much, do you?'

He shook his head again.

'What about Johnny thingy,' I said. 'Never hear from him?'

He looked up: 'Johnny?'

'Yeah,' I said, tapping the table. 'Johnny, hell-was-his-last-name?'

'Jimmy?' he said. 'Jimmy Ashworth?'

'That's it,' I nodded. 'Jimmy Ashworth. How's he doing?'

He shrugged.

'Never comes? Never writes?'

'No.'

'Christmas card?'

'No.'

'But you two were best mates, I heard?'

'Yes.'

'Thick as thieves, weren't you?' smiled Dick.

He nodded.

'Not very nice that,' I said. 'Some bloody friend he turned out to be, eh?'

Nothing.

I asked him: 'What about the others?'

He looked up.

'Your other mates?'

He shook his head.

'Who was there, remind me?'

He shook his head. He said: 'Just Jimmy in end.'

'No girlfriends? Penpals?'

He shook his head.

'What about work?'

Nothing.

'You had mates at work, yeah?'

He nodded.

'Castleford, wasn't it? Photo studio?'

He nodded again.

'Who was your mate there then?'

'Mary.'

'Mary who?'

'Mary Goldthorpe,' he said. 'But she's dead.'

'Anyone else?'

He shook his head. Then he said: 'Sharon, the new girl.'

'What was her last name?'

'Douglas,' he said.

'Sharon Douglas?' I said.

He nodded.

I turned to Dick Alderman.

Dick Alderman nodded.

I took off my glasses. I rubbed my eyes. I put them back on: 'Anyone else?'

'Just Mr Jenkins,' he said and this time I nodded –

'Ted Jenkins,' I said. 'That'd be right.'

The cage door open to the wet Scouse night, a voice shouted after us: 'Mr Jobson?'

We both turned round, a tall prison officer coming after us.

'Just thought you ought to know,' he panted. 'Myshkin had a meeting with his solicitor on Saturday.'

'Thanks,' said Dick. 'We saw his name on the visitors' list.'

'But I was there, yeah?' the prison officer said. 'In the room with them when Myshkin told this solicitor feller he didn't do it.'

'Is that right?' Dick said. 'Going to appeal, is he?'

'Myshkin said a policeman told him to say he did it,' the prison officer nodded. 'Made him confess.'

'Say which policeman, did he?' asked Dick.

'He couldn't remember the name,' said the prison officer. 'But solicitor cut him off before he could say much else.'

'Smart man,' I said.

Dick asked him: 'Myshkin say anything else?'

The officer tapped his temple with two fingers. 'He said a wolf did it.'

'Did what?' said Dick.

'Killed the little girl.'

'A wolf?' snorted Dick.

'Yeah,' the officer nodded, still tapping his temple. 'That's what he said.'

'He get many other visitors, does he?' I asked.

'Just his mad mam and the God Squad,' laughed the officer. 'Poor sod.'

'The poor sod,' I repeated.

In the visitors' car park of the Park Lane Special Hospital, we sat in the dark in silence until I asked Dick: 'What do you know about John Winston Piggott?'

'Father was one of us.'

'Jesus.' I shook my head. 'That was his father?'

Dick nodded.

'What's he look like, the son?'

'Right fat bastard,' he laughed. 'Office on Wood Street.'

'Like father, like son?'

'Who knows?' Dick shrugged. 'But he was Bob Fraser's solicitor, wasn't he?'

'Christ almighty,' I said.

'Déjà bloody vu,' said Dick.

'What's he know, Piggott?'

'Fuck knows.'

'Well, you'd better fucking well find out,' I said, the taste in my mouth again. 'And fucking fast.'

Chapter 5

You wake about eight and lie in bed eating cold Findus Crispy Pancakes –

Raw, uncooked in the middle, watching the TV-AM news on the portable:

'Police are to hold an inquiry into the death of a prisoner at Rotherhite Police Station. Mr Nicholas Ofuso, thirty-two, became unconscious and died of asphyxiation due to inhalation of vomit after nine policemen had gone to his flat in answer to a domestic dispute. Mr Ofuso struggled during the journey to Rotherhite Police Station and just before arrival he vomited. As his handcuffs were removed he went limp. He was given mouth-to-mouth resuscitation accompanied by a cardiac massage.'

It is Tuesday 17 May 1983 –

D-23.

After half an hour you make a cup of tea, then you get washed and dressed. You fancy a curry for lunch, a hot one with big fat prawns, but it is pissing down as you open the door and remember you have to see Mrs Myshkin today –

The newspaper lying on the mat, face up; Hazel Atkins:

Missing.

You go back upstairs and puke up all the pancakes and the tea, a flabby man on his knees before his bog, a flabby man who does not love his country or his god, a flabby man who has no country, has no god –

You don't want to go to work, you don't want to stay in the flat:

A flabby man on your knees.

You drive over one bridge and under another, past the boarded-up pubs and closed-down shops, the burnt-out bus stops and the graffiti that hates everything, everywhere, and everyone but especially the IRA, Man United, and the Pakis –

This is Fitzwilliam:

Back for the second time in a week, in a year.

Least it has stopped raining –

Turning out rite nice for once.

The off-licence is the only thing open so you park the car and go inside and slide the money through a slot to an Asian man and his little lad standing in a cage in their best pyjamas among the bottles of unlabelled alcohol and the single cigarettes. The father slides your change back, the son your twenty Rothman.

Two girls are sat outside on the remains of a bench. They are drinking Gold Label Merrydown cider and Benilyn cough syrup. A dog is barking at a frightened child in a pushchair, an empty bottle of Thunderbird rolling around on the concrete. The girls have dyed short rats' tails and fat mottled legs in turquoise clothes and suede pointed boots.

The dog turns from the screaming baby to growl at you.

One of the girls says: 'You fancy a fuck, fatty? Tenner back at hers.'

'I'm sorry I'm late,' you say at the front door. 'I got lost.'

'You're here now,' smiles Mrs Myshkin. 'Come in.'

'Car be all right there?' you ask her, looking back at the only one in the street.

'Yes,' she says. 'You'll be gone before the kids get out.'

You glance at your watch and step inside 54 Newstead View, Fitzwilliam.

'Go through,' she gestures.

You go into the front room to the left of the staircase; patterned carpet well vacuumed, assorted furniture well polished, the taste of air-freshener and the fire on full.

You have a headache.

Mrs Myshkin waves you towards the settee and you sit on it.

'Cup of tea?'

'Thank you,' you nod.

'I'll just be a minute,' she says and goes back out.

The room is filled with photographs and paintings, photographs and paintings of men, photographs and paintings of men not here –

Her husband, her son, Jesus Christ.

The fire is warm against your legs.

She comes back in with a plastic tray and sets it down on the table in front of you: 'Milk and sugar?'

'Please.'

'How many?'

'Three.'

'Help yourself to biscuits,' she says.

'Thank you,' you say and reach over for a chocolate digestive.

She hands you your tea and there's a knock at the door.

'My sister,' she says. 'You don't mind?'

'No,' you say.

She goes out to the door and you wash down the biscuit and take

another and think about turning down the bloody fire. You have chocolate on your fingers and your shirt again.

Mrs Myshkin comes back in with another little grey-haired woman
with the same metal-framed glasses.

'This is my sister,' she says. 'Mrs Novashelska, from Leeds.'

You stand up, wipe your fingers upon your trouser leg, then shake
the woman's tiny hand. 'Nice to meet you.'

Mrs Myshkin pours a cup of tea for her sister and they both sit
down in the chairs either side of you.

Mrs Myshkin says to her sister: 'He saw Michael on Saturday.'

The other woman smiles: 'You will help him then?'

You put down your cup and saucer and turn to Mrs Myshkin: 'I'm
not sure I can.'

Both the little women are staring at you.

'As I told you last week,' you begin. 'I don't have any experience
with appeals.'

Both little women staring at you, the fat man sweating on the small
settee.

'Not this kind of appeal. You see, what should happen, should have
happened in Michael's case, is that his original solicitor and his counsel,
they should have lodged an appeal after his trial. Within fourteen
days.'

The little women staring, the fat man roasting.

'But they didn't, did they?' you ask.

Mrs Myshkin and Mrs Novashelska put down their cups on the
table.

You wipe your face with your handkerchief.

Mrs Novashelska says: 'They couldn't very well appeal, could they?
Not when they'd all told him to plead guilty.'

You wipe your face with your handkerchief again and ask: 'But he
did confess, didn't he?'

Two little women in a little front room with its little photographs
and pictures of men gone, men gone missing –

Men not here –

Only you:

Fat, wet with sweat, and covered in chocolate and biscuit crumbs.

The two little women, their four eyes behind their metal frames,
cold and accusing –

Silent.

'It's difficult to appeal against a confession and a guilty plea,' you
say, softly.

'Mr Piggott,' says Mrs Myshkin. 'He didn't do it.'

'Look,' you say. 'I'm very sorry and I would really like to help but I just don't think I'm the man for the job and I would hate to waste your time or money. You need to find someone better qualified and a lot more experienced than I am in these matters.'

Their four eyes behind their metal frames, cold and accusing –

Silent, *betrayed*.

'Look,' you say again. 'Can I just outline what it would involve, why you really need to get someone else?'

Silent.

'Firstly you need to apply for leave to appeal. This is usually before what we call the single judge who has to be persuaded by the material prepared that we can demonstrate that there are grounds to appeal against conviction or sentence. That involves the presentation, even in very skeletal form, of legal reasons or new evidence that clearly demonstrate a reasonable degree of uncertainty as to the safety of the conviction. This is unlikely in the case of a confession, a deal with the prosecution, and the consent of the trial judge, plus the Crown and the judge and the jury's then acceptance of a guilty plea to lesser charges. But for the sake of argument, let's say such grounds for appeal against conviction can be found, if then these grounds are accepted by the single judge, and that is a very big if, leave to appeal would be granted and then the real business begins. You would need to be represented by counsel and also need to apply for legal aid for the solicitor and counsel to prepare for a full appeal. Should that aid be granted then a date would be set and eventually the case would come before the Court of Appeal. This consists of three judges who would go through the material; the evidence, arguments, what-have-you, and decide whether or not the conviction was safe, after which a ruling would be handed down detailing their decision and the reasoning behind it. In other words, it takes forever and one mistake and you're back to square bloody one. So you really need to find someone who knows what they're doing, what they're talking about.'

Four eyes, warm and welcoming –

Hands clapping.

'Mr Piggott,' beams Mrs Novashelska. 'You seem to know exactly what you're talking about.'

'No, no, no,' you say, shaking your head. 'It really isn't as simple as it sounds, plus I've never actually drawn up an application for leave to appeal and, to be frank, I don't see what grounds there would be anyway, other than Michael's changed his mind.'

Mrs Myshkin says again: 'He didn't do it.'

'So you keep saying,' you sigh. 'But that doesn't alter the fact that he

did confess and he did plead guilty to manslaughter on the grounds of
diminished responsibility, as opposed to murder, and this was accepted
by the prosecution and by the judge who did instruct the jury to do
likewise which all in all, appeal-wise, is something of an own goal
because you're basically appealing against yourself.'

'He had bad advice,' says Mrs Novashelska.

'So he doesn't need any more,' you say and stand up.

The two little women in the little front room with its little photographs and pictures of men gone, men gone missing –

Men not here –

Only you:

A fat man on fire and on his feet –

Melting –

A pool of piss on a patterned carpet.

You say: 'I'm sorry.'

Their four eyes behind their metal frames –

Silent.

You push your way along between the settee and the table, edging
towards the door, your shirt wringing, sticking to your stomach and
back.

'Mr Piggott,' says Mrs Myshkin again. 'He did not do it.'

Men not here.

You stop just to say again: 'And I'm sorry, but I wouldn't be of any
use.'

The two little women in the little front room with its little photographs and pictures of men gone, men gone missing –

Not here –

The two little women watching another man go.

In the doorway, you turn to say goodbye but Mrs Myshkin is on her
feet:

'Mr Piggott,' she says. 'I knew your father.'

You stand in the doorway with your back to her now, your mouth
dry and your clothes wet.

'He was a good man,' she says. 'I can remember him with you and
your brother, playing football on that field over there.'

Men not here.

'It's not enough,' you tell her. 'Not enough.'

'No,' she says, a hand upon your arm (upon your heart). 'It's too
much.'

You walk out into the hall.

There is an evening paper sticking through the letterbox. You pull it
out and open it up.

There's that photograph of Hazel Atkins, that word:
MISSING –
You turn back to hand the paper to Mrs Myshkin.
'It's happening again,' whispers her sister behind her.
'Never stops,' says Mrs Myshkin. 'Not round here.'
Not here –
'You know that,' she says, her hand squeezing your hand (your heart) –
Here.

Chapter 6

Phone is ringing and ringing and ringing –

Come on, come on, come on –

Hopping from foot to foot in a Bradford Bus Station phonebox –

Please, please, please –

And Clare picks up and BJ know she knows –

Knows her sister is dead, slurring: 'What now?'

'It's BJ.'

'BJ love,' she's sobbing. 'Gracie's dead.'

'I know,' BJ say. 'I was there.'

'Bastards,' she's howling. 'Bastards!'

'Clare, listen to me,' BJ whisper. 'You've got to get a cab and come and meet me.'

'Fucking filth are sending a car over, aren't they?' she's crying. 'Got to go and fucking identify – '

'You got to run – '

'I'm too fucking tired – '

'Clare, listen to me – '

'Paula and now Gracie – '

'And it'll be you next,' BJ shout. 'Come on.'

'Where are you?'

'Bradford Bus Station,' BJ say. 'Café opens in an hour.'

'But they're coming – '

'Well, fucking run – '

' . . . '

'Hello? Hello?'

Line dead, BJ hang up and dial again but it's engaged, again but it's engaged.

BJ stand in phonebox freezing BJ's tits off, staring at season's greetings:

Derek Shags Convicts Wives.

BJ dial one last time.

BJ hang up and turn and open door.

A man is sat on bench next to phonebox.

BJ look at BJ's watch:

Four in morning.

Man on bench says: 'Excuse me?'

BJ look at him: 'Yes?'

'Do you have the time?' he asks.

'You've got a watch.' BJ nod at edge of sleeve of man's coat.

'So I have,' he smiles. 'Silly me.'

BJ smile back: 'Silly you.'

He is middle-class and middle-aged and most likely married or recently divorced, dressed in corduroy trousers and an anorak. He says: 'I'm Jim. What's your name?'

'BJ.'

'That's a nice name.'

'BJ's name, BJ's game.'

'I like games,' says *Jim*.

'Me too,' BJ say. 'But they're not cheap.'

'I didn't think they would be,' he sighs.

'Ten pounds.'

He nods.

BJ look around bus station –

It's empty.

'I've got my car,' says *Jim*.

BJ shake head: 'Follow me.'

BJ and *Jim* walk across deserted platforms and into toilets and into far cubicle –

BJ put bog lid down and tell him to sit down.

He sits down.

'Give us tenner.'

Jim reaches inside his anorak and takes out a brown wallet and hands BJ two five pound notes.

BJ put them in trouser pocket and kneel down in front of him pushing his legs open.

'Just a minute,' says *Jim* and unzips his anorak.

'And trousers,' BJ say.

'They never check this place, do they?' he asks.

'Who?'

'The police? The bus company?'

'Shoosh,' BJ smile and reach into *Jim*'s fly and his underpants.

'What if – '

BJ glance at BJ's watch: 'Do you want to stop?'

'No,' he says. 'No.'

'Well, shut up and relax,' BJ hiss and pull *Jim*'s limp cock out of his vest and pants, sweet and sour smell of old talc and dry piss in BJ's face –

BJ stroke him until he is hard and then BJ start to suck –

And *Jim* closes his eyes and dreams he is fucking BJ up arse as BJ beg him to never stop, his muscular left forearm tight around BJ's thin little neck, his right fist around BJ's pale cock as his own slides in and out, in and out, in and out, in and out, in and out, in and out, in and out, in and out, in and out, in and out, in and –

Out:

Jim comes and BJ spit.

Jim does himself up and asks: 'You usually here, are you?'

BJ shake BJ's head: 'Your first time?'

Jim blushes and then nods.

'I'm just passing through,' BJ say.

'That's a shame.'

BJ nod.

'Where are you from?'

'I'm a space invader,' BJ wink and open door and step out of cubicle.

Jim stays there, smiling.

'You should go first,' BJ tell *Jim*.

'Thank you,' he says.

'Mention it.'

Jim looks confused like he wants to shake BJ's hand, but BJ look away into mirror and *Jim* hurries off home for a safer and more leisurely wank on his bathroom mat.

BJ run tap into dirty sink and splash icy water on BJ's face and rinse some round mouth and get dry with bottom of star shirt and then BJ count money and walk out across empty platforms through grey light to café and sign that promises all-day Christmas dinners today –

Christmas Eve.

BJ look at BJ's watch:

It's almost five.

BJ open door and step into café –

It's empty but warm and radio is on.

A big woman with a red face comes out of back.

'You open?' BJ ask.

'Just about,' she smiles.

'Ta,' BJ say.

'What can I get you?'

'Tea please.'

'Be five or ten minutes? I've just stuck it on.'

BJ nod and sit down opposite door.

There's a paper on one of chairs, yesterday's –

Two headlines:

RL STAR'S SISTER MURDERED.

COUNCILLOR RESIGNS.

By Jack Whitehead and George Greaves –

Two headlines and two faces:
Paula Garland and William Shaw –
Bill.
'Hello?'
BJ look up into another face –
Clare's face:
Streaked black with mascara rivers she's cried, smudged black where she's tried not to, her hair now blonde again –
'Hello,' BJ say and stand up and go towards her and take her in BJ's arms and hold her as BJ and Clare shake with tears and shock of it all until woman comes out of kitchen with tea and asks if Clare wants one as well and BJ nod and say she does and BJ and Clare sit back down across table from each other, Clare's hands in BJ's hands, and woman brings another cup and asks if everything is OK and BJ tell her everything is OK but when she's gone, Clare asks: 'What are we going to do?'
'Get out of here,' BJ say.
'Where?'
'Scotland?'
'It's where the kids are,' she says and hangs her head. 'Be first place they'll look.'
'London?'
'Second place.'
'Preston?'
Clare looks up: 'Why?'
'There's a coach at five-thirty.'
'Aye,' she nods and then she looks at BJ with her huge black eyes and asks: 'Why Gracie?'
'Loose ends,' BJ say.
'So what are we?'

Chapter 7

I woke again after less than an hour and lay in the shadows and dead of the night, the house quiet and dark, listening for something, anything: animal or bird's feet from below or above, a car in the street, a bottle on the step, the thud of a paper on the mat, but there was nothing; only the silence, the shadows and the dead, remembering when it wasn't always so, wasn't always this way, when there were human feet upon the stairs, children's feet, the slam of a ball against a bat or a wall, the pop of a cap gun and a burst balloon, bicycle bells and front doorbells, laughter and telephones ringing through the rooms, the smells, sounds and tastes of meals being cooked, served and eaten, of drinks poured, glasses raised and toasts drunk by men with cigars in black velvet jackets, their women with their sherries in their long evening dresses, the spare room for the light summer nights when no-one could drive, when no-one could leave, no-one wanted to leave, before that last time; that last time when the telephone rang and brought the silence that never left, that was here with me now, lying here with me now in the shadows and dead of a house, quiet and dark, empty –

Thursday morning.

I reached for my glasses and got out of bed and went down the stairs to the kitchen and put on the light and filled the kettle and lit the gas and took a teapot from the cupboard and a cup and saucer and unlocked the back door to see if the milk had been delivered yet but it hadn't though there was still enough milk in the fridge (there was always enough milk) and I poured it into the cup and put two teabags in the teapot and took the kettle off the ring and poured the water on to the teabags and let it stand while I washed the milk pan from last night and the Ovaltine mug and then dried them both up, staring out into the garden and the field behind, the kitchen reflected back in the glass, a man fully dressed in dark brown trousers, a light blue shirt and a green V-necked pullover, wearing his thick lenses with their heavy black frames, a man old and fully dressed at four o'clock in the morning –

Thursday 19 May 1983.

I put the teapot and cup and saucer on a plastic blue tray and took it into the dining room and set it down on the table and poured the tea on to the milk and took a plain digestive from the biscuit barrel and then put on the gas fire and switched on the radio and sat in the chair opposite the fire to wait for the news on Radio 2:

'*Peter Williams, the Yorkshire Ripper, will again appear at Newport Magistrates' Court on the Isle of Wight to give evidence against James Abbott, a fellow prisoner who is accused of wounding Williams with a piece of glass at Parkhurst Prison on January 10 this year; an attack that left Williams badly scarred and requiring surgery.*

'*Williams, dressed in a grey suit, open-necked shirt with gold cross and chain, was booed upon his appearance in court. The defence first asked him if he was not a rather unpopular person, to which Williams replied that this was an opinion based upon ignorance. Williams was also asked whether he realised that his story was worth a lot of money to the press. Williams said that this was the trouble with society today, that people were motivated by greed and that there were no moral values at all.*

'*Earlier Williams admitted that he continues to receive advice from the voices in his head. The trial of Mr Abbott continues.*'

I switched off the radio. I took off my glasses.

I was sat in the chair in tears again;

In tears –

Knowing there was salvation in no-one else –

No other name here under heaven.

In tears –

Thursday 19 May 1983:

Day 8.

I drove out of Wakefield and into Castleford, black light becoming grey mist over Heath Common, the ponies standing chained and still, the roads empty but for lorries and their lights.

I parked behind a pub called the Swan. I walked into the centre of Castleford.

On the high street a bald newsagent was fetching in two bundles of papers from the pavement.

'Morning,' I said.

'Morning,' he said, his face red.

'You know where Ted Jenkins had his studio?' I asked. 'Photographers?'

He stood upright: 'Bit early, aren't you?'

I showed him my warrant card.

He shrugged: 'Was up road on right, not there now though.'

'Since when was that then?'

Another shrug: 'Since it burned down – seven, maybe even ten years ago now.'

'So I'm actually a bit late then, aren't I?'

He smiled.

'Can I have one of them?' I said, pointing down at a *Yorkshire Post* and Hazel.

He nodded and took out a small pocket-knife. He cut the string that bound the papers together.

I handed him the money but he refused it: 'Go on, you're all right.'

'Which one was it then?' I asked him. 'His studio?'

He peered up the road: 'Where that Chinkie is.'

'Knew Ted well, did you?'

He shook his head: 'Just to say how do, like.'

'Never turned up, did he?' I said, looking up the road.

He sighed: 'Long time ago now.'

'After fire?' I said. 'No-one ever heard of him after that?'

Another shake of the head: 'Thought your mob reckoned he did a bloody Lord Lucan on us?'

I nodded: 'Long time ago.'

'Here,' he winked. 'I'll tell you who else worked there – '

'Thanks for the paper,' I nodded again and started walking away –

'Michael bloody Myshkin,' he shouted after me. 'Pervert who did all them little lasses.'

I kept walking, walking away, crossing by a shoe shop –

'Should have hung him, evil little bastard . . .'

Long time ago.

I came to the Lotus Chinese Restaurant & Take Away. I peered in over the menu in the window, white tablecloths and red napkins, the chairs and the tables, all stood there in silence and shadow –

A long time ago.

Across the road was another empty shop, just a name and a big weatherbeaten sign declaring that the property was to be redeveloped by Foster's Construction, builders of the new Ridings Shopping Centre, Wakefield:

Shopping centres –

Such a long time ago –

Fucking shopping centres –

Such a long, long time ago –

But the lies survived, those accepted little fictions we called history –

History and lies –

They survived us all.

Morley Police Station –

The Incident Room:

Alderman, Prentice, Gaskins, and Evans.

We were looking at a photograph and a poster –

One big word in red:

MISSING –

Above a picture of a ten-year-old girl with medium-length dark brown hair and brown eyes, wearing light blue corduroy trousers, a dark blue sweater embroidered with the letter *H*, and a red quilted sleeveless jacket, carrying a black drawstring gym bag.

I said: 'What happened to the *H* embroidered on the bag?'

'It was difficult – ' began Evans with the excuses.

I put up my hand to stop him. I held up the poster. 'Just tell me these'll be back from the printers by this afternoon?'

Evans was nodding: 'They'll be here for two.'

'Good,' I sighed. 'What about the school? You spoke with the Head, they know what they're doing?'

Evans still nodding: 'I said we'd be there from three.'

'*Calendar* and *Look North*?'

'Yep, but *Calendar* can only go with the photos at six; say they'll use the film after the *News at Ten*. Timing's not good.'

'Not going to be National then?'

Evans shook his head: 'Not at this stage, no.'

I turned to Gaskins: 'How many uniforms we got?'

'Hundred and fifty with roadblocks set up at both ends of Victoria Road and one at the top of Rooms Lane, another on Church Street.'

I looked up at the map of Morley pinned to the board beside her photograph: 'Where are the ones on Victoria Road?'

Gaskins stood and pointed at the map: 'One here at the junction with Springfield Road, other up here before King George Avenue.'

'They know what to do?'

'Drivers' licences and registrations,' he nodded. 'Show them the picture, spot of where were you last Thursday, and let them on their way.'

I turned to Prentice: 'Jim, you got me the unmarked cars?'

'Where you want them, Boss?'

My turn to stand and point and say: 'Junction with Asquith Avenue, here. Another up by this farm, here. Get one for centre as well, here by Chapel Hill.'

'Right,' he said.

'I want numbers,' I told him. 'Any vehicle stopping or reversing or changing direction when they see the roadblocks, take down their plate and call it through.'

Dick: 'You think he'll show.'

I nodded.

'Who?' asked Evans.

I picked up a piece of chalk. I turned to the board. I wrote up two names:

Jenkins and *Ashworth.*

Jim pointed at the first name: 'I thought he were dead?'

'Either of these names show,' I said. 'You detain them and call me. Immediately.'

1, 2, 3, 4, 5, 6, 7, all good children go to heaven –

'Fuck is this?' I said to Dick Alderman as we parked outside Morley Grange Junior and Infants, the playground full of children and parents, TV camera crews and journalists, their vans and their cars –

Reconstruction time.

'Evans,' I was shouting as I crossed the road, adjusting my glasses and looking at my watch. 'Evans!'

He was coming towards me, arms full of papers and files: 'Sir?'

'Get these fucking vans and cars out of here!' I yelled. 'Fucking circus.'

He was apologising but I wasn't listening –

'And get everyone in the fucking hall.'

'Mr Jobson?' asked the plump grey-haired woman coming towards us with the disgusted expression.

'Who are you?' I said.

'Marjorie Roberts,' she replied. 'The HT.'

'The HT?'

'The Head Teacher,' mumbled Evans.

I stuck out my hand: 'Maurice Jobson. Detective Chief Superintendent.'

'What would you like us to do, Mr Jobson?' she sighed.

'If you could ask all the children and their parents to step into the hall, that would be a big, big help.'

'Fine,' she said and walked off.

'Miserable bitch,' hissed Dick at my shoulder. 'Been up here practically every bloody day and not even a cup of tea. Just when can she expect things to get back to normal, upsetting the kids and their routine etc etc. Stupid fucking cow.'

I nodded: 'Where's Hazel?'

'In the old cow's office,' said Evans.

'And where is the old cow's office?'

'This way,' said Dick and we followed him across the playground, through the children and their parents, to the black stone building. He opened a double set of green doors and we stepped into the school and that familiar smell, that familiar smell of children and detergent.

We walked down a corridor, plastic supermarket bags hanging from the low pegs, the walls still decorated with pictures of Easter eggs. At the end of the corridor, Dick tapped on a door and opened it.

Inside a middle-aged woman was sitting with a ten-year-old girl; a ten-year-old girl with medium-length dark brown hair and brown eyes, wearing light blue corduroy trousers, a dark blue sweater embroidered with the letter *H*, and a red quilted sleeveless jacket, clutching a black drawstring gym bag.

'I'm Maurice Jobson,' I said. 'I'm the detective in charge.'

The woman stood up: 'I'm Nichola's mother. Karen Barstow.'

'Thank you very much for helping us,' I said.

'Anything to help find the poor little–'

'Hello,' I said to the ten-year-old girl with medium-length dark brown hair and brown eyes, wearing light blue corduroy trousers, a dark blue sweater embroidered with the letter *H*, and a red quilted sleeveless jacket, holding a black drawstring gym bag.

'Hello,' she said back.

'You must be Nichola,' I said.

'No,' said the ten-year-old girl with medium-length dark brown hair and brown eyes, wearing light blue corduroy trousers, a dark blue sweater embroidered with the letter *H*, and a red quilted sleeveless jacket, carrying a black drawstring gym bag –

'Today I'm Hazel.'

No other name.

I walked out on to the stage, the children sat crosslegged at the front, the teachers and journalists standing at the sides, parents mouthing messages to their kids from the back.

Mrs Roberts introduced me: 'Everybody, this is Mr Jobson. He's the policeman who's going to find Hazel. Now I know a lot of you have talked to the other nice policemen about Hazel, but today we're going to pretend it's last Thursday again. We're going to all try very hard to remember exactly what we did last Thursday and then we're all going to do the same thing again. Maybe some clever person will remember something very important and that will help Mr Jobson find Hazel.'

I stood there, nodding –

The children staring at me, silently.

Mrs Roberts had stopped speaking and was looking at me.

In a low voice she whispered: 'What about Hazel? Shall we introduce her.'

I nodded. I turned to the side. I gestured for Nichola's mother to lead her daughter out on to the stage –

There was a wave of noise across the hall, all the teachers with their fingers to their lips as all the parents strained to see their own kids who were standing up and sitting down, confused and excited.

'Children, sit down please,' barked Mrs Roberts.

I looked out at the rows and rows of children in front of me. I said: 'This is Nichola, but today she is going to be Hazel.'

'Will everybody please sit down!' shouted Mrs Roberts again. 'That means you too Stephen Tams.'

'Now,' I said, wishing WPC Martin was here and I wasn't. 'Who was with Clare last Thursday?'

Silence –

The kids were all looking at each other, then looking at their teachers and their parents, their teachers and their parents looking at me, all of them looking confused.

I turned to Mrs Roberts: 'What?'

Mrs Roberts was staring at me. She was frowning.

'What?' I said again.

Mrs Roberts, eyes wide, whispered: 'Hazel? You mean Hazel?'

I nodded. I mumbled: 'I'm sorry. Hazel. Who was with Hazel last Thursday at home time?'

Now there were hands going up, lots of hands, and the teachers and the parents were shaking their heads and then suddenly above the tiny hands, at the back of the room, I could see Mr and Mrs Atkins –

Mr and Mrs Atkins staring at me and the little girl beside me.

I turned to the girl –

The ten-year-old girl with long straight fair hair and blue eyes, wearing an orange waterproof kagool, a dark blue turtleneck sweater, pale blue denim trousers with a distinctive eagle motif on the back left pocket and red Wellington boots, carrying a plastic Co-op carrier bag containing a pair of black gym shoes.

She was holding my hand, her hand squeezing mine.

Outside it had started to rain again, the parents and journalists under their umbrellas, the kids with their hoods up, the three of us getting pissed on from up above –

And it hadn't even started yet.

'Whose fucking idea was it to have them here?' I was shouting.

'They wanted to be here,' Evans was saying. 'The press want to speak to them. Gives us more exposure.'

'You should have fucking checked.'

'I'm sorry,' he was saying for the thousandth bloody time today.

'Forget it,' I said. 'It's done.'

Dick looked at his watch: 'Home time?'

I looked at mine. I nodded at Evans: 'Let's get started.'

Evans walked back across the playground to the TV crews and the journalists at the gates; the teachers, the parents and their kids impatiently waiting for the signal to begin. The TV crews and journalists were all over Evans with their questions and demands. Finally he ducked out from under their umbrellas and curses and gave the signal and, out of this pantomime and pandemonium, in the middle of the rain at the school gates, there she was again –

Hazel Atkins:

Coming through the gates, the other kids behind her, waving and stopping and waving and stopping, hands up and hands down and hands up and hands down, waving bye-bye to the ten-year-old girl with the medium-length dark brown hair and brown eyes, wearing light blue corduroy trousers, a dark blue sweater embroidered with the letter *H*, and a red quilted sleeveless jacket, carrying a black drawstring gym bag –

Hazel:

Walking up Rooms Lane towards her home in Bradstock Gardens, behind her the TV crews and the journalists with their lenses and their pens, the kids and their parents with their whispers and suspicions, the teachers and police with their hopes and their fears, all of us walking up the road in silent procession through the rain, the rain falling down through the dark, quiet trees and into her hair, into her medium-length dark brown hair and her quiet brown eyes, staining her light blue corduroy trousers, her dark blue sweater embroidered with the letter *H*, on to her red quilted sleeveless jacket, soaking her black drawstring gym bag –

Hazel:

Watching her turn towards her house in Bradstock Gardens, the occasional car and lorry slowing, the Atkins in pieces in the rain, their tears in the road because she'd never walk up Rooms Lane again, never turn towards her home in Bradstock Gardens, never open that door and never come in from the rain, never be –

Hazel:

This was all they'd ever get –

A ten-year-old girl with medium-length dark brown hair and brown eyes, wearing light blue corduroy trousers, a dark blue sweater embroidered with the letter *H*, and a red quilted sleeveless jacket, carrying a black drawstring gym bag, a ten-year-old girl who was not their daughter, a reconstruction –

Not Hazel:

I stood in the road in tears again, a hand squeezing mine –

The hand of a ten-year-old girl with long straight fair hair and blue eyes, wearing an orange waterproof kagool, a dark blue turtleneck sweater, pale blue denim trousers with a distinctive eagle motif on the back left pocket and red Wellington boots, carrying a plastic Co-op carrier bag containing a pair of black gym shoes –

Clare:

Waving bye-bye to the ten-year-old girl with the medium-length dark brown hair and brown eyes, wearing the light blue corduroy trousers, the dark blue sweater embroidered with the letter *H*, and the red quilted sleeveless jacket, carrying the black drawstring gym bag, the ten-year-old girl who was walking away –

Hazel:

Walking away as the rain fell down through the dark, quiet trees and into her dark brown hair and her quiet brown eyes as her mother screamed and screamed, her nails in the road in the rain, screaming and screaming –

This is what you've done, this is what you've done, this is what you've done.

Then there were feet behind me, not children's feet –

But boots, police boots through the puddles –

Dick shouting: 'We got him, Boss.'

The rain falling through the dark, quiet trees –

'Up Church Street.'

The little girls gone –

'We've fucking got him.'

Just the history and the lies –

Resurrected.

Chapter 8

You have dreams –

D-20, here comes retreat; Friday lunchtime you meet Gareth in Billy Walton's and give yourself the afternoon off, it being his birthday, tea and fishcakes in teacakes with chips and peas sorting you out for the first pint of the weekend, racing pages open, Gareth still going on about Grittar losing the fucking National and how it's not right, women trainers, be women football managers next, and you're nodding along, the old woman on the table opposite you with her mouth full of lipstick, potato and fish, her eyes wrapped in bandages, she points at you with her fork.

And in your dreams –

Your bellies slopping with tea and fishcakes in teacakes, chips and peas, you cross the Springs to the indoor market and the secondhand book stall, Gareth getting his weekly additions to his porn stash, you helping him choose, the woman behind the stall pointing out a few he's missed, you treating him, it being his birthday, the rain streaming in through the roof, you wonder what the fuck will happen to this place when they finish the Ridings, Gareth with his secondhand porn in a brown paper bag, the readers' wives with their plastic carrier bags, their umbrellas and their meat, kids under their feet.

In your dreams, you have wings –

Back out in the puddles of blood, past the fish stalls, the tripe and offal shop, up the side of the Fleece, behind the back of the Bullring, out opposite the bus station and into Tickles, just in time for the afternoon stripper and that first pint of the weekend, Gareth moaning about the plastic glasses, standing room only as Disco Ken cues up *Billie Jean* and out traipses Tina, all tassels and tits, telling half the room to fuck off and forking anyone she's missed, no wink today for John Piggott, solicitor to the strippers and the deejays, the bar men and the bouncers, the spots on Tina's back catching in the lights.

But all these wings in all your dreams –

Three pints later you're next door in Hills between turns, waiting for
the two-thirty from fuck-knows-where, out of cigs and hungry again,
busting for another slash, an old bloke holding open an *Evening Post*
and a photo of Hazel Atkins with the words *Hazel: Police Arrest Local
Man in Morley*, big-black-bloody-type and doesn't-look-so-bloody-good
says Gareth and hanging-is-too-good-for-him agrees the old boy, your
brain, your bladder and your belly contorted, screaming and howling,
the old man smiling, nodding and blinking, his teeth yellow, stained
and loose in his gums bloody, black, and sore.

Are huge and rotting things –

Fifth pint and two packets of beef and onion, Gareth wants a decent
pint across the Bullring in the Strafford, you telling him to piss off cos
he only wants to go in Ladbrokes and why doesn't he anyway because
you're quite happy here watching the little stage, the mirror ball
shining and Phil Collins playing over the empty dancefloor, waiting for
Disco Ken to give it a bit of *Too Shy* which is Blonde Debbie's song,
quite looking forward to Debbie coming on, fit despite two kids and
the plasters the brewery make her put over her tattoos.

The room red.

Back out in the rain again, ducking next door for the night's cigs, forty
of them to be going on with, telling Gaz you'll see him at six down the
Waterloo, half-past at the latest, but he'll be in Clothiers opening time if
you change your mind, and you wander over the Bullring to Greggs
and buy a bag of pasties for your tea, corned beef and Cornish, then
you walk back up to St John's, past the Grammar School and on to
Blenheim Road, the tarmac coated with thousands of pieces of broken
glass from a shattered windscreen, some of them a deep, dark and
bloody red.

You have dreams –

Quarter-past five and you're soaking in Matey, a big Gordon's on the
edge of the bath, slice and ice, careful not to bloody nod off again, out
and dressed, fingers full of green super-strength Boots hair gel,
washing down the last of the pasties with another gin and tonic, out of
slice and ice, feeling better already, putting on Rod and wondering if
you shouldn't wear kegs instead of jeans, fucking the money and
calling Azads for a taxi down the Waterloo and the start of the Westgate

Run, smelling your breath on the phone and cleaning your teeth again and again and again.

And in your dreams –

Gareth's at the bar already, half-drunk Tetley's in his hand, everyone else piling in right behind you: Sarn, Kelly, Daz, Hally, Foz, Dickie, and Mark the Fireman, across the room a group of lasses starting the run themselves, hen night, everyone laughing and joking and Gareth doing the honours: a spirit for everyone in first pub then the birthday boy doesn't buy another drink all night, yours a Southern Comfort, but he knows that and there's an old man at the bar in a white coat with a tray of whelks and you quietly check your shoes for dog-shit, your ears burning.

In your dreams, you have fears –

You are in the White Hart before the hen party, Gareth and Sarn playing arrows, Kelly telling jokes and taking piss out of Hally and Foz, same old stories getting funnier and dirtier as the weeks turn into months and the months into years, Daz dissecting Leeds' season starting with Harvey back in Waterloo, now on to Thomas, Dickie stoned and half asleep and Mark the Fireman putting shit on the jukebox and getting the same in return, beer in the ashtray, beer on the table, beer on the seat, beer on the floor, Kelly reminding everyone of the time Foz shat in a girl's handbag upstairs in Raffles.

But all your fears in all your dreams –

Waggon and Horses is dead and Kelly reckons you should slow down and wait for the hen party, saying that now because he has to meet Ange in the Elephant, but a bloke at the bar reckons there's been a fight in Smith's Arms and you think you should skip it and go straight to the Old Globe, but you end up supping up even faster which pisses off Mark the Fireman because he's just put a load more bollocks on the jukebox, *Whiter Shade of Pale* for fucking starters, and someone drops a Tampax from fuck-knows-where in his pint to hurry him along, not that it's used or stops him downing the pint in one.

Are islands lost in tears –

Landlord in Smith's Arms says there was a few broken glasses was all, nothing he couldn't handle, group of lads from Stanley on a Run, heard that Streethouse were coming into town looking for them, these lads fancying their chances but getting a bit edgy, few broken glasses was all, the hen party coming in, but your seal's just gone and you're stood staring at the bloody bogies wiped on the wall above the bog where someone's written *the Paunchy Cowboys* and stuck up bits of bog roll everywhere with their own shit.

The room white.

Stopper and Norm are in the Old Globe and it's half-seven already, the big old map of the world and pictures of ships which traditionally dictates a Captain Morgan's followed by a Barley Wine and cider, Stopper shouting Ahoy! as his shipmates board, going on stoned about *Captain Pugwash*, the Black Pig and Master Bates, and you start on about *The Flying Dutchman* when you swear you hear Procul bloody Harem come on the sodding jukebox again but Hally says there isn't a fucking jukebox you pissed fat legal cunt, never has been, not here.

You have dreams –

In Swan with Two you find the hen party again, better looking by the pint, specially one with the short brown hair who's bound to be the bleeding fucking bride, not that she'd look at a fat cunt like you anyway, not that there's a wedding ring in sight on any of them says Kelly, not that a ring means any-bloody-thing thinks Dickie, and she smiles as she goes to the bogs and tells Kelly to fuck off when he does his been-for-a-shit-darling routine as she comes out, her hair smelling of shampoo and smoke and you wonder if she did have a shit or just a piss, perched over the seat, not wanting to touch it.

And in your dreams –

Daz catches up with you in Henry Boons and he's up to Hird now, the various crimes he should be shot or hung for, way he's played this season, all Eddie Gray's fault anyway, he picks the fucking team doesn't he, fat bastard, no offence John, but everyone sups up quick, except Kel because Ange and her mates will be in Elephant which you think is good news because she's got some nice mates has Ange, but you do have time for a swift one in Mid before Elephant, so you head up the back way past the Prison, everyone breaking into a chorus of *Born Free* as you go, everyone except you.

In your dreams, you see things –

The Mid stinks of damp, full of punks and students from the Tech, a couple of blokes from Labour Club who want to talk politics until it's obvious state you're in you can't, not that it stops you taking piss out of Thatcher in this morning's *Post* with her vision of a return to the eternal values of the Victorian era, ruling Britain into the 1990s, until she gets another bomb from the Yorkshire Republican Army that is, and that's you that is, the YRA, but then you think you're going to puke and you run for the bogs, the Barley Wine coming back up then straight back down your bloody nose.

But all these things in all your dreams –

Ange isn't even in Elephant and now Kel's pissed off and the pool room is packed and someone reckons Streethouse are on their way and with Stanley about it seems a bit of a bad night and then a glass smashes and everyone jumps and Sarn says it's just the speed, just the speed, but in the bogs you wonder what you ought to do and Hally says he's up for a club but none of you have ties and most of you are in jeans and none of you can be arsed to go home and change, so it'll have to be Raffles or somewhere shit like that because you'll not get in Casanovas, not dressed like this, not now.

Are big black raven things –

Fuck knows who said there are always a load of good-looking lasses in Evergreens, all you can see are a gang of Siouxsie fucking Siouxs giving you daggers until Wilf the punk dwarf who you represented when he was done for pissing against Balne Lane library after he lost one of his brothel creepers and he couldn't hop and hold it all the way home to Flanshaw, until Wilf the punk dwarf says Streethouse have been nicked at top of Westgate after a fight with some lads from Stanley, and he used to call you Petrocelli and ended up with a fifty quid fine while you and his old man got done for contempt.

The room blue.

Kelly was in Friars and says same about Streethouse when you meet him and Dickie and Ange with one of her mates back in Graziers for last, Daz and Foz still in Elephant talking to two lasses from the hen party, which is bloody fucking typical, but now it's you and Sarn talking ten to dozen, feeling top of the world, and Mark says Gareth's puking in bogs but that's only because that wasn't really a Glenfiddich in Evergreens, thinks he'll be all right for Raffles or Dolly Grays or wherever you're off but he wishes you'd make up your fucking minds, Hally suddenly silent, his eyes red.

You have dreams –

Outside Kel and them are going back to theirs or Norm's and you ought to do too he says because Raffles is going to be shit and full of fucking freaks and he's a ton of fucking draw back at his, but you always go back to his or Norm's every Friday and Saturday and it's Gareth's fucking birthday so why don't they all come up to Raffles too, but Ange is working tomorrow on an early shift so that isn't going to happen, so you tell Kel you'll see him in Billy Walton's tomorrow about two and you walk up the hill to Westgate, pissing behind back of somewhere, a light going on and then off again.

And in your dreams –

Top of Westgate's heaving, everyone stumbling around trying to get out of the pubs and into the clubs, taxis and last buses swerving and braking to miss people fighting and falling in the road with their kebabs and swamp burgers, pizzas and Indians, dropping them or puking them up, the police just sitting about in their vans with their dogs on their leads until some bloke in a crash helmet sticks his head through a window and some silly slag pushes a shopping trolley out into the road, the 127 braking and did-you-see-that, what-did-you-say, yeah-fucking-hell-you-fucking-bet-you-fucking-saw-that.

In your dreams, you cry tears –

Two quid and up the stairs into Raffles, bouncer a bloke you know giving you a slap on the back but no fucking discount because the cow on the door's screwing the boss, but it's nice to know Graham still works here because you never know what's going to happen, which is exactly what you're saying to this lass at the bar and she's all right she is and you have a bit of a dance to David Bowie and a smooch to Bonnie Tyler and you remember Gareth passing out and Sarn calling you Doctor Love and you thinking thank-fucking-Christ you didn't have any more speed.

But all your tears in all your dreams –

Her parents and brother are at the caravan for the weekend so you are
queuing among the chicken bones for a taxi on Cheapside, having a bit
of a snog every now and again, her legs nice and brown, fine fair hairs
a little bit sweaty, and you touch her cunt in the back of the taxi, the
smell of pine, puke and perspiration, and you get out in the centre of
Ossett and buy a curry to take back to hers, though she'll have to open
all the fucking windows because they'll be back Sunday lunchtime and
he hates that bloody Paki smell in the house does her dad.

Are islands lost in fears –

But after the curry she's sober and off the idea of a shag and you knew
you should have done it before you had the curry or even back behind
Raffles, but she's getting a bit funny and telling you to get off her, it's
her time of the month, and you're thinking there's always trap two, but
that's not going to happen, not now, and the curtains are beginning to
spin, the patterns in the carpet, the gold in the rug, but you can have
her brother's room if you promise not to puke or shit in his sheets,
that's if you're not going to go home which you're not, not now.

The room red, white and blue (just like you).

You wake afraid about five under a poster of Kenny Dalglish and you
go into her room and into her bed and take off her knickers and have a
good squeeze of her tits while she pretends to still be asleep as you lick
her out and shag her, she never opens her eyes so you put a finger
up her arse and have a last shag, meat and bone, fat and muscle,
blood and come, then you go downstairs and steal their paper and an
umbrella and let yourself out, standing in their drive under their
umbrella, staring at that photo on the front of their paper when you
realise this is Towngate –
     Towngate, Ossett, where Michael Williams murdered his wife with
a hammer and a twelve-inch nail back in 1974 or 75, the *Exorcist*
killing –
     About the same time they must have nicked Michael Myshkin –
     About the same time Hazel Atkins was having her first birthday –
     And you stand in their drive under their umbrella and you stare at
her photo on the front of their paper and wish you were not you –
     For there is no retreat, *no escape –*
     Not now.

Chapter 9

On back seat again –

Another empty coach:

Tuesday 24 December 1974 –

Longest Christmas Eve.

Clare slumped against window, dirty blonde hair against dirty grey glass, her best friend and her sister dead, a small suitcase in rack above her head.

BJ look across aisle and out other window at rain and moors, bleak weather and land it makes, no suitcase above BJ's head –

Just a pocket full of blood 'n' cum money, two stolen watches and some rings.

BJ look at rings on BJ's fingers –

BJ look at ring Bill put on BJ's finger –

Bill:

William Shaw.

BJ pull yesterday's newspaper out of Clare's carrier bag and look at photo –

Look at photo of his face and read that front page again:

COUNCILLOR RESIGNS

William Shaw, the Labour leader and Chairman of the new Wakefield Metropolitan District Council, resigned on Sunday in a move that shocked the city.

In a brief statement, Shaw, 58, cited increasing ill-health as the reason behind his decision.

Shaw, the older brother of the Home Office Minister of State Robert Shaw, entered Labour politics through the Transport and General Workers' Union. He rose to be a regional organiser and represented the T.G.W.U. on the National Executive Committee of the Labour Party.

A former Alderman and active for many years in West Riding politics, Shaw was, however, a leading advocate of Local Government reform and had been a member of the Redcliffe-Maud Committee.

Shaw's election as Chairman of the first Wakefield Metropolitan District Council had been widely welcomed as ensuring a smooth transition during the changeover from the old West Riding.

Local government sources last night expressed consternation and dismay at the timing of Mr Shaw's resignation.

Mr Shaw is also Acting Chairman of the West Yorkshire Police Authority and it is unclear as to whether he will continue.

Home Office Minister of State Robert Shaw was unavailable for comment on his brother's resignation. Mr Shaw himself is believed to be staying with friends in France.

Read that front page, stare at photo of his face:

Face not smiling –

Remembering when it was always smiling, smiling and laughing, laughing and joking –

That trip to Spain, mornings on beach and siestas in his arms, evenings full of fine wines and dodgy bellies, nights of –

Nights of love:

His grey hair and gentle words, his firm kisses and soft caresses before –

Before BJ fucked it all, fucked it all:

All because of what and who BJ be.

Coach slows –

BJ lean into aisle –

Blue lights up ahead in grey:

Fuck.

Single-lane traffic, red sticks waving in dawn:

Fuck.

Driver has his window down, shouting: 'What is it?'

'IRA,' comes a copper's voice.

'Not again?'

'Irish bastards,' says copper, but he waves coach through and coach picks up speed again.

Clare is staring at BJ, heavy rain against windows of coach.

'We there?' she asks, rubbing her black eyes.

'Roadblock,' BJ say.

'Jesus,' she says. 'Where are we?'

'Heading down into Manchester.'

She wipes window, but it doesn't help.

BJ say: 'Not very Christmassy, is it?'

'Used to have good ones, did you?'

BJ sigh: 'Not really. And you?'

She shakes her head: 'I'd love to see the girls though.'

'I bet,' BJ say, thinking –

Poor, poor fucking cow.

'Said I'd be back by Christmas, you know.'

'Give them a ring,' BJ say.

She sucks in her lower lip and nods.

BJ put newspaper back in bag as coach pulls into Chorlton Street Bus Station.

'Be half an hour,' shouts driver. 'You getting off?'

'Aye,' shouts Clare and walks down aisle with BJ and jumps off.

It's going up to eight and fucking freezing is Manchester.

BJ and Clare cross Portland Street into Piccadilly Gardens and go into first café BJ and Clare find:

Piccadilly Grill.

Clare has a breakfast and BJ have her toast, stomachs full of hot sweet tea.

At eight o'clock radio turns them stomachs, turns them inside out:

'West Yorkshire Police today launched a massive manhunt following an armed robbery on a Wakefield pub last night which left four people dead and two policemen seriously injured.

'The incident took place at approximately one a.m. last night at the Straf-ford Arms public house in the centre of Wakefield when a masked gang of armed men broke into a first-floor private party. Officers responding to initial reports of shots fired interrupted the robbery and were themselves attacked.

'The gang are believed to have escaped with the contents of the till and some cash and jewellery stolen from customers.

'Roadblocks were immediately set up across the county and on the M62 and M1 and initial reports that the attack might be linked to armed Irish Republican terrorists have yet to be discounted.

'Detective Chief Superintendent Maurice Jobson, the man leading the hunt for the gang, asked members of the public with any information whatsoever to contact the police as a matter of some urgency, but he also cautioned the public not to approach these men as they are armed and extremely dangerous.

'Mr Jobson admitted that the police were also taking very seriously sugges-tions that the attack upon the Strafford may be linked to a recent escalation in Yorkshire gangland violence which may also be behind the death early yes-terday morning of local Wakefield businessman Donald Foster at his Sandal home.

'Mr Jobson further confirmed that the two policemen injured in the attack were Sergeant Robert Craven and PC Robert Douglas, the two policemen who recently made headlines following their arrest of Michael Myshkin, the Fitzwilliam man charged with the murder of Morley schoolgirl Clare Kemplay. Mr Jobson described the condition of the officers as "serious but stable", but he refused to release the names of the dead as police were still trying to contact a number of relatives.

'Mr Jobson also added that he believed that some relatives may even have gone into hiding for fear of reprisals and he appealed for them to . . .'

Two steaming teas, two empty seats.

Chapter 10

Gotcha –
> Dark night –
> Day 11:
> One in the morning –
> Sunday 22 May 1983:
> Yorkshire –
> Leeds –
> Millgarth Police Station:
> The Belly –
> Room 4:

James Ashworth, twenty-two, in police issue grey shirt and trousers, long, lank hair everywhere, slouched akimbo in his chair at our table, a cigarette burning down to a stub between the dirty black nails of his dirty yellow fingers –

Jimmy James Ashworth, former friend and neighbour of Michael Myshkin, child killer –

Jimmy Ashworth, the boy who found Clare Kemplay.

I asked him: 'For the thousandth fucking time Jimmy, what were you doing in Morley on Thursday?'

And for the thousandth fucking time he told me: 'Nothing.'

We'd had him here since five on Thursday night, got him riding his motorbike into Morley, head to toe in denim and leather, the words *Saxon* and *Angelwitch* stitched into his back between a pair of swan's wings, had him here since Thursday night but hadn't technically started the questioning until Friday morning at seven which gave us another six hours with the little twat, but he'd given us nothing, nothing except the clothes off his back, his boots and his motorbike, the dirt from under his nails, the blood from his arms and the come from his cock, so we'd been over to Fitzwilliam and we'd ripped up their house, their garage and their garden, had the washing from their basket and from in off their line, the dust and hairs from their floors, the sheets and stains off their beds, the rubbish out their bins, sent it all up to forensics, then taken his mam and his dad, his whole gyppo family in, the garage where he worked and the blokes he called mates, the lass he was shagging, had them all in but had got fuck all out of them, nothing –

Yet.

*

Gotcha –

Long dark night –

Day 11:

Three in the morning –

Sunday 22 May 1983:

Yorkshire –

Leeds –

Millgarth Police Station:

The Belly –

Room 4:

We opened the door. We stepped inside:

Dick Alderman and Jim Prentice –

One with a greying moustache, the other one bald but for tufts of fine sandy hair:

Moustache and Sandy.

And me:

Maurice Jobson; Detective Chief Superintendent Maurice Jobson –

Thick lenses and black frames –

The Owl.

And him:

James Ashworth, twenty-two, police issue grey shirt and trousers, long, lank hair everywhere, slouched in his chair at our table, dirty black nails, dirty yellow fingers –

Jimmy James Ashworth, former friend and neighbour of Michael Myshkin, child killer –

Jimmy Ashworth, the boy who found Clare Kemplay.

'Sit up straight and put your palms flat upon the desk,' said Jim Prentice.

Ashworth sat up straight and put his palms flat upon the desk.

Jim Prentice sat down at an angle to Ashworth. He took a pair of handcuffs from the pocket of his sports jacket. He passed them to Dick Alderman.

Dick walked around the room. Dick played with the handcuffs. Dick sat down opposite Ashworth.

I closed the door to Room 4.

Dick put the handcuffs over the knuckles of his right fist.

I leant against the door arms folded, watching Ashworth's face –

In the silence:

Room 4 quiet, the Belly quiet –

The Station silent, the Market silent –

Leeds sleeping, Yorkshire sleeping.

Dick jumped up. Dick brought his handcuffed fist down on to the top of Ashworth's right hand –

Ashworth screamed –

Screamed –

Through the room, through the Belly –

Up through the Station, up through the Market –

Across Leeds, across Yorkshire –

He screamed.

'Put your hands back,' said Jim.

Ashworth put them back on the table.

'Flat,' said Jim.

He tried to lie them down flat.

'Nasty,' said Dick.

'You should get that seen to,' said Jim.

They were both smiling at him.

Jim stood up. He walked over to me.

I opened the door. I stepped out into the corridor.

I came back in. I gave Jim a blanket.

Jim placed the blanket over Ashworth's shoulders: 'There you go, lad.'

Jim sat back down. He took out a packet of JPS from the pocket of his sports jacket. He offered one to Dick.

Dick took out a lighter. He lit both their cigarettes.

They blew smoke across Ashworth.

Ashworth's hands were flat upon the desk, shaking.

Dick leant forward. Dick dangled the cigarette over Ashworth's right hand. Dick rolled it between two fingers, back and forth, back and forth.

Ashworth's right hand was twitching –

Twitching in the silence:

Room 4 quiet, the Belly quiet –

The Station silent, the Market silent.

Dick reached forward. Dick grabbed Ashworth's right wrist. Dick held down Ashworth's right hand. Dick stubbed his cigarette out into the bruise on the back of Ashworth's hand.

Ashworth screamed –

Screamed –

Through the room, through the Belly –

Up through the Station, up through the Market –

He screamed.

Dick let go of his wrist. Dick sat back.

'Put your hands flat,' said Jim Prentice.

Ashworth put them flat on the table.

The room stank of burnt skin:

His burnt skin.

'Another?' said Jim.

'Don't mind if I do,' said Dick. He took a JPS from the packet. He lit the cigarette. He stared at Ashworth. He leant forward. He began to dangle the cigarette over Ashworth's hand.

Ashworth stood up, clutching his right hand in his left: 'What do you want?'

'Sit down,' said Jim.

'Tell me what you want!'

'Sit down.'

Ashworth sat back down.

Dick Alderman and Jim Prentice stood up.

'Stand up,' said Jim.

Ashworth stood up.

'Eyes front.'

Ashworth stared straight ahead.

'Don't move.'

Dick and Jim lifted the three chairs and the table to one side. I opened the door. We stepped out into the corridor. I closed the door. I looked through the spy-hole at Ashworth. He was stood in the centre of the room, eyes front and not moving.

'Pity the Badger and Rudkin can't be with us,' said Jim. 'Be like old times.'

Old times.

I ignored him. I asked Dick: 'Where's Ellis?'

'Upstairs.'

'He got it?'

Dick nodded.

'Best get him then, hadn't you?'

Dick walked off down the corridor.

'Shame they can't be here,' said Jim again.

'Shame a lot of people can't be,' I said.

Jim shut up.

Dick came back down the corridor with Mike Ellis. Ellis was carrying a box under a blanket.

'Morning,' he slurred. His breath reeked of whiskey.

I said: 'You up for this Michael, are you?'

He nodded.

I leant in closer to his mouth: 'Bit of Dutch courage for breakfast, eh?'

He tried to pull his head back.

I had him by the scruff: 'Don't fuck it up, Michael.'

He nodded. I patted him on his face. He smiled. I smiled back.

'Ready?' said Jim.

Everyone nodded. Ellis put down the box. He left it in the corridor for now. I handed him a package wrapped in brown paper. I opened the door.

We stepped inside –

Room 4:

James Ashworth, twenty-two, police issue shirt and trousers, lank hair everywhere, a cigarette burn and a bloody bruise to match the dirty black nails of his dirty yellow fingers –

Jimmy James Ashworth, former friend and neighbour of Michael Myshkin, child killer –

Jimmy Ashworth, the boy who found Clare Kemplay.

Jim Prentice and I stood by the door. Dick and Ellis brought the chairs and the table back into the centre of the room.

Dick put a chair behind Ashworth. He said: 'Sit down.'

Ashworth sat down opposite Ellis.

Dick picked up the blanket from the floor. He put it over Ashworth's shoulders.

Ellis lit a cigarette. He said: 'Put your palms flat on the desk.'

'Will you just tell me what you want?' said Ashworth.

'Just put your palms flat, Jimmy.'

Ashworth put his palms flat on the desk.

Dick paced about the room behind him.

Ellis put the brown paper package on the table. He opened it. He took out a pistol. He placed it on the table between him and Ashworth.

Ellis smiled at Ashworth.

Dick stopped pacing about the room. He stood behind Ashworth.

'Eyes front,' said Ellis.

Ashworth stared straight ahead in silence:

Room 4 quiet, the Belly quiet.

Ellis jumped up. Ellis pinned down Ashworth's wrists.

Dick grabbed the blanket. Dick twisted it around Ashworth's face.

Ashworth fell forward off his chair –

Coughing and choking, unable to breathe.

Ellis held down his wrists.

Dick twisted the blanket around his face.

Ashworth was on his knees on the floor –

Coughing and choking, unable to breathe.

Ellis let go of Ashworth's wrists.

Ashworth span round in the blanket and into the wall:
CRACK –
Through the room, through the Belly.
Dick pulled off the blanket. He picked Ashworth up by his hair. He stood him up against the wall.
'Turn around, eyes front.'
Ashworth turned around.
Ellis had the pistol in his right hand.
Dick had some bullets. He was throwing them up into the air. He was catching them.
Ellis asked me: 'It's all right to shoot him then, Boss?'
I nodded: 'Shoot him.'
Ellis held the pistol at arm's length in both hands. Ellis pointed the barrel at Ashworth's head.
Ashworth closed his eyes. Tears streamed down his cheeks.
Ellis pulled the trigger –
CLICK –
Nothing happened.
'Fuck,' said Ellis.
He turned away. He fiddled with the pistol.
Ashworth had pissed himself.
'I've fixed it,' said Ellis. 'It'll be all right this time.'
He pointed the pistol again.
Ashworth still had his eyes closed.
Ellis pulled the trigger –
BANG!
James Ashworth, twenty-two, thought he was dead:
He opened his eyes. He saw the pistol. He saw the shreds of black material coming out of the barrel. He saw them floating down to the floor –
He saw us all laughing.
'What do you want?' shouted Ashworth. 'What do you fucking want?'
Dick stepped forward. Dick kicked him in the balls.
Ashworth fell to the floor: 'What do you want?'
'Stand up.'
He stood up.
'On your toes,' said Dick.
'Please tell me?'
Dick stepped forward. Dick kicked him in the balls again.
He fell to the floor again.
Ellis walked over to him. Ellis kicked him in the chest. Ellis kicked

him in the stomach. Ellis handcuffed his hands behind his back. Ellis
pushed his face down into the floor. Into his own piss.

'Do you like rats, Jimmy?'

'What do you want?'

'Do you like rats?'

Dick stepped out into the corridor. He came back into the room. He
had the box under the blanket.

Ashworth was still lying on the floor. Still lying in his own piss.

Dick walked over to Ashworth. Dick placed the box down on the
ground next to Ashworth's face.

Ellis pulled Ashworth's head up by his hair.

Dick ripped off the blanket –

The rat was fat. The rat was dirty. The rat was staring through the
wire of the cage. The rat was staring at Ashworth.

Dick tipped up the cage.

The rat slid closer to the wire. The rat slid closer to Ashworth.

'Get him! Get him!' laughed Dick.

The rat was frightened. The rat was hissing. The rat was clawing at
the wire. The rat was clawing at Ashworth's face.

'He's starving,' said Dick.

Ellis pushed Ashworth's face into the wire.

'Careful,' said Ellis.

The rat backed away.

Dick kicked the cage. Dick tipped the rat up into the wire –

It's tail and fur against Ashworth's face.

Jim Prentice was shouting: 'Turn it round, turn it round.'

'Open it,' I said.

Dick tipped the cage on its backside. The wire door of the cage was
facing up. Dick opened the wire door.

The rat was at the bottom of the cage. The rat was looking up at the
open door.

Ellis brought Ashworth's face down to the open door –

Ashworth, eyes wide –

Screaming and crying –

Ashworth, eyes wide –

Struggling and trying to get loose –

The rat was growling. The rat was shitting itself. The rat was
looking up at Ashworth.

Ellis pressed Ashworth's face down further into the open cage.

Ashworth was about to lose consciousness. Ashworth was crying
out: 'What have I done?'

I nodded.

Ellis pulled him back up by his hair: 'What did you say?'

Ashworth was shaking. Ashworth was crying.

I shook my head.

Ellis pushed his face back down into the cage.

Ashworth screamed out again: 'What have I done? Please just tell me what I've done?'

I nodded again.

Ellis pulled him back up again: 'What?'

'Tell me what I've done?'

'Again?'

'Please tell me what I've done?'

'Again?'

'Please – '

But Dick had his hand down in the cage. Dick lifted the rat out by its tail. Dick swung the rat into the wall –

SMASH!

Blood splattered across Ashworth and Ellis.

'Fucking hell,' shouted Ellis. 'You fucking do that for?'

Dick dropped the dying rat on to the floor of Room 4. Dick walked over to James Ashworth, twenty-two, slumped in Ellis's arms. Dick bent down. Dick brushed Ashworth's long, lank hair out of his face. Dick wiped his hands down Ashworth's cheeks, down his police issue shirt, down his trousers.

'Good boy, Jimmy,' smiled Dick. 'Good boy.'

I turned to Jim Prentice: 'Clean this up.'

I stepped out into the corridor. I looked at my watch:

It was almost ten o'clock –

Day 11.

I could hear footsteps coming down the steps, down the corridor, into the Belly.

I looked up:

John Murphy was coming towards me –

Detective Chief Superintendent John Murphy, Manchester CID.

'John?' I said. 'The fuck you doing here?'

Murphy looked over my shoulder into Room 4. He said: 'We've got a problem, Maurice.'

'Yeah?'

'Yeah,' he nodded. 'A big fucking problem, Maurice.'

Rochdale –

Lancashire.

Noon –

Sunday 22 May 1983:

The eleventh day –

The four thousand and eleventh day:

The gaunt, middle-aged woman was sitting alone in the gloom of her semi-detached home, sitting alone in the gloom shaking with tears, tears of sadness and tears of rage, tears of pain and tears of –

Horror –

Horror and pain, rage and sadness, raining down between her bone-white fingers, raining down between her bone-white fingers on to her broken knees, her broken knees on which was balanced –

The shoebox –

The shoebox she clutched between her bone-white fingers upon her broken knees, the shoebox damp with the tears of sadness and tears of rage, the tears of pain and tears of horror, the shoebox on which was written:

Susan Ridyard.

I looked away to the two photographs on top of the television, the one photograph of a little girl alone and smiling next to another photograph of that same little girl with her older brother and sister, the three children sat together in school uniforms –

Two girls and one boy –

That photograph of two girls and one boy which became just one girl and one boy in the photographs on the sideboard, the photographs in the hall, the photographs on the wall, the one girl and one boy growing –

Always growing but never smiling –

Never smiling because of the little girl they left behind on top of the TV, the little girl alone and smiling –

Never growing but always smiling –

Susan Ridyard –

The one they left behind:

Susan Louise Ridyard, ten, missing –

Last seen Monday 20 March 1972, 3.55 p.m.

Holy Trinity Junior & Infants, Rochdale.

I looked out of the window at the houses across the road, the neighbours at their curtains, the police cars and the ambulance, the rain hard against the double-glazing.

Beside me at the window, the doctor was fiddling with a bottle of pills, the pills that would sedate Mrs Ridyard, the pills that he desperately wanted to sedate her with so he could get away from this house, this horror –

This horror and that shoebox she clutched between her bone-white fingers, balanced upon her broken knees, that damp shoebox on which was written, written in a childish scrawl:

Susan Ridyard.

'Anyone for a cup of tea?' asked Mr Ridyard, bringing in a tray.

'Thank you,' I said, hate filling his wife's eyes as she watched her husband pouring the milk and then the tea into their four best cups.

Derek Ridyard handed me a cup, then one to the doctor.

'Love?' he said, turning to his wife –

But before I could stand to stop her, before either the doctor or I could reach her, she had knocked the tea out of his hands with the shoebox, screaming –

'How can you?'

Holding out the shoebox, crying –

'This is your daughter! This is Susan!'

The doctor and I wrestling her back down on to the sofa, the husband dripping in hot scalding tea, the doctor forcing pills down her and calling for water, uniforms coming, police and ambulance, the shoebox out of her hands –

Out of her hands and into mine –

Mine holding the shoebox, the shoebox with its childish scrawl, its childish scrawl that through my fingers and into my face screamed, screamed up through a decade or more, screamed –

Screamed and cried with her mother:

Susan Ridyard.

In their bathroom, the cold tap was running and I was washing my hands –

'*I think about you all the time –*

The people I had loved and those I had not; scattered or dead, unknown to me as to where or how they were –

'*Under the spreading chestnut tree –*

The cold tap still running, still washing my hands –

'*In the tree, in her branches –*

Washing and washing and washing my hands –

'*Where I sold you and you sold me –*

The Owl –

'*I'll see you in the tree –*

Outside the bathroom I could still hear the woman's muffled and terrible sobs, the shoebox here beside me on their pink and furry toilet mat, here amongst the smell of pine, piss and excrement –

'*In her branches.*'

*

In their doorway, Mr Ridyard and I were looking up at the black clouds.

'Do wonders for my allotment all that,' he said.

'Imagine so,' I nodded as I held in my hands –

In my dirty hands –

His daughter's little bones.

In their driveway, Mr Ridyard and I staring at the houses across the road.

'Wonders,' he shouted.

'Yes,' I whispered as I fell into the past –

Into the dark past –

The shadow of the Horns.

Chapter 11

Monday 23 May 1983 –

D-17:

'If you put your money in a sock, Labour will nationalise socks, Mrs Thatcher tells Cardiff; Britain will have the most right-wing government in the Western World if the Conservatives are returned to power, says Mr Roy Jenkins. . . '

You switch off the radio and check the telephone and the door again.

Nothing.

You sit back down at your desk, the rain coming down your office window in grey walls of piss.

Not even ten o'clock.

Sally, the woman who works part-time Mondays and Thursdays, she's off sick again because her youngest has the flu. That or she's screwing Kevin or Carl or whoever it is this week. Doesn't matter –

Four, five months later she'll lose her job and you'll lose the *firm*:

Divorce, Child Custody, Maintenance; the case-files going down as fast as the letters going out begging your clients to please, please *settle their bills.*

Fuck them –

Them and the depressing music and the grating jingles on the radio, the constant rain and the tepid wind, the mongrel dogs that bark all night and shit all day, the half-cooked food and the luke-warm teas, the shops full of things you don't want on terms you can't meet, the houses that are prisons and the prisons that are houses, the smell of paint to mask the smell of fear, the trains that never run on time to places that are all the same, the buses you are scared to catch and your car they always nick, the rubbish that blows in circles up and down the streets, the films in the dark and the walks in the park for a fumble and a fuck, a finger or a dick, the taste of beer to numb the fear, the television and the government, Sue Lawley and Maggie Thatcher, the Argies and the Falklands, the UDA and LUFC sprayed on your mother's walls, the swastika and noose they hung above her door, the shit through her letterbox and the brick through her window, the anonymous calls and the dirty calls, the heavy breathing and the dial tone, the taunts of the children and the curses of their parents, the eyes filled with tears that sting not from the cold but the hurt, the lies they tell and the pain they bring, the loneliness and the ugliness, the stupidity and brutality, the

endless and basal unkindness of every single person every single
minute of every single hour of every single day of every single month
of every single year of every single life –

You get up and switch the radio back on:

*'South Humberside Police are hoping that the ten-year anniversary of the
disappearance of Christine Markham will jog someone's memory to provide a
clue in the search for the missing Scunthorpe girl who vanished on the day
after her ninth birthday in May 1973. West Yorkshire Police meanwhile are
continuing to question a local man about the disappearance of Morley schoolgirl Hazel Atkins twelve days . . .'*

You turn the dial until you find a song:

The Best Years of Our Lives.

Just before twelve, you lock the office and go downstairs. You wave to
the pretty girl called Jenny who works downstairs in Prontoprint.

There is no rain and there is no sun.

You cross Wood Street and cut through Tammy Hall Street, past
Cateralls and your old office. You walk on to King Street and into the
Inns of Court.

You sit and drink three pints of snakebite and eat a plate of gammon
and chips. Tomorrow you'll go up the College instead, sick to death of
legal folk and all their legal talk:

'Charged him, I heard,' Steve from Clays is saying.

'Charged him with what?' laughs Derek from Cateralls. 'Can't
charge him without a bloody body.'

'Who says she's fucking dead,' says Tony from Gumersalls.

'Me,' grins Derek.

'Motoring offences and asked the magistrate for an extension,' says
Steve.

'Who's his solicitor?' asks Tony.

'McGuinness,' says Steve. 'Who do you bloody think?'

You put down your knife and fork: 'Who you talking about?'

'Aye-up,' shouts Derek. 'It speaks.'

'Who?'

'Bloke they're holding over that missing Morley lass,' says Steve.

'Hazel Atkins?'

They nod, food in their mouths, drinks in their hands.

You say: 'Well, guess who I went to see last week?'

They shrug.

'Michael Myshkin.'

They open their mouths.

'The fuck for?' says Steve.

'His mother wants him to appeal.'

'His mother? What about him?'

'He says he didn't do it.'

'So he came to you?' laughs Derek. 'Pervert must love it in there.'

'Fuck off.'

'You're never going to take it, are you?' asks Tony.

You shake your head: 'But I did recommend Derek.'

'You better fucking not have done, you fat bastard.'

You wink as you stand up: 'Told her, King of Hearts that Derek Smith.'

'Fat cunt.'

'King of Hearts.'

The telephone is ringing but by the time you've got the door open and had a piss and washed your face and hands and dried them, it's stopped. You put the three office chairs together and lie down to sleep off the gammon and chips and three pints of snakebite.

Lord, I've pierced my skin again.

You are praying for a sleep without dreams when the phone starts up again.

Undone, you pick it up.

'Have a seat,' you say with a mouthful of Polo mints.

The grey-haired woman has bucked teeth. She sits down, clutching her best handbag. She is squinting into the rare sunlight she's brought in with her.

'It was nice of Mrs Myshkin to recommend me but, to be honest with you Mrs Ashworth, I . . .'

'Least she could do,' she says, the tears already coming.

'Can I offer you a cup of tea?'

She shakes her head and opens her handbag. She takes out a handkerchief: 'He didn't do it, John. Not our Jimmy.'

You are suddenly struggling –

'The man they give him,' she says. 'This man from Bradford, he's telling Jimmy to confess. But he's done nothing.'

Suddenly struggling with your own tears –

'He's a good boy, John.'

You put your hand up to stop her, to stop yourself, to ask: 'McGuinness told him to confess?'

She nods.

'Clive McGuinness?'

She nods again.

The desk is covered in letters and files:

Divorce, Child Custody, Maintenance –

The case-files and letters bathed in sunlight, the radio and the dogs silent, the constant rain and tepid wind gone –

For now.

The grey-haired woman with the bucked teeth and her best handbag is shaking her head and dabbing her eyes with her handkerchief. It is the same handbag and handkerchief she had at the funeral, the same grey-haired woman who had shaken her head and dabbed her eyes as they'd burned your mother –

Through the holes the light shines.

'Where is he?'

She looks up: 'Jimmy?'

You nod.

'Millgarth.'

You turn your phone towards her: 'Better call Mr McGuinness, hadn't you?'

'What shall I say?'

'Tell him your Jimmy's got a new solicitor.'

Down the motorway –

The scales falling, the Pig rising:

Lord, I've pierced my skin again.

But there will be no retreat, there will be no surrender –

There will be justice and there will be vengeance:

For through the holes the light shines.

Down the motorway, the up-rising Pig –

Hear them calling you, calling:

A holy light for a holy war.

You park between the market and the bus station, a dark and steady drizzle blanketing Leeds.

It is not night and it is not day.

You cut through the market traders packing all their gear away and go up the steps into Millgarth Police Station.

'I'm here to see James Ashworth,' you say to the policeman on the front desk.

'And you are?'

'John Piggott, Mr Ashworth's solicitor.'

The policeman looks up from his paper: 'Is that right?'

You nod.

The policeman opens a large leather-bound book on the desk. He

takes out a pair of reading glasses. He puts them on. He licks a finger.
He begins to slowly turn the pages of the book.

After a few minutes he stops. He closes the book. He takes off his
glasses. He looks up.

You smile.

He smiles back: 'It appears that Mr Ashworth already has a solicitor
and it's not you.'

'That would be Mr McGuinness, who I believe was appointed as the
duty solicitor. Mr Ashworth has since dispensed with his services and
now has his own representation.'

'And that would be you?'

You nod.

The policeman looks over your shoulder: 'Have a seat, Mr Piggott.'

'Is this going to take long?'

He nods at the plastic chairs behind you: 'Who can tell.'

You walk over to the other side of the room and sit down on a tiny
plastic chair under dull and yellow strip lights that blink on and off, on
and off, a faded poster on the wall above you warning against the perils
of drinking and driving at Christmas –

It's not Christmas.

The policeman on the front desk is speaking into a telephone in a
low voice.

You look down at the linoleum floor, at the white squares and the
grey squares, the marks made by boots and the marks made by chairs.
The whole place stinks of dirty dogs and overcooked vegetables.

'Mr Piggott?'

You stand up and go back over to the desk.

'Just spoke with Mr McGuinness, the duty solicitor, and he says he
did hear from Mr Ashworth's mother this afternoon that she wished
you to represent her son but, as yet, he's not heard this from Mr
Ashworth himself, nor has he received anything written or signed by
Mr Ashworth to say he's released from his role.'

You take a letter from your carrier bag: 'That's why I'm here.'

'That's the letter?'

You hand it across the desk.

'But it's not signed, is it?'

'Course it's not bloody signed,' you sigh. 'That's why I'm asking to
see him. So he can sign it.'

'I don't think you're *bloody* listening, Mr Piggott,' the policeman
says slowly. 'You are not his solicitor, so you can't see him. Only Mr
McGuinness can.'

Fuck –

'Can I use that phone?'

'No,' he smiles. 'You can't.'

Outside, the dark and steady drizzle has turned to black and heavy rain.

You walk through the market, looking for a phone that works.

It's half-six.

You go through the double doors and into the Duck and Drake.

Order a pint and go to the phone.

You take out your little red book and dial.

The phone on the other end starts ringing.

'McGuinness and Craig,' says a woman's voice.

One finger in your ear you say: 'Could I speak to Mr McGuinness please?'

'Whom shall I say is calling?'

'John Piggott.'

'Just one moment, Mr Piggott.'

There is a pause before she's back: 'I'm sorry, Mr Piggott, I'm afraid Mr McGuinness has left for the day.'

'Really?'

'Yes,' she says. 'Really.'

'What's your name, love?'

'Karen Barstow.'

'Karen, it's very, very important that I speak with Mr McGuinness as soon as possible. So could you please tell me where I can reach him?'

'I'm sorry, I don't know where Mr McGuinness is.'

'Do you have his home phone number?'

'I'm sorry, I couldn't possibly give that number out – '

'What about if I came round and fucking beat it out of you, you stupid fucking bitch. Would that possibly help?'

'Mr Piggott – '

But you've hung up.

'That's unfortunate, that is,' smiles the policeman on the desk.

You smile back: 'Would you let his mother see him?'

'Long as she was here before eight.'

You look at your watch:

Just gone seven –

Fuck.

'Before eight?'

'Best get your skates on,' he nods.

*

M1 out of Leeds, windscreen wipers and the radio on:

'Ken, Deirdre and Mike named Personalities of the Year.'

Off the motorway, through Wakefield –

'Bonn says Hitler diaries are forged.'

Out and on the road to Fitzwilliam –

'Foot launches bitter attack on Thatcher–Tebbit Toryism as a philosophy from which all compassion and generosity of spirit has been squeezed.'

On to Newstead View, past 54, braking hard outside 69 –

'A local man arrested in Morley last week is to appear before Leeds Magistrates tomorrow morning in connection with the disappearance of Morley schoolgirl, Hazel . . .'

Up the path and banging on the door –

Mrs Ashworth, a tea-towel in her hand, the telly on –

Crossroads.

'Get your coat,' you say. 'You're coming to see Jimmy.'

'What?'

'Come on, there isn't much time.'

She shouts something into the room, grabs her coat from the hook and runs down the path behind you –

You lean across her and slam the passenger door shut –

'Clunk-click,' she says, putting on the seat belt.

You start the car, looking at the clock:

Half-seven.

Out of Fitzwilliam and into Wakefield –

Through Wakey and on to the motorway –

Down the M1 and into Leeds –

Park bang outside Millgarth and up the steps –

Through the double doors –

The stink of dirty dogs and overcooked vegetables –

The policeman on the desk on the telephone, his face white –

'She's here to see her son, James Ashworth,' you say, looking up at the clock on the wall:

Almost eight.

He's putting down the telephone, the policeman on the desk, shaking his head: 'I'm sorry, but – '

'No buts,' you're shouting. 'She's entitled to – '

But the room is suddenly full of policemen, policemen in uniform and policemen in suits, two of the policemen in suits leading Mrs Ashworth over to the tiny plastic chairs under the dull yellow strip lights that blink on and off, on and off, sitting her down beneath the faded poster warning against the perils of drinking and driving at

Christmas, you turning back to see how really bloody white the
policeman on the desk has gone, his head and hands shaking, looking
back round at Mrs Ashworth, her mouth open as she slips off the tiny
plastic chair to lie prostrate upon the linoleum floor, upon the white
squares and the grey squares, the marks made by boots and the marks
made by chairs, the policeman on the desk, his mouth dry and voice
cracking as he says:

'He's dead.'

Chapter 12

Preston:

Lunchtime –

Tuesday 24 December 1974 –

Never-ending.

Sitting in corner of a pub in centre of concrete city, office workers in their party hats already drunk and puking in bogs –

Never-ending.

Shouting along to Slade and Sweet, people snogging and glasses smashing and punches flying and coppers wading in –

Never-ending.

Walking up hill away from station, streets empty and buildings black, trains lit and cars dark –

Never-ending.

Weaving arm-in-arm through cold and dirty rain that falls from cold and dirty sky –

Never-ending.

Stepping out of one shadow and into another –

Another kind of pub, BJ and Clare's kind of pub, St Mary's –

Never-ending.

Roger Kennedy drops bloody key three or four fucking times before he finally opens door, not that Clare notices.

'Here we are,' he says, his fat face as red as stupid Santa hat he's wearing.

BJ and Clare follow him inside:

St Mary's Hostel –

Fifty yards back down road from pub of same name –

Blood and Fire etched in stone above door.

Roger Kennedy finds light switch and ducks into a small office.

BJ and Clare stand in corridor, Clare leaning against green and cream wall with her small suitcase in her hand.

Kennedy comes back out with two keys and smiles: 'Take care of the paperwork later.'

BJ and Clare follow him up steep stairs to a narrow corridor of bedrooms.

'There's only Old Walter in the end one at the moment,' says Kennedy. 'But no doubt some of the other bad pennies will turn up again after New Year.'

He opens one door at top of stairs and winks at Clare: 'You take this one, love.'

'Ta very much,' she smiles.

He hands BJ a key: 'You take the second one on the right.'

BJ walk down corridor until BJ come to second one down on right. BJ unlock door and BJ step inside:

A bed and a wardrobe that doesn't close, a chair and a window that doesn't open, stink of damp that will never leave –

Home sweet bloody home.

BJ sit down on edge of bed and BJ think about little room over in Leeds with Ziggy and Karen, records and posters, clothes and memorabilia.

BJ get up off bed and walk down corridor about to go into Clare's room when BJ hear Roger Kennedy fucking her inside. BJ go back to room and BJ sit on edge of bed and BJ count stars on BJ's shirt.

It's cold and dark and BJ lie in bed watching rain and lights on cracks in ceiling when she knocks on door and comes in with two plastic bags –

'Room for a wee one?' she asks.

'Be my guest.'

'Got some wine and some cider and some Twiglets,' she smiles. 'Thought we'd have our own Christmas party.'

'What about lover?'

'Passed out.'

'He pay?'

'No rent he said.'

'No rent?'

'Aye,' she laughs and lies down on bed next to BJ. 'No rent.'

'Maybe our luck's beginning to change?'

'Be about fucking time,' she says and pulls thin eiderdown over BJ and Clare.

'Said they were going to make me famous,' she laughs suddenly, leaning across BJ for last of wine.

'How?' BJ say, room hot and spinning.

'Here,' she says, jumping out of bed. 'I'll show you if you promise not to laugh.'

She squats down beside bed, searching through her plastic bags until she finds what she's looking for: 'Promise?'

'Cross my heart.'

She hands BJ a photograph.

BJ take it from her and sit up in bed:

Clare with her eyes and legs open, her fingers touching her own cunt.

'What do you think?'

'Doesn't look like you,' BJ say, thinking about photos they took of BJ –

Photos they took of BJ and Bill.

'Don't say that,' she's saying. 'Don't say that.'

It's night before Christmas and I'm coming up hill, swaying, bags in my hand. Plastic bags, carrier bags, Tesco bags. A train passes and I bark, stand in middle of road and bark at train. I am a complete wreck of a human being wearing a light green three-quarter length coat with an imitation fur collar, a turquoise blue jumper with a bright yellow tank top over it and dark brown trousers and brown suede calf-length boots. I turn left and see a row of six deserted narrow garages up ahead, each splattered with white graffiti and their doors showing remnants of green paint, last door banging in wind, in rain. I hold open door and I step inside. It is small, about twelve feet square, and there is sweet smell of perfumed soap, of cider, of Durex. There are packing cases for tables, piles of wood and other rubbish. In every other space there are bottles; sherry bottles, bottles of spirits, beer bottles, bottles of chemicals, all empty. A man's pilot coat doubles as a curtain over window, only one, looking out on nothing. A fierce fire has been burning in grate and ashes disclose remains of clothing. On wall opposite door is written Fisherman's Widow *in wet red paint. I hear door open behind me and I turn around and I'm –*

Screaming, Clare is screaming and screaming –

Horrible, terrible, miserable screams.

'Wake up! Wake up!' BJ shouting, shouting and shouting –

Horrible, terrible, miserable shouts.

Her eyes white and wide in dark, she tears open her blouse and pulls up her bra, three words there written in blood on her chest:

Part 2
We're
already
dead

'Madness is to think of too many things in succession too fast; – or of one thing exclusively.'

– Voltaire

Chapter 13

It's 1969 again –

July 1969:

All across the UK, they're staring at the sun, waiting for the moon –

Ann Jones, Biafra, the Rivers of Blood,

Brian Jones, Free Wales, the Dock Strikes,

Marianne Faithfull and Harvey Smith,

Ulster.

But here's the news today, oh boy –

Memo from Maurice:

Jeanette Garland, 8, missing Castleford.

It's a Sunday –

Sunday 13 July 1969.

Leeds –

Brotherton House, Leeds:

Lot of bloody suits for one little girl missing just one day; Leeds City doing their County Cousins a huge fucking favour:

Blame it on Brady, blame it on Hindley –

Blame it on Stafford and Cannock Chase.

Walter Heywood, *Badger* Bill Molloy, Dick Alderman, Jim Prentice, and me:

Maurice Jobson; Detective Inspector Maurice Jobson –

Not forgetting Georgie Boy:

George Oldman; the County Cunt himself.

A lot of blue suits, a lot more politics, all of it bullshit –

Georgie Boy getting fat and red, huffing and puffing, about to blow –

Nobody listening, everybody straining to hear the radio next door:

Across the city, up in Headingley, England playing the West Indies; trying to regain the initiative after losing Boycott LBW to Sobers.

'Be a press conference tomorrow,' George is saying, giving a toss –

No-one else but me.

'Big appeal on telly,' he says. 'We'll find her.'

'Not if GPO have their way,' I say.

'What?'

'Bloody strike coming, isn't there?' nods the Badger.

'Marvellous,' sighs George. 'Bloody marvellous.'

It's all over his face; fat and red and written as large:

Personal –
NO MOORS MURDERS HERE.

The car out to Castleford –
No-one speaking, not one bloody word –
Just the cricket on a tranny, the sky clouding over –
Bad light.

Brunt Street, Castleford –
Out on the pavement in front of the terrace, George nodding at the uniform –
In through the red door.
George with the introductions: 'Mr and Mrs Garland, this is Detective Superintendent Molloy and Detective Inspector Jobson.'
We both nod at the skinny man with the two lit cigarettes and his blonde wife with the ten bitten nails; the skinny man and his blonde wife sat behind their red front door with the curtains drawn at noon –
Poor before, poorer now.
Mrs Garland goes to the window and peeps out between the curtains –
It's 1969, the second day.

Back out on the pavement, staring across the road through the skeletons of half-built semis, the tarpaulin flapping in the breeze, watching the lines of black figures beating their way up the hills through the empty spaces with their big sticks and downward glances, the silent police dogs called Nigger and Shep, Ringo and Sambo, the white ambulance parked at the top of the street, waiting.

Cigarettes lit, George blowing his nose.
'What now?' asks Bill.
'Do neighbours again?' replies George. 'Get your hands dirty.'
I shrug, sick in the pit.
Bill grins across the street at the row of unfinished homes: 'I'll do t'other side.'
'Someone ought to,' I say, pointing at the sign –
The sign that reads:
Foster's Construction.

'Always so cheerful, she was. Always smiling. It's terrible. Broad daylight and all. There are so many bloody oddballs about these days. Not

safe in your own bloody home, are you? I bet you meet all bloody sorts,
you lot. I mean, that's the thing about mongols, isn't it? Always happy,
aren't they? Never saw her without a smile on her face. Can't say I envy
them much, her mam and her dad. Mustn't be easy on either of them.
They take so much looking after, don't they? Shocking really. Can I get
you another cup? But then they're so happy. I don't reckon they know
any better, do they? They're lucky that way. Must be nice to be always
smiling. Bet you wish you could say same, don't you? Makes you
wonder what this world is bloody coming to though, doesn't it? Just
popped down road for some bloody sweets, next door said. Broad
bloody daylight. Terrible. But you think you'll find her, don't you? You
think she's all right, don't you?'

'Terrible,' says Mr Dixon, the man in the cornershop. 'We open at three,
rain or shine, and there's always a queue of them and Jeanette's always
among them, rain or shine. Have to watch her with her money mind,
being as she is.'

   'But not yesterday, you say?'

   'No,' he shakes his head. 'Not yesterday.'

   'The other kids,' I ask him. 'How are they with her, being as she is?'

   'Right kind they are,' he nods to himself. 'Lived on street since day
she was born, Jeanette has.'

   'And yourself, you didn't see anything or anyone suspicious yesterday?'

   'No.'

   'Nothing out the ordinary?'

   'Nowt much happens round here, Inspector.'

   I nod.

   'Not till this.'

There's a familiar figure leaning against the Jensen parked outside the
shop:

   'Jack?' I say –

   Jack Whitehead, Crime Reporter for the *Yorkshire Post*.

   He offers me his open packet of Everest: 'Maurice, any news?'

   I take a cigarette. I shake my head: 'You tell me, you're the
paperboy.'

   Jack lights mine then his.

   The gentle Sunday afternoon wind is tugging at the tails of
his raincoat, its fingers through his thin hair.

   He hasn't shaved and he stinks of whiskey.

'Late night?' I ask.

He smiles: 'Aren't they all?'

'How's your Carol these days?' I ask, just to let him know I know.

He's not smiling now: 'You tell me?'

'How would I know?'

'You're the copper, aren't you?'

I look back across the road through the skeletons of half-built semis, the tarpaulin flapping in the breeze, watching the lines of black figures beating their way up the hills through the empty spaces with their big sticks and downward glances, the silent police dogs called Nigger and Shep, Ringo and Sambo, the white ambulance parked at the top of the street, still waiting, and I say:

'For my sins.'

Back inside number 11, Brunt Street:

George, Jack, and me –

Mr and Mrs Garland –

Geoff Garland holding the framed school portrait, wiping the tears from the glass with the cuffs of his shirt; Paula Garland wrapping her arms around herself, biting her bottom lip –

'I just don't understand it,' she's saying. 'Like she just vanished into thin air.'

Jack, notebook out, softly-softly –

Writing down her words, softly-softly –

Repeating her words: 'Thin air.'

'But she can't have just vanished, can she?'

Behind the curtains, there's the sudden sound of a summer shower, the noise of children's feet running for home, leaving the park and the swings, the chalk on the pavement, the wickets on the wall –

Mr and Mrs Garland are staring at the back of their red front door, their mouths half-open on the edge of their seats.

There's the sound of coins on the pavement, a child's voice shouting after the fading feet of her friends:

'Hang on! Wait for us!'

But the door stays shut, the curtains drawn, their little girl nowhere to be seen, the rain blowing through the skeletons of the half-built semis across the road, the tarpaulin flapping in the night, the lines of black figures beating their way back down the hills through the empty spaces with their big sticks and downward glances, the silent police dogs called Nigger and Shep, Ringo and Sambo, the white ambulance at the top of the street, leaving empty and silent, the little girl never to

be seen again, rain or shine, the door shut, the curtains drawn to the
sun, open to the moon –
    'Wait!'
    – for the Little Girl Who Never Came Home.

Chapter 14

She was falling backwards into enormous depths, away from this place, her mouth open, contorted and screaming and howling, the animal sound of a mother trapped and forced to watch the slaughter of her young, contorted and screaming and howling, prone upon the linoleum floor, on the white squares and the grey squares, on the marks made by boots and the marks made by chairs, contorted and screaming and howling under the dull and yellow lights blinking on and off, on and off, the faded poster warning against the perils of drinking and driving at Christmas, contorted and screaming and howling, the smell of dirty dogs and overcooked vegetables, contorted and screaming and howling as you took down their names and their numbers, telling them all the things you were going to do to them, all the shit that they were in, how fucked they really were, but they were just stood there silent, waiting for the Brass to come and take you both downstairs, the whole station silent but for her, her mouth open, contorted and screaming and howling, one young gun at the back, rocking on his chair, hands behind his head, noisily chewing his gum until you flew through them, tried to reach across and grab him, choke him, but his brother officers were holding you back, telling you all the things they were going to do to you, all the shit you were in, how fucked you truly were, her back on her feet, mouth open, contorted and screaming and howling, the sound of her glasses breaking under police boots, and then the Brass came, came to take you downstairs, down to the cells, and at the bottom of the stairs you turned the corner and they opened the door to Room 4 and there he was, his boots still turning as they struggled to cut him down, the stink of piss among the suds, his body attached to the ventilation grille, a belt holding him there by his neck, hanging in a jacket that said Saxon and Angelwitch between a pair of swan's wings, his tongue swollen and eyes as big as plates, still struggling to cut him down and take him away, to put him in a hole in the ground and make it go away, but it wouldn't and it never will, not for her, her mouth open, contorted and screaming and howling, crawling up the walls and back up the stairs on her nails and her knees, the smell of overcooked dogs and dirty vegetables, the dull and yellow lights that blinked off and on, off and on, the faded poster promoting the pleasures of drinking and driving at Christmas, the white squares and the grey squares, the marks made by boots and the marks made by chairs, the linoleum, and these men that walked these stairs, these linoleum floors, these policemen in their suits and big size ten boots, and then it was all gone; the walls, the stairs, the smell of dirty dogs and overcooked vegetables, the dull and yellow lights, the faded poster warning against the perils of drinking and driving at Christmas, the white squares and the grey squares, the marks made by boots and the marks made by chairs, the linoleum and policemen in suits and new boots, all gone as you fall backwards on a tiny plastic chair through the enormous depths of time, away from this place, this rotten un-fresh linoleum *place, and you are alone, terrified and hysterical and screeching, your mouth open, contorted and screaming and howling –*

Mouth open, contorted and screaming and howling from under the ground –

Contorted and screaming and howling from under the ground –

Screaming and howling from under the ground –

Howling from under the ground –

Under the ground –

Under the ground as they murder you –

Murdered you:

The Last Man in Yorkshire.

Your eyes are open and you are staring up at the cracks in the ceiling, listening to the footsteps above, a kettle boiling and a cup breaking, raised voices in an argument about where all the money had gone, the rain falling hard behind the words –

You lying there –

Hating this country and all the people that live here –

Lying there –

Fat, bald and full of holes –

The branches tapping against the window pane.

You get out of bed and walk into the kitchen.

It is eight o'clock –

Thursday 26 May 1983:

You put the kettle and the radio on:

'Healey accuses Thatcher of lying over the jobless; Jenkins brands Thatcher an extremist and the cause of division within the nation; reports on allegations of police corruption linked to the £3.4 million silver bullion robbery in 1980 are to be sent to the Director of Public Prosecutions; damage to Albany jail is put at £1 million; bookmakers will pay out to punters who correctly select two consecutive dry days . . .'

You open the fridge and there's nothing –

No milk, no bread –

The cupboard and there's nothing –

You turn the kettle and the radio off.

D-14.

*

The Parthenon, Wood Street, Wakefield –
   Milky coffee with a skin and a toasted teacake inside –
   Rain and umbrellas out.
   The papers, your paper, everybody's paper –
   Thatcher, Thatcher, Thatcher –
   Fuck 'em all and watch their Rome burn.
   Not one single fucking word about Jimmy Ashworth –
   Not one single word about Hazel Atkins –
   Not one.
   You look at your watch:
   Almost ten, almost time.

The drive out in the rain –
   The deserted spaces as depressing as the houses and buildings between them –
   Jimmy Young kissing Thatcher's arse on the radio, the cum drying in his y-fronts as members of the Great British Public call in –
   'Wurzel Gummidge?' repeats Jimmy with a snigger. *'That's not very nice, is it?'*
   'No Jimmy, it's not,' you shout alone in your car. 'And neither are you, you thick and greedy old cunt. But we'll not forget you and your cruel ways, not when we're round your house to do the Mussolini.'
   Alone in your car on the way to see another Jimmy –
   A very different Jimmy –
   Jimmy Ashworth –
   Alone in your car on the way to his funeral.

The funeral of a suicide –
   Your third.
   Second funeral in a fortnight –
   The same smell:
   The flowers that stink of piss, that stink of sweat.
   Wakefield crematorium, Kettlethorpe.
   Sheets of rain battering the crocuses back underground, beheading the daffodils, the petals stuck to the soles of your shoes, with the cigarette ends and the crisp packets.
   You sit near the back, seven other people down the front:
   Mrs Ashworth, her husband, and her other son –
   Two boys in denim jackets, two girls with back-combed hair –
   The vicar says the words and they shed their tears. They set fire to him and shed some more. Then everyone walks away for a cigarette and a piss, a sandwich and a pint.

There are three coppers at the back by the door, Maurice Jobson one of them.

There's a new Rover parked outside –

The window's down, the driver looking at himself in the wing mirror –

A smug cunt looking back at him.

'Give you a lift, can I, John?' says Clive McGuinness.

'No,' you say and light a cig.

'Five minutes, John?' he says. 'That's all I ask.'

'Didn't have five bloody minutes on Monday night, did you?'

'John,' he sighs. 'Look, I'm sorry about that.'

You drop your cigarette into the gutter with the yellow petals and the crisp packets. You walk around the back of the Rover. He has opened the passenger door for you. You get in. He leans across you to close the door –

'Thank you, John,' says McGuinness.

You turn to face him –

The smug cunt as immaculately turned out as ever:

Head to toe in Austin Reed and Jaeger, he stinks of aftershave.

The fat man from C&A says: 'I'm all ears, Clive.'

'There'll be an inquiry, John.'

'An internal police inquiry.'

'He confessed, John.'

'Bollocks.'

'It was too much for him, John.'

'What was? The torture? The beatings? His own fucking solicitor?'

'The guilt, John. The guilt.'

'About what?'

'John, John – '

The back door opens –

You glance in the rearview mirror:

Maurice Jobson gets in –

Detective Chief Superintendent Maurice Jobson:

The Owl.

'Afternoon, gentlemen,' he says.

You don't turn around.

'Do you know the Chief Superintendent, John?'

You nod.

'Course he bloody does,' says Jobson. 'I worked with his father.'

'Your old man was a copper, was he?' says McGuinness. 'I didn't know that, John.'

'Was,' you say as you open the door. 'Until he topped himself.'

You don't fancy the Inns but you do fancy a drink, so you cut through
the back of the Wood Street Nick and into the Jockey.

It's two o'clock so you only have an hour –

It won't be enough but it'll be a start, get some take-outs for the rest
of the afternoon, find a happy hour later and be unconscious by eight.

You take the pint, the short, and the bottle of Barley Wine through
into the pool room at the back –

Students and bikers, Vardis on the jukebox:

Let's Go –

You drink the whiskey and then the Barley Wine.

There are four people on the other side of the pool table. They are
staring at you. One of the girls gets up and walks over towards you.
She is wearing a huge gold Star of David on her chest, her hair black
and back-combed, her heavy make-up smudged.

She says: 'I was Jimmy's girlfriend.'

You say: 'I was almost his solicitor.'

'He didn't kill himself; he wouldn't.'

You nod.

'He didn't kill any little girl either; he couldn't.'

You nod again: 'What's your name?'

'Tessa,' she says.

You hold out your hand: 'John Piggott.'

'I know,' she smiles as she takes it.

'You want a drink?'

'I got one, ta.'

'You want another?'

'Twist my arm.'

'Cider and black?'

She nods.

'Sit down,' you say and stand up.

You go into the other room, order the drinks, and come back with
two pints.

Tessa's not sat at the table and she's not back on the other side of the
room.

The two lads and the other girl are still staring at you. They are
grinning now.

You look over at the toilet door and then back at the two lads and
the girl. They shake their heads. They are laughing.

You walk over to them, still carrying the two pints.

They stop laughing.

'Where's Tessa gone?'

They shrug their shoulders and play with their beer mats.

You hold out the cider and black to the girl: 'You want this?'

She looks up: 'Ta very much.'

You set it down on the table.

'You were Jimmy's mates, yeah?'

They all nod. They are not grinning now, not laughing.

You take out a biro and piece of paper. You write down your name and phone number. You put it down on the table: 'Will you give this to Tessa?'

'Why?' says one of the lads.

'Never know when you might need a solicitor, do you?'

The girl looks at the two lads and then takes the paper.

You drink your pint in one, belch, and set the glass on the table. You take out two pound notes. You put them down next to the empty pint pot.

'What's that for?' says one of the boys.

'Have one on me, lads,' you say and walk back to the bar. You buy your take-outs and leave.

Outside it's raining again. You go into the Chinky and get some lunch to take out. You get it cheap because you once defended one of the staff in an assault case.

You come out and there she is, crouched down on the other side of the road in front of the Army Recruitment, head on her knees.

You cross the road and say: 'Not thinking of joining up, are you?'

Tessa looks up: 'What?'

'After a free trip to the Malvinas, are you? See the world?'

'The where?'

You nod at the picture in the window: 'The Falklands.'

'Piss off,' she says, fiddling with one of her badges.

You point up the stairs to Polish Joe's: 'How about a haircut?'

'Fuck off.'

'OK. See you then.'

'Hang on,' she says, suddenly. 'Where you off?'

'Home.'

'Where's that?'

You point up the road past the College pub: 'Just up there.'

She looks at your carrier bags: 'What's in them?'

'Lunch.'

She smiles.

'You want some?'

She nods and holds up her hand.

You pull her up.

'You got any blow?' she asks.

'I might have.'

She smiles again: 'What we waiting for then?'

You set off up the road, past the College and the Grammar School –

'Bet you went there, didn't you?' she laughs.

'Fuck off.'

'Where you go then?'

'Hemsworth, a long time ago,' you say. 'And you?'

'Thornes.'

You turn on to Blenheim Road and walk along, the big trees keeping the rain off.

You're going up the drive of number 28 when she says: 'Isn't this where that woman was murdered? That witch?'

'Ages ago.'

'You're joking?'

You hold open the front door. 'We all live in dead people's houses.'

'Fuck off,' she says. 'Which flat was it?'

'Mine,' you say.

'You better be fucking joking?' she says.

'I have decorated.'

She is shivering and staring at you, the rain running off the guttering.

'Up to you,' you shrug. 'Do what you want.'

She looks back out at the rain and steps inside: 'Long as you're not planning any bloody seances.'

'Thought that'd be right up your street.'

'Fuck off,' she says again and follows you up the stairs.

You open the door to the flat. You go in first putting on the lights.

'Come in,' you say.

She walks down the hall and into the front room.

'Have a seat,' you say.

She sits down on the sofa.

'What do you want to drink?'

'What you having?'

'Think I'll have a lager to start with.'

She nods: 'Stick some lemonade in ours, will you?'

You go into the kitchen. You open the fridge. There's no lemonade.

'Got enough bloody records, haven't you?' she shouts.

'But no lemonade,' you call back.

'Doesn't matter.'

You wash the glasses and find a tray and bring it back through with the Chinese. You have three cans in a carrier bag on your arm. You say: 'Won't be a minute.'

She stands up: 'Where you going?'

'Just got to nip upstairs.'

'You're never going to leave me on my own in here, are you?'

'Be two minutes,' you say. 'Less you don't want any draw?'

'Two minutes?'

'Stick a record on,' you say. 'It switches on at the wall.'

'Two minutes – '

'Two minutes,' you say. 'Cross my heart and hope to die.'

You knock twice on Stopper and Norm's door. You wait and then knock once again.

'Who is it?' whispers Norman.

Two fingers up at the spy-hole, you say: 'JP.'

The three bolts slide back. The two locks turn. The door opens an inch.

'What's the password?' says Norm over the chain.

'Fuck off,' you say.

'What day is it?'

'Fucking hell, Norm, it's Thursday,' you moan. 'Just let us in, will you?'

He takes off the chain. He opens the door.

'Thank you,' you say.

He locks the locks. He bolts the bolts. He chains the door behind you.

You follow the sounds of Tomita down the hall into the front room.

Stopper's on the sofa watching the snooker.

'Aye-up, Peter,' you say.

He pushes his sunglasses up into his hair and winks.

'How much you want?' asks Norm.

You put a tenner and the cans on the table: 'Just an eighth and a couple of wraps.'

Norm picks up one of the cans and leaves the room.

You crack the other two cans. You hand one to Stopper.

'Ta,' he says. 'You out tonight?'

You look at your watch: 'Maybe. And you?'

He shakes his head: 'Tomorrow.'

Norm comes back in. He gives you an envelope.

'Thanks,' you say.

'You stopping?' he asks.

'Can't. I'll see you tomorrow though, yeah?'

'Nice one,' nods Norm.

'See you, Peter,' you say to Stopper.

'See you, John.'

You walk down the hall to the front door.

Norm unbolts the bolts. He unlocks the locks. He unchains the chain. He says: 'You haven't got a fucking lass downstairs, have you?'

'Why?'

He puts his finger to his ear: 'That's fucking *Ziggy*, isn't it?'

You smile.

'You dirty bastard,' he winks.

'Just a friend.'

Pissed and stoned, you sleep fully clothed in the same bed, dreaming of King Herod and dead kids, the Baptist and Salome –

John and Salome, the wounds of Christ and the Spear of Destiny –

Adolf Hitler and Benito Mussolini, Jimmy Young and Jimmy Ashworth –

Mouths open, contorted and screaming and howling:

'*Hazel!*'

You wake and hold her and touch her –

Hold her and touch her and fuck her –

You fuck her, hungover and hard –

Hard as her nails in your back:

'*Murder me!*'

Blood on the sheets, blood on the walls –

She opens her eyes, she looks into yours: 'This place stinks.'

'I'm sorry – '

'Of memories,' she whispers. 'Bad memories.'

Chapter 15

Clare is screaming: 'Just fucking walked up to me, bold as fucking brass, and gives it a fucking *Long time no see Clare.*'

BJ speechless.

'The cunt! Fucking cunt!'

BJ finding words: 'Where?'

'St Mary's.'

'Shit.'

'Bold as fucking brass, he was.'

'Fuck.'

Her room is trashed and smashed, her clothes and make-up lost among bottles and cans, papers and bags; wind howling around hostel, up stairs and down corridors, under doors and into room, rain hard against window –

This is Preston, Lancashire.

'How did they find us, BJ?' she cries. 'How the fucking hell did they find us?'

BJ look up from floor: 'Be kids.'

Clare is screaming.

BJ been up and down for days, Clare drunk for same –

Drunk and down since day BJ and Clare got here –

Almost one year now.

But never this down, never this drunk –

BJ a mess and Clare a mess –

Fucked.

BJ fucked, Clare fucked –

Fucked and now found.

'What we going to do?'

'Run,' BJ say.

'No fucking point,' she sighs. 'They'll find us.'

'Not if – '

'If what? They're fucking watching us!'

'So what else we going to do?' BJ cry. 'Meet him?'

'What he wants.'

'Fuck off,' BJ sob. 'It's a fucking trap.'

'I don't give a shit,' she shouts. 'I'll not keep running all my fucking life.'

'They'll kill us.'

'Good,' she mutters.

BJ under covers. BJ hiding. BJ weeping.

There's a knock on door –

BJ out from covers. Clare staring at door.

'Clare?' comes a man's voice. 'It's me.'

'Fuck, it's only Roger,' whispers Clare. 'Let him in.'

BJ get out of her bed. BJ open her door. BJ let Roger Kennedy in. BJ go down corridor. BJ get in a cold bed. BJ lie under covers. BJ peep up at cracks in ceiling.

BJ wonder what mum is doing today –

Today is BJ's seventeenth birthday.

BJ start to cry again.

BJ walk to other end of corridor. BJ knock on door.

'Come in.'

BJ step into Old Walter's room.

It's still raining outside. It's still cold inside.

Walter Kendall is sat at a table by only window. He is cutting something out of a newspaper. He sticks it into an old red exercise book.

'You're late,' he smiles.

'I'm sorry.'

He closes book: 'How's my Clare today?'

'Busy.'

He laughs. He comes across his tiny room to sit beside BJ on bed.

Outside a train goes past. Window shakes.

'Your eyes are red,' he says and takes BJ's hand. 'What is it?'

'They've found us.'

He lets go of BJ's hand. He turns BJ's face into his: 'How could they have?'

'Be her kids,' BJ say.

'How?'

'When you all went to Blackpool.'

'But how?'

BJ pull away from his grip: 'If they were watching her kids in Glasgow, they could have easy followed her Suzie when she brought them down.'

'But that was August. Why wait till now?'

'Fuck knows.'

'What you going to do?'

'Clare wants to meet them.'

'No?'

'Yes.'

'You can't let her,' he says.

'I can't stop her.'

'They'll kill her.'

'I know.'

'Kill you both,' he says.

BJ nod.

'What did she say?'

'Good.'

BJ lying in Walter's arms, BJ's head on his chest, listening to his heart. BJ remembering when mum and BJ drank a whole bottle of dandelion and burdock and ate two big boxes of chocolates for BJ's seventh birthday. BJ wondering if she remembers it too, but –

Same room, always same room; ginger beer, stale bread, ashes in grate. I'm in white, turning black right down to my nails, hauling a marble-topped wash-stand to block door, falling about too tired to stand, collapsed in a broken-backed chair, spinning I make no sense, words in my mouth, pictures in my head, they make no sense, lost in my own room, like I've had a big fall, broken, and no-one can put me together again, messages: no-one receiving, decoding, translating.

'What shall we do for rent?' I sing.

Just messages from my room, trapped between living and dead, a marble-topped washstand before my door. But not for long, not now. Just a room and a girl in white turning black right down to my nails and holes in my head, just a girl, hearing footsteps on cobbles outside.

Just a girl.

BJ wake up. BJ sweating. BJ crying –

Walter gone.

BJ run down corridor. BJ push open her door –

Clare is lying on her bed in Walter's arms. Her eyes closed –

Walter is stroking her hair –

Pair of them covered in sweat. Pair of them covered in tears.

'What happened?'

'Bad dream,' whispers Walter.

'Same dream?'

Walter nods.

'Did you look?'

Walter raises her sweater and bra, more words there written in blood:

Help me, I am in hell.

It is dawn:

Thursday 20 November 1975.

Chapter 16

We walk the hills for a third day in our black cloaks with our big sticks and our police dogs called Nigger and Shep, Ringo and Sambo, searching for the scene of a crime, walking the hills for the third day in our black cloaks with our big sticks until day becomes night and we return to our wives called Joan and Patricia, Judith and Margaret, to laughter and telephones ringing through the rooms, meals being cooked, served and eaten, to our children called Robert and Clare, Paul and Hazel, to their feet upon the stairs and the slam of a ball against a bat or a wall, the pop of a cap gun and a burst balloon, to our houses in Harrogate and Wetherby, Sandal and West Bretton, our houses safe and far from harm and –

Here.

Until the next day when we return to walk the hills for a fourth day in our black cloaks with our big sticks and our police dogs called Nigger and Shep, Ringo and Sambo, searching for the scene of the crime, the next day and the next, walking the hills in our black cloaks with our big sticks until days become night, one endless night and we've got no wives called Joan or Patricia, Judith or Margaret, no children called Robert or Clare, Paul or Hazel, only our black cloaks and our big sticks, our dogs called Nigger and Shep, Ringo and Sambo, our houses in Harrogate and Wetherby, Sandal and West Bretton, our houses big and empty and –

Full of nothing, nothing but –

Here.

Brotherton House, Leeds –

Walter Heywood, George Oldman, Dick Alderman, Jim Prentice, Bill and me.

'Come on, George,' smiles Walter Heywood, the Chief Constable. 'Bloody kid can't just vanish into thin air, can she?'

'What it looks like,' says Oldman and holds up today's paper –

Tuesday 15 July 1969:

Girl Vanishes, Fourth Day, All-out Hunt –

By Jack Whitehead, Crime Reporter.

'Cars?' asks the Chief Constable.

Oldman nods: 'Crestas, Farinas, Consuls, Corsairs, Zephyrs, Cambridges and Oxfords. You name it, we've had a bloody sighting.'

'What next then?' asks the Chief.

'Door-to-door again, outbuildings – '

Bill cutting Oldman off: 'Me and Maurice are off back up Castleford, talk to them builders again, maybe call in on Don Foster himself.'

Heywood nodding –

George Oldman: 'Don't let us keep you then, Bill.'

Morning sunlight on the windscreen –

Bill dozing, me driving –

The radio on:

Troops into Derry;

GPO Strike cuts TV;

Last day of the Test.

The A639 through Woodlesford and Oulton, Methley and Allerton Bywater, following the Aire back into Castleford –

The radio on:

Elvis –

Lulu –

Cliff.

Coming into town, policemen and their cars, women gathered on the corners in their headscarves, children tight to their apron strings, the ambulance at the top end of Brunt Street, still waiting –

I park and wake Bill: 'We're here.'

We get out and nod to the uniform outside number 11, the curtains still drawn –

Bill lights up as we cross the road to the half-built semis, the tarpaulin still flapping in the breeze –

Cross the road to the sign that reads:

Foster's Construction.

'Knock-knock,' says Bill as he pushes aside the tarpaulin and we step inside one of the partial houses.

Two men stop their hammering and look up, their mouths full of nails.

'Sorry to bother you, lads,' smiles Bill. 'Can we have a word?'

They let the nails drop from their mouths and one of them, the older one, says: 'We give statements yesterday.'

Bill sniffs. Bill stares. Bill says: 'I know.'

The older man looks at the younger one and shakes his head. They shrug and stand up.

I say: 'This is Detective Superintendent Molloy and I'm Detective Inspector Jobson.'

The men nod.

I ask: 'Anywhere we can sit down?'

'Next door,' replies the younger one.

We follow the two men into the next house, into the half-finished kitchen at the back. We sit down on wooden boxes and packing cases, among their sandwich papers and their tartan flasks, their newspapers and their cigarettes.

I take out my notebook and my pen: 'You the only two working today?'

They nod.

'That usual, is it?'

The younger of the two, he says: 'Depends, but gaffer's sick, isn't he?'

I say: 'Sorry, can I have your names?'

The younger man says: 'Terry Jones.'

'Michael Williams,' says the older man.

Bill lights up another cigarette. He walks over to where a window will be.

I say: 'You were both working Saturday, were you?'

They nod again.

I look through at the front of the house: 'Pretty good view of the other side of street, haven't you?'

Michael Williams says: 'We weren't here Saturday.'

'Thought you just said you were working?'

Williams nods: 'But like we told your mates yesterday, we were in Ponty on Saturday.'

'Why was that?'

'Gaffer wanted us to do some repairs on one of houses.'

'In Pontefract?'

They both nod.

I say again: 'That usual, is it?'

Jones looks at Williams. Williams shrugs: 'Depends how busy we are.'

'So who was working here?'

'No-one,' says Jones.

'What about your gaffer?' asks Bill from the window.

'He was sick, wasn't he,' says Jones.

Bill comes back over. He smiles: 'Not a well man your gaffer, is he?'

'Never missed a day 'fore Saturday,' says Michael Williams.

Bill is stood in front of Williams: 'Is that right?'

'Yep,' says Williams, looking at Jones –

Jones nodding along –

Both of them starting to wonder.

'I hope he's all right,' I say.

'Maybe we should go check on him,' winks Bill. 'Just to make sure it's nowt serious like.'

I ask Jones: 'What's his name?'

'Who?'

'Gaffer,' whispers Williams to Jones.

'Thank you,' I say, looking at Jones –

Jones saying: 'George Marsh.'

'And where does George Marsh hang his hat?'

'What?'

'Where does he live, Terry?'

'Mr Marsh?'

'Yes.'

'Netherton,' says Terry Jones, looking at Williams –

Williams repeating: 'Netherton.'

I stand up: 'Thank you, gentlemen.'

Two telephone calls later and we're driving through Normanton, bypassing Wakefield, heading to 16 Maple Well Drive, Netherton –

Bill pissed off no-one's been out to see this Marsh bloke, cursing them anew: 'Slack fucking County cunts the lot of them.'

Me, four eyes on the road: 'Still want to see Don Foster after?'

Bill shrugs: 'See what we get from this one first.'

I keep it shut and reach over for an *Action* form, one hand on the wheel.

We park in front of a little white van outside a little brown bungalow with a little green garden and a little blue bicycle lying on its side:

Number 16, Maple Well Drive, Netherton.

I ring the doorbell.

Bill looks at the bicycle: 'Be a waste of time this.'

A brown-haired woman opens the door, her pink washing-up gloves dripping wet: 'Yes?'

'Mrs Marsh?' I ask.

'Yes.'

'Police, love. Your George in, is he?'

Mrs Marsh looks from me to Bill then back to me. She shakes her head: 'He's up the allotment.'

'Feeling better, is he?' says Bill, like I knew he would.

Lips pursed, she says: 'Taking some air.'

'Wise man,' smiles Bill, ear to bloody ear.

Me with a kinder smile: 'Where are the allotments, love?'

'Top of field, behind here,' she gestures. 'End shed.'

'Ta, love,' I say, about to move off –

But Bill stays stood there: 'Mind if we have a quick word with you first?'

Mrs Marsh holds open the door: 'Best come in then, hadn't you?'

'Ta very much,' winks Bill.

We follow Mrs Marsh into their front room. We sit down on their pristine sofa. We are facing their brand-new TV.

I nod at the set: 'Colour?'

'Fat chance,' says Mrs Marsh and takes off her pink washing-up gloves. She wipes them on her apron. 'Not on his wage.'

'Got ours on never-never,' I say.

Mrs Marsh shakes her head: 'George doesn't believe in HP or any of that kind of business.'

'Wise man,' says Bill again and opens his notebook.

Mrs Marsh stands up: 'Sorry, can I offer you a cup of tea?'

Bill gestures for her to sit back down. 'Thank you, but we best get a move on.'

Mrs Marsh sits down again. The pink washing-up gloves are on her knees between her folded hands.

Bill looks up from his notebook: 'You know why we're here, don't you?'

'About the missing lassie? The one in Castleford?'

Bill nods. Bill waits.

Mrs Marsh says: 'George was wondering if he should call you.'

Bill: 'Why was that?'

'Thought you'd be wanting to speak to anyone who might have seen anything.'

'He saw something then, did he, your George?'

Mrs Marsh shakes her head: 'No, but he knew lass it was.'

'How's that then?'

'He'd seen her, hadn't he, working across road.'

'Must have seen a lot of kids.'

'Aye,' she nods. 'But he remembered her because she was, you know . . .'

I nod.

Bill asks her: 'So what's been up with him?'

'George? Flu.'

'Lads at work say it's first time he's missed a day.'

Mrs Marsh thinks. Mrs Marsh frowns. Then Mrs Marsh nods, just once.

'When did it start?'

Mrs Marsh thinks again. Then Mrs Marsh says: 'Sunday.'

'Right, right,' nods Bill. 'What the lads at his work thought.'

'Sunday,' she says again, says to herself.

'Remember what time he came home from work on Saturday, can you?'

Mrs Marsh says: 'I can't be right sure about that.'

'Why –'

'Took kids over to my mother's Saturday lunchtime,' she says. 'But George was here when we got back tea-time, I know that.'

'And what time's tea-time?'

'Half-six.'

Bill closes his notebook. He stands up.

'You finished?' asks Mrs Marsh.

'Yep,' nods Bill.

Mrs Marsh stands up. She leads us back out to the front door.

'End shed?' I ask her.

She nods, her eyes and brow full of worry –

Sorrow.

'Thank you, Mrs Marsh,' says Bill.

Mrs Marsh nods again.

We walk back down the little path, past the little bicycle, out of the little garden.

Mrs Marsh watches us go.

Bill stands by the car. He takes out a packet of cigarettes. He offers me one. He takes one himself. He lights us both up.

Mrs Marsh closes her front door. Minute later there's a shadow behind the nets in the front room.

I say: 'What you reckon?'

Bill shrugs. He looks at the end of his cigarette.

I say: 'Not adding up, is it?'

'Could be owt; another woman, horses, owt,' he says.

I nod.

Another car pulls up. It is a big black Morris Oxford. A man gets out. He puts on his hat. He's in black too –

A priest.

He looks at us. He touches the brim of his hat. He heads up the garden path to number 16. He rings the doorbell.

Bill raises his eyes: 'But we best make sure.'

We open the gate to the field behind the bungalows and walk up the dry tractor path towards the row of sheds at the top of the hill. The sky is blue and cloudless above us, the field full of insects and butterflies.

Bill takes off his jacket: 'Should have brought a bloody picnic with us.'

I turn around and look back down the hill at the little white van next to the two parked cars in front of their little brown bungalow and their little green garden, next to all the other little brown bungalows and their little green gardens.

I take off my glasses. I wipe them on my handkerchief. I put them back on.

I can see Mrs Marsh at the kitchen window of their little bungalow. She is watching us –

A shadow behind her.

I turn back.

Bill is up by the sheds. He shouts: 'Hurry up, Maurice.'

I start walking again.

A man comes out of the end shed in a cap and shirtsleeves, blue overalls and Wellington boots.

'Mr Marsh?' Bill is asking him as I get up to them.

'That'd be me,' nods George Marsh. 'Who wants to know?'

'My name is Bill Molloy and this is Maurice Jobson. We're police officers.'

'Thought you might be,' nods Marsh.

'Why's that then?' asks Bill.

'Be about lass who's gone missing in Castleford, won't it?'

Bill nods. Bill waits.

Marsh says nothing.

Bill keeps waiting.

Marsh looks at him. Marsh still says nothing.

Bill says: 'What about her?'

Marsh takes off his cap. He wipes his forehead on his forearm. He puts his cap back on. He says: 'You tell me.'

'No,' says Bill –

– the *Badger*: 'You tell *me* about Jeanette Garland.'

'What about her?'

'Working across road from her house, aren't you?'

'Aye.'

'Been working there a while?'

'Aye.'

'Must have seen a fair bit of her.'

'Coming and going, aye.'

'You remember her then?'

'Aye.'

'Notice owt peculiar, did you?'

'About her?'

Bill nods.

'She was slow, late in head,' he smiles. 'But I suppose you know that, being policemen.'

'*Was*?' I ask him. 'Why did you say *was*?'

'What?'

'You said *she was slow*; you're talking like she's dead, Mr Marsh.'

'Isn't she?'

Bill looks up from the hard ground: 'Not unless you know something we don't.'

George Marsh shakes his head: 'Slip of the tongue, that's all.'

I want to push him. I want to keep on –

But Bill just says: 'Remember anything else about her, do you, Mr Marsh?'

'Not that springs to mind, no.'

'What about Saturday?'

'What about it?'

'Notice owt peculiar on Saturday?'

Marsh takes off his cap. He wipes his forehead with his forearm again. He puts his cap back on. He says: 'Wasn't there, was I?'

'Where were you?'

'Sick.'

'Not what the wife says.'

'What does she know,' shrugs Marsh.

Bill smiles: 'That you weren't where you say you were.'

'Look, lads,' Marsh smiles back for the second time. 'Set off for work and I felt bloody rotten, but I didn't want her staying in and fussing. So I waited for her to take kids round to her mam's, then I came home, got some decent kip, watched a bit of sport. Not a crime, is it, lying to your missus?'

'So did you get to work?' asks Bill, not smiling –

Neither is George Marsh now: 'No.'

'So where were you exactly when you decided to turn around and come home?'

George Marsh takes off his cap again. He wipes his forehead on his forearm. He puts his cap back on. He shrugs his shoulders. He says: 'Maybe halfway.'

'Halfway where?'

'Work.'

'Where?'

'Castleford.'

'Castleford,' repeats Bill.

'Aye,' says Marsh. 'Castleford.'

Bill turns to me: 'I think that's everything, don't you?'

I nod.

Bill turns back to Mr Marsh: 'Thank you, Mr Marsh.'

Marsh nods: 'Need anything else, know where I am.'

'Aye,' smiles Bill. 'At work?'

Marsh stares at Bill. Then Marsh nods: 'That'd be right.'

Bill nods back. He turns and starts down the hill, me behind him.

Halfway down, Bill says: 'Give Mrs Marsh a wave, Maurice.'

And we both wave at the woman in the kitchen window of her little brown bungalow with its little green garden, next to all the other little brown bungalows with their little green gardens, only our car parked next to their little white van, the priest and his car gone.

Still waving at Mrs Marsh, I say to Bill: 'He's lying.'

'He is that.'

'What now?'

'Best call our Georgie, hadn't we?'

Chapter 17

She leaves. You puke. You dress. You puke again. You clean your teeth. You lock the door. You retch. You go downstairs. You heave. You run back up the stairs. You puke in your hands. You open the door. You puke on the floor. You spew. You start all over again.

It is Friday 27 May 1983 –

D-13.

A change of clothes, a change of heart –

54 Newstead View, Fitzwilliam.

Having all the fun –

The patterned carpet and assorted furniture, the taste of air-freshener and the fire on full; the photographs and paintings, the photographs and the paintings of men not here.

Up the road in 69 another man gone, a young man:

Jimmy Ashworth –

Not here.

The clock is ticking, the kettle whistling.

Mrs Myshkin comes back in with the two cups of tea and sets down the tray.

She hands you yours: 'Three sugars?'

'Thank you.'

She says: 'I'm sorry about that; once I start I just can't seem to stop.'

You mumble something crap and meaningless.

'But that poor boy,' Mrs Myshkin says again. 'His poor, poor mother.'

You mumble again. You take a sip of tea.

'I'm so happy you've changed your mind though,' she says. 'My sister, she said you would.'

Upon her settee again, you are sweating, burning, and melting again –

'I –'

'Mr Piggott,' says Mrs Myshkin. 'You do what you can for him, that's enough. You'll do your best, I know you will.'

You are about to say something else crap and meaningless, when –

Out of the corner of your eye you see something, see something coming –

Incoming –

Hard against the window:

CRACK!

Mrs Myshkin on her feet –

Hands to her mouth, shaking her head.

You hear it then, over and over –

Contorted and screaming and howling –

Hear it outside, again and again:

'It's all your fault, you fucking bitch!'

You are on your feet, over to the window.

'You fucking bitch! You Polish fucking bitch with your fucking pervert son!'

Look it straight in the eye, see it coming again –

Incoming –

You duck –

SMASH!

Broken glass everywhere, a brick at your feet.

Out into the hall, you open the door –

Open the door and there she is:

Mrs Ashworth standing on Mrs Myshkin's path, a plastic Hillards carrier bag of rocks in one hand, a half-Charlie in the other –

You walk towards her. You say: 'Put it down, love.'

'Never a moment's trouble until he met your bloody spastic son. The dirty little pervert, him they should've hung. Had bloody done.'

'Please,' you say again. 'Put it down.'

Half a house brick in one hand, her mouth white with spit and fleck, Mrs Ashworth screams again: 'Fucking bitch! You killed him. You fucking killed my Jimmy!'

You are close to her now and now she sees you –

'You!' she shrieks. 'Fat fucking lot of good you did him!'

You reach out to try and stop her arm, but it's already up in the air –

The brick away –

'You don't know how it feels, do you? I wish to God they'd show you.'

There is the sound of breaking glass again, the sound of sobs from the door –

'Please, Mary, no – '

'Don't you Mary me, you Polish fucking bitch,' cries Mrs Ashworth, trying to get her hand back into her shopping bag, trying to get her hand on a brick or a stone –

But you've got her by the tops of her arms now, trying to talk to her, talk some sense into her: 'Mrs Ashworth, let's go and sit – '

'You useless fat bastard, where were you when he needed you? I saw you sat in that posh car with bloody McGuinness. I saw you, don't think I didn't. Least McGuinness had manners not to show his fucking face inside. Not like you, you fat – '

'Mary!'

She stops –

'Mary!'

Stops at the sound of the voice behind her; stops and drops her bag of bricks.

Mr Ashworth is coming up the path: 'I'm sorry. Didn't realise she'd got out. Doctor says she's to take it easy for a bit. Shock of it all.'

You are nodding, catching Mr Ashworth's glance at Mrs Myshkin in her doorway, his glance at the broken window to her right, at the neighbours pairing up for a chat about the bother, their arms and brows folded.

But Mr Ashworth says nothing to Mrs Myshkin, just leads his wife by the shoulders back up the road to number 69, says nothing to Mrs Myshkin in her doorway with her broken window to her right, nothing to the neighbours paired up and chatting about the bother, their arms and brows crossed –

Just five more last little words from his wife –

Spinning round for one last little attack. Before the pills. Before her bed: 'Bitch! Bloody fucking Polish bitch!'

You walk back up the path. You put an arm around Mrs Myshkin. You take her back inside –

The neighbours paired up and shaking their heads.

You close the door behind you. You get a brush and shovel from under the stairs. You sweep up the broken glass as Mrs Myshkin dusts the little pieces from in between the photographs and paintings, the photographs and the paintings of men not here –

Up the road in 69 another man gone, a young man:

Jimmy Ashworth –

Not here.

'Used to happen all the time, this kind of thing,' says Mrs Myshkin. She has a splinter of glass in her palm, blood running down her wrist. 'Should have seen the place after they first arrested him.'

You nod: 'My mum said.'

You drive around looking for a DIY shop or something and eventually find one in Featherstone and you buy some chipboard, because that's all they have, chipboard like you and Pete had your trains on, then you go back to Fitzwilliam and tack the chipboard over the broken glass, Mrs Myshkin saying they'll be out the next morning to put in a new pane of glass.

You decline her offer of beans on toast, telling her you'll be in touch as soon as you have any news, and you leave her, leave her in her dark front room with the chipboard over the windows, alone with her photographs and paintings, her photographs and her paintings of men not here.

You leave her like you left your mother, alone in a dark front room with chipboard over the windows and a swastika on the door, alone with her photographs of your father, her photographs of her sons, of men not here.

You stand at the gate and look back up Newstead View, back up the road to 69 and another man gone, a young man:

Jimmy Ashworth –

Yet another young man –

Not here.

You stand at the gate and close your eyes and think of all the other young men –

Not here:

Friday 27 May 1983 –

Fitzwilliam –

Yorkshire.

On the radio on the drive back into Wakefield they are playing a record about ghosts and you wish they weren't because as you pass your old house and then the Redbeck Café and Motel, both still boarded up, you feel afraid again –

Like you've suddenly got something to lose –

For them to repossess.

You park outside the off-licence on Northgate. You switch off the radio. You go inside. The old Pakistani with the white beard is stood behind the counter with his young daughter. He is wearing white robes and she is wearing green. They do not speak. You buy vodka and fresh orange, beer and cigarettes, writing paper and envelopes, notebooks and pens –

These are your provisions –

For their coming siege.

You put the carrier bags on the passenger seat. You lock the doors. You head up the road and on to Blenheim. You park in the drive. You get out. You lock the doors. You go into the building. You go up the stairs. You let yourself in. You double-lock the doors. You close all the windows. You check all the rooms. You switch on the lights. You are afraid –

Something to lose –

Something they want.
You turn out the lights.

You can't sleep so you drink again. Drink and drink and drink again.
Drink until you puke again. Puke again and lose consciousness. Lose
consciousness and then wake on the living room floor.

It is still night. The TV still on –

The front page of an old *Yorkshire Post* is stuck over the screen:
Missing –

The colours and light from the screen illuminate the photograph of
her face. The holes in her eyes. The hole in her mouth. The colours and
light from the screen make her move. Make her live:

Hazel.

You retch. You run into the hall. You puke in your hands. You open
the bathroom door. You puke on the floor. You spew. You turn on the
taps. You wash your hands. You clean your teeth. You look up into
the mirror.

In lipstick, it says:

D-13.

The branches are tapping against the pane.

Chapter 18

Thursday 20 November 1975:
    Lost and now found –
    Preston, Lancashire:
    They mean murder.

There's banging and banging and banging on door –
    'Who is it?'
    'It's me, Walter.'
    'Not now.'
    'Let me in.'
    BJ get up, head pounding and pounding and pounding –
    BJ open door: 'What is it?'
    'It's Clare,' says Walter.
    'What?'
    'I think she's gone to meet him.'
    'What?'
    'She's not in her room.'
    'So?'
    'Way she was talking last night . . .'
    'What?'
    ' *"They're going to meet me and kill me today,"* she said.'
    Trousers and jumper on, shouting: 'When?'
    'This afternoon.'
    'Why didn't you tell me before?'
    'You weren't here, were you.'
    'Shit.'
    'Where were you?'
    'Fuck off,' BJ spit at him, pushing past him –
    Out door.

St Mary's, Preston:
    A church in Hell –
    Into saloon, heavy velvet-flowered wallpaper, leather-look seats and Formica-topped tables, lipstick on glasses and lipstick on cigs –
    A big woman in other room murdering *Superstar.*
    'Where's Clare?'
    'Just missed her, haven't you, love?'
    'Where she go?'

'Business.'
'Fuck.'
'If you want.'

Back outside in black night, black rain –
   Down hill –
   Down through town –
   Down to Roger Kennedy's house –
   Banging and banging and banging on his door –
   His wife answering door, a kid in her arms: 'Yes?'
   'Roger in?'
   'No, he's – '
   'Where?'
   'He's still at work.'
   'Hostel?'
   She nods, confused.

Black night, black rain –
   Up through town –
   Up hill –
   Into St Mary's, into hostel:
   Banging and banging and banging on door to office, fluorescent
light flickering on and off –
   But it's not Roger, it's Dave Roberts: 'What is it?'
   'Seen Roger?'
   'He's gone home.'
   'Not what his wife says.'
   Dave Roberts is frowning: 'What?'
   'Just been down his house, haven't I?'
   'Why?'
   'I can't find Clare, can I?'
   'So?'
   'I'm worried about her.'
   'What's it got to do with Roger?'
   'You got eyes in your head.'
   Dave is shaking and shaking and shaking his head: 'BJ – '
   'Fuck you,' BJ say before he even starts.
   'Listen – '
   But BJ up stairs again, checking her room again, checking BJ's again:
Nothing, no-one.
   BJ walk down to end of corridor. BJ bang on Walter's door:
Nothing, no-one, but door's open.

BJ step inside. BJ look about room.

On table in window there's his old red exercise book.

BJ walk over. BJ open it:

Cuttings about Michael Myshkin, cuttings about murdered prostitutes.

BJ close book. BJ turn to go –

But there he is, standing in doorway:

'What you doing?' he asks from out of shadow.

'I'm looking for Clare,' BJ stammer.

'In an old school exercise book?'

BJ look down at brown carpet.

'And did you find her?'

BJ look up: 'No.'

'Well, what you waiting for?' he shouts. 'There's not much time.'

'Fuck off,' BJ shout back –

Pushing old twat out of way, going back to BJ's room –

Stuffing clothes into a carrier bag –

Back into hers and doing same –

Down stairs and out hostel door.

Black night, black rain –

Back up hill –

Back up to St Mary's:

Church in Hell, last –

Back into saloon, heavy velvet-flowered wallpaper, leather-look seats and Formica-topped tables, lipstick on glasses and lipstick on cigs.

Big woman in other room now murdering *We've only just begun*.

'Clare back yet?'

'Not yet, love.'

'Will you tell her, BJ is looking for her?' BJ pant. 'Tell her I'll be down bus station waiting.'

'If you want.'

One last place –

Last place on earth:

Left on to Frenchwood Street, off Church Street –

Six narrow garages up ahead, each splattered with white graffiti, doors showing remnants of green paint –

Of evil.

Last door banging in wind, rain –

Last door.

BJ hold open door and step inside:

It is small, about twelve feet square and there is sweet smell of perfumed soap, of cider, of Durex –

Of evil, a Kingdom of Evil.

There are packing cases for tables, piles of wood and other rubbish:

Old newspapers, old clothing –

Old evil, Kingdom of Old Evil.

In every other space there are bottles; sherry bottles, bottles of spirits, beer bottles, bottles of chemicals, all empty –

Evil.

A man's pilot coat doubles as a curtain over window, only one, looking out on nothing –

Nothing but evil, Kingdom of Evil.

A fierce fire has been burning in grate and ashes disclose remains of clothing.

On wall opposite door is written *Fisherman's Widow* in red paint.

BJ touch paint. It is wet –

Red and wet.

Door opens behind BJ. BJ turn around –

'SALT!' screams a man, a vile man in black rags –

'To preserve the meat.'

BJ push him over and out way. BJ out door and into road. BJ dodging a car and its horns.

'SALT!'

Blackest night, blackest rain –

Back down hill –

Back into St Mary's –

Hell –

Back into Saloon, heavy velvet-flowered wallpaper, leather-look seats and Formica-topped tables, lipstick on glasses and lipstick on cigs.

Big woman silent, other room dead.

'You just missed her again, love.'

'Shit.'

'You tell her BJ was looking for her?'

She nods.

'About bus station?'

She nods again.

'Fuck.'

'If you want.'

*

Bus station –
   Almost midnight:
   No-one.
   BJ sit down. BJ wait –
   She is late:
   It is midnight –
   It is late:
   Thursday 20 November 1975 –
   Too late.

Chapter 19

Old times –

Dark night past –

Day 5:

One in the morning –

Wednesday 16 July 1969:

Yorkshire –

Leeds –

Brotherton House Police Station:

The Basement –

Room 4, always Room 4:

George Marsh, forty-three, in police issue grey shirt and trousers.

George Marsh, upright in his chair at our table.

George Marsh, builder's foreman on the Foster's site across the road from 13 Brunt Street, Castleford –

The 13 Brunt Street home of Jeanette Garland –

Jeanette Garland, eight, missing since Saturday 12 July 1969.

I ask George Marsh: 'For the thousandth fucking time, George, what were you doing on Saturday?'

And for the thousandth fucking time he tells me: 'Nothing.'

Old times –

Long dark night past –

Day 5:

Three in the morning –

Wednesday 16 July 1969:

Yorkshire –

Leeds –

Brotherton House Police Station:

The Basement –

Room 4, always Room 4.

We open the door. We step inside:

Bill Molloy and me –

Him with a wide streak of grey in his thick black hair, me with my thick lenses and black frames –

The Badger and the Owl.

And him:

George Marsh, forty-three, in police issue grey shirt and trousers.

George Marsh, upright in his chair at our table.

George Marsh, builder's foreman on the Foster's site across the road from 13 Brunt Street, Castleford –

The 13 Brunt Street home of Jeanette Garland –

Jeanette Garland, eight, missing since Saturday 12 July 1969.

I say: 'Put your palms flat upon the desk.'

George Marsh puts his palms flat upon the desk.

I sit down at an angle to George Marsh. I take a pair of handcuffs from the pocket of my sports jacket. I hand them to Bill.

Bill walks around the room. Bill plays with the handcuffs. Bill sits down opposite Marsh. Bill puts the handcuffs over the knuckles of his fist.

Silence –

Room 4 quiet, the Basement quiet –

The Station silent, the Headrow silent –

Leeds sleeping, Yorkshire sleeping.

Bill jumps up. Bill brings his handcuffed fist down on to the top of Marsh's right hand –

Marsh screams –

Screams –

But not much, not much at all.

I say: 'Put your hands back.'

Marsh puts them back on the table.

'Flat.'

He lies them down flat.

'Nasty,' says Bill.

'You should get that seen to,' I say.

We are both smiling at him –

Him not smiling, just staring straight ahead.

I stand up. I walk over to the door. I open the door. I step out into the corridor.

I come back in with a blanket –

I place it on George Marsh's shoulders: 'There you go, mate.'

I sit back down. I take out a packet of Everest from the pocket of my sports jacket. I offer one to Bill.

Bill takes out a lighter. He lights both our cigarettes.

We blow smoke across Marsh.

His hands are flat upon the desk.

Bill leans forward. Bill dangles the cigarette over Marsh's right hand. He rolls it between two fingers, back and forth, back and forth.

Marsh never flinches. Marsh silent –

Room 4 quiet, the Basement quiet –

The Station silent, the Headrow silent.

Bill reaches forward. Bill grabs Marsh's right wrist. Bill holds down Marsh's right hand. Bill stubs his cigarette out into the back of Marsh's hand.

Marsh screams –

Screams –

But not much, not much at all.

I say: 'Put your hands flat.'

Marsh puts them flat on the table.

The room stinks of burnt skin –

His.

'Another?' I say.

'Don't mind if I do,' says Bill. He takes another Everest from the pack. He lights the cigarette. He stares at Marsh. He leans forward. He begins to dangle the cigarette over Marsh's hand.

Marsh stares dead ahead –

Silent:

Room 4 quiet, the Basement quiet –

The Station silent, the Headrow silent.

Bill and I stand up –

I say: 'Stand up.'

Marsh stands up.

'Eyes front.'

Marsh stares straight ahead, eyes dead.

'Don't move.'

Bill and I lift the three chairs and the table to the side. I open the door. We step out into the corridor. I close the door. I look through the spy-hole at Marsh. He is stood in the centre of the room. He is staring straight ahead, not moving, eyes dead.

'He's a hard one,' I say.

'Where's Dickie?' Bill asks.

'He's here.'

'He got it?'

I nod.

'Best get him then, hadn't you?'

I walk off down the corridor.

Dick Alderman is already waiting in one of the cells at the end.

'We're ready,' I say.

He nods.

We walk back down the corridor, Alderman carrying it under a blanket.

Bill nods at Alderman: 'Morning.'

'Morning,' he slurs back. His breath reeks of alcohol.

Bill says: 'You up for this, Richard, are you?'

He nods.

Bill leans in closer to his mouth: 'Bit of Dutch courage for breakfast, eh?'

Alderman tries to pull his head back.

Bill's got him by the scruff: 'Don't fuck it up, Richard.'

Alderman nods. Bill pats him on his face. Alderman smiles. Bill smiles back.

I ask: 'Everybody ready?'

They both nod. Alderman puts down the box. He leaves it in the corridor for now. Bill hands him another package wrapped in a brown towel.

I open the door. We step inside –

Room 4, always Room 4:

George Marsh, forty-three, in police issue grey shirt and trousers.

George Marsh, upright in his chair at our table.

George Marsh, builder's foreman on the Foster's site across the road from 13 Brunt Street, Castleford –

The 13 Brunt Street home of Jeanette Garland –

Jeanette Garland, eight, missing since Saturday 12 July 1969.

I stand by the door. Bill and Alderman bring the chairs and the table back into the centre of the room.

Bill puts a chair behind Marsh. He says: 'Sit down.'

Marsh sits down opposite Dick Alderman.

Bill picks up the blanket from the floor. He puts it over Marsh's shoulders.

Alderman lights a cigarette. He says: 'Put your palms flat on the desk.'

Marsh puts his hands flat on the desk.

Bill is pacing the room behind Marsh.

Alderman puts the brown package on the table. He unwraps it. He takes out a pistol. He lays it down on the table between himself and George Marsh.

Alderman smiles at Marsh –

Marsh just stares dead ahead.

Bill stops walking about the room. He stands behind Marsh.

'Eyes front,' says Alderman.

Marsh keeps staring straight ahead into the silence –

The dead silence:

Room 4 dead, the Basement dead.

Alderman jumps up. Alderman pins Marsh's wrists down.

Bill grabs the blanket. Bill twists it around Marsh's face.

Marsh falls forward off the chair.

Alderman holds down his wrists.

Bill twists the blanket around his face.

Marsh kneels on the floor.

Alderman lets go of Marsh's wrists.

Marsh spins round in the blanket and into the wall:

CRACK –

Through the room, through the Basement.

Bill pulls off the blanket. He picks Marsh up by his hair. He stands him up against the wall.

'Turn around, eyes front.'

Marsh turns around.

Alderman has the pistol in his right hand.

Bill has some bullets. He is throwing them up into the air. He is catching them.

Alderman turns to the door. He asks me: 'It's all right to shoot him then?'

I nod: 'Shoot him!'

Alderman holds the pistol at arm's length in both hands. He points the pistol at Marsh's head.

Marsh is staring straight back into Alderman's eyes.

Alderman steps forward. The barrel touches Marsh's forehead. Alderman pulls the trigger –

CLICK –

Nothing happens.

'Fuck,' says Alderman.

He turns away. He fiddles with the pistol.

Marsh is staring straight ahead.

'I've fixed it,' says Alderman. 'It'll be all right this time.'

He points the pistol again –

Marsh staring straight back into him.

Alderman pulls the trigger –

BANG –

Marsh falls to the floor.

I think he's dead.

Marsh opens his eyes. He looks up from the floor. He sees the smoking gun in Alderman's hand. He sees the shreds of black material coming out of the barrel. He sees them floating down to the floor, over him –

He sees us all laughing.

George Marsh smiles.

Bill picks him up off the floor. Bill stands him against the wall. Bill takes two steps back. Bill takes one step forward. Bill kicks him in the balls.

George Marsh falls to the floor again.

'Stand up.'

Marsh stands up.

'On your toes,' says Bill.

Bill steps forward. Bill kicks him in the balls again.

He falls to the floor again.

Alderman walks over to him. Alderman kicks him in the chest. Alderman kicks him in the stomach. Alderman handcuffs his hands behind his back. Alderman pushes his face down into the floor.

'Do you like rats, George?'

Marsh looks up at him.

'Do you like rats?'

Marsh says nothing.

I open the door.

Bill steps out into the corridor. He comes back into the room. He has the box under the blanket. He walks over to where Marsh is lying on the floor. He puts the box down on the ground next to Marsh's face.

Alderman pulls Marsh's head up by his hair.

Bill rips off the blanket: 'Three, two, one – '

The rat is fat. The rat is wet. The rat is staring through the wire of its cage at Marsh.

Bill tips up the cage. The rat slides closer to the wire and Marsh. Bill shouts: 'Get him! Get him!'

The rat is frightened. The rat is hissing. The rat is clawing at the wire. The rat is clawing at Marsh's face.

'He's starving,' says Bill.

Alderman pushes Marsh's face into the wire.

Bill kicks the cage. Bill tips the rat up into the wire –

It's tail and fur against Marsh's face.

'Turn it round, turn it round,' Alderman is saying.

'Open it,' I say.

Bill tips the cage up on its backside. The wire door is facing up. Bill opens the door.

The rat is at the bottom of the cage. The rat is looking up at the open door. Alderman brings Marsh's face down to the open door –

Marsh, eyes wide, struggles to get loose.

The rat is growling. The rat is shitting everywhere. The rat is looking up at Marsh.

Alderman squeezes Marsh's face down further into the open cage.

Marsh struggles. Marsh says something.

I nod.

Alderman pulls him back up by his hair: 'What? What did you say?'

Marsh looks at him. Marsh smiles.

Alderman pushes his face back down into the cage. Alderman screams: 'What have you done with her? What have you fucking done with her?'

Marsh says something.

I nod again.

Alderman pulls him back up: 'What did you say?'

Marsh looks at him. Marsh says: 'I did nothing. I know nothing. So I've got nothing to say.'

'Is that right?' says Bill and Bill reaches down into the cage. Bill picks out the rat by its tail. Bill swings it around into the wall –

SMASH!

Blood splatters across Marsh and Alderman –

'Fucking hell,' shouts Alderman.

Bill drops the dead rat back into the wire cage. Bill squats down level with Marsh. Bill wipes his hands on Marsh's face, on his police issue grey shirt, and Bill says again: 'Is that right?'

George Marsh puts his hand to his face. George Marsh smears the rat's blood across his cheeks, across his tongue and lips, and George Marsh says: 'John Dawson.'

'What about him?' asks Bill.

Marsh licks his lips: 'He knows what I did. He knows what I know. He'll tell you all about it.'

Bill looks at Marsh.

Marsh winks.

Bill stands up. Bill kicks Marsh hard in the ribs.

George Marsh slumps to the floor, clutching his side, coughing –

Laughing.

I turn to Alderman: 'Clean him and room up.'

Bill and I step out into the corridor.

'He did it,' I say. 'He fucking did it.'

Bill shakes his head. Bill looks at his watch.

I look at mine:

It's almost dawn –

Day 6.

But there's no light –

Not down here.

Here just night:

Endless dark night –

Endless dark nights, past –

Past and future –
Futures and pasts:
Times old and yet to come.

Chapter 20

You are sat in the car park of the Balne Lane Library at eight o'clock on a wet Saturday morning in May –

The car doors are locked and you are shaking, unable to switch off the radio:

'*Healey wins Polaris battle with Foot; Tebbit pledges to curb unions and abolish GLC and metropolitan district councils; Thatcher seeks bumper victory to thwart Labour extremists; boy aged sixteen found hanging from window bars of a cell in the borstal allocation unit of Strangeways prison; Dennis Nilsen is committed for trial . . .'*

No Hazel.

You are sat in the car park of the Balne Lane Library at half-eight on a wet Saturday morning in May –

The radio is off but you are still shaking –

The car doors still locked.

It is Saturday 28 May 1983 –

D-12:

Does anybody know any jokes?

Up the stairs to the first floor of the library, the microfilms and old newspapers, pulling two boxes of *Yorkshire Posts* from the shelves:

December 1974 and *November 1975*.

Threading the film, winding the spools, flogging dead horses:

STOP –

Friday 13 December 1974:

Morley Girl Missing – by Edward Dunford, North of England Crime Correspondent.

Mrs Sandra Kemplay made an emotional appeal this morning for the safe return of her daughter, Clare.

STOP –

Sunday 15 December 1974:

Murdered – by Jack Whitehead, Crime Reporter of the Year.

The naked body of nine-year-old Clare Kemplay was found early yesterday morning by workmen in Devil's Ditch, Wakefield.

STOP –

Monday 16 December 1974:

Catch this Fiend – by Jack Whitehead, Crime Reporter of the Year, 1968 & 1971.

A post-mortem into the death of ten-year-old Clare Kemplay revealed that she had been tortured, raped, and then strangled.

STOP –

Thursday 19 December 1974:

Caught – by Jack Whitehead, Crime Reporter of the Year.

Early yesterday morning police arrested a Fitzwilliam man in connection with the murder of ten-year-old Clare Kemplay.

According to a police source, exclusive to this newspaper, the man has confessed to the murder and has been formally charged. He will be remanded in custody at Wakefield Magistrates' Court later this morning.

The police source further revealed that the man has also confessed to a number of other murders and formal charges are expected shortly.

STOP –

Saturday 21 December 1974:

A Mother's Plea – by Edward Dunford.

Mrs Paula Garland, sister of the Rugby League star Johnny Kelly, wept as she told of her life since the disappearance of her daughter, Jeanette, just over five years ago.

'I've lost everything since that day,' said Mrs Garland, referring to her husband Geoff's suicide in 1971, following the fruitless police investigation into the whereabouts of their missing daughter.

'I just want it all to end,' wept Mrs Garland. 'And maybe now it can.'

The arrest of a Fitzwilliam man in connection with the disappearance and murder of Clare Kemplay has brought a tragic hope of sorts to Mrs Garland.

STOP –

Saturday 21 December 1974:

Murder Hunt – by Jack Whitehead, Crime Reporter of the Year.

A fresh murder hunt was launched in Wakefield today following the discovery of the body of 36-year-old –

STOP –

STOP –

Into the library toilets, dry-heaving –

Your stomach burning, your stomach bleeding –

You retch again. You puke. You spew –

Knowing it's not over, that it'll never be over –

That you have to go back there –

Threading films, winding spools, flogging dead horses:

STOP –

Monday 23 December 1974:

RL Star's Sister Murdered – by Jack Whitehead, Crime Reporter of the Year.

*Police found the body of Mrs Paula Garland at her Castleford home early
Sunday morning, after neighbours heard screams.*
STOP –
Tuesday 24 December 1974:
*3 Dead in Wakefield Xmas Shoot-out – by Jack Whitehead, Crime Reporter
of the Year.*
STOP –
STOP –
STOP –
Back in their bogs, burning and bleeding –
Retching.
Puking.
Spewing –
Knowing what you know, damned to go back one last fucking
time –
You thread the last film. You wind the last spool. You flog the dead:
STOP –
Friday 21 November 1975:
Myshkin gets life.

In a telephone box on Balne Lane, the relentless sound of the hard rain
on the roof, you make two calls and one appointment, thinking –
Jack, Jack, Jack –
The relentless sound of the rain on the roof, thinking –
Not here.

There is a Leeds & Bradford A–Z open on your lap. Your notes and
photocopies are on the passenger seat beside you. You are driving
through the back and side streets of Morley –
It is Saturday but there are no children.
You come down Church Street to the junction with Victoria Road
and Rooms Lane. You turn right on to Victoria Road. You park outside
Morley Grange Junior and Infants School, under the steeple of a black
church –
The rain falling through the dark, quiet trees.
You look at your notes. You start the car.
'*Clare Kemplay was last seen on Thursday 12 December 1974, walking
down Victoria Road towards her home –* '
You follow Victoria Road along –
Past the Sports Ground, past Sandmead Close.
'*Clare was ten years old with long straight fair hair and blue*

eyes, wearing an orange waterproof kagool, a dark blue turtleneck sweater – '

You glance at your notes again –

You indicate left.

'Pale blue denim trousers with a distinctive eagle motif on the back left pocket and red Wellington boots – '

You turn into Winterbourne Avenue –

It is a cul-de-sac of nine or ten houses; some detached, some not.

'She was carrying a plastic Co-op carrier bag containing a pair of black gym shoes.'

A cul-de-sac.

You park outside number 3, Winterbourne Avenue.

There is a *For Sale* sign stuck in the tiny front lawn.

You get out. You walk up the drive. You ring the doorbell.

There is no answer.

A woman in the next house opens her front door: 'You interested in the house?'

'No,' you shout back over the low hedge and drives. 'I'm looking for the Kemplays?'

'The Kemplays?'

'Yeah.'

'They moved years ago.'

'You don't know where, do you?'

'Down South.'

'You remember when?'

'When do you bloody think?' she says and slams her front door.

You stand in the drive of a house that nobody wants to buy and you wonder what the Atkins will do, if they'll go down South or if they'll stay around here, stay around here and watch their neighbours' children grow, watch their neighbours' children grow while their own daughter rots in the ground, rots in the ground of the very place that took her away.

You stand in the rain in the cul-de-sac and you wonder.

You go back to the car. You get in. You lock the doors. You open the A–Z again.

You start the car. You turn right out of Winterbourne Avenue. You go back down Victoria Road –

Back past the Sports Ground, back past the school.

You turn right on to Rooms Lane. You go up Rooms Lane –

Past the church –

The rain falling through the dark, quiet trees.

You come to Bradstock Gardens. You turn right again.

Bradstock Gardens is a cul-de-sac, just like Winterbourne Avenue.
A cul-de-sac.

There are two policemen sat in a police car outside number 4.

The curtains are drawn, the milk on the step.

You turn to look at your notes:

'A ten-year-old girl with medium-length dark brown hair and brown eyes,
wearing light brown corduroy trousers, a dark blue sweater embroidered with
the letter H, and a red quilted sleeveless jacket, carrying a black drawstring
gym bag –'

Sat beside you on the passenger seat –

Hazel looks at you –

Looks at you and says –

'Help me –'

The rain falling through the dark, quiet trees –

'We're in hell.'

You reverse out of the cul-de-sac –

The Leeds & Bradford A–Z open on your lap, your notes and photocopies on the passenger seat beside you, out of Morley –

It is Saturday but there are no children –

All the children missing.

You drive out of Morley –

Down Elland Road and into Leeds –

They are playing that record about ghosts again.

You change stations but all you get is –

Thatcher, Thatcher, Thatcher.

No Hazel –

Not here.

At the *Yorkshire Post* reception, you ask the pretty girl with the nice
smile and bleached hair if she has an address for one of their former
employees.

'Jack Whitehead?' she repeats. 'Who was he?'

'A journalist,' you say. 'Crime.'

'Can't say I've ever heard of him,' she frowns. 'Do you know when
he last worked for us?'

'Saturday 18 July 1977.'

She shakes her head again. She picks up the phone: 'Hi, it's Lisa at
reception. I've got a gentleman here asking about a Jack Whitehead
who he says was a journalist here up until July 1977.'

She listens. She waits. She says: 'Thank you.'

You watch her hang up. Her roots need doing.

She looks up. She smiles: 'Someone will be down in a minute.'

The woman is in her mid-thirties and good-looking. She has a confident walk and a look of Marilyn Webb.

You stand up.

'Kathryn Williams,' she says, hand out.

'John Piggott,' you reply, holding her hand for as long as you dare.

'You're here about Jack Whitehead, I believe?'

You nod: 'I'm a solicitor and I've become involved in an appeal and I know from memory and the microfilms that Jack Whitehead covered the original case.'

She tries to smile. She's already bored. She says: 'How can I help?'

'To be honest,' you mumble, 'I don't know if you can. I know that Jack Whitehead had some sort of accident in 1977 and that he no longer – '

'Terrible,' she says. She looks at her watch.

'But I was hoping somebody might have an address, so I could maybe contact – '

She shakes her head: 'Last I heard, he was still in hospital.'

'You wouldn't happen to know which one by any chance?'

'Stanley Royd.'

You can see red brakelights through the glass walls of the building, headlights and rain against the revolving doors.

'I suppose he could be dead,' you say.

'Doubt it,' she says. 'We'd have heard.'

You nod again. And again.

'Well,' she smiles. 'If there was nothing else . . .'

'Thank you,' you say. 'Thank you very much.'

She walks you to the doors. She says: 'Nice to have met you, Mr Parrot.'

'Piggott,' you smile.

She laughs and squeezes your arm: 'I am sorry.'

'Don't worry,' you say. 'Thank you for your time.'

She has her hand out again: 'Which case was it?'

'Clare Kemplay.'

She starts to let go of your hand: 'Whose appeal? Not – '

'Michael Myshkin,' you nod.

She drops it.

Chapter 21

She's slipped on to her knees and he's come out of her. Now he's angry. She tries to turn but he's got her by her hair, punching her casually once, twice, and she's telling him there's no need for that, scrambling to give him his money back, and then he's got it up her arse, but she's thinking at least it'll be over then, and he's back kissing her shoulders, pulling her black bra off, smiling at this fat cow's flabby arms, and taking a big, big bite out of underside of her left tit, and she can't not scream and she knows she shouldn't because now he's going to have to shut her up and she's crying because she knows it's over, that they've found her, that this is how it ends, that she'll never see her daughters again, not now, not ever –

BJ awake:

    It is morning and there are sirens –

    Police sirens.

    Fuck.

    BJ get up off bench, eyes blinking in grey light –

    Heavy smell of diesel –

    BJ go into bogs and puke in sink.

    Fuck, fuck.

    Preston Bus Station –

    Friday 21 November 1975:

    Fuck, fuck, fuck.

BJ run up hill from centre, back to hostel.

    There is no-one in office –

    Just fluorescent light flickering on and off.

    BJ go upstairs and bang on her door: 'Clare!'

    But there's no-one, nothing.

    BJ try door and it opens.

    BJ step inside.

    Room is trashed and smashed, more than usual –

    More than what BJ did last night –

    Someone else was here:

    Walter.

    BJ turn to leave her room and there he is, standing in doorway.

    'Who is it?' he asks.

    'It's me,' BJ say. 'Who fuck you think it is?'

    He steps out of shadow, arms out: 'Look!'

'Fuck,' BJ say –

'Look at me!'

His eyes white, his eyes blind.

'What happened?'

'They were here,' he says.

'Who?'

'You know who.'

'What did they want?'

'You and Clare,' he says. 'They turned both your rooms upside down.'

BJ look down at carrier bag in BJ's hand. BJ tip it out on to her bed –

Clothes, make-up, a photograph:

Clare with her eyes and legs open, her fingers touching her own cunt.

'What is it?' gropes Walter.

BJ pick photograph up –

'It's not her,' BJ say.

'Where is she?' asks Walter.

'I don't know.'

'She's dead, isn't she?' he whispers, tears on his cheeks.

'We all are,' BJ say.

BJ run up hill, past other St Mary's, up Church Street and on to French –

Fuck, fuck, fuck:

Police cars and an ambulance parked in front of garages –

Last door –

Last door banging in wind, in rain –

Two policemen in black cloaks holding it open as they carry out a body on a stretcher, wind raising a bloody sheet:

A light green three-quarter-length coat with an imitation fur collar, a turquoise blue jumper with a bright yellow tank top over it, dark brown trousers, brown suede calf-length boots:

A complete wreck of a human being.

A woman is weeping at side of road, her dog barking at first train out of here –

Just like Clare used to.

Then BJ see him, standing at top of street by open door of his car –

Looking at BJ.

He smiles.

BJ run.

Chapter 22

Thursday 17 July 1969:
Apollo 11 starts with a beautiful ride on the way to the moon –
I'm on an ugly ride out to Castleford:
The overture to a new era of civilisation –
The radio full of war songs and bad news:
London Wharf explosion kills five firemen, local girl still missing –
War songs, bad news, and the moon.

The site is visible for two or three miles before we reach it, the skeleton of an enormous bungalow on the top of a hill, its stark white bones rising out of the ground.

'Must have some bloody brass,' I say –

Bill smiles. Bill nods. Bill says nothing.

I turn off the main road.

It is raining as we park at the bottom of the hill.

'He expecting us?' I ask.

'Looks that way,' says Bill –

Two men are coming down the tracks from the top of the hill. They are walking under two large red golfing umbrellas. They are wearing Wellington boots.

Bill and I get out into the drizzle and the mud.

'Long time no see, Don,' says Bill to the big man with the Spanish tan –

Donald Foster, Yorkshire's Construction King.

Donald Foster shakes Bill's hand: 'Too long, Bill.'

'Didn't expect to see you here today,' says Bill. 'Pleasant surprise.'

'The bad penny,' winks Foster. 'That's me.'

'Fair few of them too, I hear,' smiles Bill.

Donald Foster slaps Bill on the back. He laughs and gestures at the other man: 'Bill, this is John Dawson; a good man and a very good friend of mine.'

Bill sticks out his hand: 'Nice to meet you, Mr Dawson.'

Dawson takes it.

Foster says to Dawson: 'John, this is Detective Superintendent Bill Molloy; also a good man and also a very good friend of mine.'

'Nice to meet you too, Superintendent,' replies the gaunt and paler man –

John Dawson, the Prince of Architecture himself.

Bill says: 'Mr Dawson, Don; this is my colleague and friend, Maurice Jobson.'

Don Foster shakes my hand: 'Bill's told me a lot about you, Inspector.'

I say: 'Only the good things, I hope.'

Foster still has my hand in his. He grins: 'Now where would fun be in that.'

John Dawson has his hand out, waiting. He says: 'John Dawson.'

Foster lets my hand go. I take Dawson's. I nod. I say nothing.

Bill is looking up at the top of the rise, at the bones of the bungalow. He says: 'Mind if we have a look?'

'Be my guest,' says Dawson.

'We've buried bodies deep mind,' laughs Foster.

'I should bloody well hope so,' says Bill.

John Dawson hands us his large umbrella.

'Thank you,' says Bill.

I say nothing.

We start up the track towards the site. Dawson and Foster are under one umbrella, Bill and I under the other, the umbrellas failing to keep us dry –

Our shoes and our socks sinking into the sod.

Foster strides ahead back up the hill, Dawson beside him. Foster stops. He turns round: 'Keep you busy behind that desk, do they, Bill?'

'Not busy enough,' Bill shouts back.

They are waiting for us when we reach the top, waiting under their red umbrella among the stark white bones.

John Dawson asks: 'Have either of you seen the film *Lost Horizon*?'

'No,' says Bill.

Dawson shrugs. He surveys the site. He says: 'It's my wife Marjorie's favourite. In the film there's a mythical city called Shangrila; that's what I'm going to call this place – Shangrila. It's going to be her present for our Silver Wedding next year.'

'Does she know?' Bill asks.

'If she does, she's not saying,' he smiles.

The rain is falling fast on our red umbrellas, the four of us stood in the foundations, among the white scaffolding, looking out across Castleford and the Aire –

The silence and the grey sky.

'I've designed it to reflect a swan,' says Dawson.

'John loves swans,' nods Don Foster.

'Beautiful creatures,' Dawson continues. 'I suppose you both know that once swans mate, they mate for life?'

'If one of them dies,' I nod. 'The other one pines to death.'

'Very romantic,' says Bill –

There's something in his voice, something he doesn't like, something I don't –

From under our umbrella, Bill points: 'What's that going to be down there?'

Halfway back down the slope, there is a large and freshly dug hole in the ground.

'Fish pond,' says Don Foster. 'For his goldfish.'

'Not Swan Lake then?' laughs Bill.

'Not quite,' says Dawson.

Bill tilts the umbrella back so he can look at both of them; his old mate Don and his new mate John. Bill says: 'Is there somewhere we can have a word?'

'A *word*?' repeats Don Foster, his tan fading with the light and the rain.

'Aye,' nods Bill. 'A word.'

Foster looks at Dawson. Dawson looks over at a small cabin on the edge of the site. Foster looks back at Bill. He says: 'The hut?'

Bill and I follow them over there.

John Dawson unlocks the door. We go inside. Don Foster lights a paraffin heater. Dawson pours out the tea from two large flasks. Bill flashes the ash. We sit there, like four blokes about to play a hand of cards.

It is raining hard now against the hut, against the window.

I look at Bill. I look at my watch. I look at Bill again.

Bill stamps his cigarette out on the floor. He takes a swig of his tea. He asks them: 'I take it you both know we've got George Marsh at Brotherton?'

John Dawson and Don Foster glance at each other for a split second –

A split second in which you can see them thinking –

Thinking of denying that they actually know George Marsh –

A split second in which they change my life –

All our fucking lives –

A split second before Don Foster shakes his head. A split second before he says: 'I wish you'd have come to us before, Bill.'

'Why's that then, Don?'

'Could have saved us all a lot of bother.'

'How's that then, Don?'

Don Foster looks at John Dawson.

John Dawson looks at Bill.

Bill waits.

John Dawson says: 'He was with me.'

Bill waits.

John Dawson says: 'On Saturday.'

Bill waits.

John Dawson says: 'Bit of cash in hand.'

Bill waits.

John Dawson stands up. He goes over to the window and the rain. He looks out at the skeleton of the enormous bungalow, its stark white bones rising out of the ground. John Dawson says: 'He was here with me.'

I look at Bill.

Bill smiles. Bill turns to Don Foster. Bill says: 'Wish you'd have come to us before, Don.'

Don Foster doesn't smile. He just blinks.

'Could have saved us all a lot of bother,' says Bill. 'A lot of bother.'

On the road home we stop by a telephone box.

Bill makes the call.

I sit and feel hollow and sick inside.

Bill opens the passenger door. It's written all over his bloody face. All over the bloody *Action* form in his hand.

'It's bollocks,' I say. 'Fucking bollocks.'

'Got no reason to hold him now.'

'Fucking bollocks.'

'Maurice – '

'Load of fucking bollocks.'

'What? They're all fucking lying?'

'It's a load of fucking bollocks and you fucking well know it!'

'Finished?' Bill asks.

I clutch the wheel, my knuckles white when they should be bloody and scabbed.

'Have you fucking finished?' he asks again.

I nod.

'Then I hope you'll remember that we fucking owe John and Don.'

I nod again, my tongue bleeding.

'Now let's get bloody home,' says Bill Molloy, the *Badger*, scrawling across the form:

N.F.A.

Home –

Home with its children's feet upon the stairs, laughter and telephones ringing through the rooms, the slam of a ball against a bat or a wall, the pop of a cap gun and a burst balloon, the sounds of meals being cooked, served and eaten –

Home, *sod that* –

I drive through the fading summer evening, the fields of green and trees of brown, birds going home and the cattle to sleep, clouds in retreat and night upon the march with its promise of another summer's day tomorrow, of cricket and croquet and the Great Yorkshire Show, and –

Fuck it. I see under the ground –

An underground kingdom, an animal kingdom of badgers and angels, worms and insect cities; white swans upon black lakes while dragons soar overhead in painted skies of silver stars and then swoop down through lamp-lit caverns wherein an owl searches for a sleeping little princess in her tiny feathered wings –

My underground –

My underground kingdom, this animal kingdom of corpses and rats and children's shoes, mines flooded with the dirty water of old tears, dragons tearing up burning skies, empty churches and barren wombs, the fleas, rats and dogs picking through the ruin of her bones and wings, her starved white skeleton left here to weep by –

I park at the bottom of the hill, the stark white bones rising out of the ground and into the moonlight.

I get out into the moonlight, the ugly moonlight.

I walk up the hill.

My shoes and my socks sink into the sod.

In the ugly moonlight, I start to dig.

I drive home, the radio on:

Suspicious Minds –

War songs and bad news:

'David Smith, one of the chief witnesses in the Moors Murder trial, was sentenced at Chester Assizes to three years' imprisonment. Mr Smith, aged twenty-one, a labourer, pleaded guilty to wounding William Lees with intent to do grievous bodily harm. In mitigation his counsel claimed that had he not been involved in the murder trial Smith might not have been in trouble.'

War songs, bad news, and the moon:

' "Spirit of mankind is with you," says President Nixon.'

The radio off.

I park outside our house, our home –

The lights are off, the curtains drawn –

Everybody sleeping.

I get out of the car.
I stand and look up at our house, our home –
In the ugly moonlight with dirty hands:
Jeanette Garland, eight, still missing –
The little girl who never came home.

Chapter 23

Sunday 29 May 1983 –

D-11:

You push the buzzer and wait outside the door to the main building. There is the loud click. The sound of the alarm. You pull open the door. You step into the steel cage. You show the plastic visitor's tag to the guard on the other side of the bars. You tell him your name. He bangs twice on one of the bars with his black and shining truncheon. The other set of locks moves back. The other alarm sounds. You go through into the reception area. Another guard gives you the slip of paper with your number. He points at the bench. You walk over. You sit down next to a woman in grey and burgundy clothes. There is a pale and silent child upon her knee. They smell of chip shops and the rain, the grey and the damp –

The whole room still grey and damp, grey and damp with the same smell of people who've travelled hundreds of miles along motorways still grey and damp, the same overweight men in uniforms still grey and damp, the same government seats still grey and damp, the same bad news still grey and damp, as the bolts and the locks slide back and forth and the alarms sound and the numbers are called and the people cough and cough and the children stare and stare until the voice from the desk by the door cries out: 'Thirty-six'.

The pale and silent child is staring at you.

'Thirty-six!'

You look down at the piece of paper in your hand.

'Number thirty-six!'

You stand up.

At the desk, you say: 'John Piggott to see Michael Myshkin.'

The woman in the grey uniform runs her wet, bitten finger down her biro list. She sniffs and says: 'Purpose of visit?'

'Legal.'

She hands you back your pass: 'First time?'

'Second.'

She shrugs: 'The patient will be brought to the visitors' room and a member of staff will be present throughout the visit. Visits are limited to forty-five minutes. You will both be seated at a table and are to remain seated throughout the course of the visit. You are to refrain from any physical contact and are not to pass anything to the patient.

Anything you wish to give the patient must be done so through this office and can only be one of the items on this approved list.'

She hands you the photocopied piece of A4.

'Thank you.'

'Return to your seat and wait for a member of staff to escort you to the visiting area.'

Forty minutes and another paper swan later, a stocky guard with a button missing from his uniform says: 'John Winston Piggott?'

You stand up.

'This way.'

You follow him through the other door and the other lock, the other alarm and the ringing bell, through the door and up the overheated and overlit grey corridor.

At the last set of double doors, he pauses. He says: 'Know the drill?'

You nod.

'Keep seated, no physical contact, and no passing of goods.'

You nod again.

'I'll tell you when your forty-five minutes are up.'

'Thank you.'

He punches the code into the panel on the wall.

The alarm sounds. He pulls open the door: 'After you.'

You step into the small room with the grey carpet and the grey walls, the two plastic tables each with their two plastic chairs.

'Sit down,' says the guard.

You sit down in the grey plastic chair. You lean forward, arms on the marked plastic surface of the grey plastic table, eyes on the door opposite.

The guard sits down behind you.

You are about to say something to the guard when there he is again:

As if by magick –

Coming through the door in his grey overalls and grey shirt, enormous with a head twice as large:

Michael John Myshkin –

Michael John Myshkin, with spittle on his chin.

'Hello again,' you say.

'Hello again,' he smiles, blinking.

His guard pushes him down into the grey chair opposite you. He closes the other door. He takes a seat behind Michael Myshkin.

You say: 'How are you, Michael?'

'Fine,' he says, patting down his dirty yellow hair with his fat right hand.

'I've been doing some background work on your case, preparing documents for your appeal, and I'd like to go over some of the details with you.'

Michael Myshkin wipes his right hand on his overalls and smiles at you, pale blue eyes blinking in the warm grey room.

'Is that OK with you?'

Michael Myshkin nods once, still smiling, still blinking.

You take out your notebook and biro from your carrier bag. You open the pad. You ask: 'Can you remember when you were arrested?'

Michael Myshkin glances round at the guard behind him, then turns back to you. He whispers: 'Wednesday 18 December 1974. One o'clock in the morning.'

'Really? One o'clock?'

He blinks. He smiles. He nods again.

'Where were you arrested?'

Michael Myshkin is not smiling. He is not blinking. He says: 'At work.'

You look down at your notes: 'The Jenkins Photo Studio in Castleford?'

He nods his head. He looks down.

You sit back in your plastic chair, tapping your plastic pen on the plastic table. You look back across the table at him.

He is patting down his hair again.

'Michael?' you say.

He looks up at you.

'The police said they arrested you on the Doncaster Road after a chase?'

'That's not true,' he says. 'Ask my mum.'

You make a note. You ask: 'Where did they take you?'

'Wakefield.'

'Wood Street? Bishopgarth?'

He shakes his head.

'OK, then tell me why?' you ask him. 'Why did they arrest you?'

'Because of Clare,' he says.

'What about her?'

'Because they said I killed her.'

'And is that right?' you say again. 'Did you?'

Michael John Myshkin shakes his head again: 'I told you, no.'

'No what?' you say, writing down his words verbatim again.

'I didn't kill her.'

'Good,' you smile. 'Just checking.'

Michael Myshkin is not smiling.

'The actual policemen who arrested you?' you ask him. 'The ones that came to your work that night? Can you remember their names?'

He shakes his head.

'Michael, please think. This is very, very important.'

He looks up at you. He says: 'I know it is.'

'OK then,' you say. 'The policemen who arrested you, who came to the studio, who took you to Wakefield, were these the same policemen who later told you to say you killed Clare?'

Michael Myshkin blinks. Michael Myshkin shakes his head.

You look into the uniformed eyes of the man behind Michael Myshkin, another set of uniformed eyes behind you –

You ask Michael Myshkin: 'Policemen told you to say you killed Clare?'

He nods.

'But you didn't kill her?'

He nods again.

'But you signed a piece of paper to say you did?'

'They made me.'

'Who?'

'The police.'

'How?'

'They said if I signed the paper, I could see my mother.'

'And if you didn't?'

'They said I'd never see her or my father again.'

You look into the uniformed eyes of the man behind Michael Myshkin, another set of uniformed eyes behind you –

'The police said that?'

He nods.

'Who was your first solicitor?' you ask.

'Mr McGuinness.'

'Clive McGuinness?'

He nods.

'How did you find him?'

'I don't know.'

'Did you tell Mr McGuinness that you killed Clare?'

Michael Myshkin shakes his head.

'You told Mr McGuinness that you didn't kill Clare Kemplay?'

He nods.

'And what did Mr McGuinness say?'

'He said it was too late. He said I had signed the paper. He said no-one would believe me. He said everyone would believe the police. He said it would make things worse for me if now I said I didn't do it.

He said I'd never get out of prison. He said I'd never see my mother and father. He said he would only help me if I said I did it. He said I would be able to see my mother and father soon. He said I would only have to stay in prison a short time.'

You look into the uniformed eyes of the man behind Michael Myshkin, another set of uniformed eyes behind you –

'How long have you been in here, Michael?'

Michael Myshkin looks at you: 'Seven years, five months, and eleven days.'

You nod.

He starts to pat down his hair again.

You look at your notes. You say: 'Two girls told the police that they saw you in Morley on a number of occasions, including the afternoon that Clare Kemplay disappeared.'

Michael Myshkin looks up again. Michael Myshkin shakes his head. 'What?'

'It wasn't me.'

'You weren't in Morley that Thursday?'

He shakes his head.

'So where were you?'

'At work.'

'The Jenkins Photo Studio in Castleford?'

He nods.

'But the police couldn't trace Mr Jenkins and the only other member of staff, a Miss Douglas, she couldn't be sure whether you were at work or not. Not very helpful, was it?'

'They made her say that.'

'Who did?'

'The police.'

'OK,' you say. 'These two girls, they also said that the reason they remembered you so clearly was because you had once exposed yourself to them.'

He shakes his head again.

'They were lying, were they, Michael?'

He nods.

You sigh. You sit back in your plastic chair. You look across at him.

He is patting down his hair again.

'Michael,' you say. 'Do you remember Jimmy Ashworth?'

He looks up at you. He nods.

'What do you remember about him?'

'He was my friend.'

'Your friend?'

'My best friend.'

'Did he talk to you about Clare?'

He nods.

'What did he say?'

'He said she was beautiful.'

'Beautiful?' you say. 'She was bloody dead when he found her?'

Michael Myshkin shakes his head.

'What?'

'He'd seen her before.'

'What? Where?'

'When they built the houses.'

'Which houses?'

'In Morley.'

'So Jimmy knew her?'

Michael Myshkin nods.

'Did you?'

He shakes his head.

'Michael,' you say. 'Did Jimmy kill her?'

He looks at you. He shakes his head again.

'So who did?'

He is patting down his hair. He is blinking. He is smiling.

'Who?'

Smiling and blinking and patting down his hair –

You bang the table hard with your hand: 'Who?'

Michael Myshkin stares up at you –

Michael Myshkin says: 'The Wolf?'

'This wolf have a name, does he?'

He says: 'Ask Jimmy.'

You open your carrier bag. You take out a *Yorkshire Post* –

There are two photographs on the front page.

You throw the paper across the table –

You lean forward.

You point at one of the photographs –

The photograph of a young man with long, lank hair.

Michael Myshkin looks down at the paper –

You say: 'He's dead.'

You point at the other photograph –

The photograph of a little girl with medium-length dark brown hair.

You say: 'She's missing.'

Michael Myshkin is still looking down at the paper –

You say: 'The police said Jimmy took her. They caught him in

Morley. They arrested him. They say he confessed. Then he hung himself.'

Michael Myshkin looks up at you –

There are tears down his cheeks.

Michael Myshkin says: 'He's back.'

'Who?'

Michael Myshkin shakes his head.

'Who?'

Michael Myshkin turns to the guard sat behind him. Michael Myshkin whispers: 'I'd like to go back to my room now please.'

You are on your feet: 'Who?'

The guard behind you has a hand on your shoulder –

'Sit down – '

You are shouting: 'Michael, who? Tell me fucking who?'

'Sit down – '

Michael Myshkin is on his feet, his guard opening the other door –

'Who?'

'Sit down!'

Michael John Myshkin turns back –

Spittle on his chin, tears on his cheeks –

Turns back and screams: 'The Wolf!'

Doors locked, you switch on the engine and the radio news and light a cigarette and then another and another:

'Thatcher rejects TV battle with Frost; Foot finds Times *headlines malicious; Hume concerned over Kent's CND role; Hess holds key to Hitler's Diary; eleven-year-old boy strangled by a swing-ball tennis game which wrapped around his neck . . .'*

No Hazel –

Not here.

You switch off the radio and light another cigarette and listen to the rain fall on the roof of the car, eyes closed:

Fuck, fuck, fuck, fuck, fuck, fuck, fuck, fuck –

You open your eyes:

Fuck.

You feel sick again, your fingers burnt again.

You put out the cigarette and press the buttons in and out on the radio until you find some music:

Simple Minds.

'Mrs Myshkin? It's John Piggott.'

In a telephone box on Merseyside again, listening to Mrs Myshkin and the relentless sound of the hard rain on the roof –

'Yes, he's fine,' you say.

The rain pouring down, the car lights on in the middle of a Sunday afternoon in May –

'Where was Michael arrested?'

The kind of wet Sunday afternoon you used to spend in bus shelters, huddled around ten cigs and the readers' wives, afraid –

'You're certain?'

Sitting in the bus shelter, listening to the rain fall on the corrugated roof, the world outside so sharp and full of pain, listening to the relentless sound of the hard rain on the roof and not wanting to go back home, dreading it –

'I should have asked you before, but how did Clive McGuinness come to represent Michael?'

That vague fear even then –

'One last question,' you ask her. 'Who did Michael call the Wolf?'

That fear real and here –

'You're certain?'

That fear again now –

She hangs up and you stand there, listening to the dial tone –

The dial tone and the relentless sound of the rain on the roof of the telephone box, not wanting to go home, dreading it –

The fear now:

Sunday 29 May 1983 –

D-11:

That fear here –

Dogs barking –

Near.

Wolves.

You drive from Merseyside back to Wakefield –

'An active IRA unit of four or six men is thought to be planning the assassination of a leading British politician or a bombing during the General Election campaign.'

The motorways quiet –

'Mr John Gunnell, the leader of West Yorkshire County Council, has alleged that new photographs conclusively prove that British nurse Helen Smith was murdered in Saudi Arabia.'

Everywhere dead.

She is sat on the stair. She is waiting for you. She has brought cold

Chinese food and warm alcohol. She hears you on the stairs. She looks up. She is wet. She smiles.

'Thought you might be hungry,' she says.

'I am,' you lie and open the door –

The telephone ringing, the branches tapping.

Chapter 24

Breathing hard and spitting blood, running blind –

But here it is again, his car:

Fuck.

Let it get within six foot and then BJ off again –

Wind, rain, his voice:

'BJ!'

Over a fence and on to wasteland, tripping and falling on to ground on other side, bleeding and crying and praying, stumble across waste-land and into a playground, into playground and scrambling over another fence, over fence and into some allotments, drip blood through vegetable patches and over a wall and into a small street of terraces, down street and right into another street of terraces, turn left then right again –

Got to get off streets.

BJ turn off street and down side of a quiet little house –

Into their back garden:

Bingo.

A shed, black in rain at bottom of garden.

Door isn't locked, just kept shut with a brick.

BJ go inside and sit down on a pile of old newspapers beside a spade and a lawnmower, a wheelbarrow and a trowel.

BJ wait –

Wait for it to get dark –

But it's always dark.

BJ sit and BJ wait in dark, endless dark, and BJ cry –

Cry –

Cry for cuts on hands and cuts on legs, cuts on face and cuts in hair –

For mud on trousers and mud on shoes, on jacket and on shirt –

For mess –

For fucking mess BJ in –

Not only BJ:

BJ cry for mum –

Cry for mum and all other people BJ either loved or fucked or both –

Or ones BJ simply just fucked over:

For Barry Gannon and Bill Shaw –

Even Eddie Dunford and Paula Garland –

But most of all BJ cry for Grace and Clare:

Here in some nice little person's shed in a nice little garden in Preston at half-past ten in morning on a wet Friday –

Friday 21 November 1975 –

BJ crying and crying, over and over, finally crying –

Knuckles red and fingers blue, biting hands and cuffs of shirt, wishing BJ could stop –

Wishing it all would fucking stop –

Stop and rewind –

That dead be living, living never dead:

'*Clare!*'

BJ take photograph out of pocket:

Clare with her eyes and legs open, her fingers touching her cunt.

But it isn't her, it really isn't her, and BJ screw it up and hide it deep inside BJ's jacket, and BJ close eyes to make it stop and go away –

But when BJ close eyes, BJ see her body again –

Her body on a stretcher, wind raising bloody sheet:

A light green three-quarter coat with an imitation fur collar, a turquoise blue jumper with a bright yellow tank top over it, dark brown trousers, brown suede calf-length boots.

BJ open red eyes and BJ steal a glance through dirty wet window at nice little garden and nice little house with its nice little curtains and its nice little ornaments on nice little windowsill, even nice little flap for cat and nice little table for birds –

Birds with their wings, their little angel wings that raise them high –

BJ pull up BJ's shirt and with dirty wet fingers, BJ search among shoulder blades and back bones, search for stumps –

Stumps of wings –

But BJ cannot find them.

BJ pull down dirty star shirt and BJ think about BJ's mother and nice little house with nice little garden that never was; Clare and her kids and nice little house with nice little garden they never had and never will –

BJ wait in endless dark and BJ cry.

It is Friday 21 November 1975:

North of England –

Clare is dead.

It's dark when BJ open shed door –

Always dark –

There are still no lights on in house so BJ walk down side and back out on to street.

BJ jog down to end of street and peer round corner:

All clear.

BJ weave through side streets and terraces, wishing it would stop raining for just one single fucking minute.

BJ come to playing fields where on far side behind houses there is a dual-carriageway.

BJ start to cross playing fields. BJ see them:

Fuck.

A line of coppers with sticks, searching playing fields for something –

A murder weapon.

Someone –

A missing child, me.

Torches and capes in rain, fanned out like a bloody army of night marching towards BJ –

But they can't see BJ, not yet:

They are walking away from lights of road, into shadow –

BJ hit mud and ground, crouching and crawling across one pitch, rolling and tumbling on to another, slowly –

Slowly until they pass and they're gone, behind, and BJ start to crawl again –

Crawl and crouch off towards dual-carriageway and road to fuck knows where –

Anywhere but here –

Glancing back at coppers with their sticks, their torches and their capes, thanking fucking Christ they hadn't dogs out tonight –

BJ get to gardens, gardens of houses that stand between BJ and road.

BJ slink along looking for another one without its lights on, at least its curtains drawn.

BJ come to one, dark.

BJ scale wooden fence and drop down into their shrubbery and cross their neatly trimmed lawn and go along side of their house and into their front garden where BJ hide in their privets while BJ check coast is clear –

Like in a war film.

After a minute or so BJ step out into street and walk along pavement next to big and busy road, walk towards roundabout where BJ will hitch a way out of here –

Out of Nazi Germany.

And BJ is walking along, yellow lights coming, red lights leaving, practising German and thinking about trying to cross to other side where it's just more playing fields and some woods, thinking at least there'd be somewhere to run if Krauts showed their sour Nazi faces –

Thinking of somewhere to run when a car stops –

A car stops and driver winds down his window –

Winds down his window and says –

He says: 'Hello Barry, you're all wet.'

Chapter 25

We turn into Blenheim Road, St John's, Wakefield –

Big trees with hearts cut into their bark, losing their leaves in July –

Big houses with their hearts cut into flats, losing their paintwork and their lead;

We turn into Blenheim Road and I am filled again with hate –

Filled with hate at *Mystic* Mandy, the medium and the fraud –

Hate at wasted time with sideshow freaks from the Feasts and the Fairs;

Hate at Wally Heywood, Georgie Oldman, and *Badger* Billy –

Hate at who and what they are –

What they know and will not do;

But most of all this day –

Saturday 19 July 1969 –

I am filled with hate at me;

Hate at me for who and what I am –

What I know and will not do:

(*Just a lullaby in the local tongue*) –

Hate.

We park on Blenheim Road –

The big trees with hearts cut into bark, the big houses with hearts cut into flats;

We park and finally I say: 'What the fucking hell is this, Bill?'

He stinks of his lunch and guilt. He slurs: 'George reckons – '

'Since when did you give two shits what George fucking Oldman reckoned – '

'Maurice – '

'We know who fucking did it.'

'Did what?'

'Took her.'

'No, we don't.'

'Yes, we do.'

'No, we don't.'

'Yes, we fucking do.'

'Maurice, it isn't pantomime season yet.'

'Oh yes it fucking is.'

'Fuck off, Maurice,' he says and opens the car door –

(*Local, local hates*) –

I get out. I slam my door.

We walk up the drive of 28 Blenheim Road –

One big tree with hearts cut into bark, one big house with her heart cut into flats;

We walk up the drive full of shallow holes and stagnant water –

The bottoms of our trousers, our socks and our shoes, muddy in July.

George Oldman is already here, waiting under the porch with a black umbrella. He puts out his cigarette. He nods: 'Gentlemen.'

'George,' says Bill.

I've got nothing to say.

'Going up?' asks Bill.

'Best wait for Jack,' says George.

I say: 'Jack?'

'Jack Whitehead,' says George.

'Fucking hell.'

'Thought he was your mate,' says Bill.

'He is, but – '

'Him that set this up,' says George. He hands me today's *Post* –

I read aloud: '*Medium Contacts Police.*'

I shake my head. I hand the paper back to George. I look at my watch:

It's gone one –

Wasted, wasted time.

'Talk of the Devil,' says Bill –

Jack's Jensen pulls into the drive. He parks at an angle and gets out. His face is grey and his eyes are red, another one pissed up. He sparks up. He waves his cigarette: 'Hello, hello, hello. If it ain't the boys in blue.'

'Number 5, is it, Jack?' asks George.

Jack nods. Jack stumbles –

(No local angels here) –

Jack drops his fag. Jack picks it up. Jack slaps me on the back.

We go inside 28 Blenheim Road, St John's, Wakefield –

The big house with her heart cut into flats, losing her paintwork and her lead;

We go inside and walk up the stairs to Flat 5 –

The glass in the windows stained.

We walk up the stairs to Flat 5 on the first-floor landing –

The air cold and damp, the air stained.

Jacks knocks on the door: 'Police, love. Open up in the name of the law.'

Bill looks at me. I look at the floor.

The door opens a crack, a chain on –

Between the wood of the door and the wood of the frame, the pale face of a beautiful woman, the metal chain across her mouth.

'It's Jack Whitehead, love. These are the police officers I was talking about.'

Between the wood, this pale and beautiful face nods.

The door closes briefly then opens again wider, the chain gone –

The woman is in her early thirties. She is wearing a white silk blouse and a dark wool skirt.

She is truly beautiful –

(Local beauty) –

She says: 'Please, come in.'

We step inside Flat 5, 28 Blenheim Road –

A flat cut out of its heart;

We follow the woman down a dim hall, the walls hung with dark paintings, and into a big room, the walls and chairs draped in Persian rugs –

The whole flat stinks of cat piss and petunia.

Jack does the introductions: 'These two gentlemen are Detective Superintendents George Oldman and Bill Molloy, and this is Detective Inspector Maurice Jobson –

'Gentlemen, this is Mrs Mandy Denizili, or – '

'Mandy Wymer,' she smiles, shaking our hands.

'*Mystic* Mandy,' nods Jack. 'As she is known professionally.'

She looks at Jack. She sighs. She gestures at the sofa and the armchair. She says: 'Please sit down.'

George takes the armchair, Jack a cushion on the floor, Bill and I the sofa –

A low and ornately carved table pressing into our knees and shins.

'Tea?' she asks.

'That'd be grand,' smiles George, Bill and I nodding.

'Not for me, love,' says Jack. 'Never touch the stuff.'

'Excuse me for just a minute,' she says. She goes off through another door.

'Denizili?' Bill asks Jack.

'Husband was Turkish.'

I look up from the unlit candles on the table: '*Was?*'

'Not about,' says Jack.

Bill is laughing: 'You think she knows owt about the two-thirty at York?'

'I'm a medium, Mr Molloy, not a fortune-teller,' says Mandy Wymer. She is stood in the doorway with a tray in her hands.

'Sorry,' says Bill, hands up in apology. 'No offence.'

She brings in the tray of teacups and a teapot. She sets it down on the low table. She smiles at Bill: 'None taken.'

It is a truly beautiful smile.

George sits forward in the armchair. He says: 'Jack here tells us you have some information about this little girl who's gone missing up Castleford way?'

She hands him his cup of tea. She nods: 'Yes, that's right.'

'What kind of information?'

'We're desperate,' I add. 'Must be.'

She looks at me. She smiles. She hands Bill and me our cups of tea. Then she kneels down on the other side of the low ornately carved table –

'I am a medium, gentlemen,' she says again. 'And it is sometimes possible for me to hear, see, and feel things that other people perhaps cannot.'

We all nod –

Three coppers staring at the beautiful woman knelt before us, Jack struggling to keep his eyes open, Bill the grin off his chops.

'It is also the case that on occasion the dead can speak through me.'

'You think she's dead then, Jeanette?' asks George.

Mandy Wymer doesn't answer him. She lights one of the fat white candles on the low table. She stands up. She goes over to the large windows. She draws the heavy crimson curtains –

The room dark but for the candlelight, she returns to the table.

Bill: 'Mrs Denizili – '

She has her hand up in the shadows: 'Please, Mr Molloy – '

'But – '

I have my hand on Bill's arm.

She lights a second fat white candle on the low table. Then another. And another. She says: 'Now please take the hand of the person on your left and close your eyes.'

She takes George's right hand. He takes Bill's. Bill takes mine. I take Jack's –

Jack waking with a start to hold hers.

The five of us lean forward in a circle around the table and the candles, the numbers on a clock –

(Local time) –

It is Saturday 19 July 1969.

Blenheim Road, St John's, Wakefield –
　Big trees with hearts cut into their bark, losing their leaves in July;
　28 Blenheim Road, St John's, Wakefield –
　Big house with her heart cut into flats, losing her paintwork and her lead;
　Flat 5, 28 Blenheim Road, St John's, Wakefield –
　Big room with hearts dark, losing our way and our head;
　Walls hung with dim paintings and Persian rugs –
　The smell of cat piss and petunia, Bill and Jack's breath;
　My eyes are open –
　Her breasts rising and falling beneath her white silk blouse;
　Beneath the shadows –
　Low sobs, muffled sobs, she is weeping;
　Her breasts rising and falling beneath –
　Her shadows –
　Looking into my eyes –
　Rising and falling –
　Beneath her shadows –
　She is snarling, carnivore teeth:
　'This place is worst of all, underground;
　The corpses and the rats –
　The dragon and the owl –
　Wolves be there too, a swan –
　The swan dead.
　Unending, this place unending;
　Under the grass that grows –
　Between the cracks and the stones –
　The beautiful carpets –
　Waiting for the others, underground.'
　Silence –
　Silence, the circle unbroken:
　Holding George's right hand. George Bill's. Bill mine. I Jack's –
　Jack holding hers:
　Blenheim Road, St John's, Wakefield –
　Big trees with hearts cut into their bark, losing their leaves in July;
　28 Blenheim Road, St John's, Wakefield –
　Big house with her heart cut into flats, losing her paintwork and her lead;
　Flat 5, 28 Blenheim Road, St John's, Wakefield –
　Big room with dark ways, hearts and heads lost;
　My eyes are open –
　Low sobs, muffled sobs, she is weeping;

Looking into my eyes –
Weeping;
Rising and falling –
Beneath her shadows:
'It's happened once before –'
Cavernous tears:
' – and it's happening now.'
Tears, then –
Silence –
The silence, but outside:
Outside behind the heavy crimson curtains, the branches of the big tree are tapping upon the glass of the big windows, their leaves lost in July –
Wanting in;
Wanting her –
My eyes open and looking into hers;
I want to drop Bill's hand, let go of Jack –
To reach out across the table –
Free her from the chains –
The prisons:
The certain death that I see here –
That terrible, horrible voice that gloats, that boasts:
'I AM NO ANGEL –
'I AM NO FUCKING ANGEL!'
Looking into my eyes –
Weeping;
Rising and falling –
Beneath her shadows:
In the Season of the Plague, the meat –
Two black crows eating from black bin-bags, ripping through her sweet meat –
Screams echoing into the dark, sliding back on her arse up the hall, arms and legs splayed, her skirt riding up; scared sobs from behind a door, the sound of furniture being moved, of chests and drawers and wardrobes being placed in front of the door –
A faint voice through the layers and layers of wood, a child whispering to a friend beneath the covers: 'Tell them about the others . . .'
On my feet, across the table –
Teacups and teapot falling to the floor –
I shake her –
I scream: 'What others?'
Her eyes open and looking into mine –

She says: 'All the others under those beautiful carpets.'

'What fucking others?'

Bill and George are on their feet now –

The candles out –

Pulling back the curtains, Jack spewing into his palm –

I am screaming –

I am summoning her back from the Underground, the court of the Dead:

A cold and dark December place when I open up the bedroom door to find her lying cold and still upon the floor –

Bill and George taking my arms –

Pulling me off;

Her pushing me off –

Pushing me away, whispering: 'Please tell them where they are.'

'What?' I say –

Standing up in the light;

But in the light –

The dead daylight –

There are bruises on the backs of my hands –

(Local bruises) –

Bruises that won't heal.

Part 3
Dreams less sweet

'The Christian Church has always condemned magick, but she has always believed in it. She did not excommunicate sorcerers as madmen who were mistaken, but as men who were really in communion with the Devil.'

– Voltaire

Chapter 26

Tapping against the pane –

Monday 30 May 1983 –

D-10:

She is lying on her side in a sleeveless black T-shirt with her back to you –

Branches tapping against the pane;

You are lying on your back in your underpants and socks –

The branches tapping against the pane;

Lying on your back with the taste of fried rice and vodka in your mouth –

Listening to the branches tapping against the pane;

D-10:

Monday 30 May 1983 –

You are listening to the branches tapping against the pane.

It is raining again outside and they are arguing again upstairs.

You sit in the kitchen eating Findus Crispy Pancakes in silence, the radio on:

'*Sterling at new high on hopes of Tory landslide as Foot attempts to refute latest opinion polls; Mr Cecil Parkinson, the Conservative Party Chairman, dismisses suggestions that his party has been subjected to significant infiltration by far right members of the National Front and the League of St George; a report to be published today says shopping centres built in the 1960s and . . .'*

You get up. You change stations. You find some music:

Spandau Ballet –

True.

She stands up. She switches off the radio.

You go over to the sink. You rinse cold water over the plates and the grill. You turn around, hands still wet. You say: 'What was Jimmy doing in Morley?'

'What?'

'When they nicked him? Why was he in Morley?'

She shrugs. She says: 'He was coming to see me.'

'You?'

'It's where I live, isn't it?'

'I didn't know that.'

'Do now.'

She goes out of the kitchen. You follow her into the front room. She is putting on her coat.

You are stood in the doorway. You say: 'Dangerous place, Morley.'

She doesn't say anything. She walks towards you. She says: 'Excuse me.'

You say: 'Do you know Hazel Atkins? Her family?'

She shakes her head. She tries to push past you.

You grab her arm: 'What about Clare Kemplay? Did you know her?'

'You're hurting me.'

'Jimmy did.'

'Fuck off,' she hisses. 'He's dead.'

'Michael Myshkin told me.'

'What does he know.'

'He knew Jimmy; they were mates.'

'Fuck off,' she spits. 'It was years ago and they were never *mates*; they were only bloody kids.'

'*Best* mates, Michael said.'

'It was years ago and Jimmy's bloody dead because of that fucking Joey!'

And that's it:

She's gone –

Just like that.

You drive through Wakefield and out over the Calder, the car retching and then coughing, hacking its way up the Barnsley Road and out past the Redbeck –

Putting one and one together:

Michael Myshkin and Jimmy Ashworth –

Jimmy and Michael, Michael and Jimmy –

One and one to make:

' . . . and 1970s are in urgent need of repair; senior detectives searching for missing Morley schoolgirl Hazel Atkins will again travel to Rochdale having discounted the reported weekend sighting of Hazel at an Edinburgh fair . . .'

Sweating and then freezing, your clothes itching with hate, you've got shadows in your heart and a belly full of fear –

Putting two and two together:

Fear and hate, hate and fear –

Michael and Jimmy, Jimmy and Michael –

Fitzwilliam.

Another silent house on Newstead View, Fitzwilliam –

The fire and TV off –

Just the clock ticking and the whistle of another boiling kettle.

Mrs Ashworth comes back in with two mugs of tea.

She hands you yours: 'Sugar?'

You nod.

'How many?'

'Three please.'

She passes you the bag: 'Help yourself.'

'Thank you.'

She sits down. She says: 'I'm sorry about other day. I'm feeling more myself now, I suppose.'

'That's good,' you say. 'But it's going to take a bit of time.'

She nods: 'That's what the doctor says. But everyone's been very helpful, very kind.'

Just the clock ticking –

You say: 'I saw Tessa.'

Mary Ashworth rolls her tired eyes. Mary Ashworth sighs.

You wait. You wait for her to say what she wants to say –

Wait for her to say: 'She's another one, you know?'

You shake your head.

She squeezes her hands together. She leans towards you. She whispers: 'Another bloody lost cause; I tell you, if there was ever a saint for lame ducks, it was my Jimmy.'

'That how he fell in with Michael Myshkin?'

She shakes her head: 'She's been through a lot, his mother, I know. But, and may God forgive me, I wish with all my heart they'd never moved here and then Jimmy would have never met him and Jimmy . . .'

'When was that?'

'That they moved here?'

You nod.

'Must have been when Jimmy was about three or four and him, he'd have been ten or so. Not that you'd have known.'

'They knew each other a while then?'

'No,' she says. 'Wasn't till Jimmy was ten or eleven himself that they started palling around.'

'So Michael would have been a teenager? Sixteen or seventeen?'

'Physically.'

'Didn't worry you then, them two being friendly?'

'No,' she shrugs. 'He was harmless, leastways that's what folk thought.'

You nod.

'And,' she continues. 'Wasn't like it was just them two. There were others.'

'Others?'

'Four or five of them.'

'They still about?'

She sits back. She scratches her nose.

You push: 'Remember who?'

'Kevin Madeley, he would have been one of them. Little Leonard, but he was a bit younger and maybe they'd moved by then. It's such a long time ago. The Hinchcliffes' lad, Stuart maybe. There were others and all, you know how kids are?'

The clock ticking –

The bells ringing: 'They still about?'

'Kevin Madeley, he moved over Stanley way. I think the Hinchcliffe lad went down South. Birmingham somewhere.'

Distant bells: 'Their parents? They still live local?'

'The Madeleys do,' she says. 'Mrs Madeley, she worked with his mother.'

'Mrs Myshkin?'

'Aye,' she nods.

'Dinner lady?'

She nods. She finishes her tea. She keeps hold of her mug on her lap.

You pull your notebook from your pocket. You find your pen. You start to write down some of the names and dates.

She says: 'What about your brother?'

You stop writing. You look up. You say: 'What about him?'

'Always lived round here, hasn't he?'

You shrug.

'Not close these days?' she smiles. 'You and your Pete?'

You shake your head: 'Not really, no.'

'He blame you, does he?' she asks. 'Business with your father, then your mother?'

'Mrs Ashworth, I – '

'Mr Ashworth does,' she says, dabbing at her eyes with the ends of her apron. 'Blames me, I know he does. See it written all over his face every time he looks at me.'

'I'm sure he doesn't,' you lie again.

She sniffs. She tries to smile. She says: 'He might know something, mightn't he?'

'Who?'

'Your Pete.'

You shake your head. You think about your brother –

Men not here –

Your father –

Not here.

You say: 'I want to talk to you about Clare Kemplay.'

She stares at you. She says: 'Is this for my Jimmy or her down road?'

'I need to ask you – '

'Not again,' she sighs.

'It's important – '

'It's so bloody long ago – '

'But – '

'What's the point in – '

'Please – '

'Raking over – '

'Mrs Ashworth, please I – '

'Not going to bring him back – '

'Look,' you shout. 'Clare Kemplay is the bloody reason they picked Jimmy up.'

She stops speaking. She closes her eyes. She clutches the mug tight in her hands. She opens her eyes. She looks at you. She says: 'He had nothing to do with that and he had nothing to do with this.'

'He knew Clare Kemplay.'

'He didn't *know* her. He'd seen her. That's all.'

'He said she was beautiful.'

'Who did?'

'Your Jimmy.'

'No.'

'To Michael.'

She shakes her head.

'He knew her. He found her.'

'The wrong place – '

'What about Hazel Atkins?'

She shakes her head again.

'He was in Morley one week later, the exact time she'd gone missing.'

'The wrong time – '

'But why?'

She closes her eyes again.

You tell her: 'Tessa says he was there to meet her.'

She shakes her head. She opens her eyes. She says: 'He didn't . . .'

'What?'

'He didn't do it,' she says.

'Didn't do what?'

'He didn't kill Clare Kemplay. He didn't take this Hazel Atkins. And he didn't bloody kill himself.'

'But – ' you stop.

She looks at you now. She says: 'Go on, say it.'

'Say what?'

'What you want to say. What you really think.'

You shake your head.

'I'll say it for you then,' she snorts. 'You think he killed Clare Kemplay and he took this other girl and then he hung himself with guilt of it all. That's what you think, isn't it?'

'I – '

'No, *I'll* tell you. They can have all the bloody inquests and all the internal police inquiries they like, but that boy never hung himself. Never. He had no reason. He'd done nothing.'

'Mrs Ashworth – '

'Not in a month of bloody Sundays would he do that to me. Never.'

Now you close your eyes. You wait. You open them. You say: 'I'm sorry.'

She takes a deep breath. She nods.

You shake your head. You think of your father –

Men not here –

Your brother –

Not here.

She dries her eyes. She sits up. She says: 'Not going to bring him back, is it? Carrying on like this. But what can you do?'

'Depends what you want?'

She looks at you. She says: 'The truth, John. That's all.'

You look down at your notes. You close your eyes –

Not here.

You open your eyes. You look back up. You nod –

The clock ticking.

She puts her mug down on the chipped fireplace in front of her. She reaches into the front pocket of her apron. She takes out a piece of paper. She looks at it. She whispers: 'It says he hung himself by his belt until he was dead. Suicide.'

You nod.

'You've seen it then?'

You nod again.

Mrs Ashworth gets up. She walks over to the table. She picks up a single studded black leather belt. She turns to you. She holds out the belt. She says: 'You've seen this, have you?'

You look away. You shake your head. You swallow. You ask: 'Is that it?'

'That's Jimmy's belt,' she nods.

'They let you have his stuff back then?'

She shakes her head –

The clock has stopped.

You look at the belt again. You look at her. You ask: 'So how did you get it?'

She looks up at the ceiling. She says: 'I went upstairs. I opened his wardrobe door and there it was, in his other jeans.'

You look at her.

She is crying.

You swallow. You say: 'But – '

She shakes her head.

You look at the belt. You say again: 'But – '

She shakes her head again. She says: 'He only had the one belt.'

You look at her. You say: 'You're certain?'

She nods, the tears everywhere.

At the door, Mary Ashworth takes your hand in hers.

You look down at the doorstep.

'Thank you,' she says.

You shake your head.

She squeezes your hand in hers: 'Thank you.'

You nod.

She pats your hand twice. She squeezes it one last time. She lets it go.

You turn. You look down the street. You turn back to Mrs Ashworth –

She is looking at you. She is watching you.

You say: 'Do you think Michael Myshkin killed Clare Kemplay?'

She stares at you. She swallows. She looks away.

You ask again: 'Do you?'

She looks at you. She shakes her head. She shuts the door.

You walk down Newstead View –

Through the plastic bags and the dog shit.

You go up the path. You knock on number 54 –

There's no answer.

You knock again.

'She's out.'

'On her broomstick.'

You turn around –

There are a group of four young boys on enormous bicycles at the gate. They have small pointed faces and cold blue eyes. They are dressed in grey and burgundy. They are wearing boxing boots.

'She's gone to prison.'

'Gone to see her son.'

'He's in loony bin.'

'Michael Myshkin, that's her son.'

You nod. You walk back down the path towards the boys.

They rock backwards and forwards on their bicycles. They lean over their handlebars. They spit.

'He's one that killed them little girls.'

'Had it off with them.'

'Stuck birds' wings on them.'

'Cut their hearts out and ate them.'

You push through the boys and their bicycles.

They don't move.

'My dad says they should have hung him.'

'My mum says they will do, minute he gets out.'

'My dad says they'll kill her and all then.'

'My mum says she's an evil fucking witch, his mum.'

You spin round. You slap the nearest boy hard across his face.

He falls off his bicycle into a fence and a thin hedge.

He is cut. His small pointed face is bleeding. His cold blue eyes smarting.

The other three boys start to turn the bicycles around.

'Fuck you do that for fatty?'

'You fat bastard.'

'I'm fucking getting my dad on you.'

'My dad's going to fucking kill you.'

You walk to the car. You unlock the door.

'He'll fucking murder you!'

You get in. You lock the doors.

They are banging on the car:

'You're fucking dead, you are, you fat fucking bastard.'

On the radio on the way into Leeds they are playing that record about ghosts again. You pull over just past the Redbeck. You switch off the radio. You take deep breaths. You dry your eyes.

'I'd like to see the Duty Sergeant who was on the night James Ashworth killed himself.'

'And you are?'

'John Piggott, the solicitor.'

The policeman on the desk nods at the plastic chairs behind you. He says: 'Have a seat please, sir.'

You walk over to the tiny plastic chairs and sit down under the dull and yellow lights that still blink on and off, on and off, the faded poster still warning against the perils of drinking and driving at Christmas –

Still not Christmas.

The policeman on the front desk is making his calls.

You look down at the linoleum floor, at the white squares and the grey, at the boot and chair marks. The smell of dirty dogs and over-cooked vegetables is gone, pine disinfectant in its place –

They have been cleaning.

'Mr Piggott?'

You stand back up and go over to the front desk.

The policeman on the desk says: 'I'm afraid the officer in question is on holiday at present.'

'When will he be back?'

'That I don't know.'

'Could you give me his name then?'

The policeman shakes his head: 'I'm sorry, sir.'

'Regulations?'

He nods.

'Then maybe you can help me?'

The policeman stops nodding.

'You see, I represent Mrs Mary Ashworth, whom I'm sure you know is the mother of the unfortunate James Ashworth who hung himself in one of your cells. At seven fifty-five on the evening of the twenty-fourth of May to be exact. You did hear about this, I take it?'

The policeman says: 'How might I be able to help you, sir?'

'Mrs Ashworth would very much like to have her Jimmy's clothes back and any other stuff that he might have had on him when he was arrested. Not to mention his rather expensive motorbike. You know how sentimental some folks get.'

The policeman looks you up and down. He takes the end of his pen from out of his mouth. He says: 'Have a seat please, sir.'

You turn and walk back over to the tiny plastic chairs and sit down under the dull and yellow lights again, the faded poster warning against the perils of drinking and driving at Christmas –

Not Christmas.

The policeman on the desk making more calls.

You look down again at the linoleum floor, at the white squares and the grey, at the boot and chair marks. The smell of pine disinfectant strong.

'Mr Piggott?'

You stand up and go back over.

'I'm afraid everyone's over in Rochdale today, so you'll have to make an appointment for another day.'

'When?'

He looks down at the big book on the desk in front of him. He starts to turn the pages. He stops. He looks up. He says: 'Wednesday?'

You shrug your shoulders.

'Is that a yes?'

'What time?'

'Ten o'clock.'

'Thank you,' you say.

You walk through the empty market to the Duck and Drake. You go inside. You order a pint. You go to the phone. You take out your little red book. You dial.

The phone on the other end starts ringing –

Ringing and ringing and ringing.

You look at your watch –

Six.

You hang up. You leave your pint on top of the phone. You walk back out into the empty market and the rain.

It's a Bank Holiday –

Bank Holiday Monday –

Everywhere dead.

On the drive back to Wakefield you stay in the slow lane and keep the radio off.

You park outside the off-licence on Northgate. You go inside. The old Pakistani with the white beard has a black eye and a bandage over his left ear. His young daughter is not here. He does not speak. You look at the bottles. You look at the cans. You look at the papers. You buy a *Yorkshire Evening Post*. You go back outside. You get in the car. You lock the doors. You open the paper. You read:

HAZEL POLICE CROSS PENNINES
Kathryn Williams, Chief Reporter

The detective leading the hunt for missing Morley schoolgirl Hazel Atkins today denied reports that police were investigating links between the disappearance of Hazel and that of the Rochdale schoolgirl Susan Ridyard in 1972.

Susan Ridyard was ten years old when she went missing in March 1972. Her disappearance was at one time linked to the 1974 abduction and murder of ten-year-old Clare Kemplay for which Michael Myshkin was later convicted and sentenced to life imprisonment in 1975.

Although Myshkin initially confessed to taking Susan and also Jeanette Garland from Castleford in 1969, Myshkin subsequently denied any involvement and was never formally charged in connection with either disappearance. Michael Myshkin has recently begun an appeal against his conviction and life sentence for the Kemplay murder.

However, this lunchtime, Mr Maurice Jobson, the man leading the search for Hazel, described the continued presence of West Yorkshire detectives in Rochdale as 'merely routine' and denied any connection between the two disappearances, branding recent press reports as 'ultimately harmful to police inquiries'.

James Ashworth, a Fitzwilliam man who had been helping police with their inquiries, was found hanged in his cell at Millgarth police station last week.

You put the paper on the passenger seat. You start the car. You head up the road and on to Blenheim. You park in the drive. You get out. You lock the doors. You go into the building. You go up the stairs. You take your key out. You stop –

The door ajar.

You look at it. You have your key in your hand. You stand there. You shit yourself. You step forward. You push the door –

It swings open.

You stand there. You shit yourself. You say: 'Hello?'

There's no answer.

You stand there. You shit yourself. You step forward. You say: 'Hello?'

No answer.

You step forward. You go inside. You walk slowly down the hall. You say: 'Hello?'

No-one.

You look in the bedroom. The bathroom. The living room. The kitchen –

You shit, shit, shit, shit, shit yourself:

The whole place has been ransacked –

Everything smashed. Everything broken –

Every single thing –

Every single thing except the bathroom mirror:
You put your fingers to the glass –
To the lipstick:
D-10.

Chapter 27

Hate & War:

Banging on Joe's door –

Man hasn't left his room in a week –

Two sevens:

1977 –

Thursday 9 June 1977 –

Hope I get to heaven:

'Open fucking door!'

'Who is it?'

I'm not who I want to be:

'It's BJ. Open fucking door!'

Locks slide, keys turn/new locks, new keys –

I laugh at your locks:

Wide white eyes at crack –

Paranoid looks to left/paranoid looks to right –

Perilous times:

BJ push open door into this private little Chapeltown hellhole; only window boarded up with a shattered door, a battered mattress on floor covered in loose tobacco and Rizlas, broken bottles and pipes, whole room under heavy smoke and songs, every wall and every surface, whole fucking room painted with red, gold and green sevens –

'You do it?'

'No,' BJ say. 'Tonight.'

'You got the keys?'

BJ jangle them in his stoned black face: 'What these look like?'

'Keys to my heart,' he nods and rolls another one.

BJ ask him, BJ check: 'You up for this?'

Still nodding, he smiles as he lights up: 'Show me mine enemy.'

BJ take it when he passes it –

Take it because BJ need it and BJ lie back on mattress, staring at sevens on walls and sevens on door, sevens on ceiling and sevens on floor –

All them pretty little sevens, all dressed up in red, dressed up in gold and green:

Two sevens –

Joe stagger-dancing around hell, his voice of thunder chanting: *'War in the East, war in the West; War in the North, war in the South; Crazy Joe get them out – '*

Two sevens beginning to bob and beginning to weave, swaying and dancing around each other until:

They two sevens clash –

Two sevens clash and weak hearts rock –

Weak hearts drop.

It's dark:

Ten o'clock –

Sitting in a stolen Austin Allegro on Bradford Road, Batley –

Sitting in a stolen car watching a flat above a newsagent's.

BJ get out and go to phonebox and dial flat –

It just rings and rings and rings:

No answer.

BJ go back to car and tell Joe: 'All clear.'

Joe nods and gets out and follows BJ across road and round back of shops and walk down alley to a red gate to yard behind newsagent's.

'Wait here,' BJ tell Joe and open gate and go through yard to back door.

BJ unlock back door and take stairs on right.

BJ stand at top of stairs, ear to black glass of door:

Nothing.

BJ unlock white door at top of stairs and step inside –

No lights.

BJ go down passage to front of flat and look out window –

Just Allegro across road.

Phone starts ringing –

Fuck –

Ringing and ringing and ringing.

BJ let it and walk down passage to door on left.

Phone stops as BJ step inside bedroom.

BJ open wardrobe and move lights and camera bags to one side and strain in dark to find magazines piled up at back.

BJ find them:

SPUNK.

BJ go through stack until BJ find ones BJ looking for –

Ones they don't want no-one to see:

Issue 3 – January 1975.

BJ turn pages in gloom until BJ come to page BJ want –

Page they don't want no-one to see:

A bleached blonde with her legs spread, mouth open and eyes closed, fingers up her cunt and arse –

Clare.

BJ take three copies and put lights and cameras back and close wardrobe and bedroom doors.

BJ walk down passage and phone starts ringing again, ringing and ringing and ringing, making BJ jump again, but BJ lock white door and go down stairs and lock back door, phone still ringing and ringing and ringing.

Joe is stood waiting by gate: 'You get them?'

BJ nod and Joe nods back.

In another telephone box on Bradford Road, BJ dial number on slip of paper and let it ring and ring and ring until:

'Hello.'

'Jack Whitehead?'

'Speaking.'

'I've got some information concerning one of these Ripper murders.'

'Go on.'

'Not on phone.'

'Where are you?'

'Not important, but I can meet Saturday night.'

'What kind of information?'

'On Saturday,' BJ say and look across road at Joe sat in Allegro and big sign above him. 'Variety Club.'

'Batley?'

'Yeah,' BJ say. 'Between ten and eleven.'

'OK,' Whitehead says. 'But I need a name?'

'No names.'

'You want money, I suppose?'

'No money.'

'Then what do you want?'

'You just be there.'

Chapter 28

Tuesday 21 March 1972 –

I'm listening to the radio and this is what it's saying:

'The two policemen were standing next to a yellow saloon car in Donegall Street when a 100lb gelignite bomb hidden inside exploded, killing them and four civilians instantly and driving broken glass into the faces and legs of dozens of office workers as every window in the street caved in. Limbs were flung into an estate agent's premises and on to the road while nearly 100 people, most of them young girls, lay in the street covered in the shattered glass and screaming with pain and shock . . .'

The telephone is ringing.

I switch off the radio. I pick up the receiver: 'Jobson speaking.'

'You on fucking strike and all?' says the voice on the other end –

Badger Bill Molloy –

Chief Superintendent Bill Molloy.

I say: 'Had a bit of a late one last night.'

'I heard.'

'Who's been blabbing?'

'Sod them,' he snaps. 'We'll have other things to celebrate tonight.'

'Like what?'

'Like fifty fucking grand and a new business partner, that's what.'

'He agreed then?'

'Not quite,' he laughs. 'But with a bit of friendly persuasion, he will.'

'When and where?'

'Ten o'clock tonight, back of Redbeck.'

'Right,' I say. 'You about today?'

'Doubt it, got to go over bloody Rochdale with George.'

'Rochdale? What the hell for?'

He pauses. He says: 'You know George, be something and nothing.'

'What – '

'Forget it,' he laughs. 'See you tonight.'

I start to speak but the line's already dead.

I switch the radio back on and it says:

' . . . In his summing up, the Judge said he believed undoubtedly that the time these two detectives had spent trudging through the slime and the sludge of the underworld, dredging for the truth, had taken its toll and led these highly decorated officers to conspire and corruptly accept money . . .'

I switch it off again.

The wife comes in. She starts to dust. She says: 'Who was that?'

'Who was what?'

'On the telephone?'

'Bill.'

'That's nice,' she smiles. 'About work?'

I stand up. I say: 'The wedding.'

She stops dusting. She says: 'Thought it might have been about that little girl.'

'What little girl?'

'The one in Rochdale.'

'What one in Rochdale?'

She nods, the Valium not quite biting: 'Been missing since yesterday tea-time.'

Into Leeds, one hand on the steering wheel –

The other on the radio dial, searching:

' . . . *While local police remain optimistic about finding Susan safe and well, senior detectives from both Leeds City and the West Yorkshire Constabulary are expected in Rochdale later today, although police sources refused to confirm or comment on these reports . . .*'

Park off Westgate, up the steps and into Brotherton House –

Everyone talking Northern bloody Ireland.

Up the stairs to top floor and the Boss –

Julie looks up from her typing. She shakes her head.

'Five minutes,' I say. 'That's all I ask.'

She steps inside. She's out again within a minute. She's all smiles: 'Come back in half an hour.'

I look at my watch. I say: 'Eleven?'

She nods. She goes back to her typing.

Downstairs in my own office with a cold cup of tea and an unlit cig. I reach down to unlock the bottom drawer of my desk. I take out a file –

A thick file, bound with string and marked with one word.

I know what Bill's going to say and I don't give a shit –

Behind his back or not.

I light the cig. I cut the knot. I open the file –

The thick file, marked with one word –

One name –

Her name:

Jeanette.

*

'Just go straight in,' smiles Julie.

I knock once. I open the door. I step inside.

Walter Heywood, Chief Constable of the Leeds City Police, is sat behind his desk with his back to the window and the Law Courts. The desk is strewn with papers and files, cigarettes and cups, photographs and trophies.

'Maurice,' he smiles. 'Sit yourself down.'

I sit down across from the Chief Constable –

The short, deaf, blind man for whom it took three cracks and a World War to get in; the short, deaf, blind man who hears and sees everything –

The short, deaf, blind man who asks me: 'What's on your mind, Maurice?'

'Susan Ridyard.'

Walter Heywood puts his hands together under his chin. He says: 'Go on.'

'Chief Superintendent Molloy has gone over to Rochdale and . . .'

'You'd have liked to have gone with him?'

I nod.

'Why's that then?'

'I did a lot of work on the Jeanette Garland case,' I tell him.

'I know that.'

'A lot of my own work, on my own time.'

'I know that too,' he says.

I want to ask him how he knows. But I don't. I wait.

He puts his hands down flat on his desk. He looks across at me. He says: 'It was never our case in the first place, Maurice.'

'I know that,' I say. 'But once we were asked, I . . .'

'Let it get under your skin, eh?'

I nod again.

'Now you think there could be some connection between this business in Rochdale and little Jeanette and you're annoyed Bill's over there with George Oldman while you're stuck back here twiddling your thumbs talking to me?'

I shake my head. I open my mouth. I start to speak. I stop.

Walter Heywood smiles. He pushes himself up from behind his desk. He walks round the papers and the files, the cigarettes and the cups, the photographs and the trophies. He stands in front of me. He puts a hand on my shoulder.

I look up at him.

He looks down at me.

I say: 'I'd just like to be involved, that's all.'

He pats my shoulder. He says: 'I know you would, Maurice. But it's not for you, not this one.'

'But – '

He grips my shoulder tight. He bends down into my ear. He says: 'Listen to me, Maurice. You've made a name for yourself, you and Bill: the A1 Shootings, John Whitey; getting headlines, cracking cases. But you and I both know it were Bill that got them headlines, that cracked them cases. Not you. Stick with him, learn from him, and you'll get your chance. But this isn't it. Not yet. Listen to me and listen to Bill.'

I close my eyes. I nod. I open my eyes.

Walter Heywood walks back round to the other side of his desk. He sits back down. He puts his hands together under his chin again. He looks across at me. He says: 'You're in a good position, Maurice. Very good. Sit tight, wait, and let's see what the future brings.'

I nod again.

'Good man,' says Walter Heywood, Chief Constable of the Leeds City Police, sat behind his desk with his back to the window and the Law Courts. 'Good man.'

Back downstairs in my own office with a cold cup of tea and an unlit cig. I lock the door. I go to my desk. I unlock the bottom drawer. I take out the file –

The thick file, marked with one word.

I sit down. I light the cig. I open the file –

The thick file, marked with one word –

One name –

Her name:

Jeanette.

I take out a new notebook. I begin again –

Begin again to go through the carbons and the statements –

And then I stop –

Stop and pick up the phone –

Pick up the phone and dial –

Dial Netherton 3657 and listen to it ring –

Listen to it ring until it stops –

Until it stops and a woman's voice says: 'Netherton 3657, who's speaking please?'

'Is George there?'

'He's at work,' she says. 'Who is this?'

'And where's work these days? Rochdale way?'

'Who is this?'

'Jeanette.'

A black day in a black month in a black year in a black life with time to kill:

Black time –

Sat in the car in the dark with the radio on:

' . . . *Commander Kenneth Drury of the Flying Squad, the officer named in the investigation ordered by the Commissioner last week, has been suspended. The inquiry, which is being conducted by a deputy assistant chief constable of the Metropolitan Police, will look into allegations that the Flying Squad Chief spent a holiday in Cyprus with a strip-club owner and pornographer . . .'*

Sat in the car in the dark on Brunt Street, Castleford –

Tuesday 21 March 1972:

A black day in a black month in a black year in a black life –

Of black times.

Almost ten –

The Redbeck car park, the Doncaster Road.

I pull in and park, lights out.

There's a fog coming down again, the one streetlight blinking on and off.

Across the car park a dark Ford van flashes its lights twice.

I get out of my car. I lock the door. I cross the car park, my breath white against the black night.

The driver is John Rudkin, a hard man just out of uniform and on his way up:

Bill's Boy.

The man in the passenger seat next to him is Bob Craven, another cunt just out of uniform –

Another one of Bill's Boys.

Rudkin nods through the windscreen. I bang on the side of the van.

The back door opens. I get inside.

'Evening,' says Bill.

Dick Alderman and Jim Prentice are sat down the far end of the van, all in black like Bill –

Like me.

'How was Rochdale?' I ask him.

'Sod that,' he says and bangs the doors shut. 'We got some real work to do.'

He nods down the van. Dick Alderman taps on the partition and off we set –

'Some real money to make,' Bill laughs.
Off we bloody go –
No turning back.

From the Redbeck car park back into Castleford –
    Silence in the black of the back of the van –
    Dim lights down black back roads –
    Sat in the back of the black of the van –
    Yorkshire, 1972:
    You'll wake up some morning as unhappy as you've ever been before.

The van slows down. It bumps over some rough ground. It stops.
    Bill chucks me a black balaclava: 'Put that on when you get inside.'
    I put the balaclava in my coat pocket.
    Dick Alderman and Bill already have theirs on.
    Bill hands me a hammer: 'Take that too.'
    I put on my gloves. I pick up the hammer. I put it in my other pocket.
    Rudkin comes round to the back. He opens the doors.
    I jump out after Bill, Alderman and Prentice following.
    We're round the back of a row of shops somewhere in Castleford.
    'Maurice, you and Jim go round front to keep an eye out,' says Bill.
    We both nod.
    Bill pulls down his balaclava. He turns to the others: 'You lads set?'
    Alderman, Rudkin, and Craven nod once.
    We all follow Bill along the back of the shops. He stops by a metal gate in a high wall with broken glass set in the cement on the top.
    'This it?' he says to Dick Alderman.
    Alderman nods.
    'Right,' says Bill to me and Jim. 'You two look sharp.'
    We both set off jogging to the end of the alley, both turning back at the corner to see what the others are doing –
    Bill and Dick are hoisting Rudkin over the wall and the broken glass, Craven scanning the alley.
    Jim and I walk round to the front of the shops on the high street. We walk along the pavement until we come to it:
    Jenkins Photo Studio.
    'This it?' I ask Prentice.
    He nods.
    We're in the centre of Castleford and it's dead but for the odd couple walking to and from the pub.
    I turn and look at the window full of school portraits.

There's a light on in the back. I hear something break, voices raised.

I turn back to Jim: 'They're in.'

He nods again, hands deep in his pockets.

There's a tap on the door behind us. We look round and there's Alderman at the glass, balaclava raised –

He opens the door: 'Bill wants you to wait outside, Jim.'

Prentice nods.

I ask: 'What about me?'

'Come with me.'

I step inside the dark shop.

Alderman closes the door. He says: 'Put your mask on and follow me.'

I take off my glasses. I take out the balaclava. I put my glasses in my pocket. I slip the balaclava on. I follow Alderman through into the back of the shop –

No turning back.

There's a single light bulb and two men tied up and bleeding under it; five men in masks with hammers and wrenches stood over them.

One of the men is young and grossly overweight. He is gagged and bleeding from his nose. He is crying.

The other man is older; grey hair and a harsh face already swelling –

No gag.

Bill grabs the man's face. He turns it to look up at me. He squeezes it. He says: 'Just telling Mr Jenkins here how he's got himself some new business partners.'

I hear Rudkin and Craven laugh beneath their masks.

I step closer to the man. I ask: 'And what does Mr Jenkins think of that, I wonder?'

Bill dangles a bloody gag from the end of his glove. He chuckles: 'Been a bit quiet about it actually.'

I say: 'That's not very polite, is it?'

'Not very polite at all,' says Bill.

'Have to teach him some manners then, won't we?' I hiss.

Bill nods: 'He's going to need them if he wants to stay in fucking business.'

'Roll up his trouser legs,' I tell Craven.

Jenkins is squirming in the chair and his bindings: 'Please . . .'

Craven bends down: 'Both of them?'

I look at Bill.

Bill nods.

Jenkins is shaking his head: 'Please . . .'

Craven rolls up Jenkins' trouser legs.

Bill looks at me.

I take out the hammer.

Jenkins is squirming. Jenkins is shaking his head. Jenkins' eyes are wide-open: 'There's no need . . .'

I lift the hammer above my head with both my hands. I say: 'Oh, but you see there's always a need . . .'

I bring the hammer down into the top of his right knee –

'Always a need for manners, Mr Jenkins.'

Jenkins screams.

The young man howls.

Bill turns to Alderman: 'Upstairs.'

Dick Alderman takes Craven. They head up the stairs to the right of us.

Bill turns to Rudkin. He nods at the fat lad: 'Find out who this fucking lump of shite is.'

Rudkin goes into the man's pockets –

Nowt but handkerchiefs and toffee papers.

'Try them coats,' I say.

Rudkin goes over to the back of the door. He fishes two wallets out of the coats hanging there.

He opens one. He nods at Jenkins: 'His.'

Bill: 'Other one?'

Rudkin takes out a driving licence: 'Michael John Myshkin, 54 Newstead View, Fitzwilliam.'

Bill asks Jenkins: 'He work for you, this bastard, does he?'

Jenkins nods. He is white with the shock and the pain.

Craven comes back down the stairs. He tips out boxes of photographs and magazines across the floor. He says: 'Look at all this.'

'Well, well, well,' chuckles Bill. 'What kind of filth have we here?'

Skin and hair, all of them hardcore –

'Quite the European businessman,' says Alderman with another parcel.

Some of them young –

'Been a bit modest about his talents and his contacts,' laughs Craven.

Very young:

I stare down at the photograph between my feet, at the blonde hair and the blue eyes, the little white smile against the sky-blue backdrop –

I lift the hammer above my head and with both my hands I bring the hammer down into Jenkins' left knee –

Jenkins shrieks, the young man howls –

Back up for a second time –

But Bill has me by my wrists. He shouts through the masks: 'Fuck you think you're doing?'

I look down from the single light bulb at the two men tied up and bleeding under it; the five men in masks with hammers and wrenches stood over them –

Bill shouting: 'You'll fucking kill him!'

One of the men is young and grossly overweight. He is gagged and bleeding from his nose. He is crying. He has pissed himself.

The other man is older; grey hair and a harsh swollen face. Both his knees are black and bloody. He is unconscious.

I drop the hammer.

'Get him out of here,' Bill is shouting at Dick Alderman –

Alderman leads me out the back way and into the alley. I take off my balaclava. I put my glasses back on. I look up at the moon –

War songs, bad news, and the moon:

Jeanette Garland missing two years and eight months –

Susan Ridyard one day eight hours:

There's a house with no door and no windows and this where I live –

Blood on my hands –

No turning back.

Chapter 29

You drive; drive all night; drive in circles;
Disintegrating –
Disappearing –
Decreasing –
Declining –
Decaying –
Dying –
Dead –
Circles; circles of hell; local hells.

You are sat in the car park of the Balne Lane Library in the grey dawn of the last day of May 1983 –
The car doors are locked and you are staring into the rearview mirror with the radio on:
'Latest opinion polls suggest a Conservative landslide as the Tories open up an eighteen point gap on Labour; Healey accuses Mrs Thatcher of glorying in slaughter over the Falklands; a father is to sue Norman Tebbit over his son's death on a youth opportunities scheme; a fourteen-year-old boy, charged with sending a letter bomb to Mrs Thatcher, was sent for trial to the Central Criminal Court . . .'
No Hazel.

You are sat in the car park of the Balne Lane Library at half-past eight on the last day of May 1983 –
The radio is off now but you are still staring into the rearview mirror –
The car doors still locked –
Still no Hazel –
Not today:
Tuesday 31 May 1983 –
D-9.

Up the stairs to the first floor of the library, the microfilms and the old newspapers, pulling just the one box down from the shelves:
March 1972.
Threading through the film, winding the spools, searching –
STOP –
Tuesday 21 March 1972:

Rochdale Girl Missing – by Jack Whitehead, Crime Reporter of the Year.

The parents of missing ten-year-old Susan Louise Ridyard made an emotional plea late last night for information that might lead police to their daughter's whereabouts. Susan was last seen at four p.m. yesterday afternoon as she made her way home from school with friends.

STOP –

Wednesday 22 March 1972:

Oldman Joins Susan Search – by Jack Whitehead, Crime Reporter of the Year.

Detective Chief Superintendent George Oldman of the West Yorkshire Constabulary crossed the Pennines today to help his Lancashire colleagues in their search for missing Rochdale schoolgirl Susan Ridyard.

STOP –

Friday 24 March 1972:

Medium Links Susan and Jeanette – by Jack Whitehead, Crime Reporter of the Year.

Police last night refused to comment or speculate on reports that local medium and TV personality Mandy Wymer had found a connection between the missing Rochdale schoolgirl Susan Ridyard and Jeanette Garland, known as the Little Girl Who Never Came Home, *who was eight years old when she disappeared –*

STOP.

Jack, Jack, Jack –

Always back to Jack:

You turn off the main road and drive through the stone gates and up the long drive, the trees black with wet leaves and crows, the mental hospital nesting at the end of the road –

Waiting for you:

Stanley Royd Psychiatric Hospital, Wakefield.

You park in front of the old, main building and walk across the sharp, pointed gravel to the front door. The faces of mental people in their dressing gowns and cardigans are crowded at the windows. On the lawn a woman with bare feet and bloody knees is barking, her leg raised against a tree.

You open the door and go inside, thinking of your mother, thinking: *This is what she did not want.*

You ring the bell on the desk, thinking of what she got:

Graffiti sprayed on her walls, a swastika and noose hung above her door, the shit through her letterbox and the brick through her window, anonymous calls and dirty calls, the heavy breathing and the dial tone, the taunts of children and the curses of their parents, all because –

'Can I help you?' the nurse in the white uniform says again.

'I certainly hope so,' you smile. 'My name is John Piggott and I'm a solicitor. I was hoping to be able to see a patient of yours, a Jack Whitehead?'

The nurse shakes her head: 'I'm afraid Mr Whitehead is no longer with us.'

'I'm sorry to hear that, I – '

'Let me just double-check for you,' she says and walks over to a large metal filing cabinet.

Fuck.

You turn away. You look down the corridor.

A man is stood at the end of the corridor in the shape of a cross, his pyjama-bottoms around his ankles.

You hate hospitals –

Hate the institutional smell of boiling cabbages and rags, the institutional walls of heavy green and magnolia cream, the institutional floors covered with stained carpet and linoleum –

Hate hospitals because nobody you knew ever came out of one alive.

The nurse comes back with a file. She is nodding to herself. She says: 'Yes, Mr Whitehead left us on New Year's Eve, 1980.'

'Doesn't say what he died of, does it?'

'No, no, no,' she smiles. 'His son came and took him home.'

'His son?'

She nods again. She taps the file: 'What it says here.'

You strain to read the upside-down writing: 'Is there an address?'

She pulls the file back: 'I'm not sure I should – '

'It's good news,' you smile. 'Stands to inherit a small fortune.'

'Well then,' she laughs. 'Flat 6, 6 Portland Square, Leeds.'

'Thank you very much,' you wink.

'Be sure to tell him how you found him,' she giggles.

You wink again. You open the doors. You walk back down the steps and across the sharp, pointed gravel.

The woman on the lawn is chasing her tail.

You hate hospitals because nobody you knew ever came out of one –

Nobody but Jack.

Tuesday 31 May 1983 –

The first spits of another rain.

Crawling along the M62 towards Rochdale, the fields black and brown, the sky black and grey:

'She wraps herself in the Union Jack and exploits the sacrifices of our soldiers, sailors and airmen in the Falkland Islands for purely party advantage – and hopes to get away with it.'

You switch off the radio. You glance in the mirrors. You pull over on the outskirts of Rochdale beside a smashed-up phonebox –

You pray that it works.

D-9.

Fifteen minutes later you are reversing into the drive of Mr and Mrs Ridyard's semi-detached home in a silent part of Rochdale.

It is pissing down now, the houses across the road with their lights already on.

Mr Ridyard is standing in the doorway.

You get out of the car. You say: 'Afternoon.'

'Nice weather for ducks,' he says.

You nod. You shake his hand. You follow him into a small hall and through into their front room.

'The wife's having her lie-down,' he whispers. 'Afraid you'll have to make do with just me.'

'Thank you,' you say. 'It's very good of you to see me.'

'Sit down,' says Mr Ridyard. 'I'll make us a quick brew.'

You stand back up when he leaves the room. You walk over to have a closer look at the two framed photographs on top of the television –

One is of three children dressed in their school uniforms; the other of just the youngest child sat on her own:

Susan Louise Ridyard.

Mr Ridyard comes back in with the tea: 'Here we are.'

You put the photograph back down in its place. You go back over to the sofa.

Mr Ridyard sits down in the chair opposite you: 'Sugar, Mr Piggott?'

'Three please.'

He hands you your tea: 'There you go.'

You take a sip. You watch him pick up his cup –

He looks at it. He doesn't drink.

You watch him put it back down –

He looks up at you. He tries to smile. He says: 'We drink too much.'

You say again: 'I really do appreciate you seeing me. I realise it must be very upsetting for you.'

Mr Ridyard nods. He whispers: 'What is it I can do for you, Mr Piggott?'

'As I said on phone, I'm a solicitor and I have two clients who seem to have an interest or a link, should I say, with your daughter.'

'With Susan?'

You nod.

'Who are your clients?'

'One is a lady called Mrs Ashworth. Her son, James, was arrested by the police in connection with this recent disappearance of a little girl in Morley. Hazel Atkins?'

Mr Ridyard nods.

'Well, as you may already know from the news, James Ashworth hung himself while he was in police custody.'

'Hung himself?'

'Supposedly.'

'I didn't know that,' says Mr Ridyard. 'Were you his solicitor as well?'

'Supposedly,' you say again. 'But he died before I actually had a chance to speak with him.'

'But what has he to do with Susan?'

'To be honest, I'm not sure he has anything at all to do with Susan,' you stammer. 'That's half of why I'm here.'

'And the other half?'

You glance back over at the photograph on top of the television. You say quietly: 'Michael Myshkin.'

Mr Ridyard swallows. He scratches his neck. He says: 'What about him?'

'I'm representing Michael Myshkin in his appeal against his conviction,' you say and then pause –

Waiting to see if Mr Ridyard is going to say anything –

'I see,' is all he says, with a slight glance at the ceiling.

'Michael Myshkin was never actually *formally* charged in connection with your daughter's disappearance, was he?'

Mr Ridyard shakes his head: 'But he did confess to the police.'

'And then retract it?'

'Yes,' he says. 'And then he retracted it.'

'And the police never sought to press charges, did they?'

'No,' he says, shaking his head again. 'But they did close the inquiry.'

'So they obviously thought he did it?'

He nods.

'They sat you down and told you that?'

He nods again.

'When did they tell you?'

'1975,' he says. 'When they closed the inquiry.'

'And you?' you ask him. 'Do you think Michael Myshkin had something to do with the disappearance of your daughter?'

'I did,' he says.

'You *did*?' you say. 'You don't now?'

'Tell him, Derek,' says a voice from the door –

You turn in your seat:

Mrs Ridyard is stood in the doorway, drained in a scorched dressing-gown.

You stand up: 'I'm John Piggott, I – '

'I know who you are,' she says.

'We were just – ' her husband starts to say –

'Tell him!'

Mr Ridyard looks up at you in his green cardigan and his brown trousers and for the briefest of moments, the very briefest of moments, you think he is going to tell you he killed his own daughter –

But he stands up and he says: 'Sit down, Mr Piggott.'

You sit back down, trying not to stare at the woman stood in the doorway in her scorched dressing-gown, her husband on his feet –

Mr Ridyard asking her: 'Are you sure you want me to; the police said we – '

'Fuck them,' spits Mrs Ridyard, sliding down the doorframe, holding her scorched dressing-gown tight around her, the un-light catching in the scratches and sores on her neck and her legs, on the backs of her hands.

'Three weeks ago,' says Mr Ridyard, alone on his feet in the middle of the room. 'Three weeks ago when I went to get the milk in, there was a box on the doorstep.'

'A box?'

'A shoebox.'

'A shoebox?'

Mr Ridyard nods, the house silent –

The house silent but for the rain against the window and the ticking of a small clock on top of the TV, on top of the TV between the two photographs –

The one of the three children in their school uniforms; the other of only the youngest child –

Mr Ridyard crying as he sits back down then stands up again, Mrs Ridyard rocking back and forth on the floor in the doorway, you staring back across the room at that photograph –

The youngest child.

You close your eyes. You put your hands over your ears –

But the noise will not stop –

The sound of their weeping, the rain against the window, the ticking of the clock.

You open your eyes –

Mr Ridyard is alone on his feet in the middle of the room –

In the middle of the room in the shape of a cross.

You shout: 'What was in the shoebox?'

'Susan,' he sobs.

Chapter 30

'Please give a big Yorkshire Clubland welcome to the New Zombies!'

Saturday 11 June 1977 –

Batley Variety Club:

She's not there –

But he is and he doesn't remember BJ, but BJ remember him and he has aged; aged in terror, terror of witnessing execution of his ex-wife on lawn of her new house by hand of her new husband, naked under a new and bloody moon but for a hammer and a twelve-inch nail.

'Spot of late-night reading,' BJ say and pass Jack bag under table.

Whitehead takes it and daft cunt starts to open it –

'Not here,' BJ say. 'Bogs.'

Jack gets up and walks through empty tables at back towards gents, looking over his shoulder to check BJ still here –

'Give you hand if you want,' BJ shout but Jack scuttles off into toilets.

BJ finish drink as band give up on song. BJ take off every ring and put them all back on again. BJ light another cig and wonder what fuck's taking old cunt so long. Maybe he has whipped it out for a quick one. BJ smiling until BJ see them:

Fuck, fuck, fuck –

Pigs –

Fucking pigs.

BJ slide out of seat and crawl off towards stage down front. BJ keep low against lights and only in shadows. BJ get to edge of stage. BJ duck under a curtain at side. BJ start running through cables and wires. BJ following red light that shines:

Exit –

BJ push down bar and through door, letting it slam shut. BJ outside in car park at back, rain still falling –

Rain a fall –

But Allegro's round front and BJ be so fucking stupid BJ deserve all shit that's coming down –

Fuck, fuck –

Can't go back/can't go forward; can't go left/can't go right; can't go up/only down –

Fuck –

Crouched against fire door, heavy rain coming down/heavy shit with it, when out of shadows/darkness he steps –

A Black Angel –
And he says: 'You're all wet.'
My Black Angel –
BJ look up. BJ say: 'Fuck do you want?'
The Father of Fear –
He raises brow of his black hat and stares up into black night and black rain. He watch black things fall from out of black skies. He smiles his black smile and says: 'You're going to catch your death, Barry.'
'You got your car?'
'Best hurry though,' he nods. 'Police will soon tire of Our Jack.'
BJ follow him over to his old dark car parked nearby, a Morris something –
BJ looking left and right, left and then right.
He unlocks doors and in BJ get, BJ sliding over and on to backseat –
Car damp and cold, a black briefcase beside BJ.
'Keep your head down,' he says, starting car.
BJ do as he says and off he sets but then car slows at front of club –
Fuck –
Man in hat leans across passenger seat. He winds down window:
'What seems to be the problem, officer?'
'Stolen car,' says policeman. 'You haven't seen a youngish skinhead type, have you, sir?'
'Fortunately, no.'
'Thank you, sir,' says Pig.
'Goodnight, officer,' he says and winds his window back up.
Then car turns left and heads into Dewsbury.
BJ sit up in backseat –
His eyes on BJ in mirror.
BJ say: 'Where we going?'
'Church.'
It is 1977.

He found me hiding –
In Church of Abandoned Christ on seventh floor of Griffin Hotel in ghost bloodied old city of Leodis, BJ lost; all covered in sleep and drunk upon a double bed, BJ lost in room 77; hair already shaved and 8 eyes shined, BJ be Northern Son. Black Angel beside BJ upon bed; his clothes are shabby and his wings are burnt; Father of Fear is weeping, whispering from among wine his death songs:
Knew I was not happy –
'And after this Joseph of Arimathæa, being a disciple of Jesus, but secretly for fear of thee Jews, besought Pilate that he might take away

thee body of Jesus; and Pilate marveled if he were already dead and calling unto him thee centurion, he asked him whether he had been any while dead. And when he knew it of thee centurion, Pilate gave Joseph leave. He came therefore and took thee body of Jesus.'

Scratching my head –

'And there came also Nicodemus, which at thee first came to Jesus by night and brought a mixture of myrrh and aloes, about a hundred pound in weight. Then they took thee body of Jesus and wound it in linen clothes with thee spices, as thee manner of thee Jews is to bury their dead.'

Confused beyond existence –

'Now in thee place where he was crucified there was a garden; and in thee garden a new sepulchre, wherein was never man yet laid, but when they laid him out upon thee rock, they saw his wounds were bloody and bleeding beneath thee white linen, they saw he was not dead –'

Sat in the corner, shivering from fright –

'Only bleeding –'

Feeling strung up –

'And as they were afraid and bowed their faces to thee earth, he said to them: Why seek ye thee living among thee Dead?'

Out of my clothes and into the bed –

'E am here; E suffered and am now risen from thee Dead and ye are witnesses of these things. But know ye who did this thing, for only one person could do this, thee one who did not forsake me, for whom death is not thee end.'

The movements in his bed –

'And they traveled out of thee Holy Lands and through Asia Minor and across thee mountains of Europe until they arrived at thee port in France and there thee White Ship was waiting to take them to thee Land of Angels and there was a mood of celebration amongst thee party for they were in sight of their goal and eager to reach this Pagan Place they set out to sea only after night had already fallen.'

So sorry sad and so, so confused –

'But he was a jealous God and he was angry and thee White Ship hit a rock in thee gloom of thee night and thee port-side cracked wide-open to reveal a gaping hole whereupon Joseph quickly rushed thee Wounded Christ on deck and bundled Him into a smaller dinghy. They were away to safety as thee remaining crew struggled to wrest thee vessel off thee rocks. However, Christ could hear His wife calling to Him, begging Him not to leave her to thee sea and He ordered Joseph to turn around, but thee situation was hopeless.'

Between life and death –

'As Christ drew nearer once more, thee White Ship began to descend beneath thee waves. Everyone was in thee water and they fought desperately for thee safety of thee dinghy. Thee turmoil and thee weight were too much. Christ's boat was capsized and sunk without trace.'

Lost in room –

'And it is said that thee only person to survive thee wreck to tell thee tale was Mary Magdalene, thee wife of Christ, but that she never spoke or smiled again but waited alone and lost in room for thee White Ship to rise again from beneath thee waves and bear thee linen body of thee Wounded, Abandoned Christ to these pagan shores, thee shores of this, thee Land of Angels.'

They found me hiding –

In Church of Abandoned Christ on seventh floor of Griffin Hotel in ghost bloodied old city of Leodis, BJ lost; drunk and all covered in sleep upon a double bed, BJ lost in room 77; hair already shaved and 8 eyes shined, BJ be Northern Son. Black Angel is beside BJ upon bed; his shabby clothes and burnt wings; Father of Fear, he weeps and whispers from among wine:

'You must choose a side to be on.'

In the shadow –

BJ take off every ring –

In the shadow of the Horns –

Head bobbed.

Chapter 31

The telephone is ringing and ringing and ringing and I'm wondering where the fuck the wife is and why she won't bloody answer the telephone ringing and ringing and ringing wondering where the fuck the wife is and why she won't bloody answer the telephone ringing and ringing and ringing the fuck is the wife and why won't she answer the fucking telephone is ringing and ringing and ringing –

'I need to see you.'
  'I told you not to ring me here.'
  'So where am I supposed to call you? At work?'
  'I made a mistake, I – '
  'Please, I need to – '
  I hang up. I go to the bathroom. I wash my hands –
  Wash them and wash them and wash them –
  Thanking Christ the wife is out, the kids at school.

Thursday 23 March 1972 –
  Brotherton House, Westgate, Leeds:
  Downstairs in my office, the door locked –
  Cigs out and a pile of newspapers:
  Front pages full of the Belfast Station bomb and the Heath-Faulkner talks –
  Inside pages the biggest ever Littlewoods Pools win, Jimmy fucking Savile with his bloody OBE –
  Then there she is –
  Page 4:
  Susan Search Widens – by Jack Whitehead, Crime Reporter of the Year.
  That same photograph for the past two days:
  A long fringe and big teeth.
  72 hours coming up –
  Missing.
  I light another cigarette. I pick up the phone: 'News desk, please.'
  I wait. I say: 'Jack Whitehead, please.'
  I wait. I hear: 'Jack Whitehead speaking?'
  'Jack?' I say. 'Maurice Jobson.'
  'Maurice? And to what do I owe this unexpected pleasure? Got something good for your Uncle Jack, have you?'
  'I was hoping you might have something for me.'

'Oh, yeah?'

I look at my watch. I ask him: 'What you doing for lunch?'

'What I usually do for lunch.'

'Press Club?'

'I'm banned.'

'Since when?'

'Since I can't fucking remember. That's the problem.'

'Where they taking your money these days then?'

'Taking my money? I'm not fucking paying to drink with you.'

'There's no such thing as a free pint, Jack. You should know that.'

I hear him light a cigarette. Exhale. He says: 'Duck and Drake?'

'Duck and fucking Drake? Jesus, Jack.'

'You ought to drink in there more often, Maurice,' he says. 'Wouldn't need to keep crawling back to me then, would you.'

'Twelve?'

'Don't be late.'

On my way out, I stop and ask Wilson on the front desk if he's seen Bill today –

'Off, isn't he?' says Wilson.

'Yeah? Must be a first.'

'The wedding on Saturday, isn't it?'

'Fuck, yeah.'

'Don't tell me you'd forgotten, not way he's been going on.'

'You're off then?'

Wilson smiles: 'Must have invited whole bloody force and then some.'

'That's the *Badger*,' I agree, walking off.

'Going to miss him when he's gone.'

I stop. I turn back: 'You what?'

Sergeant Wilson and his boils are a deep and crimson red: 'Just a rumour.'

'Is that right,' I say. 'Is that right?'

Duck and Drake, back of the bus station, down the side of the Kirkgate market:

Not a nice pub; even when it's pissing it down on a black Thursday in March.

I'm five minutes late –

Jack's on his second pint and whiskey.

I take off my coat. I say: 'Same again?'

'You're a gentleman,' he nods.

I go over to the bar.

The big bloke behind the bar looks over at Jack then back at me: 'You feller he says is going to pay for his drinks?'

I nod: 'Same again for him and a Guinness for me.'

'That's a fucking Mick drink,' says a long-haired cunt –

A long-haired cunt with his back to me at the bar –

His mate grinning over the cunt's shoulder at me.

'You what?' I say to the back of the cunt's head.

'You heard,' says the cunt –

The cunt still with his back to me, nodding to his mate –

But his mate's not grinning now.

The long-haired cunt slowly turns around. He takes his cigarette out of his mouth, the hair out of his eyes.

The barman puts the Guinness on the counter.

'Drink it,' I tell the long-haired cunt.

'What?'

'You heard,' I say. 'Drink it.'

'Fuck off,' the cunt says, straightening up.

I take my warrant card out of my inside pocket. I put it down next to the pint of Guinness.

The long-haired cunt stands there blinking at the card on the bar next to the pint.

'Drink it,' I hiss.

The cunt glances at his mate and at the barman. He picks up the Guinness and drinks it down in one. He puts the glass back on the bar next to the card. He wipes his lips on his sleeve. He says with a smile: 'Ta very much, officer.'

'Now pay for it,' I say. 'And don't ever call anyone a Mick who isn't, you dirty little gyppo cunt.'

The dirty little gyppo cunt looks at his mate and the barman again. He shrugs his shoulders. He takes out a pound note from his jeans. He hands it across the counter to the barman.

'And these,' I say, nodding at the whiskey and Tetleys on the counter –

The barman already pulling me a fresh Guinness.

'What?'

'You heard,' I say.

'You can't fucking do that,' says the cunt.

I pick up my warrant card and the tray of drinks. I say: 'I just did.'

'Fucking hell . . .' the cunt starts to say before his mate touches his arm –

'Leave it, Donny,' says the cunt's friend. 'Not worth it.'

'Wise man,' I say.

'Fuck off.'

I walk across the room to where Jack's sat waiting –

'Making friends with the locals,' he winks.

I put the drinks down: 'How's the wife, Jack?'

'Ex-wife,' he smiles. 'Remarried and living with a builder's mate in sunny Ossett. And yours?'

'My what?'

'Wife? Family?'

'Who the fuck knows.'

Jack raises his glass: 'Ain't that the truth, Maurice.'

'Now there's a funny thing,' I nod, raising my glass. 'The truth?'

'What about it?' laughs Jack.

'Well I was rather hoping you could give me some?'

'Give you some what? Some truth? Shouldn't it be other way round, officer?'

'In a perfect world,' I smile.

Jack offers me a cig.

I lean across. I take it with a light –

'Fucking pig bastard!' comes a shout from the door –

'Wanker!' yells another –

I turn around to raise my glass but the cunt and his mate are already gone.

'Perfect world, eh?' says Jack.

I shake my head: 'What'd one of them look like, I wonder?'

Jack stubs out his cig: 'What's on your mind, Maurice?'

I sit forward. I say: 'Susan Louise Ridyard.'

'What about her?' shrugs Jack.

'Been reading your pieces.'

'Rehashes from the *Manchester Evening News*, mate.'

'You not been over there?'

'Rochdale? Nah, why?'

'George Oldman has.'

'And your boss,' nods Jack.

'You don't think this has all got a bit of a familiar ring to it then?'

Jack sits back in his chair. He shakes his head. He takes out another cigarette. He says: 'Not you and all?'

'What? Someone else talked to you about this?'

'Yeah,' he nods.

'Who?'

'Your girlfriend.'

'What you mean, *my girlfriend*?'

'*Mystic* Mandy.'

'Fuck off.'

'Come on, Maurice,' he winks again. 'Everyone fucking knows.'

'Fucking knows what?'

'That you've been having your fucking cards read a fair bit, what you think people fucking know?'

I sit there staring into my half-drunk Guinness, the sound of lorries and buses outside in the rain.

Jack stands up. He says: 'I'll get these.'

'Miracles'll never cease,' I say. I take out my own cigs and light one, the sound of the slot machine and the jukebox in rhythm.

Jack comes back with two pints and two shorts: 'Put a whiskey in your Guinness, that'll put a smile on your face.'

I say: 'Wasn't owt serious or anything.'

'Don't fucking worry about it,' grins Jack. 'Nice looking bloody woman.'

'She called you?'

'This morning.'

'Me too,' I say. 'What she say to you?'

'Same as she told you probably.'

'She didn't tell me anything.'

'Well, told me she was sensing some *connection* between Susan Ridyard and Jeanette Garland,' laughs Jack. 'You know how she talks?'

I nod, tipping the whiskey into the top of the Guinness.

'I asked her what kind of *connection*,' he says. 'Then she tells me that she's been having all these dreams but by this point, to be honest with you, I'd switched off.'

'You tell her you were going to write anything?'

Jack shakes his head: 'Said I might pop over this afternoon, if I had time.'

'And have you?'

'What?'

'The time?'

'No,' says Jack.

I pick up my pint. I drink it down in one.

'And you?' winks Jack.

From Millgarth and Leeds into Wakefield and St John's –

Big trees with hearts cut;

On to Blenheim Road –

Big houses with their hearts cut;

28 Blenheim Road, St John's, Wakefield –

Big tree with hearts cut into her bark, big house with her heart cut into flats;

I park in the drive, a bad taste in my mouth.

I put a finger to my lips. It comes away all bloody, smeared. I touch my handkerchief to my lips. There are brown stains when I look, smudged.

I get out. I walk up the drive full of shallow holes and stagnant water.

It's still raining, the branches scratching the grey sky.

I open the downstairs door. I walk up the stairs. I knock on the door of Flat 5.

'Who is it?'

'Police, love,' I say –

The door flies open, no chain, and there she is, stood in the doorway –

That pale face between the wood, that beautiful face –

Truly beautiful.

'Hello Mandy,' I say.

'I knew you'd come,' she smiles.

'I thought you weren't a fortune teller?'

'I'm not,' she laughs.

She takes my hand. She leads me down the dim hall hung with dark oils into the big room –

The smell of cat piss and petunia.

We sit side by side on her sofa, on Persian rugs and cushions –

The low ornately carved table at our shins.

She is still holding my hand, our bodies touching at our elbows and our knees.

'I'm sorry about this morning,' I say.

She tightens her hand round mine. 'No, I shouldn't call you there.'

'No-one else was home, it doesn't – '

'But you've felt it too, haven't you?'

'I – '

'You have to go and see her, you must.'

'Who? See who?'

'Mrs Ridyard.'

'Why? I – '

'She knows, Maurice. She knows.'

'Knows what?'

'Where her daughter is.'

'How? How could she?'

'She sees her.'

'Then maybe she's already told George Oldman, or – '

'No, Maurice. She's waiting for you.'

I pull her head on to my chest. I stroke her hair. I say: 'I can't do this.'

Mandy raises her head and her lips. Mandy kisses my cheek and my ear –

'You must,' she whispers. 'You have to.'

The fat white candles lit and the heavy crimson curtains drawn, there are no windows in the big room –

Dark ways, hearts lost;

Beneath her shadows –

She is sobbing, weeping;

The smell of cat piss and petunia, of desperate fucking on an old sofa strewn with Persian rugs and cushions –

She has her head on my chest and I'm stroking her hair, her beautiful hair.

Behind the heavy crimson curtains, the branches of the tree tap upon the glass of her big window –

Wanting in;

Sobbing, weeping –

Wanting in.

She kisses my fingertips and then stops, holding my fingers to the candlelight –

She lifts her head and says: 'You've got blood on your hands.'

'I'm sorry,' I say, but her face in the candlelight is white and already dead –

The branches of the tree tapping upon the glass of her big window –

Dark –

Sobbing, weeping –

Hearts –

Asking to be let in.

Chapter 32

Falling backwards into enormous depths, away from this place, her mouth open, contorted and screaming and howling, the animal sound of a mother trapped and forced to imagine the repeated slaughter of her young, contorted and screaming and howling, prone upon the floor of their front room, on the yellow squares and the red, on the marks made by crayons and the marks made by paints, contorted and screaming and howling under the dull and yellow lights blinking on and off, on and off, the faded poster warning against the perils of losing and not finding your children, contorted and screaming and howling, the smell of damp clothes and undercooked dinners, contorted and screaming and howling as you took down their names and their ages, telling them all the things you were going to do for them, all the good news you were going to bring, how happy they'd be, but they were just sat there, silently waiting for their kids to come home, to take them upstairs and put them to bed, the whole house silent but for her, her mouth open, contorted and screaming and howling, rocking back and forth, her husband in his chair and on his feet, his hands outstretched in the shape of a cross, noisily grinding his teeth as you flew across the room, tried to reach across and grab him, hold him, but your brother was holding you back, telling you all the things that he'd done, all the shit he was in, how fucked he truly was, how much better off he was dead, your mother on her feet, her mouth open, contorted and screaming and howling, the sound of her glasses breaking in her own hands, and then the Brass came, came to take you all downstairs, down to the cells, and at the bottom of the stairs you turned the corner and they opened the door to Room 4 and there he was, his gun still smoking as they struggled to clean him all up, the stink of shit among the smoke, his brains attached to the windows of the shed, a finger holding down the trigger, lying there in a uniform that said West Yorkshire Constabulary between a pair of swan's wings, his face all blown off and in bits, still struggling to mop up those bits and take him away, to put him in a hole in the ground and make him go away, but it wouldn't and it never will, not for her, her mouth open, contorted and screaming and howling, crawling up the walls and the stairs on her nails and her knees, pissing and barking and chasing her tail, the smell of overcooked cabbages and dirty old rags, the dull and yellow lights that blinked off and on, on and off, the faded poster asking the public to please help find their kids, the white squares and the grey, the marks made by bones and the marks made by skulls, the linoleum, and these men that walked these stairs, these linoleum floors, these policemen in their suits and big size ten boots, and then it was gone again; the walls, the stairs, the smell of dirty dogs and overcooked vegetables, the dull and yellow lights, the faded

poster warning against the perils of drinking and driving at Christmas, the
white squares and the grey, the marks made by boots and the marks made by
chairs, the carpets and the policemen in suits and new boots, all gone as you
fall backwards on a tiny plastic chair through the enormous depths of time,
away from this place, this rotten *un-fresh linoleum place, this place that smells*
so strongly of memories, bad memories, and you are alone now, terrified
and hysterical and screeching, your mouth open, contorted and screaming and
howling, alone with their mothers, all of these mothers, their children not
here –

    Mouth open, contorted and screaming and howling from under the
ground –

    Contorted and screaming and howling from under the ground –

    Screaming and howling from under the ground –

    Howling from under the ground –

    Under the ground –

    Under the ground as they murder you –

    Murdered you all over again:

    The Last Man.

Wednesday 1 June 1983 –

    You are listening to the branches tapping against the pane;

    Lying on your back in your underpants and socks –

    Listening to the branches tapping against the pane;

    Lying on your back in your underpants and socks, amongst the
ruins –

    The branches tapping against the pane;

    Lying on your back in your underpants and socks, amongst the
ruins of your flat –

    Tapping against the pane:

    D-8.

You drive into Leeds, the radio on:

    Searching for Hazel –

    You push the buttons. You change the stations –

    Finding only:

    'I think her appeal has always been to baser emotions like fear and
greed . . .'

    Only Thatcher –

    Thatcher, Thatcher, Thatcher –

    No Hazel –

    The radio off, you drive into Leeds.

*

'My name is John Piggott. I have an appointment.'

The policeman on the desk nods at the plastic chairs: 'Take a seat please.'

You walk over to the tiny plastic chairs and sit down under the dull and yellow lights, the faded poster warning against the perils of drinking and driving at Christmas above you –

No Christmas for Jimmy A.

The policeman on the desk making his calls –

You look down at the linoleum floor, at the white squares and the grey, at the boot and the chair marks –

'Mr Piggott?'

You stand up and go back over to the front desk.

'Someone will be down in a minute.'

'Mr Piggott?'

You look up to see a man with heavy black frames staring down at you; grey skin and suit, red eyes under thick specs, balder and thinner than he was even a week ago –

Detective Chief Superintendent Maurice Jobson:

The Owl.

You stand up. You take his hand. You say: 'About the other day, I . . .'

He stares at you. He says: 'Forget it. That's funerals for you.'

You nod.

'That's why you're here though?' he says. 'About James Ashworth?'

'Yes,' you say. 'For his mother.'

'How is she?'

'How do you think she is?' you say.

He stares at you. He says: 'So what is it I can do for you, Mr Piggott?'

'She's instructed me to ask you for Jimmy's belongings; his clothes, personal effects, his motorbike.'

'They've not been returned?'

You shake your head: 'That's why I'm asking for them.'

He stares. He says: 'If you come up to my office, I'll see what I can do.'

'Thank you.'

He doesn't move. He just stares. He doesn't blink. Just stares.

'Thank you,' you say again.

The Chief Superintendent turns and leads the way up the stairs and along the corridors, the typewriters clattering away and the telephones ringing, past the incident rooms and the murder rooms, the walls and walls of maps and photographs, past one open door –

One open door and one wall, one map and one photograph:

Hazel Atkins.

In chalk beside the map, beside the photograph:

Day 20.

You pause before the door, before the map, before the photograph.

Jobson stops. He turns round. He comes back down the corridor. He looks in the door. He walks across the room. He picks up a piece of chalk. He changes the day:

Day 21.

He drops the chalk. He walks back across the room. He passes you in the doorway. He sets off back down the corridor.

You follow him. You say: 'I thought you were over in Wakefield these days?'

'I was,' he says. 'I've lost count of the number of times I've been back and forth between there and here.'

'Which do you prefer?'

He opens the door to his office. 'Leeds City born and bred I am.'

You step inside –

It's a bare office:

No photographs, no certificates, no trophies.

Detective Chief Superintendent Maurice Jobson gestures at a seat.

You sit down on the opposite side of his desk, Jobson with his back to the window.

He says: 'I can't promise you the motorcycle today. It'll still be with forensics up at Wetherby but – '

'Forensics?'

He nods. 'I'm afraid that the late Mr Ashworth is still very much a part of our investigation into the whereabouts of Hazel Atkins.'

'I see,' you sigh. 'Actually, I did want to – '

Jobson has his palm raised. 'But I'm sure we can give you some of his clothes.'

'That would be very much appreciated.'

He passes three sheets of paper across the desk. 'Just sign these and I'll see what I can do.'

You take them. You ask: 'I was wondering if it would be possible to have a copy of the inventory, just to make sure everything is accounted for?'

'Inventory?'

'Just what he had with him when he was originally detained.'

'You want a copy?'

'For his mother.'

He stares at you. He says: 'There's going to be an inquiry, you do know that?'

'An internal police inquiry,' you nod.

Jobson stares at you. He says again: 'Sign the papers and I'll see what I can do.'

You reach inside your jacket for your pen –

It isn't there.

You look up at Jobson. He's holding one out across his desk.

'Thank you,' you say. 'I must have – '

'Forget it,' he smiles.

You sign the papers. You hand them back across the desk with his pen.

Jobson takes them. He separates them. He gives you back a copy as one of the three telephones on his desk buzzes and a light flashes –

Jobson glances at the flashing light then back at you: 'Well, Mr Piggott, if there was nothing else I – '

'To be honest with you, I do seem to have got myself up to my neck in – '

The Detective Chief Superintendent is nodding: 'Out of your depth, are you?'

'Bitten off more than I can chew,' you smile. 'Which, as you can see, is a lot.'

'Go on,' says Jobson.

'To be straight with you,' you say. 'I'm also representing Michael Myshkin.'

Jobson stares at you. Jobson doesn't blink.

You say: 'You know who I mean?'

'Yes, Mr Piggott. I know who you mean.'

'Well, I'm in the process of preparing a preliminary appeal on his behalf and I – '

Jobson has his hand raised: 'Didn't Michael Myshkin confess and plead guilty on the grounds of diminished responsibility?'

'Yes, he did.'

'So on what possible grounds is he thinking of appealing?'

'Early days yet but, in cases such as these, where a conviction is based upon a confession, it is possible for the appellant to argue that his pleas were ill-considered and out of accord with the evidence; that in the absence of the alleged confession, there was a lack of evidence to convict; that the appellant's state of mind at the time of the confession calls into question the validity of the confession; that the Trial Judge erred in accepting guilty pleas based solely upon confessions; that the very confession itself might have been gained by unlawful means – '

'Mr Piggott,' interrupts Jobson. 'That is a very serious allegation to make.'

'Examples,' you say. 'Just examples of avenues open to exploration.'

Jobson stares at you. He says: 'There were witnesses – '

You nod.

'Forensic evidence.'

You nod again. 'As I say, I am feeling somewhat overfaced.'

'That surprises me,' smiles Jobson.

'Eyes bigger than my belly, would you believe?'

Jobson shakes his head: 'I'd say you seem to have the measure of things.'

'No, no, no,' you say. 'Not at all. You see, I keep running into the same names, the same faces, again and again.'

Jobson stares at you.

'Both with Michael Myshkin and now with Jimmy Ashworth – '

'They did live on the same street,' says Jobson.

'I know, I know, I know,' you reply. 'But what with you pulling Jimmy Ashworth in over this Hazel Atkins business and her having gone missing from the same school as Clare Kemplay did nigh on ten years ago, the murder of whom Michael Myshkin is now serving life imprisonment for – '

'And to which he confessed.'

'And to which he *allegedly* confessed,' you add. 'Well – '

'Well what?'

'Well,' you say. 'Is this all just one big bloody coincidence or is there something I should know before I waste any more of Mrs Ashworth and Mrs Myshkin's money and my time?'

'Mr Piggott,' he smiles. 'You want me to tell you how to spend your time and other people's money?'

You shake your head. 'No, but I would like you to tell me if Michael Myshkin murdered Clare Kemplay?'

Jobson stares at you.

You stare at him.

He says: 'Yes he did.'

'Alone?'

Then, right on fucking cue, there's the knock at the door.

Jobson looks up and away from your face.

You turn around in your chair –

'Boss,' says a man with a moustache –

A man you recognise from the night Jimmy Ashworth hung himself downstairs, a man you recognise from the funeral –

All three of them.

'Give me two minutes, will you, Dick?' says Jobson.

But the man shakes his head: 'It's urgent.'

Jobson nods.

The door closes.

Jobson stands up, his hand out. 'If you wait downstairs, I'll make sure you get her son's belongings.'

You stand up. You reach over the desk. You take his hand. You hold it. You say: 'I went to Rochdale, Mr Jobson.'

Jobson drops your hand. 'So?'

'I know about the shoebox.'

Jobson stares at you. 'So?'

'So I know Michael Myshkin didn't kill Clare Kemplay.'

Jobson blinks.

'And I know Jimmy Ashworth didn't take Hazel Atkins and I know he didn't kill himself.'

Jobson stares at you –

You stare at him –

He says: 'You know a lot, Mr Piggott.'

You nod.

'Maybe too much,' he smiles.

You shake your head. You stare at him –

The Owl.

He says: 'Goodbye, Mr Piggott.'

You turn. You walk over to the door. You stop. You turn back round. You say: 'You won't forget about the motorbike, will you?'

'I won't forget, Mr Piggott,' says Chief Superintendent Jobson. 'I never forget.'

'See you then,' you say.

'No doubt,' he replies.

You close the door. You hear –

You swear you hear –

Hear him say:

'In the place where there is no darkness.'

You walk down the corridor and back down the stairs and over to the tiny plastic chairs and sit down under the dull and yellow lights, the faded poster warning against the perils of drinking and driving at Christmas –

No more Christmases.

The policeman on the desk is picking the scabs off his boils.

You look down at the linoleum floor, at the white squares and the grey, at the boot and the chair marks –

'Mr Piggott?'

You look up.

'Sign here please, sir,' says a young, blond policeman –

A young Bob Fraser –

Smiling and holding out a clipboard, two large brown paper bags on the desk.

You take the clipboard and the pen from him. You sign the papers.

He hands you the large brown paper bags. 'Here you go, sir.'

You stand up. 'Thank you.'

'You're welcome.'

You walk across the linoleum floor, the white squares and the grey, the boot marks and the chair marks, walk towards the double doors and out –

'Sir,' the young officer calls after you. 'Just a minute.'

You turn back round –

'Sorry,' he says. 'You wanted a copy of the inventory, didn't you?'

You nod.

He hands you a photocopied piece of A4. 'The Chief would've had my guts for garters. He said to be sure you got it.'

You sit in the car in the car park between the bus station and the market, still in the shadow of Millgarth, the two large brown paper bags open on the passenger seat with the photocopied piece of A4 in your hand:

One pair of black leather motorcycle boots, size nine.

Two pairs of blue navy wool socks, size eight.

One pair of white underpants, size M.

One pair of Lee blue denim jeans, size 30, with black leather belt.

One brown handkerchief.

One pair of medium-sized black leather motorcycle gloves.

One white T-shirt, size M.

One blue and white cotton check shirt, size M.

One sleeveless Wrangler blue denim jacket with patches and badges, size M.

One black leather jacket, marked Saxon *and* Angelwitch *with bird wing motif.*

One pair of round-framed gold spectacles.

One Casio digital calculator wristwatch.

One black leather studded wristband.

One Star of David metal key-ring with three keys attached.

One brown leather wallet containing one five pound note, driving licence in the name of James Ashworth, 69 Newstead View, Fitzwilliam, a Mass card and stamps to the value of twenty-five pence.

One packet of Rothmans cigarettes containing five unsmoked cigarettes.

One disposable white plastic cigarette lighter.

One packet of Rizla cigarette papers.

Seventy-six-and-a-half pence in loose change.

You put the list down. You root through the bags for the belt.

You find the jeans first, but the belt isn't in them –

It's at the very bottom of the second bag.

You pull it out. You hold it up:

They open the door to Room 4 and there he is, his boots still turning as they struggle to cut him down, the stink of piss among the suds, his body attached to the ventilation grille, a belt holding him there by his neck, hanging in a jacket that says Saxon *and* Angelwitch *between a pair of swan's wings, his tongue swollen and eyes as big as plates, still struggling to cut him down and take him away, to put him in a hole in the ground and make it go away –*

But it won't and it never will –

Not for her –

Nor you.

But you cannot remember if it was this belt –

Holding him there by his neck –

This belt here in your hands.

You put the belt back in the bag. You close both large brown paper bags. You fold the photocopied piece of A4. You put it in your pocket. You start the car. You pull out without looking in your mirror.

A motorcycle brakes hard behind you.

You stop.

The rider dismounts. He tears off his helmet. He is coming towards you with his angry words and violent threats.

You start the car again. You drive off up George Street, drive off thinking –

No helmet.

At the top of George Street you piss around on the various one-way systems till you come out on to the Headrow. You check the rearview to be sure Sid fucking Snot isn't still on your tail. You go up Cookridge Street.

You are looking for Portland Square –

Flat 6, 6 Portland Square, Leeds 1.

*   *

You park on Great George Street. You wander around behind the Law Courts and the Cathedral, the Infirmary and the Library –

Looking for Flat 6, 6 Portland Square, Leeds 1 –

Looking for Jack.

It is Wednesday 1 June 1983 –

D-8.

Off Calverley Street, tucked between Portland Way and Portland Crescent, up by the Poly and opposite the Civic Hall, you find it –

Suitably ruined Victorian grandeur, ill-gotten and squandered, waiting for the Wrecking Ball; two empty terraces staring down at the grass and the weeds rampant between the cracks and the stones:

Portland Square –

You pick your way along the line until you come to number 6:

The front door is wide open and there are no curtains in the windows of the ground floor. There is a tree stood in the patch of ground that sets the place back from where the pavement lies buried. The tree is taller than the building and hiding the lamppost, its branches scratching down the upstairs windows.

You walk up the three stone steps. You push the door open wider.

There is a staircase leading up to the left, leaves and crisp packets, old unopened post and papers, all scattered across the brown carpet.

You step inside. You call out: 'Hello? Hello?'

No answer.

You walk up the stairs to the first floor and Flats 3 and 4.

The carpet is cleaner here.

You cross the landing. You go up the second flight of stairs.

At the top is Flat 5 and at the end of the landing is number 6.

The carpet is clear of leaves and crisp packets, unopened post and papers.

You try the bell on the door of Flat 6, 6 Portland Square, Leeds 1.

No answer.

You knock. You shout: 'Hello? Hello?'

No answer.

There is a metal letterbox in the old wooden door.

You squat down. You lift the flap. 'Mr Whitehead? Jack Whitehead?'

No answer.

You peer in through the letterbox:

The inside of the flat is dark and the smell unpleasant.

You can hear the bells ringing for Evensong, the trees scratching at the windows.

You let the flap go. You stand back up. You drop to your knees again –

Someone has scratched a single word into the metal flap of the letterbox:

Ripper.

You let the flap go again. You stand back upright. You stare at the door –

Someone has also scratched a number on either side of the six:

6 6 6.

You are thinking of your mother again –

The things they wrote on her walls and door.

Maybe Whitehead and son don't want to be found.

Back outside among the grass and the weeds, the cracks and the stones, you follow the bells into St Anne's. You want to ask if anyone knows any Whiteheads living local, but there's no-one in a collar to pester.

Fat, bald and tired –

Scared to go home, you sit down at the back.

Down in the front pew there's an old woman with a walking stick trying to stand. A little boy is helping her to her feet, a book under his arm.

Up on the Cross, there's Christ –

Just hanging around as usual, waiting for someone to save or seduce –

Some lonely old widow trapped in her house by the endless night and its kids.

The boy is leading the old woman down the aisle. They reach the back pew where you are sat. The boy takes the book from under his arm. He opens it and hands it to you.

You look at the boy and the old woman.

They look back at you, familiar.

You start to speak but they walk off.

You look down at the pages of the book –

The Holy Bible –

Look down at the passage marked:

Job 30, 26–31.

Look down and read it:

> *When I looked for good,*
> *Then evil came unto me:*
> *And when I waited for light,*
> *There came darkness.*
> *My bowels boiled,*
> *And rested not:*

> *The days of affliction prevented me.*
> *I went mourning without the sun:*
> *I stood up,*
> *And I cried in the congregation.*
> *I am a brother to dragons,*
> *And a companion to owls.*
> *My skin is black upon me,*
> *And my bones are burned with heat.*
> *My harp also is turned to mourning,*
> *And my organ into the voice of them that weep.*

Back in the car on Great George Street, you rummage around in the bags until you find Jimmy's wallet. You take it out. You open it. You find the fiver, his driving licence, the stamps to the value of twenty-five pence –

Not the Mass card –

It isn't there.

But tucked inside the split silken lining is a photograph –

A photograph of a girl:

Not Tessa.

It's a photograph cut from a newspaper –

A cutting:

Hazel.

Chapter 33

Dawn or fucking near enough –
   Sunday 12 June 1977 –
   (You better paint your face) –
   Banging on Joe's door: 'Open fucking door!'
   'Who is it?'
   BJ hiss: 'We're fucking late!'
   Locks slide, keys turn/new locks, new keys –
   BJ: over right shoulder/over left –
   (Hair in his face, he is dressed in the black of the corner of my eye) –
   Him: wide white eyes at crack –
   (Here is your friend again) –
   Paranoid looks to left/paranoid looks to right –
   (Me, my face, my eye) –
   BJ push open door into this private little Chapeltown hellhole:
   Joe's mate Steve Barton on mattress and angry: 'You the late boy, not me.'
   BJ: 'You fucking ready?'
   Steve: 'Been waiting for you.'
   'Things to do.'
   'No shit,' nods Steve. 'You get them done, them things?'
   'Fuck off with him,' says Joe.
   'You fuck off,' he spits.
   BJ: 'Fuck is with you two?'
   'Bad night.'
   'Aren't they all?'
   Joe is shaking his head: 'Word is Janice be dead.'
   'Janice Ryan?'
   He nods.
   'Fuck that,' BJ say. 'She's protected, double I hear.'
   He snorts: 'Aren't we all?'
   Steve: 'First Marie – '
   BJ: 'Stop man, stop right there.'
   'Be out of hand, I say.'
   BJ turn to Steve: 'Then this is your fucking payback, man.'
   'Be that Pirate,' whispers Joe.
   'Fuck her,' BJ say. 'Fuck him.'
   No-one speaks.
   'We going or what?'

No-one moves.

BJ ask them again, check them two-times: 'You up for this?'

Joe, he doesn't smile, just says again: 'Show me mine enemy.'

BJ turn to Steve: 'Payback time?'

He shrugs and gets up off mattress, tracing sevens on walls and sevens on door, sevens on ceiling and sevens on floor –

All them pretty little sevens, dressed up in red, dressed up in gold and green:

Them two sevens –

Joe stagger-dancing out door, his voice of thunder still chanting: *'War in the East, war in the West; War in the North, war in the South; Crazy Joe get them out . . .'*

Steve: 'Heavy Manners.'

Heavy fucking Manners –

COMING DOWN.

Three young men sitting in a stolen Cortina:

(Down we slide, further) –

Steve Barton, Joe Rose, and BJ –

(On Satan's side) –

Edgy with cause/edgy with reason –

(Treacherous times) –

BJ look at BJ's watch:

Seven twenty-five, nineteen seventy-seven.

BJ nod.

Everybody gets out of car.

Everybody walk across Gledhill Road, Morley.

Everybody pull on their masks.

BJ knock on back door.

Everybody wait –

Wait, wait, wait:

The key turns.

The door opens.

Steve kicks it straight back in bloke's face.

Bloke goes down on other side of door (like a sack of fucking spuds):

His hair in his face, his teeth all covered in blood –

Everybody step over him –

Steve giving him a kick (just to make sure he's going to be a good boy).

'What the – '

Granny coming down stairs –

Steve straight across room to give her a slap, hard.

He bungs a bag over her head, ties her arms behind her, pretends to suck her tit:

'Please, please – '

Bound, gagged and bagged.

Steve back on his feet and through into Post Office, pointing Joe upstairs –

Joe saying: 'Upstairs?'

Steve turning and nodding, finger to his mask.

BJ stand in back with old bloke still out for count, his wife crying in a pool of her own piss.

Steve is back with a bag of cash.

Joe coming down stairs, empty-handed and shrugging his shoulders.

BJ walk over to Steve. BJ peer into bag:

NOT ENOUGH –

Not a grand, nowhere near.

Nowhere near and BJ tell him so: 'Someone's fucked up here.'

'Shut up, man,' hisses Steve. 'Deal with it later, not here.'

BJ shake BJ's head.

BJ walk out back door.

They follow.

Everybody leave –

Leave them lying in their little pools on floor of their little Post Office:

He will need thirty-five stitches in his head and in six months she'll be dead.

Everybody take their masks off.

Everybody get in Cortina.

Everybody drive back into Leeds, old sun already behind new clouds –

Steve laughing as he drives, shouting: 'Payback!'

Joe chanting to himself: *'War in the East, war in the West; War in the North . . .'*

Old sun already behind new clouds, shadows across car –

BJ say: 'We've fucked up.'

Joe counting cash: 'Still be more than seven hundred here, man.'

'We've fucked up,' BJ say again. 'It was a set-up.'

'No set-up,' Steve is saying, shaking his locks. 'Just pure fucking payback.'

BJ nodding, knowing –

(The never-never, can't go on forever) –

Knowing what's coming –
(Close my eyes but he will not go away) –
COMING –
(But I have the will to survive) –
COMING –
(I will cheat and I will win) –
COMING –
(You think I'm a raving idiot, just off the boat) –
COMING –
(But I'll be round the back of your house in the dead of the night) –
COMING –
(Watch you sleeping in your bed) –
COMING –
(When the bloody heavens clash) –
COMING DOWN –
(The Two Sevens).

Chapter 34

Saturday 25 March 1972 –

'You wake up some morning as unhappy as you've ever been . . .'

I lie alone in our double bed, listening to the sound of things getting worse:

'Protests mount over direct rule in Northern Ireland after the Government's agreement yesterday that Ulster is to be ruled direct from Westminster for a year ran into opposition immediately with both wings of the IRA saying they would fight on and militant Protestants demanding widespread strike action despite calls from Mr Faulkner for calm.

'Meanwhile Mr William Whitelaw, the new Secretary of State for Northern Ireland, yesterday described the task ahead of him as, "Terrifying, difficult, and awesome." '

I lie alone in the double bed, listening to the sound of things getting worse as my family dress for a wedding –

'Mr & Mrs William Molloy gratefully request the presence of Mr & Mrs Maurice Jobson & family at the marriage of their daughter Louise Ann to Mr Robert Fraser.'

A celebration.

'Paul!' the wife shouts up the stairs. 'Paul, hurry up, love, will you? We're all waiting.'

My wife, my daughter and I stood at the front door –

My wife looking up the stairs, my daughter in the mirror, me at my watch.

The Simon and Garfunkel abruptly stops and down he comes.

'I'll get the car out,' I say and open the door.

'I'll lock up,' nods the wife, pushing the children towards the door.

I go out. I open up the garage. I drive the car out, the family car –

The Triumph Estate.

I get back out. I lock the garage door.

'It's open,' I tell the wife and kids as they stand around the car wishing we were all somewhere else –

Someone else –

Other people.

We get in the family car.

Clare asks me to put the radio on.

'We haven't got one,' I reply.

She slouches down in the back. Paul whispers something to her. They both smile.

They are fifteen and thirteen and they hate me.

I glance in the rearview mirror. I say: 'Leeds have got Arsenal today, haven't they?'

Paul shrugs. Clare whispers something to him. They both smile again.

They are fifteen and thirteen and I hate them and I love them.

My wife Judith says: 'Hope they get a bit of sun for the photos.'

And her –

I hate her –

Hate her in her hat too big for the car.

Ossett Parish Church has the tallest steeple in Yorkshire, so they say. It stands black and tall for all to see, across the golf courses and the fields of rape and rhubarb.

We park in its shadow on Church Street, Ossett –

The whole road lined with cars in both directions.

'Big wedding,' says Judith.

No-one says a word.

We get out and walk down the road and into the churchyard where groups of coppers are gathered around their cigarettes in their court suits –

Girlfriends and wives all off to the side, battling to keep their hats on in the wind, talking to the older folk, ignoring their kids.

'He invite the whole force, did he?' laughs Judith.

I lead the way through the men and their greetings, dragging the wife and kids along –

'Sir,' says one.

'Inspector,' says another.

'Mr Jobson.'

'Maurice, Judith,' smiles John Rudkin at the church door in his morning suit –

Bill's Boy.

'Where you hid Anthea?' asks the wife.

'Bottom of Winscar Reservoir,' Rudkin laughs –

Laughs like he wishes it were true.

I say: 'Which way to cheap seats, John?'

'Anywhere on the right, but first two are for family.'

'And what are we?'

He looks confused –

'Just pulling your leg, Sergeant,' I say. 'Just pulling your leg.'

'Isn't he awful,' says the wife. 'You see what we have to put up with?'

He smiles –

A smile like he wishes us both dead.

I nod at another man in morning dress on the other side of the church. I ask: 'That Bob's brother, is it?'

Rudkin shakes his head. He says in a low voice: 'Not got any family, has Bob.'

'You're joking?' says Judith, her purple glove up over her red lipstick.

'Mam died couple of years ago.'

I say: 'His side of church is going to be a bit on thin side then.'

'Boss filled it out with a lot of blokes Bob trained with and I reckon most of Morley station must be here.'

'That's all right then,' says Judith.

'See you later,' I say and turn to my children. 'Come on.'

We walk down the aisle, nodding to Walter Heywood and his wife –

Ronald Angus and his –

They're all here:

Dick Alderman and Jim Prentice shaking my hand –

Bob Craven not.

All here but one:

No George –

George still over in Rochdale, over where I want to be.

I hear my name again. I turn round:

Don Foster and his wife, John Dawson and his –

Big smiles and waves and they'll talk to us later.

In our middle pew, Judith says: 'That's John Dawson, isn't it?'

I nod, thinking:

Other people.

'You never told me you knew John Dawson.'

'I don't.'

But she says: 'You should see that house . . .'

(Inside a thousand voices cry) –

Then Clare whispers to her mother: 'How did they meet?'

Judith looks at me. She says: 'I'm not sure.'

'What?' I say.

'How did they *meet*?' sighs Clare, wincing.

I say: 'Louise and Bob?'

'No,' she sneers. 'Queen and Prince Philip.'

'Bob's a policeman, and – '

'I don't want to marry a policeman,' she spits.

'Clare,' says my wife. 'You shouldn't say things like that.'

Me –

Her father, I say nothing.

So she says again, louder: 'I'll never marry a policeman.'

I look away at Robert Fraser –

Bob Fraser standing at the front of the church, the vicar in front of him, his best man at his side.

I don't recognise the best man –

Not a policeman –

Not one of us.

The meandering tinkling from the organist stops. He hits all his keys at once and we all stand as *Here Comes the Bride* starts, turning round to see her –

The Bride –

Beautiful in white, her father at her side –

(Beautiful as the moon, as terrible as the night) –

Proud as punch in his morning dress –

The greys of his suit matching the streak that got him his name, the black his eyes.

Then it's on with the show –

The celebration –

The hymns:

Lead us Heavenly Father, lead us;

Oh, Perfect Love;

Love Divine.

The readings –

The readings that say –

That say words like:

For the body is not one member, but many.

If the foot shall say, Because I am not the hand, I am not the body; is it therefore not of the body?

And if the ear shall say, Because I am not the eye, I am not of the body; is it therefore not of the body?

If the whole body were an eye, where were the hearing? If the whole were hearing, where were the smelling?

But now hath God set the members every one of them in the body, as it hath pleased him.

And if they were all one member, where were the body?

But now there are many members, yet but one body.

And the eye cannot say unto the hand, I have no need for thee; nor again the head to the feet, I have no need of you.

Nay, much more those members of the body, which seem to be more feeble, are necessary:

And those members of the body which we think to be less honourable, upon these we bestow abundant honour; and our uncomely parts have more abundant comeliness.

For our comely parts have no need; but God hath tempered the body together, having given more abundant honour to that part which lacked;

That there should be no schism in the body; but that the members should have the same care one for another.

And whether one member suffer, all the members suffer with it; or one member be honoured, all the members rejoice with it.

Now ye are the body of Christ, and members in particular.

I look at my family beside me in the pew –

Paul eyes closed while Judith and Clare dab theirs as Mendelssohn strikes up.

Outside in the churchyard, the groups of coppers gather around their cigarettes again –

The girlfriends and wives off to the side, battling to keep their skirts down in the wind, bitching about the older folk, their kids tugging at their hems and their sleeves, their eager handfuls of confetti slipping through their tiny fingers –

The photographer desperately trying to corral us –

A black Austin Princess sat waiting to take the newlyweds away from all this.

'He did invite the whole force, didn't he?' Judith laughs –

Laughs to herself.

I can see George –

George Oldman stood at the gates with his wife, his son and two daughters.

He sees me coming.

I shake his hand and nod to his wife. 'George, Lillian.'

'Maurice,' he replies, his wife smiling then not.

'Thought you weren't going to make it?'

'He nearly didn't,' says his wife with a squeeze on his arm.

'Any luck?'

He shakes his head. He looks away. I leave it –

Leave them to it:

George, his wife, his son and two daughters.

'Group shot, please,' the photographer pleads as the sun comes out at long last, shining feebly through the trees and the gravestones.

I walk back over to pose with my wife, my son and daughter.

Clare asks: 'Can we go home now?'

'There's the reception next, love,' smiles her mum. 'Be a lovely do, I bet.'

Paul whispers something to Clare. They both smile –

They are fifteen and thirteen and they pity their mother.

'Family for the last time,' shouts the photographer.

Judith looks from the kids to me, adjusting her hat with a shrug and smile –

We are forty-five and forty-two and we hate –

Just hate:

Married seventeen years ago this August at this church, so they say.

We drive in silence down into Dewsbury and up through Ravensthorpe to the outskirts of Mirfield, silence until Clare reminds us that Charlotte next door, her family have a car radio and her dad is *only* a teacher and, according to Paul, everyone at the Grammar School has a radio in their car and we must be the only family in the whole *bloody* world that doesn't.

'Don't use that word, please, Paul,' says his mother, turning round.

'Which word?'

'You know very well which word.'

'Why not?' asks Clare. 'Dad says it all the time.'

'No, he doesn't.'

'Yes, he does,' shouts Paul. 'And worse.'

'Well, your father is an adult,' says Judith –

'A *policeman*,' spits Clare.

'We're here,' I say.

The Marmaville Club:

Posh mill brass house turned Country Club-cum-pub, favoured by the Masons –

Favoured by Bill Molloy.

I get Judith a white wine. I leave her with the kids and the other wives and theirs. I head back to the bar –

'Don't forget you're driving,' shouts Judith and I laugh –

Laugh like I wish she was dead.

At the bar, a whiskey in my hand, there's a hand at my elbow –

'Isn't that a Mick drink?'

I turn round:

Jack –

Jack bloody Whitehead.

'What?' grins Jack. 'Didn't think the Chief Superintendent would stoop to inviting scum like me?'

'No,' I say, looking around the room. 'Not at all.'

Mr and Mrs Robert Fraser stand in the doorway to the dining room, waiting to greet their guests:

'Uncle Maurice, Auntie Jane,' says the Bride.

'Auntie *Judith*,' corrects the Groom.

'Smart lad,' I say, shaking his hand. 'You should be a copper.'

We all laugh –

All but Paul and Clare.

Louise kisses Judith on the cheek. 'It's been a long day.'

'Not over yet,' I say –

Not by a long chalk.

In the dining room we're seated at the same table as Walter and Mrs Heywood, Ronald and Mrs Angus, the Oldmans and their son and two daughters –

The Brass.

We eat grapefruit, chicken, and some kind of trifle with a fair few glasses of wine and disapproving looks from the wives and kids to wash it all down.

Then come the speeches, with a fair few glasses more to help them go down.

There's a hand on my shoulder. John Rudkin bends down to whisper: 'Bill wants us all to have a drink upstairs. When dancing starts.'

I smile, hoping he'll fuck off.

He glances at Walter Heywood and the West Riding boys. He says: 'Be discreet.'

I smile again.

He fucks off.

An upstairs room, down the red and gold corridor past the toilets –

The curtains drawn, the lamps on, the cigars out –

The sound of music coming up through the carpet –

The beautiful carpet, all gold flowers on deep crimsons and red –

Like the whiskeys and our faces.

Sat in a circle in the big chairs, a couple of empty ones –

The gang's all here:

Dick, Jim Prentice, John Rudkin, Bob Craven and –

'Lads,' says Bill. 'Like you all to meet a good mate of mine from over other side of Pennines. This is John Murphy, Detective Inspector with Manchester.'

Similar age to me but with all his hair, Murphy is a good-looking bloke –

A younger Bill Molloy –

Another one.

John Murphy stands up –

'Speech!' shouts Dick Alderman.

'I know some of you and the rest by reputation,' smiles Murphy with a nod to me. 'I also know that we're all here because of one man – '

Nods and murmurs in Bill's direction –

Bill all hands up, embarrassed and modest.

'So let's first raise our glasses,' says Murphy. 'To the *Badger* himself, on the marriage of his daughter.'

'Cheers,' we all say and stand up –

'No,' says Bill. 'We all had enough of that bollocks downstairs – '

We laugh. He pauses. We stand there waiting –

Waiting for him to say –

'Let's drink to us,' his voice and glass raised. 'The bloody lot of us.'

'The bloody lot of us,' we reply and drain our whiskeys.

We sit back down.

Bill tells Rudkin to ring down for another round. He says: 'We'll have to keep this brief, as we don't want too many questions, do we?'

'They think we're playing cards,' laughs Jim Prentice.

'Not talking about the wives, Jim,' says Bill. 'Thinking more about Old Walter and our country cousins.'

'Yeah,' I say. 'Thanks for putting us on same bleeding table.'

Hands up again, Bill grins: 'I just wanted you lads to meet John here, and – '

There's a knock on the door. Bill stops talking.

A young waitress brings in another tray of whiskeys –

Doubles.

She picks up the empties and leaves.

'And?' I say.

'And,' nods Bill. 'A couple of other things.'

We sip our whiskeys. We wait.

'John here's *acquired*,' smiles Bill. 'Acquired some offices for us on Oldham Street in centre of Manchester. Got the printing and distribution end sewn up nicely.'

'Got a few nice Vice connections too,' adds Murphy. 'Pete McCardell for one.'

Low whistles around the room.

Bill pats Murphy on the back. 'This is just the beginning; what we planned, worked so hard for, it's finally coming together – '

Nods.

'Controlled vice,' says Bill Molloy, quietly. 'Off the streets and out the shop windows, under our wing and in our pocket.'

Smiles.

'The whole of the North of England, from Liverpool to Hull, Nottingham up to Newcastle – it's ours for the taking: the girls, the shops, the mags – the whole bloody lot.'

Grins.

'It's going to make us rich men,' nods Bill. 'Very bloody rich men.'

Lots of nods, smiles, grins and *hear-hears*.

I stare around the room at all the teeth. I ask Bill: 'What about your son-in-law?'

Everyone stops smiling –

Rudkin shaking his head.

'Never,' says Bill. 'I never want Robert near any of this.'

I stare around the room again: 'Better all watch what we say then, hadn't we?'

Some of them are looking at the carpet, the beautiful carpet –

All gold flowers on deep crimsons and red –

Like the whiskeys and their faces.

'I do have some other new faces though,' smiles Bill and turns back to Rudkin. 'Invite our guests in and have them bring up some more drinks, will you, John?'

John Rudkin leaves the room.

'We've got an opportunity here,' Bill says. 'An opportunity to invest the money from our little ventures and turn it into something even bigger –

'Something great.'

There's another knock. Rudkin holds open the door for John Dawson and Donald Foster.

Bill gets up. 'Gentlemen. Please join us.'

Don and John take their seats in the circle. Bill makes the introductions –

Me thinking, *too many cooks, too many chiefs*.

The waitress brings in more drinks and leaves.

The introductions over and done, Bill gestures to John Dawson and Don Foster. 'John and Don here have their own dreams, don't you, gents?'

Foster nods. He clears his throat. 'With your help, gentlemen, we're going to build a shopping centre – '

'The biggest of its kind in England or Europe,' says Dawson.

'One place where you can buy everything you need, where you can see a film or go bowling, where you can have breakfast, lunch or tea,' says Foster.

'Whatever the weather, all under one roof,' adds Dawson. 'Make the Merrion Centre look like the rabbit hutch it is.'

'Where?' I ask.

'The Hunslet and Beeston exit of the motorway,' says Foster. 'Be ideal.'

'The Swan Centre,' beams Dawson –

Beams Foster –

Beams everyone:

Too many cooks, too many chiefs.

Bill stands back up, his left hand open in the direction of Dawson and Don Foster: 'With John's brains, Don's bricks, and our brass, we're going to make this happen – '

Everyone clapping –

'And we're going to make some bloody money too – '

Everyone joining him on their feet with their drinks –

'Some fucking real bloody money!'

All the cooks and all the chiefs –

Me too:

For the body is not one member –

Bill raises his glass: 'To us all and to the North – where we do what we want!'

But –

'The North,' we reply as one and drain our whiskeys again.

Many.

Bill looks over at me, smiling to himself: 'There's one last thing.'

We sip our whiskeys. We wait.

'You've all heard the rumours,' he says. 'But I wanted to tell you all face to face, here and now, in front of the lot of you –

'I'm retiring.'

'What?' we all say.

'I've had my time,' he grins. 'And I'm going to have plenty to keep me occupied.'

'But what – ' Jim Prentice says.

Craven: 'Who will – '

Bill looks at me. He nods. He says: 'Maurice is taking over.'

I say nothing.

'Old Walter signed the papers yesterday,' laughs Bill. 'Detective Chief Superintendent Maurice Jobson, Head of Leeds CID.'

Before I can say anything –

Before anyone can say anything –

Dick Alderman stands up, his glass raised one final time: 'To Maurice.'

Bill and Rudkin on their feet first, Dawson and Foster next, Craven and Prentice following –

Murphy bemused, confused –

As confused as me as I stand and raise my own glass to myself thinking:

Make believers of us all.

Downstairs, drunk and ugly –

Everyone dancing –

Everyone except my wife and my children, sat to the side in the dark –

Everyone dancing or falling down:

'State of her,' whispers Dick with a nod to Anthea Rudkin –

Rudkin's wife draped all over George Oldman –

Half in and half out of a long but low-cut pink dress –

Oldman's wife and children getting their coats.

Bill is shaking his head, whispering to Rudkin –

Rudkin across the dancefloor, pulling his wife off George –

Her arms already bruised in his grip, she kicks her legs out and she screams: 'Never marry a copper!'

In the family car on the drive home, Judith and Clare are asleep.

Paul puts his head between the seats. He says: 'Why do they call you the *Owl*?'

'Because of my glasses.'

'Think it's stupid,' he says and sits back.

I look in the rearview mirror. I can see him staring out of the window at the passing night, the lorries and the cars, the yellow lights and the red.

He is crying, wishing he were somewhere else –

Someone else –

Other people;

Or maybe just me –

Wishing I were someone else;

Crying and wishing we were all dead –

Or maybe just me –

Just me.

*

I lie in our double bed, listening to Simon and Garfunkel through the
wall, doors slamming and the telephone ringing, no-one answering it –
  The sound of things:
  Terrifying, difficult and awesome –
  The sound of things getting worse.
  Lying in the double bed, thinking –
  Please make me believe.

Chapter 35

You can't go to sleep; you can't go to sleep; you can't go to sleep –
You shut your eyes, you see her face –
You open your eyes, you see her face:
'If Mrs Thatcher wins, Britain's young men and women will be a lost generation, without jobs, without education – '
You shut your eyes, you see her face –
You open your eyes, you see her face:
'No hope to make the life they want for themselves.'
You can't go to sleep –
Thursday 2 June 1983:
D-7.

Down through the thunder and the rain and Wakefield, the car still retching and coughing, hacking its way over the Calder and out past the Redbeck, into Fitzwilliam –
Putting them together:
Jimmy Ashworth and Michael Myshkin –
Michael and Jimmy, Jimmy and Michael –
Putting them together and getting:
Hazel Atkins –
A photograph made of paper, cut from paper, dirty paper.
Sweating and then freezing, your clothes still itching with hate, you've got the shadows all over your heart again, a belly brimming over with fear –
Putting it all together to get:
Fear and hate, hate and fear –
A pocket full of paper, a pocketful of –
Hazel.
It is getting late –
Everywhere.

The silent houses of Newstead View, Fitzwilliam:
Fitz-fucking-william –
69 Newstead View:
Knock, knock, knock, knock.
'Took your time?' spits Ma Ashworth, almost closing the door in your face.
'I've been busy.'

She stares at the dinner medals on your shirt. She says: 'So I see.'

You put down the two large brown paper bags at her feet: 'I brought you these.'

She holds open the front door. 'Suppose you'll be wanting your cup of tea with three sugars?'

You shake your head: 'I'm not stopping.'

She shrugs. She looks at the bags. She says: 'What about the belt?'

You lean down. You open the bag nearest her, the black leather belt coiled on top.

She bends down. She picks it up.

'Was that his?' you ask.

Her shoulders are shaking, her rough hands holding the worn belt.

'Mrs Ashworth?'

She stares down at the belt in her hands, the tears falling from her face.

'What about this?' you ask. 'Was this his?'

Mrs Ashworth looks up at the tiny newspaper photograph in her face –

A photograph made of paper, cut from paper, dirty paper –

'You know who this is, don't you?'

The tears streaming down her face –

'It was in his wallet, in the lining.'

The tears down her face –

'He'd cut it out.'

The tears –

'No,' she cries.

You hold it closer to her face, to the tears and the lies –

'Why would he do a thing like that?'

But she's turned her face to the dark grey sky, mumbling hymns and whispering prayers, saying over and over: 'I went upstairs and opened his wardrobe door and there it was, in his other jeans. I went upstairs and opened his wardrobe door and there it was . . .'

'I'll see you,' you say –

In hell, another hell.

You walk down Newstead View –

The plastic bags and the dog shit.

You go up the path. You knock on 54 –

No answer.

You knock again.

'Not your lucky day, is it?'

You turn round –

There are three men at the gate. They have pointed faces and pale moustaches. They are dressed in denim and grey. They are wearing trainers.

'I'm a solicitor,' you say.

They rock back and forwards on their heels. They spit.

'You look like a fat cunt to me.'

'A fat cunt who can't keep his hands to himself.'

'Fat cunt who's going to get his head kicked in.'

They walk up the path towards you.

You swallow. You say: 'I know who you are.'

'And we know who you are,' they laugh.

You look across the road –

The neighbours paired up, arms and brows folded –

You shout: 'Will someone please call – '

The nearest man punches you hard in the face.

You put your hands up to your nose.

They grab your hair. They pull you off the step. They punch you in the stomach.

You fall forwards.

They knee you in the stomach. They hit you with a dustbin lid.

You fall on to the garden path.

They kick you in the back. They kick you in the front.

You put your hands and arms over your head. You curl up.

They smash the dustbin lid down into your head. Into your back.

You try to crawl down the path.

They grab your hair. They pull you down the path.

You reach up to your scalp.

They drop you by the gatepost. They jump on you.

You –

They close the gate in your face. Repeatedly.

'Mr Piggott?' Kathryn Williams is walking across the *Yorkshire Post* reception –

No outstretched hand today –

'What on earth happened to you?'

You are swollen and wrapped in bandages. You pull yourself up out of your seat: 'Wrong place, wrong time.'

Kathryn Williams stares at you. She says: 'You should be in hospital.'

'A mental hospital?'

She doesn't smile. She asks: 'What can I do for you, Mr Piggott?'

'Miss Williams, I – '

'*Mrs* Williams,' she says.

'OK, *Mrs* Williams,' you say. 'It's about Jack Whitehead.'

'Mr Piggott, I told you everything I know about Jack – '

'You didn't tell me about the flat.'

'The flat?'

'On Portland Square.'

'I – ' she starts then stops.

You say: '*I* what?'

'I thought he was still in Stanley Royd.'

'Well, he ain't.'

'He's at home?'

'If he is,' you say. 'He's not answering his door.'

'You're sure he's not back in Stanley Royd.'

'He was signed out into the care of his son on New Year's Eve, 1980.'

'His *son*?'

You nod. It hurts.

Mrs Williams asks: 'You know where the son took him?'

'The flat on Portland Square.'

'But there's no answer?'

You shake your head. It hurts.

She asks: 'You went today?'

'Yesterday.'

'Maybe they were just out?'

'Maybe.'

'You going round there again?'

You nod. It hurts. You stop.

She stares at you again. She says: 'This isn't just about Jack, is it?'

'Not just Jack, no.'

She closes her eyes –

The two of you stood there in the middle of the *Yorkshire Post* reception area.

You say: 'I read your piece on Hazel and Susan Ridyard. I went to Rochdale.'

She opens her eyes –

The two of you stood in the middle of the *Yorkshire Post* reception area, one of you swollen and wrapped in bandages –

Both of you in pain.

Off Calverley Street, tucked between Portland Way and Portland Crescent, up by the Poly and opposite the Civic Hall, it's still raining:

Raining on the ruined grandeur, ill-gotten, squandered and
damned –

Raining on Portland Square:

Mrs Williams and you tip-toe through the grass and weeds, the
cracks and the stones; the pair of you picking your way along
the terrace until you come to number 6, the front door still wide open
and the tree still standing.

You walk up the three stone steps and through the front door –

You call out: 'Hello? Hello?'

Still no answer.

You walk up the staircase on the left, over the leaves and the crisp
packets, the unopened post and the papers, up the stairs to the first
floor and Flats 3 and 4, cross the landing and up the second flight of
stairs to Flats 5 and 6.

You stand before the door. You look at Mrs Williams. She shrugs.

You try the bell.

No answer.

You knock. You shout: 'Hello? Hello?'

No answer.

You squat down. You lift the flap. 'Mr Whitehead? Jack Whitehead?
Anybody?'

No answer.

You let the flap go. You stand back up. You point down at the single
word someone has scratched into the metal flap of the letterbox:

Ripper.

You show her the numbers on the door –

The number someone has scratched either side of the six:

6 **6** 6.

'Be kids,' says Kathryn Williams.

'Or their dads.'

'Is it locked?' she whispers.

You press your fingertips into the wood and the door swings in and
the smell runs to greet you; a tongue warm with saved spit and an
unexpected bark that brings new tears to your black eyes.

She takes one step backwards. You take one step forwards –

This is the way.

You step inside. You can see the light at the end of the passage –

Through the old smells and the new, down the passage to his
room –

Jack's room:

Curtains billowing through the open and cracked windows, black
sails –

The books and the papers scattered to the wind, their pages turning –

The spools and the tapes, streamers from an abandoned street party –

The suit and the shirts, the shoes and the socks, all spilling out from the chests of drawers, the stately wardrobes –

The sheets and the blankets, the pillow on the bed, stained and as cracked as the ceiling and the pelmets above –

Above the photographs and the words –

The photographs upon the floor, the words upon the wall.

You stand in Jack's room and remember another room –

Room 27, the Redbeck Café and Motel:

The first and last time you met Jack Whitehead.

You remember the photographs and words upon those walls:

Clare Kemplay, Susan Ridyard, and Jeanette Garland.

Through the old tears and the new, down all those passages to that room and this –

This the place.

A mirror in four pieces, a stool with three legs –

A telephone dead in two halves, a clock stopped at 7.07 –

The time.

You swallow. You wipe your eyes –

Kathryn Williams is staring at a photograph on the mantelpiece –

A photograph of a young, handsome man with a bright, wide smile.

'You know him?'

Her bottom lip is trembling, fingers pinching the end of her nose.

'Who is it?'

'Eddie,' she says –

New tears streaming down another old face. 'Eddie Dunford.'

It is night now.

You drive alone from Leeds into Wakefield, through the dead centre and out along the Donny Road, heading towards the Redbeck –

This the place, the time –

Tuesday 14 June 1977:

'Fuck is this place?' you said stood in the doorway, two teas in your hands, a chip butty in your pocket.

'Just somewhere,' smiled Bob Fraser.

'How long you had it?'

'It's not really mine.'

'But you got the key?'

'It's for a friend.'

'*Who?*'
'*That journalist, Eddie Dunford.*'
Haunted:
1977 all over again –
This the time, the place –
The Redbeck:
There was a knock on the door, you jumped.
Bob went to the door: 'Who is it?'
'*Jack Whitehead. Let me in, it's pissing down out here.*'
Bob opened the door and in Jack stepped.
'*Fuck,*' *Jack said, looking at the walls, the words and the photographs.*
'*I'm John Piggott,*' *you said. 'I'm Bob's solicitor.*'
But Jack was still looking at the walls, the photographs and the words –
Haunted:
The words –
Jack Whitehead, Bob Fraser and Eddie Dunford –
Haunted:
The photographs –
Clare Kemplay, Susan Ridyard, and Jeanette Garland –
Haunted:
The photograph in your pocket –
Hazel.
You've got a photograph and a key in your pocket –
This the place –
The Redbeck;
The time –
1983.

You pull in behind the Redbeck –
  There is one other car parked in the depressed, coarse car park.
  A man is sat alone in the car –
  It is an old Viva.
  He is watching the row of deserted rooms –
  He has his headlights on.
  They are shining on a door –
  A door banging in the wind, in the rain.
  You don't stop. You put your foot down –
  Ninety miles an hour.

Haunted, old ghosts and new –
  Tapping against the pane;
  You are lying on your back alone –

Branches tapping against the pane;

You are lying on your back alone, swollen and wrapped in bandages –

The branches tapping against the pane;

You are lying on your back alone, swollen and wrapped in bandages, your mouth open –

Listening to the branches tapping against the pane;

You are lying on your back alone, swollen and wrapped in bandages, your mouth open, contorted and screaming and howling, listening to the branches tapping against the pane –

Wishing she was here with you now:

Thursday 2 June 1983 –

D-7.

Chapter 36

The Black Angel, the hair in his eyes and the blood on his teeth, he is standing by the window in the Church of the Abandoned Christ –

They come for BJ on Tuesday night.
    They kick in door, splinters of wood and sevens flying.
    They grab BJ.
    They slap BJ.
    They punch BJ.
    They kick BJ.
    They cuff BJ.
    They gag BJ.
    They put a bag on BJ's head.
    They drag BJ from room.
    They throw BJ down stairs.
    They kick BJ across Spencer Place.
    They toss BJ in back of a van.
    They slam doors.
    They drive away with BJ.
    They whisper.
    They light cigarettes.
    They burn BJ through shirt and trouser legs.
    They laugh when BJ scream.
    They laugh as BJ choke upon gag.
    They slow down.
    They stop.
    They open doors of van.
    They punch BJ.
    They kick BJ.
    They push BJ out of back of van.
    They throw BJ through a wooden gate.
    They pick BJ up off floor.
    They drag BJ up some stairs.
    They bounce BJ down some corridor walls.
    They stand BJ in a room.
    They whisper.
    They kick BJ in balls.
    They laugh when BJ fall to knees in pain.
    They pick BJ up off floor.

They sit BJ on a chair.
They tie BJ to it, hands cuffed behind and a bag on BJ's head.
They leave BJ.

The Black Angel, the hair in his eyes and the blood on his teeth, he is standing by the window in the Church of the Abandoned Christ on the seventh floor of the Griffin Hotel in the ghost bloodied old city of Leodis.

'Skin the cunt alive!' he screams into BJ's blindfolded face.
BJ pass out in a pool of BJ's own piss.

The Black Angel, the hair in his eyes and the blood on his teeth, he is standing by the window in the Church of the Abandoned Christ on the seventh floor of the Griffin Hotel in the ghost bloodied old city of Leodis. His clothes are shabby and his wings are burnt.

They slap BJ's face.
BJ awake inside bag.
They slap BJ again.
BJ nod.
They kick chair.
BJ try to speak through gag.
They laugh.
BJ cry.

The Black Angel, the hair in his eyes and the blood on his teeth, he is standing by the window in the Church of the Abandoned Christ on the seventh floor of the Griffin Hotel in the ghost bloodied old city of Leodis. His clothes are shabby and his wings are burnt. There is a white towel upon the bed.

There is light.
Maybe it is morning.
There is bright light.
BJ's mouth dry and cracked on gag, wrists cut and bleeding from handcuffs.
Piss has dried upon BJ's crotch, upon BJ's trousers.
Maybe BJ be alone in room.
BJ move slightly toward light.
Telephone rings.
Footsteps coming.
BJ drop down head.
Someone picks up phone.

A voice, a voice BJ know saying: 'Eric, you worry too much.'
I got to think –
'Don't say a bloody word, Eric.'
Think, think fucking fast:
'Eric for fuckssake.'
Eric Hall, Bradford Vice; dirty every which way, dealing drugs with Spencer Boys, pimping Karen Burns and Janice Ryan; Janice stepping out with Bobby the Bobby Fraser, Leeds Murder Squad and son-in-law of Badger Bill; Janice dead, some saying Eric, some saying Bobby, some saying Leeds bloody Ripper.
'Eric, I know Peter Hunter and he's not a problem.'
Peter Hunter, White Knight; Mr Manchester Clean.
'Yeah, that's what I say and you'll do what I fucking say.'
Eric shitting bricks.
'Eric, don't fucking start.'
I got to think, think –
'Eric, we're the only friends you've got,' he says. 'So stop fucking around.'
Think, think fucking fast:
'Or we'll start fucking around with you.'
They got BJ over Morley or they got BJ over Jack?
Long pause, then: 'I know you are. We all are.'
They gonna kill BJ or they gonna not?
'No, you're not.'
I got to think, think, think –
'It won't come to that.'
Think, think fucking fast:
'We'll look after you.'
Eric Hall already dead.

The Black Angel, the hair in his eyes and the blood on his teeth, he is standing by the window in the Church of the Abandoned Christ on the seventh floor of the Griffin Hotel in the ghost bloodied old city of Leodis. His clothes are shabby and his wings are burnt. There is a white towel upon the bed. He draws the curtains and places the wicker chair in the centre of the room.

Head down, out for count.
Same voice, same phone: 'It's me.'
Me: West Yorkshire Metropolitan Police Force.
'He's still out.'
Someone keeping BJ alive; someone, somewhere.
'Eric called.'

Eric, Eric, Eric.
'Hunter the Cunt.'
Peter Hunter, White Knight.
'Eric's Bob's mate; I say Bob does it.'
Bob: Craven, Douglas, or Fraser?
'Yeah? Where?'
Please god, no –
'Bring him here.'
Fuck –
'Now.'
Fuck, fuck –
'Tonight.'
Fuck, fuck, fuck.

The Black Angel, the hair in his eyes and the blood on his teeth, he is standing by the window in the Church of the Abandoned Christ on the seventh floor of the Griffin Hotel in the ghost bloodied old city of Leodis. His clothes are shabby and his wings are burnt. There is a white towel upon the bed. He draws the curtains and places the wicker chair in the centre of the room. He takes off my shirt.

They are coming –
    They are coming –
    They are coming into room –
    They are here:
    They shout: 'Wakey, wakey.'
    They kick BJ's chair.
    They slap BJ's head.
    They take bag off.
    BJ blink in light, bright morning light –
    Joe says: 'What the fuck – '
    They grab Joe.
    They slap Joe.
    They punch Joe.
    They kick Joe.
    They cuff Joe.
    They gag Joe.
    They kick Joe in balls.
    They laugh when Joe falls to his knees in pain.
    They pick Joe up off floor.
    They sit Joe on a chair.

They tie Joe to it, his hands cuffed behind him and a bag on his head.

They put bag back on BJ's head.

They leave Joe and BJ.

The Black Angel, the hair in his eyes and the blood on his teeth, he is standing by the window in the Church of the Abandoned Christ on the seventh floor of the Griffin Hotel in the ghost bloodied old city of Leodis. His clothes are shabby and his wings are burnt. There is a white towel upon the bed. He draws the curtains and places the wicker chair in the centre of the room. He takes off my shirt. He picks up the razor.

BJ awake:

It is still light.

Joe must be near, in room somewhere.

BJ try to see him, see him through bag.

But BJ can't and light is fading –

Fading fast.

The Black Angel, the hair in his eyes and the blood on his teeth, he is standing by the window in the Church of the Abandoned Christ on the seventh floor of the Griffin Hotel in the ghost bloodied old city of Leodis. His clothes are shabby and his wings are burnt. There is a white towel upon the bed. He draws the curtains and places the wicker chair in the centre of the room. He takes off my shirt. He picks up the razor. He finishes and he blows the loose hair away.

BJ awake:

It is dark now.

Joe must be near, in room somewhere.

BJ try to hear him, hear him breathing.

But BJ can't and telephone is ringing –

Ringing long and loud.

The Black Angel, the hair in his eyes and the blood on his teeth, he is standing by the window in the Church of the Abandoned Christ on the seventh floor of the Griffin Hotel in the ghost bloodied old city of Leodis. His clothes are shabby and his wings are burnt. There is a white towel upon the bed. He draws the curtains and places the wicker chair in the centre of the room. He takes off my shirt. He picks up the razor. He finishes and he blows the loose hair away. He picks up a Philips screwdriver and a ball-peen hammer.

A light goes on, telephone stops:

Head down –
Someone picks up phone.
Out for count.
That voice, that voice BJ know saying: 'Yes?'
Fuck –
'When?'
Fuck, fuck –
'We'll be waiting.'
Fuck, fuck, fuck.

The Black Angel, the hair in his eyes and the blood on his teeth, he is standing by the window in the Church of the Abandoned Christ on the seventh floor of the Griffin Hotel in the ghost bloodied old city of Leodis. His clothes are shabby and his wings are burnt. There is a white towel upon the bed. He draws the curtains and places the wicker chair in the centre of the room. He takes off my shirt. He picks up the razor. He finishes and he blows the loose hair away. He picks up a Philips screwdriver and a ball-peen hammer. He stands behind me.

They are coming –
   They are coming –
   They are coming into room –
   They are here:
   They shout: 'Wakey, wakey.'
   They kick BJ's chair.
   They slap BJ's head.
   'Put your masks on,' says one of them. 'And take their bags off.'
   They take bag off.
   BJ blink in light, light from single light bulb.
   'Take their gags off.'
   They take gag off.
   Joe says: 'What the fuck – '
   They punch Joe.
   BJ know where this place be:
   Flat above shop on Bradford Road –
Flat above shop where two men are tied up and bleeding under a single light bulb; three men in overalls and masks with hammers and wrenches stood over Joe and BJ.

The Black Angel, the hair in his eyes and the blood on his teeth, he is standing by the window in the Church of the Abandoned Christ on the seventh floor of the Griffin Hotel in the ghost bloodied old city of Leodis. His clothes are shabby and his wings are burnt. There is a white towel upon the bed. He draws the

curtains and places the wicker chair in the centre of the room. He takes off my
shirt. He picks up the razor. He finishes and he blows the loose hair away. He
picks up a Philips screwdriver and a ball-peen hammer. He stands behind me.
He puts the point of the screwdriver on the crown of my skull.

They grab Joe's face in their hands.
    They say: 'You been a busy boy, haven't you, Joseph?'
    BJ can hear them laughing beneath their masks.
    They step closer to Joe: 'Wonder why that would be?'
    They laugh: 'Bit quiet about it.'
    They say: 'That's not very polite, is it?'
    'Not very polite at all,' they say.
    'Have to teach him some manners then, won't we?' they hiss.
    'We will,' they nod.
    'Take his trousers down,' they say.
    Joe is squirming in his chair and bindings: 'Please – '
    They take his trousers down.
    They take out hammer.
    Joe is squirming and shaking, cock small and eyes big: 'There's no
need . . .'
    They lift hammer above their head and say: 'Oh, but you see there's
always a need . . .'
    They bring hammer down into top of his right knee –
    'Always a need for manners, Joseph.'
    Joe is screaming.
    BJ howling.
    They lean into Joe's face and say: 'Gledhill Road, Morley. Whose
idea was that?'
    Joe is shaking. Joe is crying.
    They ask him: 'You still work for Eric, do you?'
    Joe is wide-eyed –
Following them and their hammer as they pace beneath single
white bulb –
    Joe not daring to blink.
    'Joseph,' they say. 'Who set it up?'
    Joe is opening and closing his stupid fat lips.
    'You do know who it was?'
    Joe is nodding.
    They lean down into his face and hiss: 'So tell us.'
    Joe is sniffing and Joe is stammering: 'The one in Morley?'
    'Yes?'
    'Eric, it was Eric.'

'Eric?'

Joe is nodding and nodding and nodding.

'No-one else?'

'No.'

'You didn't think it up all on your lonesome, did you?'

'No.'

'Didn't think you'd use the money to get away, did you?'

'No.'

'Get away from your obligations, your commitments?'

'No.'

'To us? To your friends?'

'No.'

'Not to drop your friends in the shit and do a runner; that not your plan?'

'No.'

'Payback?'

And Joe Rose looks up at BJ for a split fucking second –

A split fucking second in which he ends his life.

The Black Angel, the hair in his eyes and the blood on his teeth, he is standing by the window in the Church of the Abandoned Christ on the seventh floor of the Griffin Hotel in the ghost bloodied old city of Leodis. His clothes are shabby and his wings are burnt. There is a white towel upon the bed. He draws the curtains and places the wicker chair in the centre of the room. He takes off my shirt. He picks up the razor. He finishes and he blows the loose hair away. He picks up a Philips screwdriver and a ball-peen hammer. He stands behind me. He puts the point of the screwdriver on the crown of my skull. He brings the hammer down –

Down for a second time –

Down for a third –

Until they say: 'He's dead.'

He looks up at single, blood-specked light bulb and then down at man tied up and soaked in blood under it; two other men in overalls and masks with hammers and wrenches stood over Joe –

He takes off his mask and he looks at BJ, stares at BJ –

Tied up and splattered in Joe Rose's blood under a single white light bulb.

He comes towards BJ.

He takes BJ's face in his hands.

He wipes away Joe's blood with BJ's tears.

He kisses BJ's forehead and he kisses BJ's cheek.

He takes a photograph from inside his overalls.
He shows it to BJ.
It is BJ's mother.
BJ mouth open and –
He puts a finger to BJ's lips.
He says: 'I think you need a new friend, Barry.'
BJ nod.
He says: 'Can I be your friend?'
BJ nod.
He taps photograph of BJ's mother: 'I'll help you then.'
BJ nod.
'Will you help me?'
BJ nod.
'Will you go to the Spencer Boys for me?'
BJ nod.
'Will you tell them Joe is dead?'
BJ nod.
'Will you tell them Eric Hall killed him?'
BJ –
'Will you?'
BJ –
He taps photograph again: 'I'll help you, if you help me.'
BJ –
'Isn't that what friends are for?'
Head bobbed and wreathed, BJ nod –
It is 1977 –
Not heaven.

Chapter 37

The family gone –

The telephone is ringing and ringing and ringing.

I don't answer it –

I haven't time.

Sunday 26 March 1972:

'I think about you –'

Crawling through Huddersfield and on to the M62, over the moors and on to Rochdale, the stage bare but for the wraiths and the sheep, the pylons and the pile-ups, the sky black:

'Heath names Roman Catholic as Minister of State in Northern Ireland as strikes cripple Ulster and soldiers face angry Protestant crowds and buildings blaze . . .'

I switch off the radio, talking to myself:

'Susan Louise Ridyard, aged ten, missing seven days. Last seen at 3.55 p.m. on Monday 20 March outside Holy Trinity Junior and Infants School, Rochdale . . .'

The hard rain –

'She knows, Maurice. She knows.'

The wraiths and the sheep –

'She sees her.'

The pylons and the pile-ups –

'She's waiting for you.'

The sky black and only black –

'I think about you all the time.'

I pull up on the outskirts of Rochdale beside a telephone box. It is the colour of dried, spilt blood.

Fifteen minutes later and I'm parking two doors down from Mr and Mrs Ridyard's semi-detached home in a strained part of Rochdale –

Strained by the waiting ambulance, the two police cars and the men at the door.

It's pissing down and there's no sign of George.

Mr Ridyard is standing in the doorway talking to one of the uniforms.

I walk along the pavement and up their path, the rain in my face.

'Nice weather for ducks,' says Derek Ridyard.

I nod. I shake his hand. I show my warrant card to the uniform. I follow Mr Ridyard inside –

Through into their front room, dark with the rain –

Dark with their pain –

The seventh day:

Mrs Ridyard is sitting on the sofa in her slippers. She has her arms tight around her older son and other daughter, the children looking at the hands in their laps –

The patterns in the carpet.

'Sit down,' says Mr Ridyard. 'I'll make us a cup of tea.'

I sit down opposite the sofa. I smile at the kids. I look at Mrs Ridyard.

Mrs Ridyard is staring at the framed photograph on the top of the television –

The framed photograph of three children sat together in school uniforms, the older son and other daughter with their arms around the youngest girl:

Susan Louise Ridyard –

All big white teeth and a long fringe, smiling.

The framed photograph of two girls and one boy that'll become just one girl and one boy in the photographs on the sideboard, the photographs in the hall, the photographs on the wall, the one girl and one boy growing –

Always growing but never smiling –

Never smiling because of the little girl they'll leave behind on top of the TV, the little girl who'll be always smiling –

Never growing but always smiling:

Susan Ridyard –

The one they'll leave behind.

I look away out of the window at the new and detached houses across the road, the neighbours at their curtains, the rain hard against their windows.

'Here we are,' says Mr Ridyard, coming back in with the tea on a tray.

I smile.

Mr Ridyard puts down the tray. He looks up at me. He says: 'Sugar?'

'No, thank you.'

'Sweet enough already,' he says, quietly.

I try not to stare –

Not to stare at the woman on the sofa in her slippers, arms tight around her older son and other daughter.

I look away again out of the window at the new and detached houses across the road, the neighbours at their curtains, the rain hard against their windows –

That same rain hard against the Ridyards' leaking, rotting frames –

The only sound.

I say: 'My name is Maurice Jobson and I'm with Leeds CID. Three years ago a little girl called Jeanette Garland went missing over Castleford way and I was involved in that investigation – '

They are looking at me now –

The children blankly, their father intently –

Their mother, his wife nodding –

Nodding and saying: 'You never found her, did you?'

'Not yet, no.'

'Not yet?'

'The investigation is still open.'

There are trails of tears down Mrs Ridyard's face –

Trails of tears that leave red scars upon her cold, white skin.

Mrs Ridyard looks up through her tears and their trails –

Looks up through her tears and their trails with hate –

Hate and blame –

With hate and blame she looks into my face;

A face where she can see no trails of tears, no red scars upon my cold, white skin.

I say: 'Mrs Ridyard, I think you know where your daughter is.'

Silence –

The rain hard against her leaking, rotting frames, the only sound –

The only sound before she howls –

Her mouth open, contorted and screaming –

She howls –

Her bone-white fingers digging into the faces of her older son and daughter –

Her husband on his feet: 'What? What are you saying?'

I say: 'You see her, don't you?'

Howling –

Contorted and screaming, her mouth open –

Her face to the ceiling, her eyes wide with the pain –

The pain in the belly where she grew her –

Digging –

Digging bone-white fingers into the faces of her older son and daughter –

Shaking –

Shaking with tears, tears of sadness and tears of rage, tears of pain
and tears of –

Horror –

Horror and pain, rage and sadness, raining down between her
bone-white fingers, raining down between her bone-white fingers on to
her children, the children she clutches between her bone-white fingers
and broken arms, arms shaking with the tears, the tears of pain and the
tears of horror, the tears of sadness and the tears of rage, the tears for –

Susan –

All big white teeth and a long fringe, smiling.

I ask: 'Where is she?'

Her mouth open, contorted: *'Those beautiful new carpets – '*

Screaming: *'Under those beautiful new carpets – '*

And howling: *'I see her – '*

Bone-white fingers pointing through the trails of tears –

Pointing through her leaking, rotting frames –

The rain hard against their windows, all our windows –

Her husband on his feet, on his knees –

The children looking at the hands in their laps –

The patterns in the carpet –

The patterns that once were roads for their toys –

Roads now flooded with tears –

Mrs Ridyard pointing across the road –

She is pointing at the new and detached houses across the road –

The neighbours at their curtains, the rain hard against their
windows –

Their lights already on.

In their bathroom, the cold tap is running and I am washing my
hands –

'I think about you all the time –

Judith, Paul and Clare, unknown to me as to where they've gone or
how they are, if they'll come back or if they'll not; thinking of Mandy;
thinking of Jeanette and now Susan –

'Under the spreading chestnut tree –

The cold tap still running, still washing my hands –

'In the tree, in her branches –

Washing and washing and washing my hands –

'Where I sold you and you sold me –

Maurice Jobson; the *new* Detective Chief Superintendent Maurice
Jobson –

Stood before the mirror in their bathroom, stood behind these thick

lenses and black frames, stood staring back into my own eyes, into
me –

The Owl –

'I'll see you in the tree –

Outside the bathroom I can hear the woman's muffled and terrible
sobs, here amongst the smell of the pines, piss and excrement –

'In her branches.'

In the doorway, the uniform and I are looking at the detached houses
across the road.

'You checked them out, did you?'

He nods; cold, wet and insulted.

'When were they built?'

He shrugs; cold, wet and unsure. 'Couple of years ago.'

'Who by?'

'What?'

'Who built them?'

He shakes his head; cold, wet and stupid.

'You tell Mr Oldman and Mr Hill that Detective Chief Superintendent Jobson suggests they find out.'

He nods; cold, wet and humiliated.

Mr Ridyard steps into his doorway, red eyes up at the black clouds
above.

'Do wonders for the allotments, that,' he says.

'Imagine so,' I nod –

His daughter's little bones already cold and underground.

Beneath her shadows –

Dark hearts.

Kissing then fucking –

Cat piss and petunia, desperate on a sofa stripped of rugs and
cushions.

Fucking then kissing –

She has her head upon my chest and I'm stroking her hair, her
beautiful hair.

Behind the curtains, the branches of the tree tap upon the glass –

Wanting in.

'I thought I'd lost you,' I say –

'Never want to lose you,' I say.

The branches of the tree tapping upon the glass of her big
window –

Wanting in.

Laughing, she says: 'You couldn't lose me – '
Laughing, she whispers: 'Even if you wanted to.'
Sobbing, weeping –
Wanting in.
She kisses my fingertips and then stops, holding my fingers to the candlelight –
The ugly candlelight.
She lifts her face and says: 'You can find them, you know you can.'
But her face in the candlelight, her face is white and still dead –
Lost –
Sobbing, weeping –
Hearts –
Asking to be let in.

The windows look inwards, the walls listen to your heart –
Where one thousand voices cry.
Inside –
Inside your scorched heart.
A house –
A house with no doors.

I wake in the dark, beneath her shadows –
'I'll see you in the tree – '
Tapping against the pane.
She's lying on her side in a white bra and underskirt, her back to me –
Branches tapping against the pane.
I'm lying on my back in my underpants and socks, my glasses on the table –
The branches tapping against the pane.
Lying on my back in my underpants and socks, my glasses on the table, terrible tunes and words in my head –
Listening to the branches tapping against the pane.
I'm lying on my back in my underpants and socks, my glasses on the table, terrible tunes and words in my head, listening to the branches tapping against the pane.
I look at my watch –
'In her branches.'
Past midnight.

I reach for my glasses and get out of the bed without waking her and I go through into the kitchen, a paper on the mat, and I put on the light and fill the kettle and light the gas and find a teapot in the cupboard and two cups and saucers and I rinse out the cups and then dry them and then take the milk out of the fridge and I pour it into the cups and put two teabags in the teapot and take the kettle off the ring and pour the water on to the teabags and let it stand, staring out of the small window, the kitchen reflected back in the glass, a married man undressed but for a pair of white underpants and glasses, these thick lenses with their heavy black frames, a married man undressed in another woman's flat at six o'clock in the morning –

Monday 27 March 1972.

I put the teapot and cups and saucers on a tray and take it into the big room, stopping to pick up the paper, and I set the tray down on the low table and pour the tea on to the milk and I open the paper:

POLICE CHIEF'S SON KILLED IN CRASH
George Greaves, Chief Reporter

The son of top local policeman George Oldman was killed when the car his father was driving was involved in a head-on collision with another vehicle on the A637 near Flockton, late Saturday night.

Detective Superintendent Oldman's eldest daughter was also described as being in a serious condition in intensive care at Wakefield's Pinderfields Hospital. Mr Oldman and his wife, Lillian, and their other daughter were being treated for minor injuries and shock and it was believed they would be discharged later today.

The driver of the other vehicle is described as being in a serious but stable condition, although police have yet to release the driver's name.

It is believed that Mr Oldman and his family were returning from the wedding reception of another policeman when their car collided with a vehicle travelling in the opposite direction.

Mr Oldman's son John was eighteen.

'What is it?' says Mandy behind me –

I hold up the paper.

She says nothing –

'You knew?' I ask.

Nothing –

Just the branches tapping against the pane, whispering over and over:

'We'll see you in the tree, in her branches.'

Part 4
There are no spectators

'There are truths which are not for all men, nor for all times.'
— Voltaire

Chapter 38

You can't sleep; you can't sleep; you can't sleep –

Your head hurts, your mouth hurts, your eyes hurt;

But you drive; drive all night; drive in circles –

Circles of hell; local, local hells:

'The mother of the missing Morley child, Hazel Atkins, yesterday renewed her appeal for information about the disappearance of her ten-year-old daughter.

' "I know in my heart that Hazel is alive and that someone somewhere is keeping her. I would like to ask that person to please bring Hazel home to her family and we will help you in any way we can. But we need you to bring her home today because we miss her very, very much."

'Hazel disappeared on her way home from school in Morley three weeks yesterday. Police have made a number of arrests since that day but have yet to charge anyone in connection with the case nor have they had any confirmed sightings of the missing girl since her disappearance on May 12.'

It is Friday 3 June 1983 –

You can't sleep because you hurt; you hurt so you drive; you drive in circles;

Circles of tears; local, local tears:

D-6.

Shangrila –

An enormous white bungalow lain bare on a wet black hill.

You walk up the drive, past the goldfish and the new Rover, the rain on your bandages and your bruises.

You press the doorbell. You listen to the chimes.

It is six-thirty and the milk is on the doorstep.

The door opens –

He is in his silk dressing-gown and best pyjamas. He blinks. He says: 'John?'

'Clive.'

'Look like you've been in the wars, John?'

'I have,' you tell him. 'A fucking long one and it isn't over.'

'That which doesn't kill us – '

'Fuck off, Clive.'

McGuinness looks at you. He says: 'So what brings you out to my house at six-thirty on a Friday morning, John?'

'Answers, Clive. I want some fucking answers.'

'And you can't just pick up a bloody phone and set up a meeting like anyone else, can you?'

'No.'

'John, John,' he sighs. 'He was guilty. He hung himself. End of fucking story.'

You don't say anything.

'Give it up as a bad job, mate.'

You wait.

'OK?' he says.

You cough. You turn. You spit once on his drive.

'I'll take that as a yes, shall I?' he says. 'Now if you don't bloody mind, John, I want to get dressed and have my breakfast. Some of us have still got an office to go to.'

You have your foot in his door. You say: 'Michael Myshkin.'

'What?'

'I'm here about Michael Myshkin, Clive.'

'What about him?'

'He's appealing. I'm representing him.'

He looks at you.

'What?' you say. 'Didn't Maurice Jobson tell you?'

He blinks.

'Not had a falling out, have you? You and the Chief?'

'What do you want, John?'

'I told you; answers.'

He swallows. He says: 'I haven't heard any questions yet, John.'

You smile. You say: 'Well, I've heard quite a few about you, Clive.'

'From Michael Myshkin?'

You nod.

'So fucking what?' he says. 'He did it. He confessed.'

'Just like Jimmy.'

'Yes,' he says. 'Just like Jimmy.'

'Except Michael tells me that he didn't do it. That his confession was gained under duress. That he told you this. But Michael says you advised him to stick to the confession. That you would help him. That he would only stay in prison for a short time.'

'He did it, John.'

'You were his solicitor, Clive. You were supposed to advise him of his legal rights. You were supposed to defend him.'

'He –'

'Protect him.'

'Look,' he shouts. 'He *fucking* did it.'

You shake your head.

'There was forensic evidence, John. Witnesses.'

You shake your head.

'You know what hypogonadism is, do you, John? It means your balls don't grow. That's what Myshkin had. Doctors shot him full of fucking hormones. Cranked him up to ten. Poor bastard couldn't control himself. Week before he did what he did to that poor little lass, he was wanking himself off in front of two teenage girls in the fucking graveyard next to Morley Grange Infants. He did it. He might not have been able to help himself, John, but he did it. He fucking well did it.'

You stand on his doorstep, the rain in your bandages and your bruises. You say: 'What were their names, Clive?'

'Who?'

'The girls in the graveyard.'

'I can't remember, John,' he sighs. 'Be in the court records.'

'He pleaded guilty, Clive. They were never called. Remember?'

'For the life of me, after all these years, John, I couldn't tell you.'

You look into his eyes, look into the lies –

The lies and the greed –

The stains from the hours before the mirror:

The lies, the greed and the guilt.

'John, John,' he says. 'There's no need for it to be like this.'

'Be like what?'

'Just look at the state of you, man.'

You stare at him.

'Walk away, John,' he tells you. 'Walk away.'

You stare at him in his silk dressing-gown and his best pyjamas.

'There's nothing but pain here,' he says. 'Nothing but pain, John.'

'You're going to be the one in fucking pain, Clive.'

'I hope that's not a threat, John?'

'Call it a prediction.'

'In the fortune-telling business are you now, John?'

'And what business are you in, Clive?'

He starts to speak –

You say: 'How about the intention to pervert the course of justice business?'

He shrugs. He says: 'You do like your lost causes, don't you, John?'

You turn. You say: 'See you in court, Clive.'

'Don't doubt it, John,' he says. 'Don't doubt it.'

You walk down the drive, past the new Rover and the goldfish, the rain in your bandages and your bruises.

'Maurice told me about your father, John,' McGuinness shouts down the drive. 'Sounds like brave men run in your family.'

You stop. You turn round. You walk back up the drive.

He starts to close the door –

You start to run.

'Fuck off, John!'

You crash into the door. Into him –

'Fuck off – '

You have him by his silk dressing-gown and best pyjamas –

'Fuck – '

You clench your fists. You raise them. You look down at him –

He is struggling on the floor, wriggling –

Struggling and wriggling in his silk dressing-gown and best pyjamas –

Pleading with you:

'John, John – '

You pull him up towards you. You look at him –

'John – '

You spit in his face. You let him go.

He falls to the floor.

You walk away.

You park in the lay-by. You turn off the engine. You wait. You watch.

Twenty minutes later, the Rover pulls out of the end of the road.

You wait for a moment. You watch it go round the bend.

You turn on the engine. You follow the Rover:

Methley –

East Ardsley –

Tingley –

Bruntcliffe Road on to Victoria Road, left up Springfield Avenue –

Morley.

You pull up on Victoria Road. You turn the car around. You park opposite Morley Grange Junior and Infants School, in the shadow of the black steeple –

The graveyard.

You are facing Springfield Avenue. You get out. You lock the doors. You cross the road. You run back along Victoria Road. You turn up Springfield Avenue. You can see his new Rover parked outside a semi-detached house on the right. You walk back to your car. You get in. You wait. You watch.

Forty minutes later, the Rover comes out of Springfield Avenue. It turns left. It comes towards you.

You duck down in your seat –

McGuinness alone. McGuinness gone.

You get out. You lock the doors. You cross the road. You run back along Victoria Road. You turn up Springfield Avenue. You walk up the drive of the semi-detached house on the right. You knock on the door.

'Spot of afters,' she says as she opens the door. She is wearing a sleeveless black T-shirt and a pair of yellow knickers. Her mouth is open –

'Hello, Tessa,' you say.

She tries to shut the door in your face.

You put your foot in the way. You lean on the door. You force your way in. You slam the door shut.

'Fuck off,' she spits and picks up the phone. 'I'm calling – '

'Calling who?' you laugh. 'Your solicitor?'

You snatch the phone out of her hands. You rip the cord out of the wall.

'What do you want?'

You grab her hair. You tip her head back.

'You're hurting me!'

'You set Michael up. You set Jimmy up.'

'No!'

'Yes.'

'No!'

You wrap the telephone cord around the tops of her arms.

'Please . . .'

You pull it tight.

'It's not what it looks like,' she is saying. 'Not what you think.'

You knot it. You push her through into the front room. You throw her on the floor. You draw the curtains. You switch the TV off. You light a cigarette.

'John,' she says. 'Please, listen to me . . .'

You are stood over her.

'I know what you're thinking,' she whispers. 'But you're wrong.'

You shake your head. 'You called Jimmy.'

'No – '

'You told me you did.'

'No – '

'He came to meet you.'

'No – '

'The police were waiting for him.'

'No – '

'You planned it with McGuinness.'

'No – '

'You set him up.'

'No – '

'You set Jimmy up just like you set Michael Myshkin up.'

'No – '

'You had to, because it was you who told the police about Michael. It was you who said he exposed himself. You who said he'd been wanking in the graveyard.'

'It's – '

'You were one of the girls they were going to call.'

'I – '

You look down at her.

She nods.

You shake your head.

She looks away.

'How could you?' you say. 'How fucking could you?'

She looks up at you.

You look away.

'It was during summer holidays. Jimmy was working on the new houses. Michael used to pick him up from work in his van every night. We used to see them mucking around in churchyard. We started talking to them, me and some of the others. Michael could get us booze and cigs from off-licence. Used to all get pissed. Just mucking about in churchyard. I started to go out with Jimmy. But Michael was always about because of his van and fact he could get us the booze and stuff. Jimmy used to say Michael had never had a girlfriend. Never been kissed or anything. Jimmy was dead rotten to him. Just used him. Teased him. Bullied him. Made Michael try and get off with some of the lasses or Jimmy would pay some of lasses to get off with Michael. It was fucking cruel, I know. But Michael wasn't bothered. He wasn't interested. He had eyes – '

You look down at her.

'He only had eyes for one girl.'

'No,' you say.

'He went on about her all the time.'

'No – '

'How he could save her.'

'No – '

'He had a photo – '

'How – '

'From his work.'

'No – '

'All the time – '

'No – '

'He'd look at it all the time – '

'No – '

'For hours.'

'No – '

'He talked to it.'

'Shut up!'

'It's the truth – '

'I don't believe you.'

'It's the truth, John!'

'Fuck off!' you shout. 'You ever actually see them together, did you?'

She looks up at you. She shakes her head.

'Rumours. Innuendo. Circumstantial fucking – '

'Not Clare,' she whispers.

You look at her.

'Jeanette.'

You close the door. You walk down the drive. Back down Springfield Avenue. You turn on to Victoria Road. You go back down the road towards the graveyard, the Church and the school. You cross the road. You take out your car keys. You unlock the car door. You open it –

'Help me,' she says –

A ten-year-old girl with medium-length dark brown hair and brown eyes, wearing light brown corduroy trousers, a dark blue sweater embroidered with the letter H, and a red quilted sleeveless jacket, holding a black drawstring gym bag –

'We're in – '

You fall backwards into the road –

An election van brakes –

A woman drops her shopping –

You lie in the road in a ball –

The rain falling through the dark quiet trees –

The rain in your bandages, the rain in your bruises –

A man shouts: 'Somebody call the police!'

You pull into the car park behind the Redbeck Café and Motel –

The Viva is gone –

Hazel too.

You park. You wait. You watch –

You watch the row of deserted rooms –
Their boarded glass, their padlocked doors.
You get out. You lock the car door. You walk across the car park –
That depressed, coarse car park –
Puddles of rain water and motor oil underfoot.
You walk across the rough ground to the bogs round the side –
They reek. The tiled floor covered in old, black piss. The mirror broken and the light smashed. The sink stained with brown water from a busted tap. There is one cubicle without a door, the toilet inside without a seat. The whole room engrossed in a thousand different inks and words of –
Hate.
Always hate, always –
Fear –
Fear and hate, hate and fear;
You've been here before –
Now you're back for more –
Always back to here;
This the place –
The place you never left:
Never left the motel room of a forgotten café on a tedious road in a barren place; the place you've been for the last six years –
Stolen wine/stolen time.
Piss on your bandages and down your trousers, you walk out of the toilets and along the row, past the broken windows and the graffiti, the mountains of rubbish and the birds and the rats that feast here, walking towards the door –
The door to one room in a row of disused motel rooms –
The door banging in the wind, in the rain –
You stop before the door:
Room 27 –
The place you've been for the last six years.
You pull open the door –
The room is dark and cold.
You step inside –
The remains of a devoured mattress against the window;
No light here –
No words upon the wall, no photographs –
Nothing but pain.
You walk across the floor –
Shattered furniture and splintered wood underfoot;
Walk across the floor to stand before the wall.

You take the photograph from your pocket –
A photograph made of paper, cut from paper, dirty paper;
You take the photograph and you stick it on the wall.
You sit down upon the base of the bed –
The relentless sound of the rain on the window and the door;
The door banging in the wind and the rain.
You close your eyes –
The Fear here –
The place you never left;
The dogs barking –
The Wolf at the door.

Chapter 39

It's Christmas and I'm coming up hill, swaying, bags in my hand. Plastic bags, carrier bags, Tesco bags. A train passes and I bark, stand in middle of road and bark at train. I am a complete wreck of a human being wearing a light green three-quarter-length coat with an imitation fur collar, a turquoise blue jumper with a bright yellow tank top over it and dark brown trousers and brown suede calf-length boots. I turn left and see a row of six deserted narrow garages up ahead, each splattered with white graffiti and their doors showing remnants of green paint, last door banging in wind, in rain. I hold open door and I step inside. It is small, about twelve feet square, and there is sweet smell of perfumed soap, of cider, of Durex. There are packing cases for tables, piles of wood and other rubbish. In every other space there are bottles; sherry bottles, bottles of spirits, beer bottles, bottles of chemicals, all empty. A man's pilot coat doubles as a curtain over window, only one, looking out on nothing. A fierce fire has been burning in grate and ashes disclose remains of clothing. On wall opposite door is written Fisherman's Widow *in wet red paint. I hear door open behind me and I turn around and I'm –*

In same room, always same room; ginger beer, stale bread, ashes in grate. I'm in white, turning black right down to my nails, hauling a marble-topped washstand to block door, falling about too tired to stand, collapsed in a broken backed chair, spinning I make no sense, words in my mouth, pictures in my head, they make no sense, lost in my own room, like I've had a big fall, broken, and no one can put me together again, messages: no-one receiving, decoding, translating.

'What shall we do for rent?' I sing.

Just messages from my room, trapped between living and dead, a marble-topped washstand before my door. But not for long, not now. Just a room and a girl in white turning black right down to my nails and holes in my head, just a girl, hearing footsteps on cobbles outside.

Just a girl –

Just a girl on my knees and he's come out of me. Now he's angry. I try to turn but he's got me by my hair, punching me casually once, twice, and I'm telling him there's no need for that, scrambling to give him his money back, and then he's got it up my arse, but I'm thinking at least it'll be over then, and he's back kissing my shoulders, pulling my black bra off, smiling at this fat cow's flabby arms, and taking a big, big bite out of underside of my left tit, and I can't not scream and I know I shouldn't because now he's going to have to shut me up and I'm crying because I know it's over, that they've found me, that this is how it ends, that I'll never see my daughters again, not now, not ever.

*

BJ wake up, sweating:

It is Saturday 27 December 1980.

BJ lie in bed and watch rain and lights and cracks in ceiling.

There's someone at door –

(Always someone at door) –

Someone knocking on door: 'Phone.'

'Ta,' BJ say. 'Ta very much.'

It is Saturday 27 December 1980 –

BJ back in Preston –

St Mary's Hostel:

Blood and Fire etched in stone above door.

'What?'

'Did you call him?'

'Yes.'

'And?'

'Tomorrow.'

'Where?'

'You know where.'

'You've got the picture?'

'I've got picture.'

BJ hang up and stand in institutional corridor. BJ's eyes black and lips raw, nose broken and hand bandaged. These green and cream walls defaced with insults and with numbers.

BJ staring at sevens, but they mean nothing now –

Not now in 1980 –

Now is time of sixes:

Six six sixes –

Illuminated.

BJ go back up steep stairs and walk down narrow corridor to room at end.

Door is open.

BJ go inside.

It is cold in here.

Light doesn't work.

BJ sit at table by window.

It is raining outside.

There are pools of water forming on windowsill.

A train goes past.

A dog barks.

The window shakes –

Rattles.

BJ wish BJ were dead.

Chapter 40

Saturday 14 December 1974:

100 miles an hour –
North up the motorway:
Never leave home, never leave home, never fucking leave home ever –
Through the night, screaming:
Noooooooooooooooooooooooooooooooooooooooooooooooooooooooooooooooooooooo!

8.15 a.m.

Millgarth, Leeds:
Up the stairs to my old office –
'He in?' I say to Julie, my old secretary –
Julie on her feet: 'He's in a meeting.'
'Who with?' I say, not waiting –
'Journalist from the *Post*.'
Fingers on the handle: 'Jack?'
'No.'
I let go of the handle.
'You'll have to wait,' she says.
'I can't.'
She nods. She picks up the phone on her desk. She presses a button.
I hear his phone buzz on the other side of the door.
'Thanks, love,' I say.
She smiles. She says: 'How's Bishopgarth?'
'Don't ask me. I was in London until three o'clock this morning.'
'Mr Oldman knows you're back?'
'If he's any bloody brains, he does.'
She shakes her head. She says: 'Won't you sit down.'
I look at my watch. 'I can't.'
She picks up the phone again. She presses the button. The phone
buzzes on the other side of the door.
'Thank you,' I say again.
The door opens a fraction. George is talking to someone inside. I
hear him say: 'You do your digging and I'll do mine.'
I look at my watch.
I hear George laugh, hear him say: 'Bismarck said a journalist was a
man who'd missed his calling. Maybe you should have been a copper,
Dunstan?'
I look at my watch again.

Julie presses the button. She keeps her finger on it.

George Oldman opens the door wide. He leads out a young man –

A young man I've never seen before.

'Not a word,' George is telling him. 'Not a bloody word.'

George lets go of the young man's hand.

The man walks off.

George Oldman turns to me. He's pissed off.

'Maurice,' he says with a sigh. 'Thought we'd have seen you sooner.'

'I was in London at the conference,' I say. 'Nobody told me. Nobody called.'

'Somebody must have – '

'I sleep with the fucking radio on, George.'

He smiles. 'What about them psychic contacts of yours?'

I ignore him. I walk past him into my old office.

He follows me inside.

I shut the door. I want to take my seat behind my desk. I don't –

He does. He says: 'It's Leeds, Maurice.'

'Jeanette Garland wasn't. Susan Ridyard wasn't.'

'You're as bad as that bloody journalist,' he spits –

'I'm not alone for once then?'

'Early days, Maurice, you know that,' he says. 'Early days.'

I shake my head. I say: 'It's been over five years, George.'

'Look in long run, it doesn't bloody matter who – '

'Long run?' I laugh. 'I'm the fucking long run, George. Not you.'

He sighs. He rubs his eyes. He looks at me across my old desk –

His eyes empty. His hands shaking. He says: 'What do you want to know?'

'Everything.'

He picks up a file off the desk. He flings it across at me. It lands on the floor. 'There you go,' he says.

I pick it up. I open it. I look at the photograph –

Clare Kemplay.

'Was there anything else?' he sighs.

I look up at him sat behind my desk. I tell him: 'I want in.'

'Talk to Angus,' he says. 'His call, not mine.'

'George – '

He stands up. 'I've got a fucking press conference in five minutes.'

The Conference Room, Millgarth Police Station, Leeds.

I stand at the back. I wait. I watch the faces –

Looking for the man who'd been upstairs with George.

There's a nudge to my ribs. I turn around –

'Jack,' I say. 'Just the man I wanted.'

'That's what all the girls say,' grins Jack, fresh whiskey on his breath.

'Thought it was someone else from the *Post* on this one?'

Jack laughs. He points down the front: 'You mean him?'

The young man from upstairs is talking and laughing with the rest of the pack –

Hounds, the lot of them.

'What's his name?'

'Scoop,' laughs Jack.

'Very funny, Jack,' I sigh. 'His fucking name please?'

'Edward Dunford, North of England Crime Correspondent.'

'Thought that were you?'

Jack rolls his red eyes. 'Crime Reporter of the Year, if you don't mind.'

'And I can see why,' I say. I look at my watch:

Nine.

Down the front the side door opens:

Everyone quiet as Dick Alderman, Jim Prentice, and Oldman troop out.

'Here,' whispers Jack. 'Your Mandy got any messages for us, has she?'

'Fuck off,' I hiss and leave him to it –

The whole bloody lot of them.

I go up the stairs and along the corridor –

Lots of nods and handshakes and pats on the back as I go.

In the Leeds half of the Incident Room, a familiar face:

John Rudkin in a bright orange tie –

'Boss,' he says. 'They let you out then?'

'Day release.'

'How are you?' he asks.

'Who can say?'

He nods –

Both staring across at the enlarged photograph of another missing schoolgirl –

Trapped in the claws of Time –

Tacked up on the far wall between a map of Morley dotted with pins and flags and a blackboard covered in chalk letters and numbers, her physical measurements and a description of her clothing –

Orange waterproof kagool; dark blue turtleneck sweater; pale blue denim trousers with eagle motif on back left pocket; red Wellington boots –

A telephone is ringing:

Somewhere on the other side of the room someone picks it up. They shout something to Rudkin. John picks up the one on his desk. He listens. He looks up at me –

His face full of shadow –

He hands me the phone.

I swallow. I say: 'This is Maurice Jobson speaking.'

Mandy says: 'Maurice – '

The telephones all ringing at once, every single fucking one –

'Bloody wings – '

People picking them up –

'I've seen her – '

People shouting to Rudkin –

'Down by the prison – '

Rudkin picking them up one after another –

'In a ditch – '

Rudkin listening –

'She's dead – '

Rudkin looking at me –

'Maurice,' she's crying. 'Maurice – '

I drop the receiver –

'She had wings, bloody wings – '

The room, the building, the whole fucking place full of shadow:

The shadow of the Horns.

100 miles an hour back down the motorway –

I see her –

Lights and sirens –

Down by the prison –

Into Wakefield –

In a ditch –

My new patch –

She's dead –

Patch of sheer fucking, bloody hell.

Devil's Ditch, Wakefield –

In the shadow of the prison:

The wasteland beside the Dewsbury Road –

Across from St Michael's.

Drive straight on to the rough ground, two police cars already here –

More on their way;

Door open before the car's stopped –
Boots in the mud;
George barking at the uniforms –
My uniforms.
I'm out the car, my hand on his shoulder –
'You don't work round here any more,' I tell him. 'I do.'
'Fuck off, Maurice!' he shouts –
But I'm past him, waving at the gallery, telling my lads: 'Get them
out of here.'
Barking my orders to my boys –
360° as I cross the ground;
Oldman, Alderman, Prentice, Rudkin –
Everyone else in my wake;
Rain in our faces –
Cold and black.
180° I see it –
Big bold letters flapping in the piss:
Foster's Construction –
Cold and fucking black.
Another 180° and I'm there –
The edge of the ditch;
I stop –
Stop dead:
The air that I breathe, choking me –
The rain;
I look away –
Look up at the bloody grey sky;
I'm crying –
Tears, cold and fucking black;
The air that I breathe, killing me –
I drop to my knees, my hands together:
I see her –
I SEE HER NOW;
On my knees, hands together –
Praying:
In the shadow of his Horns –
Sleep, silent angel, go to sleep.

Dark times –
No darker day –
This Third Day:
Eleven in the morning –

Saturday 14 December 1974:

Yorkshire –

Wakefield:

Wood Street Police Station –

Down the long, long corridor –

Room 1:

Terry Jones, thirty-one, in his black wet donkey jacket at our table –

Terry Jones of Foster's Construction –

Terry Jones who was working on Brunt Street, Castleford, in July 1969 –

Terry Jones, working where we just found Clare Kemplay in December 1974.

I ask Terry Jones: 'So tell us again, Terry, what happened?'

And Terry Jones tells me again: 'Ask Jimmy.'

Back upstairs they're shitting fucking bricks, already talk of bringing in outside Brass, the fucking Yard even, like we're some gang of monkeys can't find our arses without a bloody map, and I'm wishing to Christ there'd been no amalgamation, no West Yorkshire fucking Metropolitan Police and –

'Maurice?'

Ronald Angus is looking at me –

Chief Constable Ronald Angus –

My Chief Constable.

I say: 'Pardon?'

'I said, George will do the Press Conference if you've no objections.'

I stand up. I say: 'None.'

'Where you going?' asks Angus.

'Well, if you've no objections,' I smile. 'I thought someone ought to try and catch the fucking cunt. If that is, you've no objections.'

Long dark times –

Endless dark day –

The Third Day:

Three-thirty in the afternoon –

Saturday 14 December 1974:

Yorkshire –

Wakefield:

Wood Street Police Station –

Down the long, long corridor –

Room 2:

We open the door. We step inside:

Dick Alderman and Jim Prentice –
One with a long moustache, the other one with fine sandy hair:
Moustache and Sandy.
And me:
Maurice Jobson; Detective Chief Superintendent Maurice Jobson –
Thick lenses and black frames –
The Owl.
And him:
James Ashworth, fifteen, in police issue grey shirt and trousers, long
lank hair everywhere, slouched in his chair at our table, dirty black
nails, dirty yellow fingers –
Jimmy James Ashworth of Foster's Construction –
Jimmy Ashworth, the boy who found Clare Kemplay.
'Sit up straight and put your palms flat upon the desk,' says Jim
Prentice.
Ashworth sits up straight and puts his palms flat upon the desk.
Prentice sits down at an angle to Ashworth. He takes a pair of
handcuffs from the pocket of his sports jacket. He passes them to Dick
Alderman.
Dick Alderman walks around the room. He plays with the
handcuffs.
I close the door to Room 2.
Dick Alderman puts the handcuffs over the knuckles of his fist. He
leans against one of the walls.
I sit down next to Jim Prentice, opposite Ashworth, watching his
face –
In the silence:
Room 2 quiet –
Jimmy Ashworth looks up. He sniffs. He says: 'You talk to Terry, did
you?'
I nod.
'He tell you same, did he?'
I shake my head. I say: 'One more time, Jimmy.'
He slouches back in his chair. He sighs. He picks at his dirty black
nails.
'Sit up straight and put your palms flat upon the desk,' says Jim
Prentice.
Ashworth sits up straight and puts his palms flat upon the desk.
I push an open pack of fags his way. I say again: 'One last time,
Jimmy.'
He sniffs. He flicks his fringe out of his face. He takes a cigarette.
Jim Prentice holds out a lighter.

Ashworth leans in for a light. He looks up across the table at me. He smiles.

I turn away. I nod at Dick Alderman.

Dick takes two small steps from the wall. Dick smacks Jimmy Ashworth hard across the face.

The boy falls from his chair on to the floor.

Dick leans down. Dick shows him his right fist, the handcuffs over his knuckles. Dick says to Jimmy Ashworth: 'Be this one next time, lad.'

Jim Prentice picks the scrawny little twat up off the floor. He plonks him back down in his seat.

'Are we ready now?' I ask.

'I told you,' he says.

I turn away. I look at Dick Alderman –

'No, no,' Ashworth screams. 'No, wait . . .'

We wait:

'I told you, we were hanging about for Gaffer. But he never come and it was raining so we were just arsing about, you know, drinking tea and stuff. I went over Ditch to have a waz and that's when I saw her.'

'Where was she, Jimmy?'

'Near top.'

'So what did you do?'

'I just froze, didn't I?'

'That's when Terry came over, is it?'

He nods.

'When you was all frozen?'

Jimmy Ashworth sniffs. He says: 'Yes.'

I turn away. I nod.

Dick takes two steps from the wall. Dick smacks Ashworth hard across the face.

Ashworth falls from his chair again on to the floor.

Dick leans down. Dick shows him his right fist, the handcuffs over his knuckles. Dick says: 'That was last with left, lad. I promise you.'

Jim Prentice picks the scrawny little twat up off the floor again. He plonks him back down in his seat.

'The truth please, Jimmy?'

'I must have gone back,' he moans. 'I can't remember exactly.'

'You want that gentleman over there to help jog that memory of yours, do you, Jimmy?'

'No, no,' he screams again. 'No, listen will you . . .'

We listen:

'I went back to shed, you're right. I was hoping Gaffer would be there because he'd know what to do. But it was just Terry, wasn't it?'

'What about the others?'

'They were off in van somewhere.'

'So you and Terry Jones, the two of you went back over to Ditch?'

He shakes his head. 'No. Terry told me to phone you lot.'

'So that was what you did?'

'Yes.'

'Which phone you use?'

'One on Dewsbury Road.'

'We'll check, you know that, don't you?'

He nods.

'Is that everything, Jimmy?'

Jimmy Ashworth nods again.

I look at Dick.

Dick shrugs.

I say: 'Thank you, Jimmy.'

Dick takes the handcuffs off his knuckles. He steps out into the corridor.

Jim Prentice stands up. He says: 'Good boy, Jimmy.'

I wait until he's out in the corridor with Dick. I lean across the table. I bring the lad's head towards me. I whisper into Jimmy's ear: 'One last question.'

Ashworth looks at me from under his fringe, his face swelling beneath his eyes.

I ask him: 'What's your Gaffer's name?'

'Mr Marsh,' he whispers back.

'George Marsh?'

He nods –

He nods. My heart pounds –

My heart pounds. My fists clench –

My fists clench. There is blood in my mouth.

I brush his long lank hair out of his face. I touch his cheek. I hold his cheek. I say: 'Good boy, Jimmy.'

He nods.

'Not a word,' I tell him. 'Not a word.'

He nods again.

I stand up. I step out into the corridor –

Dick and Jim are waiting.

I look at my watch –

It's almost five:

They'll be finishing the post-mortem –

The little thing cut to bits for a second time –

George Marsh sitting down for his tea.

I look up. I can hear footsteps coming down the corridor –

Familiar footsteps –

Bill Molloy coming towards me –

Retired Detective Chief Superintendent *Badger* Bill Molloy –

The black hair gone grey, his skin a terrible yellow.

I close the door to Room 2. 'Bill?' I say. 'What you doing here?'

Bill Molloy tries to see over my shoulder. He turns back to me. He winks: 'Helping hand, that's all.'

I lock the door. I dial *Netherton 3657*.

I listen to it ring. It stops –

'Netherton 3657, who's speaking please?'

'Is your dad there?'

'No, he's – '

'Where is he?'

'He's in hospital.'

'Hospital? What's wrong with him?'

'I'm not sure.'

'Which hospital?'

'I don't know.'

'Can I speak to your mam?'

'She's not here.'

'Where is she?'

'She's gone to see me dad.'

'When she gets back, will you – '

There's a knock at the door. I hang up.

Back upstairs with the brand-new West Yorkshire Metropolitan Police Brass, the brand-new West Yorkshire Metropolitan Police Brass in their nice new suits and polished shoes with their nice new sheepskins hanging by their trophies and their tankards, the West Yorkshire Metropolitan Police Brass with their beer guts and their wallets bulging in those nice new suits, the brand-new West Yorkshire Metropolitan Brass plus one ex-Brass:

Badger Bill Molloy –

The helping hand.

Plus one guest Brass:

Detective Superintendent Peter Noble –

The man who nicked Raymond Morris.

Ronald Angus, fingers in a church beneath his chin: 'The Hunslet gypsy camp – '

Fuck, I'm thinking –

'George,' says Angus. 'Would you care to brief the troops on the latest.'

Here we fucking go again:

'Witness has given us a positive sighting of a white Ford Transit in Morley last Thursday night. This witness has been shown photos taken by surveillance at the Hunslet camp of a similarly described van and we now have a positive ID. I've got officers over in Rochdale picking up the Lamberts who also made a statement about a white van and some gypsies spotted around the time of Susan Ridyard's disappearance,' pants Oldman.

'When we going to hit the bastards?' asks Dick.

'Midnight,' says Oldman.

Prentice: 'Bring the cunts back here?'

Oldman: 'Split them between here and Queen's.'

'Briefing will be downstairs at ten,' nods Angus. 'Anything else?'

Bill Molloy looks across the table. He says: 'You're very quiet, Maurice.'

'Not like you,' smiles Oldman.

'Not a crime, is it?' I say.

Bill looks at me. He says: 'It's a coincidence, Maurice.'

'What else could it be?' I nod –

In my nice new suit and polished shoes with my nice new sheepskin on the wall, my beer gut and my wallet bulging in that nice new suit –

I nod because there's nothing more to say –

They're going to die in this hell –

We all are.

I drive out of Wakefield –

Up to Netherton.

I park at the end of Maple Well Drive –

The night here now.

All the bungalows but one have their lights on –

All the bungalows but number 16.

I get out –

I walk along the road.

Their house dark –

No van parked outside.

I go up the path –

Fucking bird table on the small lawn;

I ring the doorbell:

No answer.

I try again –

No answer.
I go round the back –
The curtains not drawn;
No fire left on –
Nothing.
I go back down the path –
Back to the car.
I get in and I wait –
I wait and I watch;
Wait and watch –
Nothing.

It's gone nine when I turn into Blenheim –
Hearts cut, leaves lost;
I park in the drive. I open the car door. I spit –
That taste in my mouth;
I get out. I walk up the drive full of shallow holes and stagnant water –
Ugly moonlight and black rain;
The bottoms of my trousers, my socks and shoes, muddy –
Devil's Ditch.
I open the downstairs door. I go up the stairs. I knock on the door of Flat 5 –
'Maurice?'
'Yes,' I say. 'It's me, love.'
The door opens without the chain and there she is –
So truly fucking beautiful.
'I saw her,' she says.
I nod.
She takes my hand. She pulls me towards her –
'I can't,' I say.
She looks at me –
'I have to go back.'
'She had wings, Maurice. Bloody wings – '
I nod.
'I saw her.'
'I know.'
She squeezes my hand –
'I'll be back in a bit,' I say.
'Promise?'
'Cross my heart.'
She squeezes my hand again –

'Lock the door,' I tell her.

There are three envelopes on my desk. I sit down with an unlit cig. I open the top envelope. I pull out two sheets of typed A4 and three enlarged black and white photographs:

The post-mortem.

I wipe my eyes. I look at my watch:

Eleven-thirty –

Saturday 14 December 1974.

I reach for the phone book. I turn the pages. I find the number I want. I pull the telephone closer. I dial, a handkerchief over the mouthpiece.

The number rings. And rings –

'Ossett 256199. Who's speaking please?' a woman asks.

'Is Edward there?'

'Just a minute, please.'

There's a pause –

Beethoven down the other end of the line.

'Edward Dunford speaking.'

I ask him: 'Saturday night all right for fighting?'

'Who's this?'

I wait.

'Who is it?'

'You don't need to know.'

'What do you want?'

'You interested in the Romany Way?'

'What?'

'White vans and gyppos?'

'Where?'

'Hunslet Beeston exit of the M1.'

'When?'

'You're late,' I say. I hang up –

4 LUV.

Chapter 41

You are sat in the car park of the Balne Lane Library for the last time –

It is Saturday 4 June 1983:

The car doors locked, you are staring into the rearview mirror and then the wing; the rearview and then the wing; rearview and then wing –

The relentless sound of the rain on the roof, the radio on as loud as it can go:

'*200 arrests at USAF base at Upper Heyford in Oxfordshire; VC's widow accuses Healey of despicable and cheap conduct over his remarks about Mrs Thatcher and the Falklands; Dr Owen warns that the Tories need a constraining force to combat Mrs Thatcher and Norman Tebbit and that voters are afraid of Big Sister . . .*'

No Little Sister –

Rearview then wing; rearview wing; rearview:

Not today –

D-5.

The key turns in the lock and you are up the stairs two at a time, pulling the last box down from the shelf –

July 1969.

Threading film, winding spools –

STOP –

Monday 14 July 1969:

Local Girl Missing – by Jack Whitehead, Crime Reporter.

The parents of missing eight-year-old Jeanette Garland made an emotional plea late last night for information that might lead police to their daughter's whereabouts. Jeanette was last seen on Saturday on her way to buy sweets at a local shop.

Tuesday 15 July 1969:

Girl Vanishes, Fourth Day, All-out Hunt – by Jack Whitehead, Crime Reporter.

STOP –

Saturday 19 July 1969:

Medium Contacts Police – by Jack Whitehead, Crime Reporter.

STOP –

Back to the shelf, back to 1972 –

Friday 24 March 1972:

Medium Links Susan and Jeanette – by Jack Whitehead, Crime Reporter of the Year.

Police last night refused to comment or speculate on reports that local medium and TV personality Mandy Wymer had found a connection between the missing Rochdale schoolgirl Susan Ridyard and Jeanette Garland, known as the Little Girl Who Never Came Home, *who was eight years old when she disappeared from her Castleford street in 1969.*

STOP.

STOP.

STOP –

Into the library toilets, dry-heaving –

Your stomach burning, bleeding again –

You retch. You puke. You spew –

Knowing it'll soon be over, soon –

But you have to go back there:

Back to the room (back to all their rooms) –

Back to the shelf again (take them all down again):

The films, the spools –

STOP –

AGAIN –

Saturday 21 December 1974:

Murder Hunt – by Jack Whitehead, Crime Reporter of the Year.

A fresh murder hunt was launched in Wakefield today following the discovery of the body –

STOP –

AGAIN AND AGAIN –

Monday 23 December 1974:

RL Star's Sister Murdered – by Jack Whitehead, Crime Reporter of the Year.

Police found the body of Mrs Paula Garland at her Castleford home early Sunday morning, after neighbours heard screams.

STOP –

AGAIN AND AGAIN AND AGAIN –

You retch. Puke. Spew –

Blood in your mouth, blood on your shirt, blood on your hands –

Again and again and again –

Until it stops.

You drive through Wakefield and up the Barnsley Road, out of Wakefield and along the Doncaster Road, past the Redbeck into Castleford –

You pull up by a red telephone box. You get out. You walk over to the telephone box and open the door.

The phone is ringing.

You pick up the receiver. You listen –

There is a foreign voice on the other end;

You hang up. You wait –

No-one phones.

You stand in the red telephone box. You listen to the relentless sound of the rain on the roof of the telephone box. You watch the silent cars with all their killers at the wheel, watch them speed up and down the road, watch them point and laugh at you, missing children in their boots, tiny hands pressed to their back windows –

You pick up the receiver. You listen –

There's no-one there;

The world outside so sharp and full of pain.

Brunt Street, Castleford –

You've been here before.

The car stinks of sick. You wind the window down. You stare across at 11.

The red door opens. A woman comes out under a flowered umbrella. She locks the door behind her. She walks past the car, her boots on the wet pavement as she goes –

Down Brunt Street –

Echoing.

'Terrible,' says the old woman for the third time, her arms folded against the rain and the memories, the bruised and bandaged fat man on her doorstep.

You nod.

'Just seemed to be one bloody thing after another,' she says, shaking her head. 'All started with the little lass though.'

You nod again.

'If that'd never have happened,' she sighs. 'They could have had everything.'

And you nod again.

'But he goes and kills himself, husband. Next their Johnny, he starts getting in all kinds of bother, letting his talent go to waste. Then – '

You look up.

She is staring down the street. 'Then she's murdered, mother. Right there.'

You follow her pointing bones down the street to number 11.

'Right there on our own bloody doorstep,' she sighs again. 'I don't know.'

'Terrible,' you say.

'Terrible,' says the old woman across the road. 'Never same again, mother was.'

You shake your head.

'You wouldn't be, would you?'

You shake your head again.

'Lovely little lass,' she sighs, folding the tea-towel in her hands. 'Always so cheerful, she was. Always smiling.'

And you shake your head again.

'I mean,' she says. 'That's the thing about mongols, isn't it? Always happy, aren't they? I don't reckon they know – '

You look up.

She is staring across the road. 'They're lucky that way.'

You turn round and look across at the red door.

'Broad daylight it was,' she sighs again. 'Broad bloody daylight.'

'Terrible,' you say.

'Terrible,' says Mr Dixon, the man in the cornershop. 'Back then didn't used to open up until three of an afternoon so there always be a queue of kiddies and she'd be among them. Had to watch her with the money mind, being how she was.'

You nod.

'Wasn't there that last Saturday though,' he sighs. 'I remember that.'

You nod again, looking at the sweets and the crisps, the cigarettes and the alcohol, the pet food and the local papers.

You say: 'Heard husband topped himself?'

'Aye,' says Mr Dixon. 'Be a couple of years later, mind.'

You nod towards the door. 'In that house?'

Mr Dixon shakes his head. 'Wife would know, good with stuff like that she is. Know it wasn't here though.'

'The mother?' you ask. 'That was here though?'

Mr Dixon nods. 'Oh aye, that was here.'

'Not a very lucky family,' you say.

'This bloody street,' whispers Mr Dixon, the bloody street listening at the door. 'You know who else lived on here, don't you?'

You shake your head.

'The Morrisons,' he says. 'Clare and Grace?'

You stop shaking your head. You swallow. You stare. You wait.

'Grace was one of them that got shot when them blokes did over Strafford in centre of Wakey?'

'And Clare?'

'They thought Ripper did her, over in Preston,' he smiles. 'He's always denied it mind, has Ripper.'

'Clare Strachan,' you tell him.

He nods. 'That'd be her married name.'

'What about him?' you say. 'Ever see him round here?'

Mr Dixon takes the photo from you. He stares at the twenty-two-year-old face of Michael Myshkin –

Round and smiling.

Mr Dixon shakes his head. 'No,' he says. 'I'd remember him.'

You drive into Leeds. You park under the arches –

The Dark Arches;

Two black crows fighting with a fat brown rat over a bin-bag –

UK DK sprayed in white on a damp green wall;

You lock the car. You walk through the arches and out into the night –

It is Saturday 4 June 1983.

'You shouldn't keep coming here,' says Kathryn Williams. 'Folk'll start talking.'

'I wish they bloody would.'

'What do you mean?'

'Tell me what you know about Jeanette Garland.'

'I – '

'Her father?'

'John, I – '

'Her mother?'

'Please John, I – '

'Her uncle?'

Kathryn Williams is squeezing her hands together in her lap, her eyes closed.

'Her neighbour?'

She opens her eyes: 'Who?'

'Clare Strachan,' you say –

She stands up: 'Not here.'

You grab her arm –

She looks down at it. She says: 'You're hurting me.'

'Am I?'

'Please John, I – '

'I want to know if you think Michael Myshkin killed Jeanette Garland?'

'John, I – '

'Susan Ridyard?'

'I – '

'Clare Kemplay?'

She looks at you. She closes her eyes. She shakes her head.

The Press Club –

In the sights of the two stone lions –

Leeds City Centre:

Almost ten.

You are waiting outside in the rain.

They come along the road under two separate umbrellas.

'John Piggott,' says Kathryn Williams. 'This is Paul Kelly.'

Paul Kelly juggles his briefcase and umbrella to shake your hand.

'Thanks for agreeing to meet,' you say.

He looks at you. Your bandages and your bruises.

'He's had a bad week,' says Kathryn.

Paul Kelly shrugs. He opens the Press Club door:

Members Only.

'After you,' you say to Kathryn.

She smiles.

You follow her down the steps.

It is badly lit and half empty.

You sit down at a table against the far wall.

'What can I get you?' you ask them both.

'Nothing,' says Paul Kelly.

'You sure,' you say.

'You're not a member,' he smiles. 'They won't serve you.'

Kathryn Williams stands up. 'I'll get them.'

You hold out a fiver. 'At least let me pay.'

She waves it away: 'What do you want?'

'Bitter,' says Paul.

'Water,' you say. 'If they've got any.'

Kathryn Williams looks at you. She smiles. She walks over to the bar.

You're sitting across the table from Paul Kelly, your back to the bar and the door –

In the corner is a pool table with a game in progress.

'Used to be a stage there,' says Paul Kelly.

'Really?'

'A long time ago,' he says.

You look up at the walls, the dark walls with their dim photographs of the famous and the dead. You look back –

Paul Kelly is staring at you.

You smile.

'Recognise anyone?' he asks.

'John Charles, Fred Trueman, Harvey Smith,' you say.

'Had them all in here,' he nods.

'Not Sir Geoffrey?'

He smiles. He shakes his head. 'More's pity.'

Kathryn brings the drinks over on a tray. She sets them down. She hands you your water. 'Having a nice time?'

'Just chatting,' you say.

She lights a cigarette. She says: 'What about?'

'Yorkshire,' you say, looking at Paul Kelly. 'And the past.'

Paul Kelly glances at his watch.

Let's Dance is on the jukebox.

Kathryn's knee touches yours beneath the table –

(You say run) –

You move your knee closer into hers. She doesn't move away –

(You say hide) –

'So go on,' Kathryn tells you. 'Ask him.'

Paul Kelly looks up at you. He is waiting –

His pint already gone.

You cough. You shift your weight. You say: 'I wanted to ask you about your cousin Paula. Her daughter Jeanette.'

Kathryn moves her leg away from yours –

(For fear tonight) –

Paul Kelly looks at you again. He tips his glass up.

You say: 'Do you want another?'

'Murdered cousin and missing niece?' he says and shakes his head. 'No, thanks.'

Kathryn stubs out her cigarette. She says: 'Same again?'

You both look up at her, but she's already at the bar.

You turn back to him –

He is staring at you again.

'I'm sorry,' you say. 'I'm representing a man called Michael Myshkin and – '

'I know.'

'I do appreciate – '

He nods towards Kathryn at the bar. 'I only came here because she asked me.'

'I appreciate that,' you say. 'It was very good of you.'

He shakes his head. He looks at his watch again. 'Not really. She suffered as much as anyone.'

You take a cigarette from the pack she's left on the table. You light it.

'I suppose you know about Eddie? Jack Whitehead?'

'Yes,' you nod.

Kathryn brings the next round over on a tray. She sets them down.

'Still having a nice time?' she laughs, handing you another water.

You hold up the cigarette: 'I took one of yours, sorry.'

'Forget it,' she says. 'Everyone else does.'

Kelly takes a big sip from his bitter. He says: 'This is fun.'

Let's Dance has finished.

'I'm sorry,' you say again.

'Look, Mr Piggott,' he says. 'Ask your questions. But I think you'll find you're talking to the wrong Kelly.'

Down by the dark arches under the railway –

She pulls you up, bringing your mouth to hers as you topple on to the back seat –

A pretty young damsel chanced my way –

Her tongue pushes down harder on yours –

Down by the dark arches under the railway –

The taste of her own cunt in her mouth pushing her harder –

Singing Vilikens and Dinah, so blithe and so gay –

You take off her knickers –

Then I stepped up to her so gay and so free –

And she takes your cock in her right hand and guides it in –

To her did I say will you my sweetheart be?

Using your right hand to move your cock clockwise around the lips of her cunt –

Oh no, my gay young man that cannot be –

She digs her nails into your arse, wanting you in deeper –

There is a chap here in blue and he is a-watching me –

You go in hard, your stomach fat and sick –

And if he should see me, what would he say –

Kiss her hard, moving from her mouth to her chin and on to her neck –

Down by the dark arches under the railway –

'Eddie,' she whispers –

Pop goes the weasel –

You slip out of her cunt and off her –

Down by the dark arches –

'I'm sorry,' she says.

You want to go home and drink sweet white wine and smoke some fine Red Leb watch TV with Pete and Norm and fall asleep on their sofa and wake up about five go downstairs and wank yourself back to sleep and get up late eat crispy pancakes and listen to records and do the crossword on the bog meet Gareth for Yorkshire Pudding and onion gravy on the Springs then sit in half-empty pubs playing the jukebox and pool end up in a disco dancing to Culture Club with ugly girls in Boots No. 7 buying them an Indian or a Chinky and tapping off having a shag planning an away day a cheap holiday, wishing you were far away –

But you're not:

You're here –

Where everybody knows.

Break my heart in two –

In the black, broken heart of the black, broken night, you pull into the Redbeck –

The Viva back.

A man sat alone in the car –

Headlights on.

They are shining on a door –

The door banging in the wind, in the rain:

Room 27 –

A light on inside;

A photograph stuck on a wall –

A photograph made of paper, cut from paper, dirty paper;

A light on inside –

You don't stop, you don't stop, you don't fucking stop –

For fear tonight is all.

Chapter 42

This man is at door to hell –

Preston, Sunday 28 December 1980.

Door is banging in wind and rain –

From station to station, this his destination:

The door to hell.

He pulls it back and he sees BJ.

'Afternoon,' BJ say.

'Who are you?' he asks. 'You got a name?'

I am not who I want to be –

'No names.'

He points to his own wounds: 'What happened to you?'

'Occupational hazard,' BJ say. 'Goes with places I go.'

He looks around hell and he says: 'Is this what you wanted to talk about? The places you go? This place?'

'You been here before, have you, Mr Hunter?'

He nods: 'Have you?'

I don't know how to leave –

'Oh yes,' BJ say. 'Many times.'

'Were you here on the night of Thursday 20 November 1975?'

BJ brush hair out of two black eyes. BJ try to smile: 'You should see your fucking face?'

'Yours isn't that good.'

'How's that song go: *if looks could kill they probably will*?'

'I don't know.'

BJ take piece of paper out of jacket. BJ hand it to him. BJ say: 'Well, I do.'

He opens it. He looks at it:

Clare with her eyes and legs open, her fingers touching her own cunt.

He looks up at BJ then back at piece of paper:

Murdered by the West Yorkshire Police, November 1975.

He looks up at BJ again.

BJ say: 'Here comes a copper to chop off your head?'

'You do this?'

'What?'

'Any of it?'

'No, Mr Hunter.' BJ say. 'I did not.'

'But you know who did?'

BJ shrug. BJ wait.

'Tell me.'

BJ shake BJ's head.

'I'll fucking arrest you.'

'No, you won't.'

'Yes, I will.'

'For what?'

'Wasting police time. Withholding evidence. Obstruction. Murder?'

'That's what they want.'

'Who?'

'You know who.'

'No, I don't.'

'Well then, you've obviously been overestimated.'

'Meaning?'

'Meaning a lot of people seem to have gone to a lot of bother to make sure you're not in Yorkshire and not involved with Ripper.'

'So why do they want you arrested?'

'Mr Hunter, they want me dead,' BJ say, spinning truths from lies and lies from truths. 'Arresting me's just a way to get their hands on me.'

'Who?'

BJ shake BJ's head again. BJ try not to laugh: 'No names.'

Not yet:

It isn't working yet –

Hunter's pissed off.

'Stop wasting my time,' he shouts and opens door –

The door out of hell.

But BJ there first, at door –

The door to hell.

BJ slam it shut.

'Here,' BJ tell him. 'You're not going anywhere.'

He holds piece of paper up to BJ's face. He says: 'Start fucking talking then.'

BJ push him and paper away: 'Fuck off.'

'You called me,' he shouts. 'Why?'

'I didn't bloody want to, believe me,' BJ say, moving away from him. 'I had some serious doubts.'

'So why?'

'I was going to just post picture,' BJ mutter. 'Then I heard about your suspension and I didn't know how long you'd be about.'

'Just this,' he says, holding up piece of paper. 'That was all?'

BJ nod.

'Why?'

'I just want it to stop,' BJ say. 'Want them to stop.'

'Who?'

'No fucking names!' BJ scream. 'How many more times?'

He looks at BJ then back down at Clare: 'So why here? Is this where it all started? With her?'

'Started?' BJ laugh. 'Fuck no.'

'Where it ended?'

'Beginning of end, shall we say.'

'For who?'

'You name them?' BJ whisper. 'Me, you, her, – half fucking coppers you've ever met.'

He looks back down at piece of paper in his hands:

Clare with her eyes and legs open, her fingers touching her own cunt.

'Why Strachan?' he asks. 'Because of the magazine? Because of *Spunk*?'

'Why they murdered Clare?' BJ shake BJ's head. 'No.'

'Not the porn? Strachan's murder had nothing to do with MJM?'

'No.'

'I want names – '

'I'll give you one name,' repeating today's instructions for today's mission, BJ whisper. 'And one name only.'

'Go on?'

'Her name was Morrison.'

'Who?'

'Clare – her maiden name was Morrison.'

'Morrison?'

'Know any other Morrisons, do you, Mr Hunter?'

'Grace Morrison.'

'And?'

'The Strafford,' he says. 'She was the barmaid at the Strafford.'

'And?'

'They were sisters,' he whispers.

'And?'

He looks down at piece of paper in his hand:

Clare with her eyes and legs open, her fingers touching her own cunt.

He looks up again, his eyes open: 'The Strafford.'

'Bullseye.'

'How do you know this?'

'I was there.'

'Where? You were where?'

'Strafford,' BJ say and BJ open door –

The door out of hell.

But he is there first, at door –
The door to hell.
He slams it shut.
'You're not going anywhere, pal,' he says. 'Not yet.'
'But that's your lot, Mr Hunter.'
'Fuck off,' he screams. 'You tell me what happened that night?'
'Ask someone else.'
'You mean Bob Craven? There isn't anybody else, they're all dead.'
Mission for Dead accomplished, BJ smile: 'Exactly.'
'Fuck off,' he says, grabbing BJ's jacket.
BJ push him away.
He grabs BJ again.
BJ punch him.
He goes down.
BJ have fingers round his throat but he still has hold of BJ. BJ shout:
'What fuck are you doing?'
'Time to stop running,' he hisses.
BJ kick him but he still has hold of BJ. BJ say: 'Get fucking off me.'
'What happened?'
BJ kick him again: 'I'm saying no more.'
'Tell me!'
BJ break free and at door –
The door out of hell.
BJ tell him: 'They haven't finished with you.'
'You're dead,' he shouts from floor of hell. 'You're dead.'
'Not me,' BJ laugh. 'I got my insurance. How about you?'
'They'll find you and they'll kill you if you don't come with me.'
'Not me.'
'Go on, run.'
'Fuck off,' BJ say, opening door –
Door banging in wind, in rain –
The door out of hell.
'It's you who should be running,' BJ tell him. 'You, they haven't
finished with you.'
BJ stand at door –
The door into hell –
Stand at door and BJ see him now:
On his knees on his lawn in rain, his finger on trigger of shotgun in his mouth.
'You're dead,' he shouts –
BJ step outside –
'Dead.'

BJ start walking, walking up to top of street, when BJ see *him* –
See *him* standing at top of street by open door of his car –
Looking at BJ –
Unblinking –
He smiles.
BJ run –
Run like hell.

Chapter 43

No sleep, no food, no cigarettes –
   Just this:
   Netherton/Wood Street/Netherton/Wood Street/Netherton/Wood Street –
   Back to Netherton:
   Sunday/Monday/Tuesday –
   The evening of Tuesday 17 December 1974:
   Nothing –
   No sleep, no food, no cigarettes:
   No George fucking Marsh.

There's a tap on the glass –
   I jump:
   Badger fucking *Bill* –
   He tries the passenger door.
   I lean across. I open it.
   He gets in. 'Christ, it fucking stinks in here.'
   'How'd you know I was here?'
   'Fucking hell, Maurice,' he snorts. 'You're an open fucking book, mate.'
   'Not a crime, is it?' I smile.
   'A broken fucking record.'
   'Is that what you came to tell me?'
   'No,' he says. 'It's not.'
   'What then?'
   He pauses –
   I turn to look at him:
   He's staring up the road at Maple Well Drive; the black bungalow on the right.
   'What is it?' I ask again.
   'Eddie Dunford,' he says.
   'Who?'
   Bill turns to look at me. He smiles. He says: 'Fuck off, Maurice.'
   'What?'
   'He's a bloody nuisance and he doesn't need any fucking encouragement.'
   I've got my hands on the steering wheel, holding it tight.
   Bill says: 'He's already been up Shangrila.'

'So?'

'So we've got enough bloody problems with Derek fucking Box. I don't need any fucking more. Thank you.'

'Dunford's not a problem,' I say.

Bill doesn't reply –

I turn back to look at him:

He's looking at me.

'He doesn't know anything,' I say.

'He knows enough to have been round your bird's house this afternoon.'

'What?'

He winks. He opens the passenger door. He gets out. He turns back. He says: 'You and your ladyfriend best remember, reckless talk costs lives.'

I drive back through the dark and on to Blenheim Road, St John's, Wakefield –

Big hearts cut, lost;

28 Blenheim Road, St John's, Wakefield –

Heart cut, lost;

I park. I close my eyes. I open them. I see stars –

Stars and angels –

Silent little angels:

Jeanette, Susan, and Clare.

I get out. I lock the car door. I spit –

The taste of flesh;

I walk up the drive –

Shallow ugly moonlight, black stagnant rainwater;

The bottoms of my trousers, my shoes and socks, muddy –

Everything mud;

I go inside out of the rain. I go up the stairs to Flat 5 –

The air damp, stained –

Hearts lost;

The door is open –

Wide open, the metal chain loose –

In the Season of the Plague, the meat;

My heart thrashing –

The air suddenly thick with murder –

Two black crows eating from black bin-bags;

I step inside, listening:

Low sobs, muffled sobs –

Ripping through her sweet meat;

Stood before the bedroom door, whispering: 'Mandy?'
Low sobs, muffled sobs, weeping –
Screams echoing into the dark;
I try the door: 'Mandy?'
I close my eyes. I open them. I see stars –
Sliding back on her arse up the hall –
Stars and angels –
My angel: 'Mandy?'
Arms and legs splayed, her skirt riding up;
Close my eyes. Open them –
Stood before the bedroom door, whispering: 'Mandy?'
Scared sobs from behind a door;
Listening to the low sobs –
The muffled sobs, the weeping –
The sound of furniture being moved;
I lean into the wood of the door. I push –
The door opens a fraction then stops –
Chests of drawers and wardrobes being placed in front of the door;
The sobs louder, the weeping more –
I push again: 'Mandy?'
A faint voice through the layers and layers of wood;
The sobbing, the weeping –
Another fraction, another inch: 'Mandy?'
A child whispering to a friend beneath the covers;
Sobbing, weeping –
My arm inside then a leg, pushing the fractions and the inches –
'Tell them about the others –'
It is Tuesday 17 December 1974 –
A cold and dark December place when I open up the bedroom door;
Behind the chests of drawers and the wardrobes –
To find her lying cold and still upon the floor;
Beneath the shadows.
I take her into my arms –
I look into her eyes;
Beneath her shadows –
She is snarling, carnivore teeth:
'This place is worst of all, underground;
The corpses and the rats –
The dragon and the owl –
Wolves be there too, a swan –
The swan dead.
Unending, this place unending;

Under the grass that grows –
Between the cracks and the stones –
The beautiful carpets –
Waiting for the others, underground.'
Silence –
Holding her;
Low sobs, muffled sobs, she is weeping –
Beneath her shadows:
'It has happened four times before – '
Tears –
'Four times–'
Cavernous tears:
' – and it will happen again.'
Tears, then –
Silence –
The silence, but outside –
Behind the chests of drawers and the wardrobes, the broken doors
and the heavy curtains, outside the branches of the big tree are tapping
upon the glass of the big windows, their leaves lost in December –
For only moon has shone upon them;
Cold and wanting in –
Wanting her –
Where the wind cannot rest;
My eyes open –
Looking into hers –
Winter lights for the dead;
I want to free her from the chests of drawers and the wardrobes, the
broken doors and the heavy curtains –
Free her from the chains –
The prisons:
The certain death that echoes here –
The terrible, horrible voice that gloats, that boasts:
'I AM NO ANGEL –
'I AM NO FUCKING ANGEL!'
Looking into my eyes –
Weeping;
Rising and falling –
Beneath her shadows;
'I'm sorry,' I say –
'Where were you?' she whispers.
'Who was it?' I sob –
Her eyes open and looking into mine: 'Please tell them where I am.'

'What?' I am screaming –
Summoning her back from the Underground, the court of the Dead:
This cold and dark December place –
'Who?'
She is pushing me off –
Pushing me away, whispering: 'You weren't here.'
'I'm sorry,' I say –
Standing up in the light –
But in the light –
The dead moonlight –
There are bruises on the backs of my hands again –
Bruises that won't heal –
Ever.

Beneath her shadows –
Lost hearts.
Fucking –
The cat piss and petunia, desperate.
Fucking then fucking –
Desperate.
Fucking then kissing –
Her head upon my damp chest, I stroke her hair, her beautiful wet
hair.
The branches of the tree tap upon the glass –
Sobbing, weeping –
Soaked and wanting in.
'I love you,' I say.
The branches tapping –
Sobbing, she whispers: 'I can't live like this.'
Sobbing and weeping –
Wanting out.
'We'll go,' I tell her –
Her face in the candlelight: 'Where?'
'Far away.'
Her face white: 'When?'
'Tomorrow night.'
Her face white and already –
Dead –
Sobbing, weeping –
Hearts –
Asking to be let out.

*

The windows look inwards, the walls listen to your heart –
  Where one thousand voices cry.
  Inside –
  Inside your scorched heart.
  There is a house –
  A house with no doors.
  The earth scorched –
  Heathen.

I wake suddenly in the dark again, beneath her shadows –
  'I'll see you in the tree – '
  Tapping against the pane.
  She's lying on her side in a black bra and underskirt, her back to me –
  Branches tapping against the pane.
  I'm lying on my back in my underpants and socks, my glasses on the table –
  The branches tapping against the pane.
  Lying on my back in my underpants and socks, my glasses on the table, that terrible tune and its words in my head –
  Listening to the branches tapping against the pane.
  I'm lying on my back in my underpants and socks, my glasses on the table, that terrible lonely tune and her words in my head, listening to the branches tapping along against the pane –
  'In her branches.'
  I look at my watch –
  It is one o'clock in the morning –
  Wednesday 18 December 1974.

I reach for my glasses and get out of the bed without waking her and I go through into the kitchen and I put on the light and fill the kettle and light the gas and find the teapot in the cupboard and the two cups and saucers and I rinse out the cups and then dry them and then take the milk out of the fridge and I pour it into the cups and put two teabags in the teapot and take the kettle off the ring and pour the water on to the teabags and let it stand, staring out of the small window, the kitchen reflected back in the glass, a divorced man undressed but for a pair of white underpants and glasses, these thick lenses with their heavy black frames, a divorced man undressed in the other woman's flat at two o'clock in the morning –
  Wednesday 18 December 1974:
  'Under the spreading chestnut tree – '

I put the teapot and cups and saucers on the tray and take it into the big room and I set the tray down on the low table and pour the tea on to the milk when –

There are boots upon the stair, the doorbell ringing, the knocking heavy –

She is standing in the hall.

I ask: 'Tomorrow night?'

'Tomorrow night,' she nods.

The doorbell ringing, the knocking heavy –

I open the door –

Dick's stood there, panting. 'They've got someone.'

'What?'

'For Clare.'

'Who?'

'Someone we fucking know – '

'Who?'

'Michael Myshkin.'

'What?'

'He's coughing.'

'What?'

'Come on. Get dressed.'

I turn back round –

She's not there;

Just the branches tapping against the pane, saying over and over:

'Where I sold you and you sold me.'

Dark hours –

Dark, dark hours –

Before the cock crows:

Three in the morning –

Wednesday 18 December 1974:

Yorkshire –

Wakefield:

Wood Street Police Station –

We walk down the long, long corridor –

Uniforms stood around, drinking and laughing, singing fucking carols –

Jingle Bells –

Jimmy Ashworth sat at the table in Room 1 –

Jingle Bells –

Two teenage girls sat at the table in Room 2 –

Jingle –

Room 3 empty –

Fucking –

In Room 4 –

Bells –

Three big kings in their shirtsleeves:

Ronald Angus, George Oldman and Pete Noble –

Three big men in their shirtsleeves stood over *him*:

Michael John Myshkin, twenty-two, in police issue grey shirt and trousers –

Michael John Myshkin of Jenkins Photo Studio, Castleford –

Michael John Myshkin the man who is saying he murdered Clare Kemplay:

'. . . she wouldn't let me kiss her, so I kissed her anyway and then she wouldn't shut up. Said she was going to tell her mam and dad and police, so I strangled her. Then I cut her and put the rose up her and the wings in her back . . .'

He is grossly overweight, his enormous head bowed and shaking –

Handcuffed, spots of blood are dropping from his nose on to the table.

He is crying. He has pissed himself.

Dick and I step inside.

Angus, Oldman and Noble turn round –

'Maurice,' says George. 'This is Michael John Myshkin.'

I look back at Myshkin –

Head bowed and shaking.

'Michael's just been telling us what a bad boy he's been, haven't you, Michael?'

Myshkin doesn't answer.

Noble bangs both palms down loud on the table. 'Answer the man!'

Myshkin nods –

A fat and stupid moon in a black and cruel night;

'Tell these gentlemen what you just told us, Michael,' says Ronald Angus.

Michael Myshkin looks up at me –

Trembling and blinking through his fears and tears.

I say: 'We're listening, Michael.'

Michael John Myshkin smoothes down his hair. He blinks. He nods. He whispers: 'I was driving the van in Morley and I saw her and I fancied her and I stopped and got her into the van but she wouldn't let me kiss her, so I kissed her anyway and then she wouldn't shut up. Said she was going to tell her mam and dad and police, so I strangled her. Then I cut her and put the rose up her and the wings in her back. Just like the others.'

'Which others?' I say.

'Them two others.'

'You did them too, didn't you, Michael?' says Noble.

He nods.

Noble: 'Susan Ridyard?'

He nods.

Noble: 'Jeanette Garland?'

Michael Myshkin looks from Noble to me for a split second –

A split second in which you can see him –

See him see her –

See Jeanette –

A split second in which he loses his life –

A split second before he nods.

'Did what?' shouts Noble.

'Killed them.'

I say: 'Michael? Where did you kill them?'

'Under the grass, between the cracks and the stones – '

'Where?'

'Those beautiful carpets.'

'Where is this?'

'My kingdom,' he says. 'My underground kingdom.'

Noble steps forward. He slaps him hard across the top of his head. He shouts: 'You're going to have to do fucking better than that, you dirty fat fucking bastard!'

'Come on,' says Oldman. 'Leave him to think on. I need a drink.'

'A bloody whiskey,' laughs Angus. 'A bloody big one.'

Dick follows them out into the corridor.

I wait until they're all out in the corridor. I lean across the table. I lift the lad's head up. I look him in the eye. I tell him: 'You didn't really do it, did you, Michael?'

Michael Myshkin stares back. He doesn't blink –

He shakes his enormous head.

'But you know who did, don't you, Michael?'

He looks at the table. He smoothes down his hair.

'Who was it, Michael?'

He looks up –

There is blood on his face, tears on his cheek –

This fat and stupid moon in this black and cruel night;

He looks up. He blinks. He smiles. He laughs. He says: 'The Wolf.'

*

They are waiting for me outside Room 4.

We walk back down the long, long corridor.

The two girls are still sat in Room 2.

They are wearing long skirts, tight sweaters and big shoes. They are about thirteen or fourteen years old.

'Who are they?' I ask Oldman.

'These are two that first told us about Myshkin.'

I stand in the doorway of Room 2. I stare at them –

They have love bites on their necks.

'One of them goes out with the lad that found the body,' says Oldman.

'Jimmy Ashworth?'

He nods: 'Him and Myshkin live on same street out Fitzwilliam. He's been driving Jimmy up and down to Morley to see her. They reckon he's on some kind of pills to make his balls grow and his tits shrink. The lasses say he's always whipping it out in churchyard. The one next to Morley Grange – '

'Who pulled him?'

'Girls went into Morley Station with their mams last night. Morley phoned it through. I sent John Rudkin up Fitzwilliam. He gets there. Myshkin's done a runner. White Ford fucking Transit no less. Bob Craven and Bob Douglas spot him on the Doncaster Road. They chased him. They nicked him. Their collar.'

'That's it? A wank in the graveyard and he does a runner?'

George shakes his head.

'What else you got?'

George hands me an envelope.

I open it –

A school photograph:

Blue-sky background –

Eyes and smile shining up in my face;

One pair of mongol eyes –

One crooked little smile:

Jeanette Garland.

'It was in his wallet,' says Oldman. 'His fucking wallet.'

Ronald Angus stands between me and George Oldman. He already smells of whiskey. He puts an arm around each of our shoulders.

I try to move away.

Angus grips my shoulder. He says: 'He did it, Maurice.'

I look at him.

'You know it in your heart,' he says.

I turn. I walk down the corridor –

'In your heart,' shouts Angus.

I walk past Room 1 –

Jimmy Ashworth still sat at the table, long lank hair everywhere. He is crying.

So am I –

In my heart.

Back upstairs they're choosing Myshkin a solicitor, calling in Clive McGuinness and a thousand fucking favours, the talk now of Chivas Regal and press conferences, new tankards and trophies, like we're some gang of monkeys who've just found their own arses without a fucking map, but I'm still wishing there'd been no amalgamation, no West Yorkshire fucking Metropolitan Police, wondering where the fuck the *Badger* is –

'Maurice?'

Ronald Angus is looking at me –

My Chief Constable.

'Pardon?'

'I said, George will do the Press Conference if you've no objections.'

I stand up. I say: 'None whatsoever.'

'Where you off now?' asks George.

'Well, if you've no objections,' I say. 'I thought someone ought to go up the pervert's house and get some fucking evidence. If that is you've no objections?'

Out of Wakefield and up the Doncaster Road, past the Redbeck –

Blue lights spinning, the sirens screaming like the undead but buried –

Screaming all the way into Fitzwilliam –

Dick shouting: 'You remember him, yeah?'

Nodding –

'You know who nicked him?'

Nodding –

'You know who they got him for a solicitor?'

Nodding –

'You think he did it?'

Foot down –

'I fucking hope he did.'

Foot down, nodding.

One, two, three, four –

Five o'clock:

54 Newstead View, Fitzwilliam –
Three police cars and a van, parked angular –
Doors open, hammers out –
His mam and his dad at the front door in their nightclothes –
Dick knocking them to one side on to their tiny front lawn –
Shouting: 'We have a warrant to – '
Old man Myshkin coughing his blood and guts up, her screaming –
I give her a slap. I push them both back inside –
'Upstairs,' I say to Dick and Jim Prentice –
Old man Myshkin, hands full of stringy blood trying to comfort his
wife –
I push them down into their tatty old sofa. 'Sit down and shut up!'
'Where's Michael?' she's crying. 'What have you done to Michael?'
'Boss,' says Dick –
Dick and Jim are standing in the doorway:
Jim is holding up a huge drawing of a rat –
A rat with a crown and wings –
Swan bloody wings.
Dick with a box full of photographs –
Photographs of ten or twelve young girls –
The windows look inwards, the walls listen to your heart;
School photographs –
Where one thousand voices cry;
Eyes and smiles shining up in my face –
Inside;
Ten pairs of blue eyes –
Inside your scorched heart;
Ten sets of smiles –
There is a house;
That same blue-sky background –
A house with no door;
One pair of mongol eyes –
The earth scorched;
One crooked smile –
Heathen and always winter.

100 miles an hour out of Fitzwilliam and down into Castleford, the
undead but buried spinning and howling –
Spinning and howling all the way into Castleford –
Dick shouting: 'You tell Oldman where we're going?'
Shaking my head –
'You called Bill, didn't you?'

Shaking my head –

'You think we should call him?'

Shaking my head –

'I fucking hope you know what you're doing?'

Foot down, shaking.

Heathen and always winter –

The car slows down. It bumps over the rough ground. It stops.

I chuck Dick and Jim their black balaclavas: 'Put them on when you get inside.'

I stuff my balaclava in my coat pocket.

I hand them a hammer each.

I put on my gloves. I pick up another hammer. I put it in my other pocket.

We get out of the car –

We're at the back of a row of shops in the centre of Castleford.

'Jim, go round the front to keep an eye out,' I tell him.

He nods.

I pull down my balaclava. I turn to Dick: 'You set?'

Dick nods.

They follow me along the back of the shops. I stop by the metal gate in the high wall with the broken glass set in the top. I look at Dick.

Dick nods.

He gives me a leg up and over the wall and the broken glass.

I land on the other side in the backyard of Jenkins Photo Studio:

There's a light on upstairs, a hammer in my pocket –

A photograph.

I open the gate for Dick.

I pick up one of the metal dustbin lids. I drop it on the floor with a crash –

We stand flat against the wall in the shadows by the back door –

In the shadows by the back door, waiting –

The door stays shut, the light on upstairs.

I nod.

Dick picks up the metal dustbin. He hoists it up. He hurls it through the back window –

Glass and wood everywhere.

He pulls himself up on to the ledge. He shoulders in through the broken glass and splintered frame. He jumps down on the other side to open the back door –

No turning back.

In and down the corridor to the front of the shop, Dick straight up the stairs –

Me past the window full of school portraits. I tap on the door. I open it for Jim.

He steps inside.

I point at the ceiling.

He puts on his balaclava. He follows me through to the back stairs –

Up the narrow steep stairs past a dark room on the right and into a living room-cum-bedroom on the left.

Dick is standing alone in the room on a carpet of photographs –

Photographs of young girls –

School photographs –

Thousands of eyes and hundreds of smiles shining up in our faces:

Pairs of eyes and sets of smiles all against that same blue-sky background –

That same sky-blue background favoured by Mr Edward Jenkins, photographer.

I take the photograph from my pocket –

The photograph of a young girl –

A school photograph –

Eyes and smile shining up in my face:

Mongol eyes and crooked smile against that same blue-sky background –

Jeanette Garland.

I take off my balaclava. I put my glasses back on –

Their thick lenses and black frames –

The Owl:

I am the Owl and I see everything from behind these lenses thick and frames black, everything in this upstairs room with its carpet of innocent eyes and trusting smiles, abused and exposed under a single dirty light –

Unblinking –

A single dirty light bulb still left on.

I put the photograph of Jeanette back in my pocket.

'He's gone then,' says Jim.

I nod.

Dick hands me a large black *Letts* desk diary for 1974. 'Forgot this in his haste.'

I turn to the back. I flick through the names and addresses –

Initials and phone numbers listed alphabetically.

I turn the pages. I read the names. I see the faces:

Looking for one name, one number, one face –

I see John Dawson. I see Don Foster –
I see me –
I see Michael Myshkin, John Murphy, the _Badger_ and then –
That name, that number, that face:
GM: 3657.
I close the book –
They're all going to die in this hell;
· Close my eyes –
We all are.
'What now?' Jim is asking.
I open my eyes.
They are both staring at me.
'Torch the place,' I tell them.
They nod.
I walk back down the stairs. I go out into the alley.
It is daylight now.
I take off my glasses. I wipe them. I put them back on. I look up at
the sky –
The moon gone –
No sun –
Jeanette Garland missing five years and six months –
Susan Ridyard missing two years, ten months –
Clare Kemplay dead five days –
Dead:
The windows look inwards, the walls listen to your heart –
Where one thousand voices cry;
Inside –
Inside your scorched heart;
There is a house –
A house with no doors;
The earth scorched –
Heathen and always winter;
The room murder –
This is where I live:
The grey sky turning black –
Fresh blood on my hands –
No turning back.

I drive out of Castleford –
Over to Netherton.
I park at the end of Maple Well Drive –
The morning sky black.

All the bungalows have their lights on –
Even number 16;
Fuck –
Never leave, never leave, never leave;
I get out –
I walk along the road.
The living room light is on –
Their white Ford Transit parked outside.
I go up the path –
I ring the doorbell:
A grey-haired woman opens the door, pink washing-up gloves dripping wet: 'Yes?'
She's put on weight since last we met.
I say: 'Mrs Marsh?'
'Yes.'
'Police, love. Is your George in?'
She looks at me. She tries to place me. She shakes her head. 'No.'
'Where is he?'
'He's at his sister's, isn't he?'
'I don't know,' I say. 'That's why I'm asking you.'
'Well, he is.'
'Where's that then? His sister's?'
'Over Rochdale way.'
'When did you last see him?'
'What do you mean?'
'When did you last see your husband?'
'Day he left.'
'Which was?'
'Last Thursday.'
'Heard he was sick?'
'He is. He's gone for a break.'
'Is that right?'
'That's what I just said, isn't it?'
I want to push the door back hard into her face. I want to slap her. To punch her. Kick her. Beat her.
'Is everything all right?' asks a man from the doorway to the kitchen –
A tall man in black, his hat in his hands –
A priest.
I smile. I say: 'Thank you for your time, Mrs Marsh.'
She nods.
I turn. I walk away, back down the garden path.

Back at the gate, I turn again –

Mrs Marsh has closed her front door, but there's that shadow again –

Behind the nets in the front room –

Two shadows.

I walk back down Maple Well Drive –

Back to the car.

I get in and I wait –

I wait and I watch –

I wait.

I watch.

Chapter 44

You sleep in the car. You wake in the car. You sleep in the car. You wake in the car –

You check the rearview mirror. Then the wing –

The passenger seat is empty.

The doors are locked. The windows closed. The car smells. You switch on the engine. You switch on the windscreen wipers. You switch on the radio:

'*Latest opinion polls have the Conservatives still 15% ahead of Labour; Mrs Thatcher accuses SDP leaders of lacking guts; Britain faces a 1929-style economic crash within two years whatever party wins, according to Ken Livingstone; Michael Foot speaks at a Hyde Park rally attended by 15,000 people at the end of the People's March for Jobs . . .*'

You switch everything off.

You can hear church bells, the traffic and the rain:

It is Sunday 5 June 1983 –

D-4.

You are parked below the City Heights flats, Leeds.

Halfway to the tower block, you turn back to check the car is locked. Then you walk across the car park. You climb the stairs to the fourth floor. You read the walls as you go:

Wogs Out, Leeds, NF, Leeds, Kill a Paki, Leeds.

You think of your mother. You don't stop. You turn one corner and there's something dead in a plastic bag. *Your father.* You don't stop. You turn the next and there's a pile of human shit. *Fitzwilliam.* You don't stop. You are walking in another man's shoes, thinking of lost children –

Hazel.

On the fourth floor you go along the open passageway, the bitter wind ripping your face raw until there are tears in your eyes. You quicken past broken windows and paint-splattered doors –

Doors banging in the wind, in the rain;

New tears in your old eyes, the lights are already going on across Leeds –

But not here –

Not here before a door marked *Pervert.*

You knock on the door of Flat 405, City Heights, Leeds.

You wait.

You listen to the smash of glass and the scream of a child down below, the brakes of an empty bus and an hysterical voice on a radio in another flat –

The church bells gone.

You press the doorbell –

It's broken.

You bend down. You lift up the metal flap of another letterbox. You smell staleness. You hear the sounds of a TV.

'Excuse me!' you yell into the hole.

The TV dies.

'Excuse me!'

Through the letterbox, you can see a pair of dirty white socks pacing about inside.

You knock on the door again. You shout: 'I know you're in there.'

'What do you want?'

You stand up. You say to the door: 'I just want a word.'

'What about?'

'Your sister and her daughter.'

The latch turns. The door branded *Pervert* opens.

'What about them?' says Johnny Kelly –

The Man who had Everything;

'What about them?' he says again –

The Man who had Everything –

In a tight pair of jeans and a sweater with no shirt, his hair long and unwashed, his face fat and unshaven;

'They're dead,' he says.

'I know,' you say. 'That's why I'm here.'

'Fuck off,' he hisses.

'No.'

Johnny Kelly steps forward. He pokes you in the chest. 'Who the fuck do you think you are?'

'My name is John Piggott,' you reply. 'I'm a solicitor.'

'I've got no fucking money,' he says. 'If that's what you're after.'

'No,' you say. 'That's not what I'm after.'

'So what are you after?'

'The truth.'

He swallows. He closes his eyes. He opens them. He looks past you at the grey and black sky. He hears the glass smash and the child's screams, the brakes and the voices. He sees the dead and the shit –

'About what?' he says.

'The truth about your Paula and her Jeanette. About Susan Ridyard and Clare Kemplay. About Michael Myshkin and Jimmy Ashworth. About – '

The dead and the shit –

The tears old and new –

The windows and the doors branded *Pervert* –

'About Hazel Atkins,' you say.

'What makes you think I know anything?'

'It was just a hunch,' you shrug.

'You fucking psychic, are you?' he says, closing the door.

You put your right foot forward between the door and the frame. You stop him.

'Fuck off!' he shouts. 'I don't know anything.'

You push the door back in his face. You say: 'Is that right? Well, you know all those names, don't you?'

And Johnny Kelly –

The Man who had Everything –

Johnny Kelly looks down at his dirty white socks. He nods. He whispers words you cannot hear –

'You what?' you say.

'They're dead,' he says again, looking up –

The tears old and new –

The tears in both your eyes –

'All of them,' he says. 'Dead.'

'Not quite,' you say.

He looks down again at his dirty white socks.

'You going to let me in?' you say.

Johnny Kelly turns. He walks back into his flat, the door open.

You follow him down a narrow hall into the living room.

Kelly sits down in an old and scarred vinyl armchair, racing papers and a plate of uneaten and dried-up baked beans at his feet –

An empty bottle of HP stood on its head –

He has his face in his hands.

You sit on the matching settee, a colour TV showing *The World at War*.

Above the unlit gas-fire and its plastic-surround, a Polynesian girl is smiling in various shades of orange and brown, a tear in her hair and one corner missing, the walls running with damp.

You sit and you think of faces running with tears –

Think of the missing –

Of Hazel.

Next door a dog is barking and barking and barking.

Johnny Kelly looks up. He says: 'It never goes away.'

You nod.
'So what do you want to know?'
'Everything,' you whisper.

You drive from Leeds back into Wakefield. You do not put the radio on. You repeat as you drive:
Everybody knows; everybody knows; everybody knows –
Everybody knows and –

It is about four o'clock in the afternoon with the sun never shining and the hard, relentless, endless fucking drizzle of a dull, dark, soundless fucking Sunday running down the windscreen of the car.
You check the rearview mirror. Then the wing.
You park up on the pavement of a quiet dim lane in front of tall wet walls:
Trinity View, Wood Lane, Sandal –
The posh part of Wakefield; the garage owners and the builders, the self-made men with their self-made piles, their double drives and deductible lives, the ones who never pay their bills and always dodge their taxes –
Self-satisfied and shielded, gilded against the coming war –
Against John Piggott.
You walk up the long drive towards Trinity View, past the neat lawn with its tainted, plastic ornaments and stagnant, plagued pond.
There are no cars in the drive. There are no lights on inside –
Only the hateful gloom of bad history –
The hateful, hateful gloom of bad, bad history, hanging in the trees, the branches –
Their shadows long.
You ring the doorbell. You listen to the dreadful, lonely chimes echo through the inside of the house.
'Yes? Who is it?' calls out a woman from behind the door.
'My name is John Piggott.'
'What do you want?'
'I want to talk to you.'
'About what?'
'About Johnny Kelly.'
'Go away.'
'About your late husband.'
'Go away.'
You have your face and lips to the door: 'About Jeanette.'
Silence –

Hanging in the trees –

'About Clare.'

Silence –

In the branches.

'Mrs Foster,' you say. 'I'm not going to go away until you open that door and I see your face.'

There is hesitation. Then a lock turns. The door opens.

Mrs Patricia Foster is in her early fifties with grey hair in need of a perm. She is dressed all in black and holding a lighter and an unlit cigarette in her hands.

There's already lipstick on the filter and her hands are shaking.

She turns back inside. She sits down on the steps of her grand, carpeted stairs. She shakes her head. She says: 'The things we do.'

'Pardon?'

She looks up at you. She lights her cigarette. She says: 'I knew you'd come.'

'Me?'

'Someone.'

You tell her: 'I went to see Johnny Kelly.'

She smiles at the carpet. 'A man's got to do what a man's got to do, eh?'

You hold up a newspaper photograph of Hazel Atkins.

She looks up, dark eyes and tall nose, the face of an eagle –

An iniquitous, flesh-eating bird of prey.

She looks away. She says: 'So what do you want to know?'

'Nothing,' you say.

She stares at you. She says: 'Nothing?'

You nod. You turn –

'Wait!' she screams –

You walk –

'Where do you think you're going?'

You keep on walking –

'You can't leave!'

Walking away through the hateful gloom, the stained class that she is –

On her doorstep, screaming: 'No!'

Past the neat lawn with its tainted, plastic ornaments and stagnant, plagued pond –

The neat lawn on which her husband was murdered on December 23, 1974 –

Under these very trees;

You walk down the long drive away from Trinity View –

Mrs Patricia Foster screaming and screaming and screaming;
Her screams and her memories –
Hanging in the trees, in the branches –
Your memories;
You are walking in another man's shoes –
A dead man's.

Chapter 45

Breathing blood and spitting blind, running hard –

Here it is again, his car –

Fuck.

Gets within six foot and BJ off again –

Door, wind and rain –

His voice: *'BJ!'*

Over fence and on to wasteland, tripping and falling on to ground on other side, bleeding and crying and praying as BJ stumble over land and into playground, into playground and scrambling across fence, across fence and into allotments, dripping blood through vegetable patches and over wall and into small street of terraces, down street and right into next street of terraces, BJ turn left and then right again and into privets –

The shrubbery.

After a minute BJ step out into street and walk along pavement next to big and busy road, walk towards roundabout where BJ will hitch out of here –

Out of Nazi Germany.

BJ walking along, yellow lights coming towards BJ like stars, red lights leaving BJ like sores, practising German and thinking about trying to cross to other side where it's just factories; fires burning and smoke rising, crows picking at white bones of babies and their mothers, screaming:

'*Hex, hex, hex, hex, hex, hex –*

'*Hex, hex, hex, hex, hex, hex –*

'*Hex, hex, hex, hex, hex, hex.*'

Thinking at least there'd be somewhere to hide –

Somewhere to hide.

Then car stops –

His car –

His car stops. He winds down window –

He says: 'You're going to catch your death, Barry.'

'Please,' BJ say. 'Help me.'

He raises brow of his black hat. He looks up at black afternoon sky and black rain. He says: 'Are you sorry?'

BJ nod.

'Sorry for all the things that you've done?'

BJ looking left and right, left and then right. BJ say: 'I am sorry.'

He unlocks door. BJ get in, sliding over into back –
Car damp and cold, black briefcase beside BJ.
He starts car. He says: 'Keep your head down.'
BJ do as he says.
On motorway, BJ look up from leather seat: 'Where we going?'
'Church,' he says.
It is 1980.

He found me hiding –

In Church of Abandoned Christ in sixth flat on second floor of sixth house in Portland Square in ghost bloodied old city of Leodis, BJ lost again; all covered in sleep and drunk upon a double bed, lost in another room; hair shaved again and eight eyes shined, BJ be once more Northern Son. Black Angel beside BJ upon bed; his clothes shabby and wings burnt; he is Hierophant, Father of Fear, and he is weeping, whispering old death songs:

Knew I was not happy –

'Through thee Church, E met Michael and Carol Williams at their house in Ossett in December 1974 where E had been invited to lecture on thee Irvingites. We took communion of ready-sliced bread and undiluted Ribena. During prayers thee next day Michael spoke in glossolalia for thee first time. Thee three of us wept for it is thee gift of thee Holy Spirit. It is beautiful and it is frightening.

Scratching my head –

'And suddenly there came a sound from heaven as of a rushing mighty wind. It filled all their house on Towngate where we were sitting. And there appeared unto us cloven tongues as of fire and they sat upon Michael. And he was filled with thee Holy Ghost and began to speak with other tongues as thee Spirit gave him utterance.

Confused beyond existence –

'In January 1975 Michael suddenly visited me. He said he had seen thee Devil who had told him to go and kill himself in his car. He then kissed me upon thee lips. It was not a Christian kiss and we bounced off each other, repelled.

Sat in the corner, shivering from fright –

'Thee following day Michael approached neighbours in thee street. He told them thee world was coming to an end. He came to thee Church and told me he had been seduced by thee Devil. E recited a prayer of absolution, thee Infilling of thee Holy Spirit. He was strained and tired and went home before night fell. He was afraid of thee dark.

Feeling strung up –

'On Friday 24 January Michael told Carol to get rid of all thee

crosses and religious books in thee house and she did so. When it was
time to go to bed he left thee radio on. He was frightened of thee silence
of thee night.

Out of my clothes and into the bed –

'On thee Saturday E decided to give Michael and Carol a rest from
their troubles. They would, E believed, benefit from a car ride in thee
fresh air of thee Yorkshire Dales. As E drove out Wharfedale way, Carol
seemed relieved until Michael suddenly uttered a piercing scream. It
was as if all his prayers vociferated in one high-pitched cry full of pent-
up blasphemies and curses. "He desperately needs help," said Carol.

The movements in his bed –

'E turned thee car around and headed back to thee Church. By
7.30 p.m., Michael was behaving irrationally, violently and noisily. He
picked up my cat and flung it through thee window. Food was placed
before him to placate and occupy his mind, but he threw it on thee
floor. It was my view that an enormous force of evil was emanating
from Michael and that this was undoubtedly a case of demonic pos-
session. It was clear from Carol's words that she was convinced that
her ex-husband Jack was connected with some Satanic group and
that he had pledged Michael to thee Devil. Michael's violence of speech
and action, his threat to murder someone and thee fact that he invoked
thee power of thee moon persuaded me that thee exorcism should
begin immediately without further delay.

So sorry, sad and so, so confused –

'E took him to thee vestry at thee side of thee Church and there E
laid him on his back on a pile of red, gold and green cassocks. E stood
over him asking him questions, finding answers, putting suggestions,
saying prayers, and casting out thee devils one by one. E named each
devil by its own evil: bestiality, lewdness, blasphemy, heresy, maso-
chism and so forth. A wooden crucifix given to him by his wife was
repeatedly put in his mouth as E prayed for him. He writhed and
thrashed on thee floor. Carol and E had to hold him down forcibly.
Every time he puffed out his cheeks and gasped and panted for breath,
another demon had been expelled. However, by noon on thee Sunday
we were all exhausted. He was rid of forty demons but alas there were
two still inside of him: violence and murder.

Between life and death –

'E felt that there was a doll somewhere for Michael like thee witch-
craft dolls into which people stick pins; unless it was found and burned
E would never be able to cast out thee spirit of murder for E had had
thee word from God that if Michael went home that afternoon he
would kill his wife. E tried to contact a medical officer of some sort but,

as it was a Sunday, E could find none. E called thee police but Carol
said Michael would be cross if thee police were called into this matter.
So at 8.30 p.m., E drove Michael and Carol home. E left at 9 p.m. in
search of thee doll and Carol's ex-husband. Thee last thing Carol said
was, "My husband is going to have a good rest."

Lost in room –

'E finally returned with her ex-husband, Jack. Michael Williams was
on his hands and knees with his forehead touching thee lawn. He
was naked except for his socks and his wife's rings on his fingers. It was
with these very fingers he had torn out her eyes and her tongue and, as
she lay choking on her own blood on thee grass, he had hammered a
twelve-inch nail into thee top of her skull. His hands, arms and body
were bloody and beside him was thee hammer. Thee first policeman
asked him, "Where did all that blood come from?"

' "It is thee blood of Satan."

' "Did you kill your wife?"

' "No, not her," he said. "E loved her."'

They found me hiding –

In Church of Abandoned Christ in sixth flat on second floor of sixth
house in Portland Square in ghost bloodied old city of Leodis, BJ still
lost; all covered in sleep and drunk upon a double bed, lost in so, so
many rooms; hair shaved again and eight eyes shined, BJ be this
Northern Son. Black Angel beside BJ upon bed; his clothes shabby and
his wings burnt, he has dolls in his pocket; he is Hierophant, Father of
Fear, and he whispers:

'It is time to bring Jack home again.'

In the shadow –

Rings upon the bed –

In the shadow of the Horns –

BJ, head bobbed and wreathed.

Chapter 46

I watch –

No sleep, no food, no cigarettes –

I just watch and I listen:

'*A Fitzwilliam man will appear before Wakefield Magistrates later today charged with the murder of Clare Kemplay, the Morley schoolgirl whose body was found on Saturday in Wakefield. The man is also charged with a number of motoring offences and is expected to be remanded in custody for questioning in connection with offences of a nature similar to those with which he has already been charged. This is widely believed to refer to the disappearance of eight-year-old Jeanette Garland from her Castleford home in 1969, a case which became nationally known as the* Little Girl Who Never Came Home *and which remains unsolved to this day . . .'*

Thursday 19 December 1974 –

Netherton, Yorkshire.

I wait.

Dawn, I watch a grey-haired woman come out of her front door with a parcel under her arm. I watch her close the door. I watch her come down her garden path. I watch her open her gate. I watch her carry the parcel round the back of Maple Well Drive. I watch her open the gate behind the bungalows. I watch her walk up the tractor path towards the row of sheds at the top of the hill. I watch her slip. I watch her get back up. I watch Mrs Marsh disappear into the end shed with her parcel.

I wait.

Thirty minutes later, I watch Mrs Marsh come out of the end shed. I watch her walk back down the tractor path. I watch her slip. I watch her get back up. I watch her open the gate behind the bungalows. I watch her come back round on to Maple Well Drive. I watch her open her garden gate. I watch her go back up her garden path. I watch her open her front door. I watch her go back inside, empty-handed.

I wait.

Twenty minutes later, I watch a car pull up.

It is a big black Morris Oxford. The driver is all in black. He is wearing a hat. He doesn't get out. He sounds his horn twice.

I watch Mrs Marsh open her front door. I watch her lock it. I watch her come back down the garden path. I watch her get inside the car. I watch them talk for a minute. I watch them set off.

I toss a coin –

I look at the top of my hand:

Tails –

I wait.

Ten minutes later, I open the gate to the field behind the bungalows. I walk up the tractor path towards the row of sheds at the top of the hill. The track is muddy and the sky grey above me, the field full of dark water and the smell of dead animals.

Halfway up the hill, I turn around. I look back down at the little white van outside their little brown bungalow and their little brown garden, next to all the other little brown bungalows and their little brown gardens.

I take off my glasses. I wipe them on my handkerchief. I put them back on.

I start walking again –

I come to the top of the hill. I come to the sheds:

An evil sleeping village of weatherbeaten tarpaulin and plastic fertiliser bags, damp stolen house bricks with rusting corrugated iron roofs.

I walk through this Village of the Damned. I come to the end of the row –

To the one with the blackest door and the rotten sacks nailed over its windows.

I knock on the door –

Nothing.

I open the black door –

I step inside:

There is a workbench and tools, bags of fertiliser and cement, pots and trays, the floor covered with empty plastic bags.

I step towards the bench. I step on something –

Something under the sacks and bags.

I kick away the sacks and bags. I see a piece of rope, thick and muddy and hooked through a manhole cover –

I wrap the rope around my hands. I hoist the cover up. I swing it off to one side –

There is a hole.

I look into the hole –

It is a ventilation shaft to a mine. It is dark and narrow. The sides of the shaft are made of stone, metal rungs hammered into them.

I can hear the sound of dripping water down below. I look closer –

There is a light, faint but there –
Fifty feet down there.
I take off my coat. I take off my jacket. I lower myself down into the
shaft, hands and boots upon the metal ladder –
Everything dark. Everything wet –
Everything cold, down I go.
Ten feet. Twenty feet –
Thirty feet, down I go.
Forty feet. Fifty feet –
Towards the light, I go.
Then the wall at my back ends. I turn around –
There is a passageway. There is a light.
I heave myself out of the vertical shaft into the horizontal tunnel –
It is narrow. It is made of bricks. It stretches off into the light.
I can hear strange music playing far away:
The only thing you ever learn in school is ABC –
I crawl upon my belly across the bricks towards the light –
But all I want to know about is you and me –
Crawl upon my belly across the bricks towards the light –
I went and told the teacher about the thing we found –
Upon my belly across the bricks towards the light –
But all she said to me is that you're out of bounds –
My belly across the bricks towards the light –
Even though we broke the rule I only want to be with you –
Belly across the bricks towards the light –
School love –
Across the bricks towards the light –
School love –
The bricks towards the light –
You and I will be together –
Bricks towards the light –
End of term until forever –
Towards the light –
School love –
The light –
School love –
Light –
The music stops. The ceiling rises. There are beams of wood among
the bricks.
I stagger on, arms and legs bleeding –
Stagger on through the shingle and the shale. The sound of rats here
with me –

Near.
I put out my hand. I touch a shoe –
A child's shoe, a sandal –
A child's summer sandal. It is covered in dust –
I wipe away the dust –
Scuffed.
I put it down. I move on –
My back ripped raw from the beams, the burden.
Then the ceiling rises again. I stand upright in the shadow of a pile
of rock –
I breathe. I breathe. I breathe.
I turn the corner past the pile of fallen rock and –
THWACK! THWACK! THWACK!
I am falling –
Falling –
Falling –
Falling:
Backward from this place –
This rotten *un-fresh* place –
Her voice, Mandy's voice –
She is calling –
Calling –
Calling –
Calling:
'This place is worst of all, underground;
The corpses and the rats –
The dragon and the owl –
Wolves be there too, the swans –
The swans all starved and dead.
Unending, this place unending;
Under the grass that grows –
Between the cracks and the stones –
The beautiful carpets –
Waiting for the others, underground.'
I am on my back –
Eyes closed –
I am dreaming –
Dreaming –
Dreaming –
Dreaming:
Underground kingdoms, animal kingdoms of pigs and badgers, worms and
insect cities; white swans upon black lakes while dragons soar overhead in

painted skies of silver stars and then swoop down through moonlit caverns
wherein an owl guards three silent little princesses in their tiny feathered
wings from the wolf that waits for them to wake –
On my back –
Eyes half open –
I am not dreaming –
I am underground:
In the underground kingdom, this animal kingdom of corpses and
rats and children's shoes, mines flooded with the dirty water of old
tears, dragons tearing up burning skies, empty churches and barren
wombs, the fleas, rats and dogs picking through the ruin of their bones
and wings, their starved white skeletons left here to weep by the wolf –
On my back –
Eyes wide open –
Under the ground:
Lying on a bed of dying red roses and long white feathers –
Looking up at a sky of bricks painted blue, white cotton wool clouds
stuck here and there among bright swinging Davy lamps –
Lying here, I watch a dark figure rise out of the ground –
Rise out of the ground into the swinging lamplight –
Into the lamplight, a hammer in his hand:
George Marsh –
A hammer in his hand, limping towards me.
I do not move. I wait for George Marsh –
A hammer in his hand, limping towards me.
I do not move. George Marsh almost upon me –
A hammer in his hand, limping towards me.
I do not move. Then I raise my right leg. I kick out hard –
Hard into his leg.
George Marsh howls. He tries to bring down the hammer –
The hammer in his hand.
I kick out hard again. Then I roll over. I rise up –
George Marsh howling, trying to stand.
But I am behind him now and I have his hammer in my hand.

Blind and black with his blood, I stop.
Under this painted sky of bricks of blue, in this one long tunnel of
hate, there are two walls made up of ten narrow mirrors, ten narrow
mirrors in which I can see myself –
See myself among the Christmas tree angels, the fairies and their
lights, among the stars that hang from the beams, that hang and dangle
among the swinging Davy lamps but never ever twinkle –

See myself among the boxes and the bags –
The shoeboxes and the shopping bags –
The cameras and the lights –
The lenses and the bulbs –
The tape recorders and the tapes –
The microphones –
The feathers and the flowers –
The tools;
I see myself and him among the tools –
The tools black with his blood.
His mouth opens and closes again.
I put the hammer down.

I stagger and crawl back the way I came, past the child's summer sandal, through the tunnel until I come at last to the shaft –
I can see the grey light above.
I haul myself up the metal rungs towards the light, weak and fit to drop into the endless dark below.
I reach the top. I scramble out of the hole. I pull myself on to the floor of the shed. I turn on to my back, panting –
Panting and wanting out.
I use the workbench to get to my feet, my glasses gone.
Blind, I move the manhole cover back into place. I camouflage it with the plastic sacks, kicking them over the cover and the rope.
Then I hear it –
Behind me.
I stop. I turn:
There is a figure, a shape here in the shed with me now –
Quiet and hooded.
Crouched down in the corner by the workbench and the tools, hidden here among the bags of fertiliser and cement, the pots and the trays –
Small hands.
A thin shape, with black hair and raggedy clothing –
Bleeding.
It steps forward –
Arms raised in the air with the appearance of menace and implacable famine.
I reach out towards it –
Blind and groping, covered in dried black blood, I whisper: 'Who is it?'
The figure darts to the left. I follow –

Darts to the right. I have it –
Then it is away –
Out of my arms and out of the door.
I stumble after it –
Out into the field and the rain –
But it is gone –
Gone.
I fall to my knees in the mud.
I raise up my eyes and heart, blind and raw up towards the vast grey sky and I let the coarse black rain wash away the blood –
From my eyes and heart, his heart and mine –
I let the rain wash away the blood, wash it into the earth –
This scorched and heathen earth –
These scorched and heathen hearts.

Thursday 19 December 1974 –
Midnight –
I am late:
Blenheim Road, St John's, Wakefield –
Hearts cut, lost –
I am late;
28 Blenheim Road, St John's, Wakefield –
Heart cut –
I am late;
I park. I get out. I lock the car door. I walk up the drive. I go inside.
Up the stairs to Flat 5 –
Heart –
Late;
I knock on the door –
The air stained –
Silent.
I try the door –
It opens.
I step inside –
Listening:
No low sobs, no muffled sobs –
No weeping here tonight;
Only silence.
Stood before the bedroom door, I whisper: 'Mandy?'
I close my eyes. I open them. I see stars –
Stars and angels –
My angel –

I try the door: 'Mandy?'
The door swings open.
There are loud animal sobs –
Contorted, screaming and howling –
The weeping is mine.
She is naked but for her blood –
Her hair all gone –
She is hanging from the light.

Beneath her shadows –
Dead hearts.
The cat piss and petunia, desperate on an old sofa –
Her head upon my chest, I am stroking her beautiful, bloody scalp.
Behind the heavy stained curtains, the branches of the tree tap upon
the window –
Sobbing and weeping;
Soaked in blood and wanting in –
'I love you.'
Sobbing –
'We'll go.'
Weeping –
'Far away.'
Her face in the candlelight white and dead –
The branches of the tree tapping upon the glass;
Sobbing and weeping –
We are kissing –
Asking to be let in –
Kissing and then fucking.

The windows look inwards, the walls listen to your heart –
Where one thousand voices cry.
Inside –
Inside your scorched heart.
There is a house –
A house with no doors.
The earth scorched –
Heathen and always winter.
The rooms murder –
Here is where we live.

I wake in the dark, beneath her shadows –
'We have her in the tree –'

Tapping against the pane.

She's lying on her side, naked –

Branches tapping against the pane.

I'm lying on my back in my underpants and socks –

The branches tapping against the pane.

Lying on my back in my underpants and socks, terrible laments and their dreadful elegies inside my head –

Listening to the branches tapping against the pane.

I'm lying on my back in my underpants and socks, terrible laments and their dreadful elegies inside my head, listening to the branches tapping along against the pane –

I look at my watch –

'Have her in the branches.'

It's stopped.

I reach for my glasses but they are gone and I get out of the bed without moving her and I go through into the kitchen and I put on the light and fill the kettle and light the gas and find the teapot in the cupboard and two cups and saucers and I rinse out the cups and then dry them and then take the milk out of the fridge and the bottle smells bad but I put two teabags in the teapot anyway and take the kettle off the ring and pour the water on to the teabags and let it stand, staring out of the small window, the kitchen reflected back in the glass, an un-dead man undressed but for his white underpants, an un-dead man undressed in a dead woman's flat at six o'clock in the morning –

Friday 20 December 1974:

'Under the spreading chestnut tree – '

I put the teapot and cups and saucers on the tray and take it into the big room and I set the tray down on the low table and pour the tea and switch on the radio:

'A Fitzwilliam man yesterday appeared before Wakefield Magistrates and was charged with the murder of Clare Kemplay, the Morley schoolgirl whose body was found on Saturday by the Calder in Wakefield. The man was also charged with a number of driving offences and was further remanded in custody for questioning in connection with offences of a nature similar to those with which he was charged. This is widely believed to refer to the disappearance of eight-year-old Jeanette Garland from her Castleford home in 1969, a case which became nationally known as the Little Girl Who Never Came Home *and which remains unsolved to this day . . .'*

I switch off the radio and take the tray back into the kitchen, one cup untouched.

I rinse out the cups and then dry them and put them away.

I go back into the bedroom –
I lie down beside her.
There are sirens and there are brakes –
I close her eyes.
Boots upon the stairs, fists knocking on the door –
I kiss her.
Boots down the hall –
I close my eyes.
Fists pounding on the bedroom door –
I kiss her for the last time.
Bill is shaking me –
I open my eyes.
I hold up her hand in mine –
There are bruises on the backs of both our hands;
Bruises that will never heal –
Never.
Bill is saying: 'I think you need a friend, Maurice.'
I nod.
The branches tapping against the pane, screaming:
'Where I sold you and you sold me.'

Chapter 47

Falling backwards into enormous depths, away from this place, her memories open, contorted and screaming and howling, the animal sound of an unfaithful wife trapped and forced to watch the slaughter of her husband upon their own neat lawn, contorted and screaming and howling, prone upon the carpet in the hall, on the golden flowers and the crimson leaves, on the marks made by piss and the marks made by shit, contorted and screaming and howling under dull Christmas tree lights that blink on and then off, on and then off, the faded poster warning against the perils of drinking and dying at Christmas, contorted and screaming and howling, the smell of dirty clothes and unshaven faces, contorted and screaming and howling as you took down their names and their memories, telling them of all the hells they were in and all the fresh hells you'd bring, how damned they truly were, but they just sat there silently waiting for new hells to come to their houses and flats, to take them upstairs and fuck them on their bed with their eyes open wide and their mouths shaped like fish, the whole house silent but for her, her mouth open, contorted and screaming and howling, her husband rotten in his box, already on his way back down underground, a tie around his neck and truncheon by his side, stitched up stones for his teeth, as you flew across the church, tried to reach across the pews and grab Badger Bill, to kill him here and kill him now, but your brother Pete was holding you back, telling you all the things that your dad had done and had not, all the shit he was in, how fucked he truly was, how he was better off dead and now she could get back on her feet and on with her life, better off without him, her mouth open, contorted and screaming and howling, the sound of her glasses breaking in her fingers, and then came the Brass, came to tell you how sorry they were, he was one of their own he was, one of the best that there was, how they were all going to miss Big John the Pig, his gun still smoking as they struggled to clean this all up, the stink of bullshit among the smoke, their lies smeared all over the windows of your shed, their fingers holding down the trigger, lying in their uniforms that said Leeds City Police, your father dead between a pair of swan's wings, his story blown to bits, still struggling to tidy up those little loose ends and file them away, to put him in the ground and make him go away, but it didn't and it never would, not for her, her mouth open, contorted and screaming and howling, crawling up her walls and her stairs on her hands and her knees, the bricks through her windows and LUFC on her walls, the swastikas and noose they hung above her door, the kids and their dogs chanting and barking, chasing her home from the shops in packs, home to the shit through her letterbox and the dirty phone calls, the dull thuds in the night and the torchlight that blinks off and on, on and off through her windows all night, the feeble voice asking her sons to please, please come help stop these kids and their dads, the white swastikas and the black, the marks made by kids and the marks by their dads, burning paper through her letterbox and a dead cat on her step, these policemen in suits and big size ten boots who check all her locks and drink all her tea and remember her John and then are all gone; the walls covered in wet painted words, the stink of shit up the stairs, the smell of dirty dog muck and rotten old eggs, the fruit and the veg and the endless days and nights of hate, these long days and long, long nights spent alone in her bedroom afraid to go downstairs, afraid to go out, for the kids and their dads, their mams and their nans, their chants and their taunts, their sticks and their stones, the words and the bricks that always hurt always, her husband dead and her sons that never call, alone on her bed in her own shit and piss with no food in the house, the doors and windows all locked and the dog fucking starved, she falls backwards alone on her bed through the enormous depths away from this place, this terrible rotten un-fresh place, this place that smells so strongly of memories, bad memories and history; this place where you are now, alone; terrified and hysterical and screeching, your mouth open, contorted and screaming and howling, alone with your mother on her bed in the piss and the shit with no food in the house and the wolf fucking starved at the door, alone with your mother in her bed, your mother and –

Mouth open, contorted and screaming and howling from under the sheets –

Contorted and screaming and howling from under the sheets –

Screaming and howling from under the sheets –

Howling from under the sheets –

Under the sheets –

Under the sheets as he first buggers and murders thee all over again –

Buggers and murders thee:

The Last Yorkshire Son –

Thee and then her –

Hazel.

Monday 6 June 1983 –

You are on your back, back in the flat, listening to the branches;

Everybody knows; everybody knows; everybody knows –

Listening to the branches tap;

Everybody knows; everybody knows; everybody knows –

Listening to the branches tap against;

Everybody knows; everybody knows; everybody knows –

Listening to the branches tap against the pain:
D-3.

The old woman with the walking stick and the small boy are staring at
you.

'Number forty-five!'

You look down at the piece of paper in your hand.

'Number forty-five!'

You stand up.

At the desk, you say: 'John Piggott to see Michael Myshkin.'

The woman in the grey, damp uniform runs her wet, bitten finger
down the biro list. She sniffs and says: 'You're not on the list.'

You say: 'I'm his solicitor.'

'Neither of you are,' she spits.

'There must be some mistake . . .'

She hands you back your visitor's pass: 'Return to your seat and a
member of staff will be down to explain the situation to you.'

Fifty minutes and two paper swans later, a plump man in a doctor's
coat says: 'John Winston Piggott?'

You stand up.

'This way.'

You follow him to a different door and a different lock, a different
alarm and a different bell, through another door up another overheated
and overlit grey corridor.

At a set of double doors, he pauses. He says: 'I'm afraid Mr Myshkin
is in the hospital wing of our facility.'

'Oh,' you say. 'I had no – '

'His family didn't contact you then?'

You shake your head. 'I've been away.'

'Mr Myshkin has been refusing food for just over a week now. He
had also taken to smearing his excrement on the walls of his room.
He refused to wear the regulation clothing provided to him. Both the
staff and his family felt that he might possibly attempt to take his own
life. As a result, Mr Myshkin was hospitalised late Saturday night.'

You shake your head again. 'I had no idea.'

'It is possible for you to still see Mr Myshkin,' he says. 'However,
I'm afraid that it can be only for a very, very short period.'

'I understand,' you say. 'Thank you.'

'Certainly no longer than ten minutes.'

'Thank you,' you say again.

The doctor punches a code into a panel on the wall.

An alarm sounds. He pulls open the door: 'After you.'

You go through into another corridor of grey floors and grey walls.

There are no windows, just doors off to your left.

'Follow me,' says the doctor.

You walk down the corridor. You stop before the third door on the left.

The doctor punches another code into another panel on the wall.

Another alarm sounds. He pulls open another door: 'After you.'

You step inside a large grey room with no windows and four beds.

The beds are all empty but one.

You follow the doctor across the room to the bed in the far-left corner.

'Michael,' says the doctor. 'You have a visitor.'

You step forward. You say: 'Hello, Michael.'

Michael Myshkin is lying strapped to the bed in a pair of grey pyjamas, staring at the ceiling –

His hair shaved. His mouth covered with sores. His eyes inflamed –

Michael John Myshkin, the convicted murderer of a child.

He turns from the ceiling to you –

There is spittle on his chin.

He looks at you. He doesn't speak.

You stop staring at him. You look at your feet.

The doctor pulls a set of screens around you both. He says: 'I'll be outside.'

'Thank you,' you say.

He nods. 'I'll be back in ten minutes.'

'Thank you,' you say again.

The doctor leaves you stood beside the bed –

Michael Myshkin looking up at you from beneath the straps.

'I didn't know,' you say. 'Nobody told me.'

He looks away, his face to the wall.

'I'm sorry,' you say.

He doesn't turn his head back.

It is hot in here. It is bright. It smells of shit. Of disinfectant. Of lies.

'Michael,' you say. 'I want you to tell me about Jeanette Garland.'

He doesn't turn back. He doesn't speak.

'Michael,' you say. 'Please . . .'

He is lying on his back with his face to the wall.

'Michael,' you say. 'I've tried to help you. I still want to help you, but – '

He turns his face from the wall to the ceiling. He whispers: 'Why?'

'Why what?'

He looks at you. 'Why do you want to help me?'

You swallow. You say: 'Because I don't think you should be here. Because I don't think you killed Clare Kemplay. Because I don't think you're guilty.'

He shakes his head.

'What?' you say. 'What?'

He stares at you. He smiles. 'So why do you want to know about Jeanette?'

'Because you knew her, didn't you?'

He is still staring at you –

'I went to see Tessa. You remember Tessa?'

He sighs. He blinks.

'She said you had Jeanette's photo. That you carried it everywhere. That you talked to it.'

He is crying now.

'She said you got it from work. Is that right?'

He nods.

'How? Why?'

'We went to her school,' he says. 'Jeanette's school.'

'Who?'

'Me and Mr Jenkins. It was my first week.'

'To take school photos?'

'I didn't know what to do. Mr Jenkins was shouting at me. The children were all laughing at me. But not Jeanette.'

'So you kept her photo?'

'No,' he says. 'That was later.'

'So you never saw her again?'

He looks away.

'What?' you say. 'Tell me – '

'I used to see her on the High Street sometimes with her dad or her uncle.'

'Johnny Kelly? In Castleford?'

He turns back. He nods. 'She always smiled and waved but . . .'

Strapped to the bed in a pair of grey pyjamas –

Hair shaved. His mouth sores. Eyes inflamed –

He is sobbing.

'You saw her one last time, didn't you?'

He closes his eyes. He nods.

'When, Michael?'

He opens his eyes. He looks up at the ceiling.

'When?'

'That day,' he whispers.

'Which day?'

'The day she disappeared.'

'Where?'

'In Castleford.'

'Where in Castleford?'

'In a van.'

Shaved. Sore. Inflamed –

He is weeping –

'She wasn't smiling,' he cries. 'She wasn't waving.'

'Who – '

He sighs. He blinks. He says: 'I loved her.'

You nod. You say: 'Who was she with, Michael?'

He looks at you.

'In the van?'

He smiles.

'Who was it, Michael?'

He says: 'You know.'

Hot. Bright. The smell of shit. Of disinfectant. Of lies –

'I want you to tell me.'

'But you know.'

'Michael, please – '

'Everybody knows,' he shouts.

You look at the floor.

'Everybody knows!'

You stare at your shoes.

'Everybody!'

You look back up at him. You say: 'The Wolf?'

He nods.

'Why didn't you say?'

'I did,' he says. 'Why didn't you?'

'I didn't know.'

Michael Myshkin stares at you –

You turn away again.

'Yes, you did,' he whispers. 'Everybody did.'

'About the Wolf?'

'Everything.'

This heat. The brightness. This shit. The disinfectant. These lies –

'I didn't know,' you say again. 'I didn't.'

Michael John Myshkin laughs. 'Your father did.'

Spittle on his chin, tears on his cheeks –

Tears on yours.

*

Doors locked, you check the rearview mirror then the wing. You switch
on the engine and the radio news and light a cigarette:
   *'The stars came out last night for Mrs Thatcher at a packed Wembley
Conference Centre: Bob Monkhouse and Jimmy Tarbuck, Steve Davis and
Sharon Davies, Brian Jacks and Neil Adams, Terry Neill and Fred Trueman;
Kenny Everett shouted* Let's Bomb Russia *and called on the crowd to* Kick
Michael Foot's Stick Away; *Lynsey de Paul composed and sang a song
entitled* Tory, Tory, Tory . . .'
   You are crying again:
   No Hazel.
   You switch the radio off. You light another cigarette. You listen to
the rain fall on the roof of the car, eyes closed:
   *Fourteen years ago, you waited in the same piss outside Wakefield Station
for your dad to pick you up. Just graduated. A lawyer at last. The Prodigal
Son. Your dad never came. You got the bus out to Fitzwilliam. There was no-
one home. You had no key. You went round the back of the house to wait in the
shed, the shed with your old trains and tracks. You thought you could see your
dad inside. You opened the door –*
   You open your eyes.
   You feel sick. Your fingers burning.
   You put out the cigarette. You press the buttons in and out on the
radio. You find some music:
   Iron Maiden.

There's no answer –
   You are listening to Mrs Myshkin's telephone ring and the relentless
sound of the hard rain on the roof –
   Nobody home –
   The rain pouring down, car lights on a wet Monday afternoon in
June –
   *The kind of wet Monday afternoon you used to spend in your office
answering and asking questions about marriage and divorce, children and
custody, maintenance and money, eating Bourbon or digestive biscuits, sitting
behind your desk, listening to the rain fall on the windows, the raindrops on
the wall outside so sharp and full of pain, listening to the relentless sound
of the hard rain on the windows and the walls, not wanting to visit your
mother, dreading it –*
   This fear even then –
   You hang up:
   This fear real –
   This fear real and here again:
   In a telephone box on Merseyside, listening to the dial tone –

The dial tone and the relentless sound of the hard rain on the roof, not wanting to leave the telephone box, dreading it –

This fear now:

Monday 6 June 1983 –

D-3:

This fear here –

The Wolf.

You park outside the off-licence on Northgate. You get out of the car. You go to the door of the shop. It is locked but there is a light on behind the handwritten postcards and the stickers for ice-cream and beer. You knock on the door. The old Pakistani with the white beard appears at the glass. He looks at you. He shakes his head. You rap on the door again –

'I just want a paper,' you shout.

The old Pakistani appears at the glass again. He shakes his head again.

'Mr Khan,' you say. 'Please – '

He is crying.

You turn round. You walk back to the car. You get in. You lock the doors. You start the car. You go up Northgate and turn on to Blenheim. You park in the drive. You get out. You lock the doors. You go inside your building. You go up the stairs. You take your key out –

The door is not open. There is no-one on the stair.

You open the door. You go inside. You lock the door. You walk down the hall. You do not go into the bathroom. You do not look in the mirror. You go into the ruined front room. You take some paper from a drawer on the floor. You take out your pen. You sit down on a pile of broken records –

The telephone ringing. The branches tapping –

Everybody knows; everybody knows; everybody knows –

You start writing.

Chapter 48

Big car turns off main road and passes through stone gateposts and up long drive, trees bare and black, up to main building of hospital –
Stanley Royd Mental Hospital, Wakefield.
He parks in front of old house and BJ and him crunch across gravel to front door.
BJ hold open door then follow him into reception area.
A nurse with a nametag that says M. *White* is sat behind desk; she is listening to a local radio news report about arrest of Yorkshire Ripper.
'Good afternoon,' he says.
'Good afternoon,' smiles woman. 'Can I help you?'
'I do hope so,' he smiles. 'We've come for Mr Whitehead.'
'Pardon?' she says, turning down radio.
'We've come to take him home.'
'Jack Whitehead?'
'Yes,' he nods.
'And you are?'
'The Reverend Laws.'
Confused, she says: 'I'll have to get Dr Papps.'
Reverend takes off his black hat and smiles at her, his nose broken and bandaged: 'We can wait.'
M. White picks up a phone with one hand and points at some chairs with other: 'Have a seat.'
BJ and him sit down and wait, staring through open double doors into day room –
Day room staring back in their pyjamas and paper hats.
It is New Year's Eve, 1980.

A short and fat man is coming down stairs: 'Gentlemen?'
BJ and Reverend stand up.
He has his hand out: 'I'm Dr Papps, Senior Consultant.'
'Reverend Laws.'
They shake hands. Papps says: 'Nurse White tells me you're here about Mr Whitehead?'
'Yes,' nods Reverend Laws. 'We've come to take him home.'
Papps is looking at BJ, trying to place top of BJ's head –
Suddenly trying not to remember BJ –
But BJ remember him:
BJ never forget a cock.

Papps suddenly blushes. He stammers: 'I'm afraid it's not as simple as you might think.'

Reverend puts an arm around Dr Papps. He turns him to look at BJ. He says: 'This young man is a relative.'

Good doctor tries not to look at BJ. He whispers: 'A relative?'

'His son.'

Dr Papps leads BJ and Reverend up stairs and down corridors, out of main building and into one of wings, unlocking and locking doors until last corridor and last door.

Dr Papps, key in hand, says: 'He hasn't been well, has Mr Whitehead; in fact he's only just returned from Pinderfields.'

'I know,' says Reverend.

'He won't be easy to care for, to administer to.'

'His son is aware of the commitment.'

Dr Papps glances at BJ.

BJ smile. BJ wink.

Papps unlocks door.

Everybody steps inside.

Room is cold and grey, just a toilet and a bed:

Jack Whitehead is lying flat upon bed in a pair of white pyjamas –

Staring up at light from window high in wall –

His head shaved, his hole in shadow.

'Jack?' whispers Reverend.

'Father,' he smiles.

'We have come to take you home.'

Jack sighs, eyes watering –

Tears slipping down his face –

Down his cheek –

His neck –

Off his pillow –

From mattress –

On to floor –

Puddles –

Rivers –

Rivers of tears upon stone floor –

Lapping around tips of all our wings.

Jack turns his head towards door: 'So many broken hearts.'

'So many pieces,' Reverend softly says.

'But do they fit?' BJ ask.

'That's the question,' whispers Jack. 'That is the question.'

*

Papps leads Jack in his white pyjamas out of door and down corridor, unlocking and locking doors, crossing from wing back to main building, along corridors and down stairs.

At reception, Reverend hands bad doctor a fat brown manila envelope and smiles: 'I believe this will help take care of any outstanding paperwork.'

Papps is touching envelope and his lips, nodding.

Reverend puts on his black hat: 'Good day, Dr Papps.'

'Good day, Father.'

Nurse White holds open front door as BJ and Reverend help Jack down stone steps and across gravel to car.

'Wait,' cries Nurse White. 'He hasn't any slippers, any shoes!'

BJ look down at Jack's bare feet, a tiny trail of blood upon cold, sharp gravel –

Reverend is holding open car door: 'He'll soon be home, don't worry.'

BJ push Jack's head down into back seat. BJ slide in next to him.

Reverend puts seat back and gets in. He closes door –

'Soon be home,' he repeats as he turns car around and heads back down long drive to stone gateposts and main road, trees black and bare but for old nests and carved hearts that cry:

'Hex, hex, hex, hex, hex, hex –

'Hex, hex, hex, hex, hex, hex –

'Hex, hex, hex, hex, hex, hex.'

It is raining and it is night in ghost bloodied old city of Leodis when big black car turns off Calverley Street and on to Portland Square, in shadows of Cathedral and Court.

Reverend parks before number 6.

There is a light in a second-floor window.

Reverend opens door and pulls back seat.

BJ help Jack from car and up three stone steps and through front door. BJ lead him across carpet of brittle leaves and buried letters and up staircase to first floor, across landing and up stairs to second –.

To door of Flat 6 –

Door where someone has written on letterbox:

Ripper –

Door where someone has added two sixes to first:

6 6 6 –

But there are so many, many doors:

Many doors to hell;

Open –

All of them open:

Everybody steps inside.

There is smell of amaranth and aldehyde.

BJ and Jack walk down passage into front room:

There are curtains whipped and candles fervid, there are words upon walls and photographs upon floor, there are shadows and there are sounds:

' . . . *no not she e loved her e destroyed thee evil within her it had to be done e am relaxed what had to be done has been done thee evil in her was destroyed carol was good but they had put thee evil into her e had to kill it he primed me to do it this last night we went to his church in fitzwilliam and stayed all night he will tell you it was a long night he danced around me and he burned my cross but he was too late my cross was tainted with evil he tried oh how he tried but e had to do it e had to destroy it e am relaxed e am at peace it was terrible he had me in thee church all night look at my hands e was banging them upon thee floor thee power was in me e could not get rid of it and neither could he e was compelled by a force within me which he could not get rid of e felt compelled to destroy everything living within thee house everything living including thee dog everything living but that was a lesser evil it is done now it is done thee evil in her has been destroyed it was in carol it used my wife my love oh hell e loved that woman no not carol she was good e loved her . . .'*

Tape stops.

There is a white towel upon bed.

Reverend Laws draws curtains.

He places a wicker chair in centre of room.

'Come here,' he says.

Jack doesn't move.

'Come to me,' he says again.

He is not looking at Jack –

He is looking at BJ.

BJ do as he says.

He takes off BJ's shirt.

'Sit here,' he says.

BJ do as he says.

He picks up a razor from white towel.

Jack is stood in middle of his room in his white pyjamas and his bleeding feet, tears in his eyes.

Reverend finishes. He blows across top of BJ's head. He brushes loose hairs away. He walks back over to bed. He puts down razor. He stands behind BJ.

He is facing Jack, whispering:

'Thy way is thee sea and thy path in thee great waters, and thy footsteps are unknown.'

Bathroom door opens.

A big skinhead in blue overalls is standing in doorway.

He has a Philips screwdriver in one hand and a ball-peen hammer in other.

'This is Leonard,' says Martin Laws. 'You remember Little Leonard?'

BJ close his eyes.

BJ wait.

BJ feel cold point of screwdriver on crown of skull –

Head bobbed and wreathed, this is BJ's choice.

Chapter 49

It was the night before Christmas. There was an enormous bungalow made of white feathers sat on the top of a big black hill, fat white candles burning in the windows. I was walking up the hill in the rain and the sleet, past the giant orange goldfish in the pond. I rang the doorbell. There was no answer. I opened the door. I went inside. A fire was burning in the hearth, the room filled with the sounds and smells of good cooking. Under a perfect Christmas tree, there were boxes of beautifully wrapped presents. I went down the hall to the bedroom. I stood before the door. I closed my eyes. I opened them. I saw stars, stars and angels. I tried the door. It swung open. I saw her; my star, my angel. She was lying on the bed under a beautiful new carpet, her beautiful, beautiful hair splayed out across the cushions, her eyes closed. I sat down on the edge of the bed, unbuttoning my uniform. I slid quietly under the carpet, nuzzling up to her. She was cold. She was wet. Her hair all gone. I tried to get up out of the bed but arms held me down, children's arms, branches –

'Uncle Maurice! Uncle Maurice!'

I open my eyes.

Bill's daughter is looking down at me.

I breathe. I breathe. I breathe.

'Are you OK?' she asks.

I blink. I am lying in a big double bed. I am wearing a pair of pyjamas.

'It's me,' she says. 'Louise.'

I sit up in the bed. It is not my bed. Not my pyjamas.

'You're at John and Anthea's house,' she says. 'In Durkar.'

I blink. I nod.

'Can I get you anything?' she asks. 'A cup of tea?'

'What happened?' I ask.

'My dad said you needed to rest.'

'What day is it?'

'It's Monday,' she says. 'Monday morning.'

I look at my watch. It's stopped.

'It's just after ten,' she says.

'Where is everybody?'

She starts to speak. She stops. She puts her hand to her mouth.

'Tell me, love,' I say. 'Please – '

'Sandal,' she says.

I look at her. I wait.

She sighs. She says: 'Donald Foster's dead.'
'What?'
'Bob found him.'
'Your Bob?'
'At his house this morning,' she nods. 'Murdered.'
I push back the covers. I get up.
'Where are you going?'
'I can't stay here, love.'
'But my dad said – '
'Where are my clothes?'
She points at the stool in front of the dressing table. 'Over there.'
On the stool are a clean set of clothes and my spare pair of glasses.
'I went to your house,' she says. 'I hope you don't – '
'Not at all,' I say. 'Thank you.'
'Where are you going?' she asks again.
'Wood Street,' I say. 'Can I borrow your car?'
'Your Triumph's outside.'
'Thank you,' I say again.
'But are you sure, you're – '
'I'm fine,' I smile. 'Honestly.'
'Do you want me to call my dad?'
'No,' I say. 'You know how he worries.'

I drive from Durkar into Wakefield. I don't turn off to Sandal. I go
straight to Wood Street. I don't go in the front way. I go in the back. I
don't speak to anyone. No-one speaks to me. I run up the stairs. I go
into my office. I unlock the bottom drawer. I take out two thick old files
and a third thin new one. I close the drawer. I pick up the files. I leave
the office. I walk back down the stairs. I go out the way I came in. I
don't see anyone. No-one sees me. I run back to the car. I drive out of
Wakefield past the Redbeck. I come to the edge of Castleford –
     To Shangrila.
     I don't stop –
     There is a dark red Jaguar parked at the bottom of the drive.
     I drive to the end of the road. I turn left. I drive to a lay-by. I turn the
car around.
     I wait.
     I don't close my eyes. I don't dare.
     I watch.

Thirty minutes later, I watch the dark red Jaguar pull out of the end of
the road –

There are two big men in the car.

I know the big man sat in the passenger seat –

Derek fucking *Box.*

The Jag turns right. It disappears around the bend in the road.

I start the car. I go back the way I came.

I park at the bottom of the drive. I get out. I look up the hill –

Shangrila.

I remember this place when it was only bones –

Stark white bones rising out of the ground;

I remember this place in the moonlight –

The ugly moonlight;

I remember this place and I remember the lies –

'He was here with me.'

I walk up the drive. I pass the goldfish –

I am not empty-handed.

I come to the door. I press the bell. I listen to the chimes.

The door opens:

John Dawson, the *Prince of Architecture* himself –

'Maurice?' he says. 'This is an unexpected – '

'Shut up,' I tell him.

'What?'

I push him back into his hall.

His wife is coming down the stairs in her dressing-gown: 'Who is it now?'

'It's the police,' I say.

'Maurice?' she says. 'What on earth's going on?'

I point to the living room on the left. 'Both of you in there.'

They go into the large white living room.

I follow them –

The whole room white. The whole room decorated with images of swans.

'I hope you know what you're doing,' says Dawson.

I punch him in the back of his head. 'Sit down and shut up.'

They sit down on the huge cream sofa, side by side.

On the glass table in front of them are architect's plans and today's paper –

I stare down at an upside-down photograph:

Paula Garland.

I read an upside-down headline:

RL STAR'S SISTER MURDERED.

I look back up at them. I say: 'You know why I'm here.'

'No, I don't actually,' says Dawson. 'And what's more, I believe Bill Molloy – '

'Fucking shut up!' I shout. 'Shut up!'

'Mr Jobson, I – '

'John,' whispers his wife. 'Please be quiet.'

I look at Marjorie Dawson –

Her expensive dressing-gown. Her tired, lonely eyes;

I look at her and I know she knows.

I look at her husband –

His expensive clothes. His timid, licentious eyes;

I look at him and I know he knows –

Knows she knows, knows I know.

'Ted Jenkins,' I say.

'Who?' asks Dawson.

'Photographer and purveyor of pornography. Child pornography to be exact.'

Mrs Dawson looks at her husband.

I take out a large black *Letts* desk diary for 1974. I open it. I turn to the addresses and telephone numbers at the back. I find the names beginning with the initial *D*. I turn it around. I put it down on top of the newspaper and the plans. I point to one name and one number.

Marjorie Dawson leans forward. John Dawson doesn't.

I smile. I say: 'He's got your number, has Mr Jenkins.'

Marjorie Dawson looks at her husband.

'He's got a lot of numbers,' I say.

John Dawson is biting his lip.

'Don Foster for one,' I say. 'Not that he'll be answering his phone again.'

Marjorie Dawson looks at me.

'He's dead,' I say.

She is opening and closing her mouth.

'Sorry,' I say. 'I thought you knew.'

Dawson tries to hold his wife's hand –

She moves away from him.

He tells his wife. 'I only just heard.'

'That what Derek Box came to tell you, was it?' I ask.

John Dawson puts his hands over his face.

'Well, I'm afraid I've got some more bad news,' I say.

Dawson looks up from his hands.

'George Marsh is dead too.'

'What?' says Dawson.

'Yes,' I nod. 'I killed him.'

'What?' he says again. 'Why – '

I smile again. I put three photographs down on the table on top of his plans –

Jeanette. Susan. Clare.

His wife looks down at them. His wife looks up at him –

'I wish you were dead,' she says. 'I wish we all were.'

I pick up the photographs.

He has his head in his hands again.

She stands up. She slaps him. She claws at his hands. She screams.

I leave.

I drive from Shangrila back home –

Home.

I park outside the house, my home.

There are no lights on, the curtains are not drawn –

Everything gone –

The children's feet upon the stairs, the laughter and the telephones ringing through the rooms, the slam of a ball against a bat or a wall, the pop of a cap gun and a burst balloon, the sounds of meals being cooked, served and eaten –

Everybody –

Judith, Paul, my Clare;

Jeanette, Susan, Clare Kemplay;

Mandy –

Everybody gone.

I drive back into Wakefield and on to Blenheim Road, St John's, Wakefield –

I park on the road beneath the big trees with the hearts cut into their bark;

I look down the street at 28 Blenheim Road –

I stare at the policemen sat in the dark in their cars;

I close my eyes. I open them. I see no stars –

No stars or angels;

I look up at Flat 5 –

No star, no angel;

Not tonight.

There's a tap on the glass –

I jump:

Bill –

He tries the passenger door.

It's open. He gets in.

His hair grey. His skin yellow –
He stinks of death;
We both do.
'Don's dead,' he says. 'So's John Dawson.'
'How?'
'Derek fucking Box did Don. Looks like John and his wife topped themselves.'
I turn to look at him. 'His wife too?'
Bill nods.
'What we going to do?'
Bill looks at me. He smiles. He says: 'We're late.'

Sleigh bells ring, are you listening?
    The Marmaville Club:
    Posh mill brass house turned Country Club-cum-pub, favoured by the Masons –
    Favoured by Bill Molloy:
    The Badger.
    The upstairs room, next to the toilets –
    The curtains drawn, the lamps on, no cigars –
    No cigars tonight:
    Monday 23 December 1974 –
    Christmas bloody carols up through the carpet –
    The beautiful carpet, all gold flowers on deep crimsons and red –
    Like the Chivas Regals and all our faces –
    Stood and sat in a circle of big chairs, a couple of upturned and empty ones –
    The gang half here:
    Dick Alderman, Jim Prentice, John Rudkin and Murphy –
    John Murphy on his feet and off his rocker –
    'Sit down!' Dick is shouting at the bastard –
    The Manc bastard not listening:
    'No, I fucking won't sit down,' Murphy shrieks. 'Not until someone fucking tells me what the hell is going on over here . . .'
    Bill palms up, asking for calm: 'John, John, John – '
    'No! No! No!' Murphy shouts. 'John Dawson and Don Foster are fucking dead. I want some fucking answers and I want them fucking now!'
    We say nothing.
    Murphy looks around the room. He points at me. 'And that fucking cunt – '

Points and screams at me: 'Now you tell me that fucking headcase has only gone and burned down half our fucking business!'

I say nothing –

'Fuck only knows what he's done with Jenkins.'

Nothing.

Bill is on his feet: 'Believe me, John, we're all as concerned as you are.'

We don't nod.

Murphy stops. He stands in the centre of the circle. He is panting and staring –

'John,' Bill tells him. 'What we've planned, what we've all worked so hard for; it's not going to be thrown away.'

Murphy is shaking his head.

'I won't let that happen,' Bill promises –

Just so we know –

Reminds us all: 'Off the streets, out of the shop windows; under our wings and in our pockets.'

We all stare at Bill –

Bill smiles. Bill winks. Bill says: 'Our very rich pockets.'

We don't smile.

Bill puts an arm around Murphy. He sits him back down –

Tells him and the rest of us how it's going to be: 'We have got a bit to sort out, but then it'll all be over and our investments secure.'

Jim Prentice shakes his head. He snorts: 'A bit?'

'Not talking about much,' says Bill. 'Two little problems, that's all, Jim.'

We wait –

Wait for him to tell us what we know: 'Derek fucking Box for bloody one.'

'Two-faced fucking cunt,' Dick spits –

'Where is the twat?' Jim asks.

'Bastard's meeting Bob Craven and Dougie at midnight,' Bill says.

'The heroes of the hour,' smiles Rudkin.

'More ways than one,' nods Bill. 'Upstairs in the Strafford.'

There's a tap on the door. The waitress brings in another tray of whiskeys:

Doubles.

She picks up the empty glasses. She leaves.

Murphy asks Bill: 'So what's on the agenda for this meeting of the minds?'

'You'll find out,' he winks –

'What do you mean?' says Murphy

Bill turns to Rudkin. 'You got the guns?'

Rudkin nods.

'Go get them then,' he tells him.

Rudkin leaves the room.

Bill gets to his feet. He shouts: 'Stand up!'

Everybody joins him on their feet, fresh drinks in their hands –

Me too:

For the body is not one member –

'To us,' Bill raises his glass. 'The bloody lot of us.'

But –

'The bloody lot of us,' we mumble –

Many.

'And the North,' I shout. 'Where we do what we want!'

'The North,' they reply and drain their whiskeys.

We sit back down.

'And the second little problem,' says John Murphy. 'You said there were two?'

Bill turns. He looks over at me –

They all turn. They all look over at me.

'Eddie Dunford,' says Bill.

I close my eyes –

I see my star, my angel –

My silent bloody angel;

I open my eyes. I nod. I start to say: 'I'll take – '

But there are boots on the stairs –

Heavy boots.

Rudkin bursts through the door: 'They got fucking shots fired at the Strafford!'

Bill and Dick on their feet first –

Jim and me right behind them –

Murphy fucked;

Everybody down the stairs fast, drunk and ugly –

Everybody shouting –

Everybody except Bill;

Down the stairs and into the cars –

100 miles an hour;

Bill, Dick, and John Rudkin in the one car –

110 miles an hour;

Jim driving ours, Murphy in the back seat –

120 miles an hour;

Police radio still reporting shots fired –

120 miles an hour;

Me screaming at Jim: 'Can't you go any fucking faster?'

120 miles an hour;

Hammering into the radio: 'This is Chief Superintendent Maurice Jobson, repeat: Do not approach the scene – '

120 miles an hour;

I tell them: 'Armed officers are being deployed – '

120 miles an hour;

I order them: 'Establish roadblocks in a five-mile radius, extending radius five miles every ten minutes – '

120 miles an hour;

I warn them: 'DO NOT APPROACH THE CRIME SCENE!'

120 miles an hour;

John Murphy, head between the front seats –

Drunk and laughing, fucked forever –

'Fuck they all call you the *Owl* for?' he shouts.

'Because of my glasses,' I reply.

'I see,' he grins –

'Now fuck off and let me do my job.'

He sits back –

I look into the rearview mirror. I can see him staring out of the window at the dark Yorkshire night, the Christmas lights already broken or off –

Murphy crying, wishing he were somewhere else –

Someone else –

Other people;

Crying and wishing we were all dead –

Or maybe just me –

Just me.

Fuck him –

Fuck them all –

The bloody lot of them:

I am the Owl.

Prentice slams on the brakes:

It is 1.30 a.m. –

Tuesday 24 December 1974:

The Bullring –

Wakefield.

There is an ambulance and a couple of Pandas at the bottom of Wood Street –

Our two cars with all doors open;

Bill sat in the passenger seat of one car telling us how it's going to be:

'Dick and Jim, get up Wood Street and wait for the call. Start rewriting this; times, calls, the whole fucking thing.'

They nod. They go.

'You hold the line here,' he tells Rudkin. 'Everyone out of sight, especially Brass.'

Rudkin nods.

Bill looks at his watch: 'Put the call in for the SPG in three minutes.'

Rudkin nods again.

'Me?' asks Murphy.

'You get fucking lost and fucking lost fast,' hisses Bill. 'Not your patch.'

He nods. He goes.

Bill looks at me –

I nod.

He stands up. He walks over to the back of the car –

I follow.

He hands me the Webley. He takes the L39 for himself.

He closes the boot of the car.

There are faint, distant screams on the wind.

Bill Molloy looks at me. He stares at me –

I stare back at him:

There is cancer in his eyes and he knows it; no-one at his bedside when he dies.

'Know what we're going to have to do, don't you?' he asks –

I nod.

'Let's get going then.'

I follow him across the Bullring –

Towards the screams.

I look up at the first floor of the Strafford –

The lights are on.

Bill looks at his watch. He opens the door –

The screams loud.

We go up the stairs. We go into the bar –

Into the screams. Into the smoke. Into the music:

Rock 'n' Roll.

The record on the jukebox stuck –

In hell:

A woman is standing behind the bar with blood on her. She is screaming.

An old man is sat at a table by the window. He has one hand raised.

Bob Craven is standing in the centre of the room. He is not moving.

Bob Douglas is lying on his stomach by the toilets. He is crawling.

A big man is on his back on the floor. He is opening and closing his eyes –

Derek Box next to him, dead.

Bill walks up to Craven. He asks him: 'What happened here, Bob?'

There is blood running from Craven's ear –

He can't hear.

Bill hits him across the face –

Craven blinks. He doesn't speak.

I go over to Bob Douglas. I turn him over on to his back –

He stares up at me.

I ask him: 'Who did this?'

He speaks but I cannot hear him.

I lean closer to his mouth: 'Who?'

I listen –

I look up –

Bill Molloy standing over us –

I repeat: 'Dunford.'

'Kill the cunt,' he says. 'Kill them all.'

I nod.

Bill turns. He shoots the old man sat at the table by the window.

He shoots him dead.

Bill looks at his watch. He looks back down at me –

I stand up.

I walk over to the woman behind the bar.

She has stopped screaming.

She is curling herself into a ball on the floor between the open till and the bar.

She stares up at me –

I know her:

Her name is Grace Morrison.

I know her sister too –

Her name is Clare Morrison.

I have my finger on the trigger of the gun in my hand. I close my eyes –

I see my star, my angel –

My silent bloody angel –

In hell.

I open my eyes –

We all are –

The record on the jukebox stuck –

In hell –

'Kill them,' Bill is shouting. 'Kill them all!'

Chapter 50

You stop writing.
 There is light outside among the rain –
 The branches still tapping against the pane;
 You put down your pen.
 There are seven thick envelopes before you –
 The branches tapping against the pain;
 You seal the envelopes.
 It is Tuesday 7 June 1983 –
 The branches tapping against the pain;
 D-2.

You open the bathroom door. You step inside. You stand before the sink. Your eyes are closed. You turn on the taps. You take off your bandages. You stand before the sink. Your eyes are closed. You wash your wounds. You dry them. You stand before the sink. You open your eyes. You look up into the mirror.
 In lipstick, it says:
 Everybody knows.

You drive out of Wakefield for the last time, the radio on:
 'The pathologist who examined Mr Roach told the inquiry yesterday that he believed the injury was self-inflicted and that Mr Roach had put the gun in his own mouth. He admitted, however, that he could not be 100% certain. The inquiry was also told that Mr Roach was hearing voices before his death. Colin Roach, aged twenty-one, died of shotgun wounds in the entrance of Stoke Newington police station in January . . .'
 You drive over the Calder for the last time, the radio on:
 'Mr Neil Kinnock said yesterday that it was a pity that people had had to leave their guts on Goose Green to prove Mrs Thatcher's strength. Meanwhile, polls continue to predict a Tory landslide with the Alliance and Labour battling for a poor second . . .'
 You drive into Fitzwilliam –
 For the last time.

Fitz-fucking-william –
 Newstead View –
 The street quiet:
 No fathers, no sons –

The men not here.

You pull up outside 69 –

What's left of 69:

There are boards across the windows and the door.

There are black scorch marks stretching up the walls.

There are piles of burnt furniture and clothes in the garden.

There are letters sprayed upon the boards:

LUFC, UDA, NF, RIP.

There are words:

Pervert, Pervert, Pervert, Pervert.

You start the car. You drive slowly down the road to 54:

There is an Azad taxi parked outside, waiting.

Mrs Myshkin and her sister are coming down her garden path. They are wearing headscarves and raincoats. They are each carrying two suitcases.

You get out of the car.

Mrs Myshkin stops at her gate.

'Where are you going?' you ask her.

She looks back up the road at 69. She says: 'You seen what they did?'

You nod. 'When?'

'Two nights ago, a mob of them just set the place ablaze.'

'Terrible,' says her sister.

'Where are you going?' you ask again.

Mrs Myshkin nods at her sister. 'Leeds eventually.'

You step forward. You take their cases. You say: 'Eventually?'

'I need to be near Michael,' she says. 'I'm going over to Liverpool today.'

'I saw him yesterday,' you say.

'I know,' she says. 'Thank you.'

'You've spoken to them today?'

'Yes,' she nods. 'Every day at the moment.'

You carry the cases round to the boot of the taxi. You bang on the boot.

The driver releases it.

You put the cases inside.

'Thank you,' say Mrs Myshkin and her sister.

'Just hang on a minute,' you say.

They nod.

You go over to your car. You take out two of the envelopes. You walk back to the two little women. You hand the two envelopes to Mrs Myshkin.

'What are these?' she asks.

'One's for you and Michael,' you say. 'The other is for Mrs Ashworth.'

'You want me to give it to her?'

'If you don't mind.'

'But I don't know when I'll next – '

'I'm sure you'll see her before me.'

Mrs Myshkin looks at you –

There are tears in her eyes –

Tears in yours.

'Thank you,' she says. 'For everything.'

'I didn't do anything,' you say.

Mrs Myshkin steps forward. She stands on her tiptoes. She kisses your cheek.

'Yes, you did,' she says. 'Yes, you did.'

You shake your head.

She takes your hand. She squeezes it. She says: 'I heard what they did to you.'

You shake your head again. 'It wasn't about Michael.'

She squeezes your hand once more. She lets go. She walks back over to her sister.

They get in the taxi. They close the doors. They wave at you.

You stand in Newstead View –

Among the plastic bags and the dogshit.

You wave back. You watch them go –

Your dried blood on the gatepost.

You park outside another boarded-up house on another street in another part of Fitzwilliam.

You get out. You walk up the path. You read the letters:

LUFC, UDA, NF, RIP.

You read the words:

LEEDS, LEEDS, LEEDS, LEEDS.

You stare at the swastika and noose painted above the door.

You turn away.

You look down the side of the house. You can see the edge of the back garden.

You walk slowly down the side of the house. You turn the corner. You stop –

You look down the back garden. You see the shed –

The shed with your trains and your tracks;

The shed –

Where you thought you could see your dad inside;

The shed –
You walked towards the door;
The shed –
You opened the door;
The shed –
You smelt the smoke;
The shed –
You saw the blood;
The shed –
You saw your dad;
The shed door banging in the wind, in the rain –
Your mother's mouth open, contorted and screaming and howling;
You turn away –
'Why?'
You close your eyes –
'Why?'
You open your eyes –
You look over the broken fence. You stare up at another empty house next door –
You remember a family that lived there a long time ago –
The two little kids, the mother and father –
'A very nice man'.
The father –
'So good with the kids.'
The father –
George Marsh.

Haunted, you drive –
She is dripping wet and as skinny as a rake;
Haunted –
Silently she points.

You park in front of a little white bungalow with a little green garden and nothing in it:
16 Maple Well Drive, Netherton.
You knock on the glass door. You have a mouthful of brackish water. You spit.
A chubby woman with grey permed hair opens the door.
You wipe your mouth. You ask: 'Mrs Marsh?'
She shakes her head. She says: 'No.'
'I'm sorry,' you say. 'I thought – '
'They used to live here, the Marshes,' she nods. 'Years ago.'

'Don't know where they went, do you?'
She shakes her head again. 'They flit, didn't they?'
'Flit?'
'Almost ten year ago,' she says. 'Bank repossessed place.'
'They just vanished?'
'Thin air,' she nods.
'I remember they had an allotment or something – '
She shakes her head. 'Some up field behind here, but we don't – '
'Didn't come with the house then?'
'No,' she laughs.
'Who owns them then?'
'Them allotments?'
You nod.
'Don't know,' she says. 'Coal Board, maybe?'
'Thanks,' you say.
She nods.
You turn. You walk back down the garden path.
'Sorry,' she calls after you. 'Who are you anyway?'
'Solicitor,' you say. 'John Piggott.'
'No trouble is there, I hope?' she asks. 'About the house?'
'No,' you say. 'Friends of my parents, that's all.'

The gate to the field behind the bungalow won't open.
You climb up over the stone wall. You lumber up the muddy tractor
path towards the row of dark sheds at the top of the hill.
The sky is heavy and about to piss all over you again.
Halfway up the hill, you turn around. You look back down at the
little white bungalow and the little green garden next to all the other
little white bungalows and little green gardens.
You can see the chubby woman with the grey permed hair at her
kitchen window.
You take out your handkerchief. You wipe your face.
Your breath smells of shit.
You spit again. You start walking again.
You reach the row of sheds –
You peer in through the gaps in the wood, the cracks between the
bricks:
Seed trays and yellow newspapers, plant pots and old copies of the
Radio Times –
All seed trays and plant pots until you come to the last one:
The one with the bricked-up window. The padlocked black door.
You knock on the door –

No answer.
You rattle the padlock –
Nothing.
You pick up half a house brick. You batter the padlock off the door.
You open the door –
You open the door and you see the pictures on the wall –
Pictures you've seen on a wall once before:
Jeanette Garland, Susan Ridyard, Clare Kemplay and –
One new photograph, cut from paper, dirty paper –
Hazel.
You know where she is.

Part 5
Total eclipse of the heart

'Every man is guilty of all the good he did not do.'
– Voltaire

Chapter 51

There is a light summer rain falling on empty flowerbeds below my window.

Doctor shines torch in my eyes again. He gives me three injections. Nurse cleans my wounds. She administers to my bandages. Doctor smiles. He shakes my hand. Nurse nods. She kisses my cheek. They leave me to dress.

Rain has stopped and there is sunshine somewhere behind clouds.

I get out of bed. I put on a heavy army greatcoat. I straighten my cap. I turn my collars up. I walk down corridor. I go into dayroom. I walk across carpet with a swastika held high in hand, rest of room prostrate at my feet in their dressing-gowns –

Fugitive sunshine caught in their tears –

I've been so far away;

I say my goodbyes –

So far from her arms;

Hospital clock strikes thirteen –

Hate Week.

This is North –

Where they do what they want –

Wellington Street, Leeds.

I get off bus. I go into coach station toilets. I take off my cap and coat. I unravel bandages. I look at my face in mirror. I tilt my head down. I stare up into glass –

It gets dark.

I take out my scissors. I cut my hair. I shake my head. Loose hairs fall into sink. I run taps. I take out my razor. I mix soap and water in my hand. I rub it over my scalp. I pick up razor. I shave my neck. I shave my face. I shave my head. I look at my face in mirror. I tilt my head down. I stare up into glass –

It gets dark and –

There are visions of sixes and sevens, swastikas and crucifixes inside my head, big black and white ones all splattered with blood in an underground bunker, in an upstairs bar, on a motel wall, in a hotel room on seventh floor –

A toilet wall.

It gets dark and I get confused.

I put my cap and army coat back on. I shine my best badge:

UK Decay.

I walk over to a phonebox. I step inside. I close door. I pick up phone. I
dial her number. She does not answer phone:
   Never answers her phone, she never answers her phone; that is her way –
   It is a war of nerves.

I am hungry now. I go into café. A lovely girl asks me what I want. I
take a cup of tea from her and a hot toasted teacake. I give her money.
She smiles at me. I take my tea and toast over to a table. I sit down. I
watch her work. I enjoy my tea and toast. I thank her. I pick up my bag
and leave.

I walk down Wellington Street into City Square –
   There are voices from vans;
   Past two stone lions and Leeds City Station –
   There are posters on walls;
   Along Boar Lane, past Griffin Hotel –
   There are ghosts on every corner;
   Across Vicar Lane and along Call Lane –
   In windows and doorways;
   Through Market into Bus Station and Millgarth –
   A black winged gargoyle looming;
   It watches me with talons pointed as memories are dull –
   It is dark now. I am confused;
   I wait for bus to Fitzwilliam –
   A shadow on wall.

Bus comes. I get on. I sit upstairs –
   Backseat hard.
   I light matches. I smoke cigarettes. I read seats –
   Thornhill Whites; Jeff is gay; LUFC; Barry 4 Clare.
   I light matches. I remember faces. I remember hers –
   I think about her all time.
   I light matches –
   Will she like me? Love me? Let me in? Let me stay, way people say –
   Or will she remember me? Hate me? Wish me dead, way people do.
   I let them fall to floor –
   Fucking cunts treat us like pricks.
   I light another match –
   Why this person is liked and that one is not –
   Why this one is loved and that one is not.

It burns my fingers. I let it fall –
A lie to him but not to her –
A kiss for him and a slap for me.
I close my eyes –
It gets dark.
I want to open them again. I cannot –
My trousers are round my ankles. Your hands are on my cock. Your own is
in my mouth. You come in my face. You beat me. You rape me all over again.
You give me money. You tell me to shut my mouth. Shut my mouth or you'll
kill my mum –
My stop is next –
I am nine years old.

1, 2, 3, 4, 5, 6, 7 –
All good children go to heaven.
I cross road. I cut through Corporation Cemetery. I come out on to
street –
My street, our street:
Newstead View.
This is where it started:
Fitzwilliam, 1967 –
Not heaven.

I look at watch again. It says thirteen o'clock –
Hate Week.
I walk down street –
Our street;
I come to house –
Our house;
I open gate. I walk up path –
It is dark now. I am confused;
I press doorbell. I wait –
A shadow on her wall in silence of her night;
I hear footsteps. I see a small body through glass –
I think about her all time;
Wait almost over –
I've been so far away, so far from her arms;
Now I'm home –
Back from underground.

Chapter 52

I have found her. She is safe and well. I hold her hand. We get into my car. Her family will be overjoyed. I start the car. We drive. She needs the toilet. We pull into a motorway service station. I park among the lorries and the coaches. We get out of the car. I lock the doors. We walk across the tarmac. I hold her hand. She goes into the ladies. I stand outside. I wait. Her family will be overjoyed. I wait. It starts to spit. I wait. Lorries come and lorries go. I wait. She does not come out. I go inside to look for her. There is blood on the floor. Blood up the walls. I push open the cubicle doors. I come to the last one. It is locked. It will not open. I knock. I knock and knock and knock. Blood on the floor. Up the walls. I step back. I kick in the door. She's not there. I run outside. She's not there. The lorries and the coaches gone. Not there. The car park empty. Blood on my shoes. On my socks. A Bloody Tide, lapping at my ankles. Up my legs. I start to run. The waters rising. The Bloody Waters. The rain coming down. The Bloody Rain. I slip. I fall to the ground. I cannot stand. I am drowning here. The Bloody Tide, a Bloody Flood.

I woke on my knees, my hands in prayer, in the shadows and dead of the night, the house quiet and dark, listening for something, anything: animal or bird's feet from below or above, a car in the street, a milk bottle on the step, the thud of the paper on the mat, but there was nothing; only the silence, the shadows and the dead, remembering when it wasn't always so, wasn't always this way, when there were human feet upon the stairs, children's feet, the slam of a ball against a bat or a wall, the pop of a cap gun and a burst balloon, bicycle bells and front doorbells, laughter and telephones ringing through the rooms, the smells, sounds and tastes of meals cooked, served and eaten, of drinks poured, glasses raised and toasts drunk by men with cigars in black velvet jackets, their women with their sherries in their long evening dresses, the spare room for the long summer nights when no-one could drive, when no-one could leave, no-one wanted to leave, before that last time; that last time the telephone rang and brought the silence that never left, that was here with me now, lying in the shadows and dead of a house, quiet and dark, empty –

Tuesday morning.

I reached for my glasses and went down the stairs to the kitchen and put on the light and filled the kettle and lit the gas and took a teapot from the cupboard and a cup and saucer and unlocked the back door to see if the milk had been delivered yet but it hadn't and there wasn't any milk in the fridge but I still put two teabags in the teapot and took the kettle off the ring and poured the water on to the teabags and let it stand while I washed the soup pan from last night and the bowl and then dried them both up, staring out into the garden and the field behind, the kitchen reflected back in the glass, a man fully dressed in dark brown trousers, a light blue shirt and a green v-necked pullover, wearing his thick lenses with their heavy black frames, an old man fully dressed at four o'clock in the morning –

Tuesday 7 June 1983.

I put the teapot and cup and saucer on the plastic blue tray and took it into the dining room and set it down on the table and poured the tea and lit a cigarette and then switched on the radio and sat in the chair and waited for the news on Radio Leeds:

'*Police searching for missing Morley schoolgirl, Hazel Atkins, are expected to come under renewed pressure for a breakthrough in the investigation following criticisms of the police handling of the case made by Hazel's parents.*

'*In a newspaper article in this morning's* Yorkshire Post, *Mr and Mrs Atkins say they have not been kept informed of the progress of the inquiry into their daughter's disappearance and have only learned of certain key developments through the press or television. Mr and Mrs Atkins were particularly critical of Chief Superintendent Maurice Jobson, the man leading the investigation. Hazel's parents say that Mr Jobson spoke to them on just three occasions early in the inquiry but that he has since been either unavailable or unwilling to meet them.*

'*Mr Jobson has so far refused to comment on . . .*'

Radio off, glasses off –

I was sat in the chair in tears again;

In tears –

For I knew there was salvation in no-one else –

No other name under heaven.

In tears –

Tuesday 7 June 1983:

Day 27.

Just gone seven –

Morley Police Station –

The Incident Room.

No-one here but me –

No-one and nothing here but two dozen four-drawer filing cabinets, nearly two hundred card-index drawers, a two-tier wooden rack for the scores of *Action* books and ten trestle tables with five huge computers and twenty telephones, the telephones on tables fitted out as

desks for writing up *Actions*, statements and reports, card-writing and
cross-checking the house-to-houses and the cars, cross-indexing and
entering data, updating files and sending out for more –

Or not, marking them:

No Further Action.

I opened the door to a small adjoining room:

Officer-in-Charge Investigation.

I sat down at my desk opposite a huge, pin-spattered map of
Morley –

A huge, pin-spattered map of Morley and a photograph –

A photograph of a little girl –

A little girl, still lost.

I turned on to Blenheim Road, St John's, Wakefield –

Old trees with old hearts cut, losing their leaves in June;

I parked in the drive of 28 Blenheim Road –

One big old tree, one big old house, one big old cut;

I closed my eyes. I opened them. I saw a star –

A single star, an angel –

A silent little angel;

I got out. I locked the car door. I spat –

Flesh;

I walked up the drive –

Shallow ugly daylight, brown stagnant rainwater;

The bottoms of my trousers, my shoes and socks, bloody –

Everything bloody;

I went inside. Up the stairs to Flat 5 –

Damp and stained –

Hearts still lost;

The door was open –

I stepped inside. I stood in the hall. I said: 'Hello?'

There was no answer.

I walked down the hall.

The doors were all closed.

I stood before the bedroom door. I whispered her name.

Silence –

The branches tapping upon the glass.

I tried the door.

The door swung open.

The room and everything in it had been destroyed.

I went across the hall.

I stood before the bathroom door. I whispered her name again.

Silence –
The branches tapping upon the glass, their leaves lost.
I tried the door.
The door swung open.
The bath taps were on. The sink too. The room flooded.
I stepped inside. I turned off the bath taps. I pulled out the plug. I went over to the sink. I turned off the taps. I took off my glasses. I washed my face and hands in the water. I pulled out the sink plug. I dried my face and hands on my coat. I put my glasses back on. I looked into the mirror above the sink. I put my fingers to the glass –
The lipstick:
Everybody knows.

I ran back down the stairs. I ran back down the drive. I got in the car. I locked the doors.
I stared back up at the flat. I took off my glasses. I closed my eyes again;
The windows that looked inwards, the walls that listened to your heart –
Where one thousand voices cried.
Inside –
Inside our scorched hearts.
There was a house –
A house with no doors.
The earth scorched –
Heathen and always winter.
The rooms murder –
Here was where we lived:
Jeanette, Susan, Clare, Mandy and –
Caught in the branches and the tree –
An angel –
The branches tapping upon the glass, their leaves lost and never found –
Wanting in –
Sobbing, weeping, and asking to be found –
Hazel.
I looked down at the bruises on the backs of my hands –
The bruises that never healed.

Hazel, Hazel, Hazel –
The motorway across the Pennines, raining with occasional shotgun blasts of thunder and lightning as I drove over the Moors –
More missing children, more lost children –

More children, taken and murdered;
More voices –
Terrifying, hysterical, and screeching voices of doom, disaster and death.
I drove. I drifted –
Underground kingdoms, evil kingdoms of badgers and pigs, worms and
insect cities; screaming swans upon black lakes while dragons soared overhead
in painted skies of fading stars and then swept down through lamp-lit caverns
wherein a blind owl searched for the last princess in her tiny feathered wings,
the wolf back –
Past Manchester and on to Merseyside, that familiar taste in my
mouth:
Flesh –
Fear.

I looked down at Michael Myshkin strapped to the bed.
He looked up at me –
His face sore. His eyes raw.
He whispered: 'Only you today?'
'Only me.'
'Can't keep away,' he said.
I nodded. I smiled.
He didn't smile back.
I opened my briefcase. I took out a photograph. I held it over him.
Michael Myshkin tried to turn away.
I pushed it towards him.
He closed his eyes.
'She's missing,' I said. 'Been missing twenty-seven days now.'
Silence –
'I want you to tell me everything, Michael.'
Silence –
'Everything – '
Silence –
'About the Wolf.'
Michael Myshkin looked up at me. He said: 'But you already know.'
I swallowed.
'I told you,' he said.
I fought tears.
'A long time ago.'
I took a pen from my pocket. I wrote four words on the back of her
photograph. I held it over him.
Myshkin looked up at the four untidy words:
I REGRET WHAT HAPPENED.

He began to cry.

I leant over the bed. I took his huge shoulders in my hands. I held him. I put my head on his chest. I listened to his heart. I held him in his dumbness –

In his dumbness and my blindness.

In both our tears.

I said: 'It's not too late – '

'I still see the Underground Kingdom. It is evil and an animal place; a kingdom of lost corpses and children's shoes, mines flooded with the tears and blood of the dead – '

'Other times,' I whispered –

'A dragon howling at the burning skies and the empty churches, while local mobs search me out – '

'Not your fault,' I said –

'For I was the Rat Man, Prince of Pests,' he cried. 'And I, I could have saved her. I could have saved them all. But – '

'Never mind,' I shouted.

Michael stopped. He was looking over my shoulder.

I turned around and there they were –

Stood in the open doorway:

Mrs Myshkin and Mrs Ashworth.

I let go of Michael. I stood. I started to speak –

Mrs Ashworth stepped forward. She slapped me hard across my face:

'Rot in hell,' she spat.

I nodded.

'We're all going to rot in this hell . . .'

I nodded.

Mrs Myshkin holding Michael –

His straps in one of my hands;

Michael rocking back and forth in his mother's arms –

The photograph of Hazel Atkins in my other hand.

'This hell,' Mrs Ashworth shouted again.

Mrs Myshkin whispering: 'Why didn't you say, Michael?'

Michael looking up at me from his mother's arms –

Trembling and blinking through his sores and his tears;

He looked up –

Blood on his face. Tears on his cheeks –

His face as beautiful as the moon, as terrible as the night;

He looked up. He blinked. He screamed: 'He told me not to!'

I turned away. I turned back to the doorway –

'This hell!'

Dick was standing there, panting. 'Boss – '
Michael Myshkin screaming over and over: 'He told me not to!'

Chapter 53

Tuesday 7 June 1983 –
  'Do not let us fall into the trap –'
  60 miles an hour –
  'Of voting for a schoolyard bully –'
  70 miles an hour –
  'Or we will deserve to live on our knees.'
  80 miles an hour –
  'Mr Scargill warned yesterday –'
  90 miles an hour –
  'People will have to stand and fight –'
  100 miles an hour –
  'Sooner or later.'
  Foot down –
  Everybody knows; everybody knows; everybody fucking knows.
  The hate nailed to the shadows of your heart –
  The fear stitched into the fat of your belly –
  Hate and fear, fear and hate –
  Putting hate and fear and fear and hate –
  Putting them together and getting –
  The Kingdom of Evil.
  The key in your pocket –
  The key to the Kingdom –
  D-2.

You pull in behind the Redbeck Café and Motel. You park in the empty car park –
  The Fear here –
  The dogs barking, the waiting over –
  The Wolf near.
  You get out. You lock the car door. You run across the car park –
  Puddles of rain water and motor oil underfoot;
  You run across the rough ground to the row of disused motel rooms –
  The broken windows and the graffiti, the rubbish and the rats;
  You run along the row towards the door –
  The door banging in the wind, in the rain.
  You stop before the door:
  Room 27.

You pull open the door –
The room is dark and cold.
No light here:
Only pain –
Someone has been decorating:
The walls inscribed with pain –
Maps, charts, photographs of pain:
Photographs of little girls –
Pale skin, fair hair, white wings.
Across the maps, the charts, and the photographs –
Swastikas and sixes;
Across every surface –
Six six sixes.
You step inside –
You try the light switch again –
No light here:
Only pain and darkness.
You step further inside:
Shattered furniture, splintered wood –
The base of the double bed pulled out into the centre of the room –
On the base of the bed, a portable tape recorder –
A cassette case marked:
On care to be had for the Dead.
You walk towards the bed –
You walk towards the bed and then you see her –
See her –
See her feet first –
Her tiny, tiny feet –
Her –
On the floor, between the bed and the wall –
Between the bed and the wall, on her face –
Her –
Hazel Atkins.
You look –
You look away.
You look –
You look down.
You kneel upon the base of the double bed. You lean against the wall.
You reach down. You turn her over –
In pen upon her chest:
6 LUV.

You collapse on the base of the bed and the portable tape recorder –
'*The only thing you learn in school is ABC –*
But all I want to know about is you and me – '
You switch it off.
Silence –
The weeping the only sound;
Sat among the silent sixes, weeping on the base of the double bed –
Staring up through your tears at the photographs and the sixes –
The silent sixes, waiting –
Six six sixes.
The silence –
The long silence until you hear car tyres on the car park –
Puddles of rain water and motor oil under their wheels.
Doors banging, slamming –
Car doors slamming.
Boots across the car park –
Puddles of rain water and motor oil underfoot.
You look down at the baby on the floor –
You look away;
Sat among the silent sixes, on the base of the bed –
Your wings, huge and rotting things –
Big black raven things that weigh you down, heavy –
That stop you standing –
Leave you sitting on the base of the double bed –
Staring through your tears at the photographs and the sixes –
The silent sixes, waiting –
Six six sixes.
They come to the door –
This door banging in the wind, in the rain.
They stop before the door:
Room 27.
They open the door –
Two figures in the doorway.
They step inside:
Maurice Jobson and another man.
They look at the walls –
The photographs and the sixes.
They look at the floor –
The girl on the floor.
They look at you –
The fat man on the double bed –
His wings, huge and rotting things –

Big black raven things that –
That weigh him down, heavy and burnt –
That stop him standing.
Maurice Jobson walks across the room –
He stands before you.
He reaches out to your face –
His cold fingers touch your damp cheek.
You bob your head forward –
You lean into him.
He holds you –
Holds you and strokes your hair.
You raise your hands –
You clasp your hands around his.
You squeeze his hand with yours –
His bruised hand in your bruised hand.

Chapter 54

Hate week:

I press doorbell again –

Again clock strikes thirteen.

I knock upon door. I bang upon door –

Never answers her phone, never answers her door; that is her way.

I sit down on doorstep with my back to door. I reach inside my army greatcoat. I take out an orange. I start to peel it.

Door opens a crack.

I turn round. I hold out a piece of orange.

Little lad, he tiptoes out into gloom. He reaches for outstretched orange –

Tips of our fingers touch.

I take his hand. I hold him by his wrist. I place a piece of orange in his mouth. It breaks skin of his little lips. He can taste old orange and his own blood. He is unable to speak. He is unable to tell me his mum's not here, that she is at shop –

But she'll soon be back, I nod.

I swing him through door and back inside his house, which is our house now –

Our house in middle of our street.

I close door. I wait.

Television is on: *Play your cards right; Give us a clue; Only when I laugh –*

I have no idea, I am a shadow.

I turn out lights –

Only television lights now: *Dynasty, Fall Guy, Kids from Fame –*

I have no fucking idea.

I take other orange from inside my army greatcoat. I offer it to little lad.

He shakes his head.

I say: 'Your name is Barry, is it not?'

Little boy, he nods.

'My name was Barry too,' I tell him.

Little boy looks at his feet.

'Here,' I say. 'Would you like this badge?'

Little boy looks up at badge in my hand:

UK Decay.

He shakes his head.

I hear key turn in door once –
(We think of key, each in his prison) –
and turn once only.
She opens door and her mouth. She turns to go, but I am on my feet across room.
I pull her back inside our house –
This was where we used to sleep (to dream, to scream) –
I spin her across room on to settee. I slam door –
(We keep pain on inside round here) –
'Dream on,' I say.
She sits on settee. She looks up at me, chest rising and chest falling –
Little lad watching us both.
'Hello,' I say. 'Hello from one that got away.'
She just sits and stares.
'You don't remember me, do you?'
She sits. She stares. She says: 'I thought you were dead?'
'Oh no, not me,' I say.
She starts to cry.
I sit down beside her. I put my arm around her.
Her hair smells of fat and smoke –
They are big tears that are falling on her old clothes.
'Oh, don't start with them waterworks, now will you?' I smile.
She stops. She sniffs. She rubs her red nose. She dries her red eyes –
Little lad still watching us both.
'Do you believe in ghosts, little Barry?' I ask him.
He shakes his head.
'Well, you bloody ought,' I swear. 'Didn't he, mum?'
Then I hear them –
Hear them coming;
Coming to our house –
Our house in middle of our street (our house in middle of our hell).

Chapter 55

Sirens down the Doncaster and Barnsley Roads, into Wakefield:

Two cars, a van, and an ambulance –

No sirens on the ambulance.

Piggott cuffed and bagged on the floor of the van as we swept into Wood Street, taking him underground before the pack had either a hint or a whiff –

Just our lot all lined up and waiting for him, punching and kicking and spitting on him as we dragged him by his heels up and down the corridors –

Up and down the corridors.

Then we stripped him. We fingerprinted him. We photographed him –

Threw him in a cell.

'Keep him sweet,' I told Dick.

'With the exception of the slight ligature marks on the ankles and wrists,' Dr Alan Coutts was saying, 'there are no wounds.'

I stopped writing. I said: 'Cause of death then?'

'Preliminary – '

'What?'

'Starvation and – '

'What?'

'Hunger and – '

'What?'

'Possibly vagal inhibition.'

'Strangled?'

He shook his head: 'A sudden and unexpected shock can also be enough to stimulate the vagal nerve and cause death – '

'She died of fright?'

'Or hunger.'

'When?'

'I can't be precise yet,' he said. 'But – '

'Approximately?'

'Within the last 72 hours.'

'Where?'

'Initial examination of particles from the skin and nails have revealed the strong presence of coal dust.'

'Local?'

He nodded.
'Underground?'
He nodded.
I looked down at my hands –
History and lies.

They were standing at the end of the corridor, black shadows under the white lights –
'*Under the spreading chestnut tree* –'
I walked down the corridor towards them.
They were waiting for me.
'Mr and Mrs Atkins,' I said.
They were staring at me.
I gestured to the four grey plastic seats against the cracked magnolia wall. I said: 'I think we should sit down.'
There were staring –
'I'm very sorry to have to tell you that we have found a little girl and – '
They were waiting –
'The little girl is not alive.'
They held each other's hands in their own. They squeezed them.
'The body was discovered earlier today in a disused room at the old Redbeck Café on the Doncaster Road.'
They both looked at the linoleum. They shook.
I had nothing more to say to them.
Mr Atkins looked up. Her father said: 'How did she die?'
'It would appear she died from a combination of a lack of food and water and – '
They were both looking up at me now.
'Fright.'
'When?'
'Possibly within the last 72 hours but – '
Mrs Atkins' mouth was open, contorted and screaming and howling –
She was slapping and scratching and punching me, trying to murder me –
Murder me –
Murder me –
Murder me –
Murder me –
I wished her mother would murder me –
'*Where I sold you and you sold me.*'

'I'm sorry,' I said.

'Can I see her?' asked Mrs Atkins, quietly.
I looked up.
WPC Martin had her by the arm, trying to ease her away.
I nodded.

Dr Coutts opened the door.
He switched on the overhead lights.
They flickered and then came on.
She was lying under a sheet on a gurney in the middle of the room.
Dr Coutts pulled back the sheet as far as her shoulders.
They stepped forward.
They fell on her.

Chapter 56

They take you naked into a ten by six interrogation room with white lights and no windows. They sit you down behind a table. They handcuff your hands behind your back. They throw a bucket of piss and shit across your face. They hose you down with ice water until you fall over in the chair. Then they leave you alone.

You are lying on the floor, handcuffed to the chair.

You can hear screams from other rooms –

You can hear laughter –

Dogs barking.

The screaming goes on and on for what seems like hours.

Then it stops.

You close your eyes.

You have dreams –

And in your dreams –

In your dreams, you have wings –

But all these wings in all your dreams –

Are huge and rotting things –

The room red.

The door opens. Three men in suits come in. They are carrying chairs.

One man has a grey moustache. The other is bald but for tufts of fine sandy hair:

Moustache and Sandy.

The last man you know:

Maurice Jobson; Detective Chief Superintendent Maurice Jobson –

Thick lenses and black frames:

The Owl.

They pick you up. They sit you in the chair. They undo your handcuffs.

'Put your palms flat upon the desk,' says Sandy.

You put your palms flat upon the desk.

Sandy sits down. He takes a pair of handcuffs from the pocket of his sports jacket. He passes them to Moustache.

Moustache walks around the room. Moustache plays with the handcuffs. Moustache sits down next to Sandy. Moustache puts the handcuffs over the knuckles of his fist. Moustache stares at you.

Maurice closes the door. He leans against it, arms folded. He watches you.

They all smile.

Moustache jumps up. Moustache brings his handcuffed fist down on to the top of your right hand.

You scream.

'Put your hands back,' says Sandy.

You put them back on the table.

'Flat,' says Sandy.

You try to lie them down flat.

'Nasty,' says Moustache.

'You should get that seen to,' says Sandy.

They both smile at you.

Sandy stands up. He goes out of the room.

Maurice follows him.

Moustache says nothing. He just stares.

Your right hand is red and throbbing.

Sandy comes back in with a blanket. He puts it over your shoulders. He sits back down. He takes out a packet of JPS from his sports jacket. He offers one to Moustache.

Moustache takes out a lighter. He lights both their cigarettes.

They sit back. They blow smoke at you.

Your hands are shaking.

Moustache leans forward. Moustache dangles the cigarette over your right hand. Moustache rolls it back and forth between two fingers.

Your hand is twitching –

You pull your hand back a bit.

Moustache reaches forward. Moustache grabs your right wrist. Moustache holds down your right hand. Moustache stubs his cigarette out in the bruises on the back of your hand.

You scream.

Moustache lets go of your wrist. Moustache sits back.

'Put your hands flat,' says Sandy.

You put them flat on the table.

The room stinks of burnt skin –

Yours.

Moustache sweeps the ash and tobacco off the table.

'Another?' says Sandy.

'Don't mind if I do,' says Moustache. He takes a second JPS from the packet. He lights the cigarette. He stares at you. He leans forward. He begins again to dangle the cigarette over your hand.

You stand up: 'What do you want?'

'Sit down,' says Sandy.

'Tell me what you want!'

'Sit down.'

You sit down.

Moustache and Sandy stand up.

'Stand up,' says Sandy.

You stand up.

'Eyes front.'

You stare straight ahead.

'Don't move.'

You don't move.

Moustache and Sandy put the three chairs and the table to the side. Maurice opens the door. They step outside into the corridor.

You can hear screaming –

Laughter –

Dogs barking.

They close the door.

You stand in the centre of the room. You stare at the white wall. You are naked. You want a piss. You listen to the screaming. You listen to the laughter. You listen to the barking. You do not move. You close your eyes.

You have dreams –

    And in your dreams –

    In your dreams, you have fears –

    But all your fears in all your dreams –

    Are islands lost in tears –

    The room white.

The door opens again. Moustache and Sandy come back in.

Maurice does not.

Moustache and Sandy walk around you in silence.

They smell of drink and curry. They smell of sweat.

They bring the chairs and the table back to the centre of the room.

Moustache puts a chair behind you. He says: 'Sit down.'

You sit down opposite Sandy.

Moustache picks up the blanket from the floor. He puts it over your shoulders.

Sandy lights a cigarette. He says: 'Put your palms flat on the desk.'

'Please tell me what you want.'

'Just put your palms flat.'

You put your palms flat on the desk.

Moustache walks about behind you.

Sandy puts a brown paper package on the table. He opens it. He takes out a pistol. He lays it down on the table. He smiles at you.

Moustache stops walking about. He stands behind you.

'Eyes front,' says Sandy.

You stare straight ahead.

Sandy jumps up. Sandy pins your wrists down.

Moustache grabs the blanket. Moustache twists it around your face.

You fall forward off the chair. You cough. You choke. You are unable to breathe. You hit the edge of the table –

Crack.

Sandy holds down your wrists.

Moustache twists the blanket around your face.

You kneel on the floor. You cough. You choke. You are unable to breathe.

Sandy lets go of your wrists.

You spin round in the blanket into the wall –

Crack.

Moustache throws off the blanket. He picks you up by your hair. He stands you against the wall.

'Turn around, eyes front.'

You turn around.

Sandy has the pistol in his right hand.

Moustache has some bullets. He is throwing them up. He is catching them.

'Maurice says the cunt wants to die,' whispers Moustache. 'So just make it look like he topped himself.'

Sandy holds the pistol with both hands at arm's length. He points the gun at the side of your head.

You close your eyes, tears streaming down your cheeks.

Sandy pulls the trigger –

Click.

Nothing happens.

'Fuck,' says Sandy.

He turns away. He fiddles with the pistol.

You have pissed yourself.

'I've fixed it,' says Sandy. 'It'll be all right this time.'

He points the pistol again.

You close your eyes.

Sandy pulls the trigger –

Bang.

You think you are dead.

You open your eyes. You see the pistol. You see shreds of black material coming out of the barrel. You watch them float down to the floor.

Moustache and Sandy are staring at you.

You shout: 'What do you want?'

Moustache steps forward. Moustache kicks you in the balls.

You fall to the floor.

'What do you want?'

'Stand up.'

You stand up.

'On your toes,' says Moustache.

'Please tell me?'

Moustache steps forward again. Moustache kicks you in the balls again.

You fall to the floor.

He whispers: 'Man had his balls removed after being kicked by the Leeds SPG.'

Sandy walks over. Sandy kicks you in the chest. Sandy kicks you in the stomach. Sandy handcuffs your hands behind your back. Sandy pushes your face into the floor –

Into your own piss.

'Do you like dogs, Johnny?'

'What do you want?'

'Do you like dogs?'

'What do you fucking want?'

'I don't think you do, do you?'

The door opens.

A uniformed policeman comes in with an Alsatian on a lead.

Moustache sits astride your back. Moustache pulls your face up by your hair.

The dog is staring at you, panting –

Tongue out.

Moustache shouts: 'Get him! Get him!'

The dog is growling. The dog is barking. The dog is straining on its leash.

'Careful,' says Sandy to the uniform.

Moustache pushes your head forward –

'He's starving,' he says. 'Just like little Hazel was.'

You struggle.

The dog is getting nearer –

'Just like little Hazel.'

You try to get loose.

Moustache pushes your face in closer –
'Starving.'
You cry.
The dog is a foot away.
'Alone in that room.'
You see its gums. You see its teeth. You smell its breath. You feel its
breath.
'Starving.'
The dog growling. The dog barking. The dog straining on its leash.
'Starving to death alone in that room.'
You shit yourself.
'Fucking knew, didn't you?'
The dog is inches from your face.
'Did nothing.'
Everything going black –
'Nothing!'
Going black –
'Tell me what I've done.'
'Again!'
'Please – '
'Please what?'
Black –
'Please tell me what I've done.'
'Again!'
'Please tell me what I've done!'
'Clever boy,' he says –
Everything black now.
You fall backwards, handcuffed upon a tiny plastic chair –
Through the floor of the cell, through the walls of the Station –
Through the earth and through the oceans –
Through the atmosphere into outer space –
To the gulfs between the stars –
Always away from the dog –
Away from this place –
This *rotten*, un-fresh linoleum place;
Light years distant, Jobson still standing at your side –
The dog gone.

You have dreams –
  And in your dreams –
  In your dreams, you see things –
  But all these things in all your dreams –

Are big black raven things –
The room blue.

You open your eyes.

Maurice Jobson is staring back at you.

You are still in the room with white lights and no windows.

But you are dressed in your own clothes again.

Maurice Jobson takes off his glasses. He rubs his eyes.

'I didn't do it,' you say.

'Not guilty?' he smiles.

'Not guilty.'

He puts his thick lenses and black frames back on. 'We're all guilty, John.'

You shake your head. 'Not me.'

He nods. 'We all are.'

You close your eyes.

When you open them again, he is still staring at you –

Still waiting.

'Will you make it right?' he asks.

You nod –

'Yes, sir,' you say. 'I will.'

You have dreams –
And in your dreams –
In your dreams, you cry tears –
But all your tears in all your dreams –
Are islands lost in fears –
The room red, white, and blue (like you).

He leads you down the corridor to the double doors and the courtyard.

A black van is waiting, its back doors open.

Moustache and Sandy are sitting inside.

'You're not coming?' you ask.

He shakes his head. 'I've been there before.'

There are tears in your eyes again. 'We'll meet again?'

'Don't know where, don't know when,' he says without a smile.

'Some sunny place?' you ask.

'Where there is no darkness.

Chapter 57

Here come sirens, here come blue lights –

I turn back from window. I say: 'They're here.'

She is kneeling before settee. She is sobbing. She is clutching her rosary.

I drag her to her feet, left arm round her neck, right arm on shotgun.

I manoeuvre us over to door.

I yank it open just as two uniforms come through garden gate up path.

'Get back!' I shout. 'Get back or I'll blow her fucking head off.'

She is screaming, legs half off ground.

Uniforms scramble off back down garden path and out gate, back behind their car.

I lower shotgun. I pull trigger –

BANG!

Through hedge into side of their car –

Lights out.

I drag her back up path into house. I slam front door shut.

I push her back into living room. I tie her hands and feet together.

I pull back curtain. I break glass. I let off another shot into night –

BANG!

I reload:

We've only just begun.

I head straight into kitchen. I tip dresser and fridge in front of back door.

I break milk bottles. I break all her best china. I scatter it across barricade.

I tear back through into front room. I start shifting stuff in front of window.

She is just lying in middle of it all, teeth chattering.

I put my boot through TV. I take petrol. I splash it all over –

All over kitchen, all over front room.

'Right,' I say. 'Time for bed.'

I drag her out front room upstairs into back bedroom.

I toss her on spare bed. I rush into front bedroom.

I tip bed and mattress on their ends. I put them over window, wardrobe behind them.

Downstairs I can hear phone ringing.

I take doors off bathroom and front bedroom. I put one over bathroom window and other across top of stairs.

I return to back bedroom. I move her off bed on to floor. I make sure she is secure. I upend bed. I put it low along bottom of window.

Downstairs telephone is still ringing.

I go back down stairs into hall, low as I go, no lights on:

Keep pain on inside.

I pick phone up. I say nothing –

Listen –

I say: 'I want to talk to Maurice Jobson. Tell him I need a friend.'

I hang up.

I go halfway up stairs to wait.

It starts ringing again, phone.

I can see them moving about in garden.

I take off my shoe. I lob shoe at phone. I knock receiver off hook.

I hear them shout: 'Go.'

I point shotgun at door. Just before it opens, I do –

BANG!

'FUCK! FUCK! – '

Both barrels:

BANG!

'FUUUUUUUUUUUUUUUUUUUUUUUUUUUUUUUUUCK!'

I go back upstairs. I put door across top again. I go into back bedroom.

She is lying on floor, skirt up around her ears as bloody usual –

Bawling, waterworks.

I can hear more sirens.

I look up –

There are posters on bedroom walls, Karen and Richard –

Yesterday Once More.

'Where's Barry?' I yell at her. 'What fuck you done with him?'

Chapter 58

Darkness –

Pitch black fucking darkness:

Wednesday 8 June 1983.

Thunder, no lightning –

Never-fucking ending:

Cars across the night, the sirens and the blue lights.

Heart of a darkness, belly of a nightmare –

Fitz-fucking-william:

My darkness, my nightmare.

Two radios on –

Police and fucking local –

Stereo hell:

'*A man is believed to be holding a woman hostage in Fitzwilliam following an incident in which shots were fired at police officers responding to reports of a break-in at an address in Newstead View.*

'*Armed officers have been deployed but Mr Ronald Angus, the Chief Constable, issued a statement insisting that the police were anxious to end this incident without injury to anyone. This comes after mounting criticism in recent weeks over revelations that armed police are now deployed on routine patrols in Greater Manchester and West Yorkshire.*'

I cut that crap off with the heel of my fucking boot –

One, two, three –

Crack!

Ellis driving, eyes and foot down on wet streets: 'Sir?'

Fourth, final kick –

Craaaaaaaaaaaaaaaaaaaaaaaaaaaaaaaaaaaaack!

Plastic flying, radio dead.

Into the handheld, shouting: 'Alderman? Prentice?'

Static: 'No, sir.'

'Where the fuck are they?'

'Netherton.'

'That was fucking hours ago.'

'Sir – '

'Fuck it,' I screamed.

'We have got a description – '

'Give it!'

'White male, mid to late twenties; shaved head with a deep indentation – '

'Indentation?'

'A hole, sir.'

'Name?'

'We're working on it – '

'Work fucking harder,' I yelled, tearing the flex out –

The radio dead in my hand –

The rain and the night all over the windscreen –

Tears and blood all over my cheeks.

'It's him, isn't it?' whispered Ellis –

I raised my right leg. I put my boot through that fucking windscreen –

Smaaaaaaaaaaaaaaaaaaaaaaaaaaaaaaaaaaaaaaaaaash!

The rain and the night all over us now –

The tears and the blood, the tears and the blood –

Everywhere.

Parked at the end of the road among the other blue lights –

We waited. We watched.

A sergeant came crouching up the street. He leant in the window.

'Sir?'

'What is it, Sergeant?'

'He's asking for you, sir,' he panted. 'The man inside the house.'

'By name?' asked Ellis.

'Yes.'

'What's he say?'

'Says he needs a friend, sir.'

I opened the door. I got out of the car, my wrists and ankles all bloody.

'He'll kill you,' said Ellis –

I nodded. I walked up the road through the blue lights –

The white floodlights –

The red rain.

I came to the house –

Ellis running up the street. Ellis shouting: 'Kill you – '

I nodded again. I opened the gate, thinking –

Murder me.

Chapter 59

They take off the handcuffs. They take off the blindfold. They open the back doors.

The van slows.

They throw you out on to the road. They drive away.

You lie in the road. You don't know if it is dawn or dusk.

It is raining.

You get up off the ground. You stand up.

There is a green Viva parked outside the little white bungalow.

There are no lights on. The curtains aren't drawn.

You go round the back. You climb over the stone wall into the field. You walk up the tractor path towards the row of sheds at the top of the hill.

It is pissing down now.

You are ankle deep in mud and animal shit.

You slip.

You fall.

You get up.

You look back down the hill at all the little bungalows tucked up together, sleeping soundly –

Day in, day out.

You wipe the mud off your hands. You start walking again.

You slip again.

You fall again.

You get up again.

You reach the row of sheds. You walk along. You come to the last one:

The one with no windows and the black door –

The black door banging in the wind and the rain:

The door to hell.

You step inside –

The pictures on the wall have gone.

There is a workbench and tools, bags of fertiliser and cement, pots and trays.

There is a hole in the ground. It is surrounded by sacks and a piece of thick and muddy rope hooked through a manhole cover.

You look into the hole –

It is a ventilation shaft to a mine.

You squeeze yourself down into the shaft –

Your hands and boots upon the metal ladder;
You start down –
Everything is wet. Everything is cold. Everything is dark;
You come down to a second horizontal passage –
There is a dim light from the end of the passage;
You turn around. You pull yourself out of the shaft into the tunnel –
It is narrow and made of bricks. It stretches off into the faint light;
You think you can hear familiar music playing far away:
The only thing you ever learn in school is ABC –
You crawl upon your fat bleeding bloody belly across the bricks
towards the light:
But all I want to know about is you and me –
Crawl upon your fat bleeding bloody belly across the bricks
towards the light:
I went and told the teacher about the thing we found –
Upon your fat bleeding bloody belly across the bricks towards the
light:
But all she says to me is that you're out of bounds –
Your fat bleeding bloody belly across the bricks towards the light:
Even though we broke the rule I only want to be with you –
Fat bleeding bloody belly across the bricks towards the light:
School love –
Bleeding bloody belly across the bricks towards the light:
School love –
Bloody belly across the bricks towards the light:
You and I will be together –
Belly across the bricks towards the light:
End of term until forever –
Across the bricks towards the light:
School love –
The bricks towards the light:
School love –
Bricks towards the light:
School love –
Towards the light:
School love –
The light:
Love –
Light.
The music stops. The roof rises. There are beams among the bricks.
You stagger on, on fat legs and fat feet –
Through the muck and the mud, the sound of rats here with you –

Near.

You stumble on a shoe –

A child's summer sandal, covered in dust –

You wipe away the dust –

A child's summer sandal, scuffed.

You leave it. You go on –

Back ripped raw from the beams and the bricks –

Until the roof rises again and you can stand in the shadow of a pile of rock.

You wait. You wait. You wait.

You turn the corner past the pile of rock and –

Fuck –

You see two skeletons lying on a bed of dead roses and old feathers, skulls turned up to a faded sky of bricks once blue, black cotton wool clouds stuck here and there among dim swinging Davy lamps –

Two skeletons entwined in osseous embrace –

Their black son rising out of the ground into the dim lamplight –

Into the lamplight, a hammer in his hand:

Leonard Marsh –

Little Leonard Marsh, a hammer in his hand –

Head shaved and chest bare, coming towards you –

His chest in bloody scars, it reads:

O LUV.

You do not move. You wait for Leonard Marsh –

A hammer in his hand, coming towards you.

You do not move. You wait until Leonard Marsh is almost upon you –

A hammer in his hand, coming towards you.

You raise the brick in your fist. You bring it down hard into the side of his head –

Leonard Marsh howls. He tries to bring the hammer down –

The hammer in his hand.

You raise the brick in your fist again. You bring it down hard again –

Leonard Marsh howling, trying to stand.

But you are behind him now and you have his hammer in your hand–

'Remember me?' you whisper.

Blind with his blood, you stop –

In this one long tunnel of hate, you see yourself;

In the ten broken mirrors –

The boxes and the bones –
The shadows and the lights –
The tape recorders and the screams –
The dead flowers and the feathers –
You see yourself and Leonard among the feathers –
Among the wings;
Your feathers and your wings –
Both stuck with his blood.
His mouth opens and closes again –
You put the hammer down.
'No-one even looked,' he whispers.
'I know,' you nod.
'No-one.'
You wipe the tears from his cheek. You kiss his head. You say: 'I know.'
He closes his eyes.
You put your wings over his mouth –
'The children of sinners are abominable children –
Your wings, huge and rotting things –
'And they frequent the haunts of the ungodly.
Big black raven things –
'Children will blame an ungodly father –
Heavy and burnt, over his mouth.
'For they suffer disgrace because of him.
He tries to raise his hand –
'But whatever comes from the earth returns to the earth –
Tries to stop you –
'So the ungodly go from curse to destruction.'
Stop you –
D-1.

Chapter 60

He walks up path. He knocks on door.

'It's not locked,' I shout downstairs.

He opens door. He steps inside.

'Up here.'

He turns. He starts to walk upstairs. He reaches top of stairs. He stops.

Door is on its side, blocking his path.

He can see my mother lying on floor of back bedroom.

He climbs over door –

I turn –

Turn from out of front bedroom –

I thrust knife though his coat –

Through his coat, deep into his belly:

'Hello,' I say.

I pull knife out. I push it back in –

Back in, up and under his ribs.

'Hello from back seat hard on last bus home, one that got away and lived to tell tale, from Barry Gannon and Eddie Dunford, Derek Box and his mate Paul, from my mate Clare and her sister Grace, Billy Bell and his spilt pint, from John Dawson and his brother Richard, Donald Foster and Johnny Kelly, from Pat they fucked and left behind, Jeanette Garland and her mum Paula, from Susan Ridyard and Clare Kemplay, Hazel Atkins and every missing child in this whole fucking world, from Graham Goldthorpe and his murdered Mary, Janice Ryan and Bad Bobby Fraser, from Eric Hall and his wife Libby, Peter Hunter and Evil Ken Drury, from Steve Barton and his brother Clive, Keith Lee and Kenny D, from Two Sevens and Joseph Rose, Ronnie Angus and George Oldman, from lovely Bill Shaw and Blind Old Walter, poor Jack Whitehead and Ka Su Peng, from Strafford Public House and Griffin hotel, Millgarth and Wood Street nicks, from Gaiety and both St Marys, motorways and car parks, from parks and toilets, idle rich and unemployed, from Maggie Thatcher and Michael Foot, from SWP and National Front, IRA and UDA, from M&S and C&A, Tesco and Co-op and every shopping centre in this wounded, wounded land, from shit they sell and shit we buy, my old mum and Queen sodding Mum, from kids with no mum and mums with no kid, Black Panther and Yorkshire Ripper, from Liddle Towers and Blair Peach, black bodies in Calder and ones in Aire, from all dead meat and my dead friends, pubs

and clubs, from gutters and stars, local tips and old slag heaps, from
ladies of night and boys in bogs, headlights and brake-lights, high life
and low, from mucky mags and dirty vids, silent pits and page three
tits, from Nazis and Witches, West Yorkshire coppers and their bent
mates, from all little shits and things we get to see, dead bodies piled
up in first-floor bars, stink of shotguns mixed with beer, sirens that
howl for ten long years bloodstained with fear, from one that got away,
un-lucky one, from Dachau to Belsen, Auschwitz to Preston, from
Wakefield to Leeds, Stanley Royd and fucking North, from West bloody
Riding and Red Riding Hood, final solution and wrath of God, from
Church of Abandoned Christ and her twenty-two disciples, Michael
Williams and Jack's wife Carol, from pictures and tapes, murders and
rapes, from whispers and rumours, cancers and tumours, from badgers
and owls, wolves and swans – '
  I twist knife:
  'This is for all things you made me do, for all things you had me see,
for every cock I've ever sucked and every night I've never slept, for
voices in my head and silence of night, for hole in my head and scars
on my back, words on my chest, for boy I was and them boys that saw,
Michael Myshkin and Jimmy Ash, fat Johnny Piggott and his brother
Pete, Leonard Marsh and his dad George, for every little lad you ever
fucked and all their dads who liked to watch, with their cameras in
their hands and their cocks in my arse, your tongue in my mouth and
your lies in my ear, loving you loving me, his nails in my hands
and yours in my head, for that knife in my heart and this one in you – '
  'Goodbye Dragon,' I spit –
  I pull knife back out again and –
  With one last kiss –
  I let him fall –
  Backwards –
  Down –
  Stairs.
  Bare-chested and soaked in blood –
  I turn. I see myself in bathroom mirror:
  Hole in my head –
  Stumps in my back –
  Seven letters on my chest:
  One Love.
  'Barry!' she is screaming. 'Barry!'
  I follow him downstairs to front door –
  I open it.
  Maurice is coming up garden path.

I strike a match.
He stops. He stares.
I let it fall –
Our house starts to burn.
I step over dead body of Martin Laws –
Into red rain, white floodlights and police lights blue.
My shoes gone, I walk barefoot into garden.
Head bobbed and wreathed, I drop knife and raise shotgun.

Chapter 61

There were no sirens, only silence –
No lights, only darkness.
We parked under Millgarth. I did not go upstairs –
Angus would be waiting:
More crimes and more lies, more lies and more crimes.
I walked through the market. I walked through the dawn –
Thursday 9 June 1983.

I cut through the backstreets. I ran up the Headrow.
I turned on to Cookridge Street.
I opened the door into the Church of Saint Anne.
I staggered down the side aisle.
I fell before the Pietà.
I took off my terrible glasses. I closed my tired eyes.
I prayed:

'Lord, I do not understand my own actions.
I know that nothing good dwells within me, in my flesh.
I do not do what I want, but I do the very things that I hate.
I can will what is right but I cannot do it.
I do not do the good I want, but the evil I do not want is what I do.
When I want to do what is good, evil lies close at hand.
Wretched and damned man that I am!
Will you rescue me from this body of death?'

I opened my eyes. I looked up at Christ –
The wounded, dead Christ.
I was crying as I stood –
I was crying as I turned to go –
I was crying when I saw him.
He was sat among the Stations. His head shaved –
He was dressed in white, bleeding from his hands and his feet.
There were children sat around him –
Little girls and little boys.
'Jack?'
He smiled at me.
'Jack?'
He stared through me.

'What?' I cried. 'What can you see?'

He was smiling. He was staring at the Pietà –

'How can you still fucking believe?' I shouted. 'After all the things you've seen?'

'It's the things I've not seen,' he said.

'I don't understand.'

'During an eclipse there is no sun,' he smiled. 'Only darkness.'

'I don't – '

'The sun is still there,' he said. 'You just can't see it.'

'I – '

'But in your heart you know the sun will shine again, don't you?'

I nodded.

'Faith,' he whispered –

'The substance of things hoped for, the evidence of things not seen.'

I turned again to the Pietà. I turned back to the wounded Christ –

No other name.

There was a hand squeezing mine –

A ten-year-old girl with blue eyes and long straight fair hair, wearing an orange waterproof kagool, a dark blue turtleneck sweater, pale blue denim trousers with a distinctive eagle motif on the back left pocket and red Wellington boots, holding a plastic Co-op carrier bag in her other hand.

I looked down at my hand in hers –

There were no bruises on the backs of my hands.

'He was not abandoned,' smiled Clare. 'He is loved.'

Chapter 62

Thursday 9 June 1983 –
D-Day:
Flat 5, 28 Blenheim Road, St John's, Wakefield –
Heart lost.

You can't go to sleep; you can't go to sleep; you can't go to sleep –
The branches still tapping against the pane –
Everybody knows;
You are lying on your back in your underpants and wings –
The branches tapping against the pane –
Everybody knows;
You are lying on your back in your underpants and wings, black
with his blood, black with all their blood –
The branches banging against the pane –
Everybody knows;
You are lying on your back in your underpants and wings, black
with his blood, black with all their blood, that terrible tune and her
words in your head –
Everybody knows; everybody knows, everybody knows and –
The branches cracking the pane.

You look at your watch. You see it is time:
2.25 a.m.
You get out of bed. You walk across the floor upon your knees.
You switch on the radio. The TV too –
The Hate:
'Where there is discord, may we bring harmony –
The Hate:
'Where there is error, may we bring truth –
The Hate:
'Where there is doubt, may we bring faith –
The Hate:
'Where there is despair, may we bring hope.'
Radio off. The TV too –
The branches have smashed the pane.
The rain pouring in –
No hope for Britain.

*

You open the bathroom door. You step inside. You turn on the bath taps. You put a circle of salt around the bath. You take out a pair of scissors. You cut your hair. You cut your nails. You take out a razor. You shave your head. You place the hair and the nails in an envelope. You put the envelope in the sink. You light a match. You burn the envelope. You look up into the mirror.

In blood, it states:

Nobody cares.

You get in the bath. You lie in the bath in your wings –

The water is warm.

You see the scenes; see the scenes as you could not at the time –

The shadows in your heart, the fear and the hate –

The hate and the fear.

You put all your fear and all your hate together and get:

Yorkshire, England, 1983.

You pick up the razor blade from the side of the bath:

My county, my country, right or wrong.

Four tears trickle down the sides of your nose.

But it's all right, everything is all right, the struggle is finished –

The water red.

You write three last words on a piece of damp paper.

Acknowledgments

I would like to thank the following people for their support during the writing of the *Quartet*:

James Anderson, Marcel Berlins and the *Times*, the staff of *Books Etc* Covent Garden, *Borders* Leeds, Jenny Boyce, George and Gill Chambers, Hiroyuki Chida, Julian Cleator, *Crime Time*, Jim Driver, Simon and Chiaki Evans, Judith and Reg Eyles, Max Farrar, Anne and Dave Francis, Robert and Astrid Fraser and family, Gregory Gannon, Leland and Carolyn Gaskins, Shigeko and Daisuke Goto, François Guérif, Alan Hadden and family, Richard and Alison Hall, Tamako Hamaguchi, Paula Hammerton, Seishu Hase, Nick Hasted, Hiroshi Hayakawa and all the staff of *Hayakawa Publishing*, Michael Hayden and Sam Dwyer, Jon Haynes, Shizuyo Ide, Jonathan Kelly, Darren Kemplay, Mrs Lambert, Paul Landymore, Pete and Persis Lunt, Maxim and all the staff at *Murder One*, Hamish Macaskill, Takashi Matsuki, Yumiko Mikado, the Nash family, Chris Nelson and the *Big Issue in the North*, Yasuko Nomura, Joseph O'Neill, Basil and Felicity Peace, Jonathan Peace, George P. Pelecanos, Ruth Petrie, Justin Quirk, Jon Riley, Junzo Sawa, Yukako Higuchi and all the staff at the English Agency Japan, the staff of Serpent's Tail, Stephen Shoebridge, Mario Tauchi, Stuart Turnbull, Cathi Unsworth, Nicola Upson at the *New Statesman*, Anna Vallois, Marco Vicentini, Andrew Vine and the *Yorkshire Post*, Tomohiro Yoshida, the staff of Waterstone's Leeds and Manchester, Sarn and Tara Warbis, Daina and Keri Warbis, Paul Westlake, Lynda Wigelsworth and family, Bob and Celia Wilkinson and family, Gareth and Sophia Williams, Mark and Susan Williams, Michael Williams, and last but most of all Izumi, George and Emi Peace. Thank you.